JOSEPH ROTH (1894–1939) was a prolific journalist and novelist and was one of the greatest writers of the 20th century. His work traces the decline of the Austro-Hungarian Empire and the rising fascist threat in Europe. On Hitler's assumption of power, he was obliged to leave Germany for Paris, where he died in poverty a few years later. His books include *What I Saw*, *The Legend of the Holy Drinker*, *The Hotel Years*, *Job* and *The Emperor's Tomb* and *The Radetzky March*, all published by Granta Books.

MICHAEL HOFMANN is the highly acclaimed translator of Joseph Roth, Franz Kafka, Hans Fallada, Bertolt Brecht, and many more writers. The author of several collections of poetry and a book of criticism, he teaches at the University of Florida.

'I re-read this book every two or three years, captivated anew by its low-key melancholia and its wry take on the human predicament' William Boyd

'Roth's masterpiece is one of the greatest novels written in the last century even though, at least in the English speaking world, it is also still one of the least known of those that may unequivocally be called great. This should now change ... There is a magnificent unity to this novel. It all holds together. You feel Roth knows everything there is to be known about his characters, their circumstances and their destiny: that, in writing he holds the whole unfolding steadily in his mind ... Exhilarating, life-enhancing to read. That is the magic of art and *The Radetzky March* is a great work of art. Buy it, read it, and then read it again. You will be well rewarded' *Scotsman*

'In Michael Hofmann's triumphant new translation, Roth's masterpiece rears from the past, its intellectual authority matched by the thrill of great writing ... a symphony, timeless and full of impact' *The Times*

'Roth can evoke an unknown place and time with an exactness of sensory detail that is particularly alive to sounds and to changing light. His sharp but sympathetic wit is present throughout, and scene after scene is brightened by unexpected, comic detail ... a historical novel that retains all its power in our not-so-post-imperial age' *Economist*

'A superb new translation ... a dark disturbing novel of eccentric beauty ... Read all his books, his stories, his observations and wonder at the intelligence, natural poetry and humanity of a gifted and candid master storyteller' *Irish Times*

'A heartfelt evocation of an empire in which he discerned virtues that outweighed all the burdens of a mindless officialdom ... Roth's masterpiece is of such enormous relevance to our times that we must be grateful that it has found in Michael Hofmann, a translator who does justice to its understated grief' Roger Scruton, *The Times*

'Unquestionably his masterpiece ... a historical novel of the highest order' *Jewish Quarterly*

'The most leisurely of Joseph Roth's great novels. Once again Michael Hofmann has rendered us a service by bringing us a fresh and lively translation of a 20th-century masterpiece' *Telegraph*

'One of the great traditional novelists of the last century ... likened in quality to Thomas Mann yet inexplicably overlooked ... Fiction of the highest, and most heartfelt order ... Roth's is a voice to heed – even better, to relish' *Herald*

'There are passages here so fine that, childlike, one ekes the book out, postponing the bereavement of finishing it' *RTÉ Guide*

*Also by Joseph Roth*

# The Radetzky March

## JOSEPH ROTH

**Translated by Michael Hofmann**

**With an introduction by Jeremy Paxman**

GRANTA

Granta Publications, 12 Addison Avenue, London W11 4QR
First published in Great Britain by Granta Books, 2002
First paperback edition published by Granta Books, 2003
This edition published by Granta Books, 2022

A CIP catalogue record for this book
is available from the British Library.

3 5 7 9 10 8 6 4 2

ISBN 978 1 78378 845 3

Typeset by M Rules
Printed and bound by CPI Group (UK) Ltd, Croydon, CR0 4YY

www.granta.com

MIX
Paper | Supporting
responsible forestry
FSC® C171272

# INTRODUCTION BY JEREMY PAXMAN

You are in for a treat. *The Radetzky March* is the perfect historical novel, packed with incident and beguiling characters, all set among the trumpeting brass of the Habsburg empire.

The challenge for writers of historical fiction is much more than capturing what things looked like: they have to show readers how the unchanging impulses, lusts and kindnesses of humanity *felt* in that context. Most historical novels are paper cups full of coloured water made from instant granules. Joseph Roth is a strong black coffee on a Viennese sidewalk. There are some scenes in this novel – like the one in which the young hero visits an army sergeant to offer his condolences on the death of his wife (who has also been the young man's secret lover) that are cinematic in their vividness. For some reason, it has become a term of praise to say that you read a novel in one sitting. I'm afraid I ration myself to so much per day, so that I always have something to look forward to. There is so much here to luxuriate in, to marvel, laugh and weep at.

It is not, however, grandiloquently or stuffily written. In Michael Hofmann's wonderful and lively translation of Roth's German manuscript, you can feel Roth wrestling with the words to fit the predicament in which one of his heroes finds himself, from despair and shame to bafflement and, occasionally, pride. 'Yes,' you say, 'this is how people talk and think.'

The only explanation for the fact that Joseph Roth is persistently overlooked in the tiresome lists of great twentieth-century novelists is that he is too continental for Anglo-Saxon taste. *The Radetzky March* is set in the dying decades of the Austro-Hungarian empire, an elaborate exercise in pomp and glitter. On thousands of walls hang portraits of the emperor in white tunic and red sash. The sinews of the state are visible in railway lines, gendarmeries and red tape.

Roth's masterpiece follows one family through three generations, and the fortunes of the Trotta dynasty are emblematic of the fate of the empire of the double-headed eagle. Happenstance and quick-wittedness elevates the first Trotta to become 'the Hero of Solferino', a dull man who, by impulsive heroism, saves the Emperor from a bullet amid the appalling carnage of the 1859 battle. He is promoted, raised to a baronetcy and thereby cut adrift from a long lineage of peasants. His son is a decent man who wears the inherited title dutifully, as a benign provincial official, while the debt-ridden grandson of the Hero of Solferino loses his way among the officer class, for whom imperial military service is just an opportunity to whore and gamble.

The novel is about identity and belonging. 'In those days before the Great War when the events narrated in this book took place, it had not yet become a matter of indifference whether a man lived or died,' Roth writes. 'When one of the living had been extinguished another did not at once take his place in order to obliterate him: there was a gap where he had been.' Roth never misses an opportunity for his readers to see the empire through the eyes of his character. The genius of this book is its ability to capture the bars, houses, railways and dusty roads of Austria-Hungary through highly distinct individuals.

Austria-Hungary was a quintessentially continental invention, prefiguring not merely other nation states, but the ambitions of the European Union. In this novel, the empire breathes and sighs like a massive bear, its enormous, haughty shadow laid across the many different peoples over which it ruled. As the world discovered in the summer of 1914, anyone who prodded a stick at the bear took their life in their hands. But, for as long as it lasted, Roth suggests, the empire was an ordered, secure place to be. It may have encompassed a cacophonous variety of peoples, but it offered a place to belong.

The author's life was a picaresque tragedy: even Roth's most devoted fans are unsure of some of the details (which he did little to clarify). He was certainly born to a Jewish mother in the bustling Jewish community of Brody, in Galicia (Austrian Poland), on the eastern outer reaches of the empire. The town had a majority Jewish population and earned the nickname 'the Galician Jerusalem'. Roth's father was unknown to him, committed to a lunatic asylum before he was born. The family was sufficiently assimilated to speak German at home, rather than Yiddish. Like Freud, Roth loved Austria-Hungary: it was, he said, his 'only one'. When the First World War broke out, he wore the imperial army's uniform, after which he made a living from his pen, churning out newspaper articles and novels, of which *The Radetzky March* is the masterpiece.

The title refers to the Johann Strauss's jaunty tune, popular with town bands and brothel pianists, written in homage to the greatest general in the Austrian army. Field Marshal Joseph Radetzky died before the Battle of Solferino in 1859 – Europe's last military clash in which all armies were led by their monarchs. The Emperor Franz-Joseph, though, was no military genius and the battle resulted in defeat for Austria-Hungary. All that remained of Radetzky's military skill was a marching tune.

The soldiers swung off to the First World War to the tune of the Radetzky March, and when the bloodletting was over, so was Austria-Hungary. The only place that Joseph Roth could call 'home' had vanished. Nationalistic states which emerged from the dismembered corpse, whether Croatian, Czech or Polish, were a disaster for the Jews, who had nowhere they could claim as a homeland. Like many of those disinherited by the war, Roth became an exile. He moved to Berlin, and wrote for liberal and left-wing papers, for whom he signed himself 'Joseph the Red'. In 1925, the leading liberal paper, *Frankfurter Zeitung*, appointed him its Paris correspondent. He lost the job after a year, but his furious energy enabled him to file pieces of journalism from all across Europe.

Hitler's rise to power made it impossible for a left-wing Jew like Roth to remain in Germany, and he had anyway already fallen in love with Paris. It was there that he spent the rest of his life, repeatedly drinking himself senseless. (One of the many spectacular pieces of writing in the novel is Roth's description of the effects of strong liquor.) For a while he had been, for someone making a living with their pen, tremendously well paid. It did not bring lasting comfort. His letters disclose a man living on loans and publishing advances.

'I am unfitted to hold down a job anywhere unless they were to pay me for getting angry at the world,' he wrote in *Flight Without End*. During one outbreak of skin trouble, after being sacked by the *Frankfurter Zeitung*, he described himself as 'completely covered in red boils. I can only go out after dark ... slathered in sulphur and stink.' His health did not improve, but his industry was undimmed. The alchemy of exile brought something magical from him. Living in a hotel room, Roth worked at a table downstairs in the Café Tournon, Saint-Germain-des-Prés. Here he sat scribbling away furiously on article and novel after article and novel. In May 1939 he collapsed there and died. He was forty-four. A year later Hitler's army marched into Paris. Had Roth still been alive, his fate would have been a concentration camp.

Photographs show a round-faced, slightly rat-featured individual, growing more pudgy and ill-favoured as the years passed. Great quantities of drink did not help his appearance, and a picture taken in the Café Tournon in 1938 shows an overweight, balding, bow-tied man with a brush moustache, sitting behind two wine glasses, cigarette in hand. He looks like the manager of a minor bank.

From such an apparently unprepossessing individual came one of the great novels of the twentieth century. *The Radetzky March* is his memorial.

Jeremy Paxman
London, May 2018

# TRANSLATOR'S INTRODUCTION

*The Radetzky March* has a prominence in the work of the Austrian novelist Joseph Roth that is magnificent and entirely merited, and yet still troubling. Like any great book, it distorts its author. The novel is taken, almost reflexively, as tantamount or equivalent to Roth. In a game of literary consequences, if A. says Joseph Roth, B. says *The Radetzky March*. Most people who have read Roth have read it, and most who have read it have stopped there. I spoke out of exasperation, but I think truthfully, when I remarked that the consensus on Roth is that he is 'a one-book author with fourteen or however many titles to his name'. It can seem a lot to ask, but one should remember that *The Radetzky March* has a crown around it.

Roth came to write *The Radetzky March* in the autumn of 1930. After a string of restless, contemporary, occasionally satirical books (*Zeitromane*) that led ultimately to his brief commitment to documentary fiction – *Neue Sachlichkeit* – in *Flight Without End* (subtitled *A Report*) in 1927 and *Right and Left* in 1929, he found himself dissatisfied, and in a sort of literary cul-de-sac. Indicative of this is the fact that one more book of this sort, *Perlefter: The Story of a Bourgeois*, remained a fragment, as did the remarkable *Strawberries* (included in *The Collected Shorter Fiction*). Roth ended up by breaking with the present, and with the politics and perspectives of the *entre deux guerres* period, and taking up the past in *Job: The Story of a Simple Man*, published in 1930. Set in the 1890s in Russia – crossing the physical border always seems to confer anteriority in Roth, as witness also the novella *The Leviathan* – written in short, highly coloured, descriptive sentences, and told in an almost naïve, fabulist manner, this book was Roth's first great success in Germany and abroad. (An American translation promptly appeared, by Dorothy Thompson; and Marlene Dietrich always claimed it as her favourite novel. When it came to be filmed, admittedly, in the late 1930s, Hollywood would not permit the figures and setting to remain Jewish, but made them Catholic; 'Mendel Singer Gets Baptised' was the – not unreasonably – waspish title of a review that appeared in Jerusalem.) It says everything about Roth – and about the necessity of reading all of him – that this 'most Jewish' of his books was followed by his 'most Austrian'; his shortest and simplest sentences by his most elaborate; one of his most spoken books by one of his most written.

How he did it is a mystery – as much as how he wrote the charmingly effervescent and optimistic *Legend of the Holy Drinker* in his last months, or, indeed, how he managed, over the last fifteen years of his life, to combine a novelist's oeuvre with a journalist's calling and habits. *The Radetzky March* was in many ways a favoured book: his new publisher Kiepenheuer (no doubt happy and relieved after the success of *Job*) paid him a monthly stipend; for the one and only time he did a little research (not that there is any necessary correlation between research and end product in fiction); he took the best part of two years to write it (again, there is no correlation between time taken and quality); and he tried hard to free himself from other deadlines and obligations. On the other hand, the distractions and adverse circumstances were, as was always the case with Roth, formidable. The list of places where Roth lived in the period in which he was working on *The Radetzky March* includes, but is probably not limited to, the following (in his correspondence, there are letters headed from all of them): Frankfurt, Goslar, Leipzig, Berlin, Cologne (Germany), Paris, Marseilles, Antibes (France), Badenweiler, Baden-Baden (Germany) and Rapperswil (Switzerland). (For a time, curiously, the two great epics about the end of the Dual Monarchy, *The Radetzky March* and Robert Musil's *The Man Without Qualities*, were being written in two Berlin cafés perhaps a couple of hundred yards apart; the respective authors did not like one another.) Then, after years of dread and treatment – wonder rabbis, analysis, shock treatment – Friedl, his wife, was diagnosed as a schizophrenic, and caring for her became a source of constant expense and unimaginable anguish; finally she was committed to the Steinhof asylum outside Vienna (where the Nazis later murdered her in the interest of eugenics). Her condition and fate are reflected in those of Deborah in *Job* and Chojnicki in *The Radetzky March*. These were the years, incidentally, in which Roth became a confirmed alcoholic.

Roth, as I say, at least tried to steer clear of competing or distracting work. His letters show that he was very aware of what was riding on his '*altösterreichischer Roman*', his novel of old Austria – elsewhere he can be rather casual, almost bored-sounding about his books; when he does refer to one, often it's not even clear which one he means, as though it were unprofessional to ponder such things overmuch – but his awareness often comes with an agonizing dread and sense of failure. On 22 August 1930, he writes: 'I am old and tired, and writing is a huge effort'; on 20 November 1930: 'How I wish I could be working on my book about old Austria!'; on 6 February 1931: 'I have to write a new novel, and with a completely skewed head, God knows if I'll succeed. With all my debts, I've had to give up writing for the paper, which means a loss of earnings, but what else can I do, I can't tear myself in half'; on 20 March 1932: 'I have been chronically ill and unhappy, and working desperately on *The Radetzky March*. The material is too much for me, I am too feeble to be able to shape it'; on a 'Sunday' in 1932: 'I have tried to take refuge in the pre-war era, but it's appallingly difficult to write it the way I feel it. I fear,

I fear, I'm botching it'; and on 'Wednesday': 'I am working inhumanly, it's monstrous, I have an incredible fear that the novel will turn out INADEQUATE. I have a sense of what's good, but whether God will give me the strength to make it good, that seems highly debatable to me.'

It seems, in fact, truer to say that the conditions, both internal and external, under which *The Radetzky March* was composed were awful, and Roth's ability to keep them out, or to mute their entry into his manuscript, was nothing less than heroic. He, who once submitted a novel with the order to himself, 'Must complete novel in three days,' accidentally included among the pages – which promptly secured its rejection – still and always worked in that fashion. *The Radetzky March* stretched as he wrote it. Originally, we know, it was conceived as running from 1890 to 1914; it moved both forwards, beyond the end of World War One, and back, to the battle of Solferino, in 1859: what has been called 'his first successful multi-generational novel' was actually substantially improvised. The personal appearance in it of the Emperor Franz Joseph was similarly determined at a fairly late stage. Newspaper serialization of the book in the *Frankfurter Zeitung* was well under way at a time when Roth still didn't know how – in either sense – he was going to finish it. He was pursued by creditors, bills, journalistic work, the publishers of a coffee table-type book on the Orient Express which he hadn't written but for which he had accepted payment, love affairs, a painful and troublesome eye disease (some of Dr Demant's erratic vision is perhaps informed by this). He was so haunted by Friedl's condition that he was unable to go to Vienna, even as he wrote pages of luminous and plausible description of its imperial ceremonial and protocol. Nor, unlike, say, Thomas Mann, was he able to blind himself to contemporary political developments: 'Europe,' he wrote in 1930, 'is committing suicide, and what has caused the peculiarly extended agony of this suicide is the fact that it is a corpse that is killing itself.' At the same time, what he was able to set down survives as infinitely more than a record of the combination of a hypertrophic sense of duty, and a protracted absence in the ostrich position, as seems to me the case with Mann's Joseph tetralogy.

Joseph Brodsky wondered – archly, provocatively – 'why/we need the twentieth century when we already/have the nineteenth'. It is a question that Joseph Roth would have relished and put as well. Most of the great literary works of the twentieth century celebrate the triumph of style over matter. Even where matter is present, trivially or abundantly or often both at once (Joyce, Broch, Svevo), it is ironized into an adjunct of style (the pages on the weather at the beginning of *The Man Without Qualities*). The aim of the enterprise was to freight and ultimately to sink the novel: to produce more and more about less and less. Consciousness, especially self-consciousness, ballooned, the less there was to be conscious about – in Proust, in Faulkner, in Woolf. Joseph Roth is a spectacular exception to both these (related) tendencies. Big things happen in his books. Not even by synecdoche or symbolism or *multum in parvo*, but blatant and undeniable big things, at the most attended and lit by detail. Roth's novels and stories always depict the great turnings of a life: love, loss, honour, career, betrayal, frustration, death. What in Musil is Zeno-ishly kept at arm's length – that calamitous August 1914 that is postponed over fifteen hundred pages in splintering subdivisions and intrigues and ramifications – Roth impatiently pulls down in his reckless appetite for disaster: the salted dramatic irony he begins to crush over Part Two of his novel, once the action has reached the border garrison town of B.: 'And none of the Tsar's officers, and none of the officers of His Apostolic Majesty knew then that over the glass bumpers from which they drank, Death had already crossed his bony invisible hands.' And, correspondingly, consciousness and self-consciousness are both at an absolute premium in his work, and where they do occur, do so as mere tragic ornaments, confined to characters – Chojnicki is one of them – who, Cassandra-like, have and are nothing else. In Roth, nothing comes between the human and the abyss where he is headed. (It is, at least in part, the scriptural note on the inadequacy of 'taking thought'.) In Roth's world, the idea of consciousness is, if not trivial, then at least unavailing, against the big and old-fashioned ideas of a relentless, mechanical fate, of human folly, of evil, even – though not in *The Radetzky March* – of the Devil.

This boldness is a principal source of Roth's appeal. His stories have an *élan* and a rush to them that, as far as the twentieth century is concerned, seem like a memory, unexpected and disreputable. The word drastic – to do with drama and action, from the Greek word *dran*, to do – suggests itself as one of the aptest descriptions of these for the most part short, headlong books that seem always to accomplish so much. Verifiable, freestanding character, like consciousness, is in short supply (though the books are never embarrassed by their 'solo' or soliloquizing scenes). Like Chekhov, Roth took his beginnings in sketches, humoresques, satire, and, like Chekhov, he never seems to have abandoned his belief that the human character is basically flat. Trotta in *The Radetzky March*, Tunda in *Flight Without End*, Taittinger in *The String of Pearls*, are basically all one and the same: dutiful, helpless, out of their depth. The view propounded in his books that though the world and our lives are complicated, we are simple, seems to me to have much to be said for it. Roth seems to have applied the tragic maxim of character in action. This takes him, actually, into the unlikely company of 'progressives' like Brecht and his anti-psychological 'epic theatre' and Kafka, with his K-ciphers. But then, it has always seemed to me the gravest error to condescend to Roth, or to mistake his simplicity for lack of sophistication.

What sets *The Radetzky March* apart from almost all the rest of Roth's production – though from the very beginning, and throughout his career, he had a way of writing 'big scenes' – is how it seems to have been done in oils. Elsewhere, there is something rapid, sketched, sometimes caricatural, at any rate linear, about his novels. Here, the scenes follow one another like broad discs overhanging one another, like the records cued on an old-fashioned gramophone: Sunday lunch, the visit to Frau Slama's, passing out and the trip to Vienna, the encounter with Moser, and so on. What one remembers of the book between readings are its expressive outdoor and indoor pageants, the scenes like floats in a parade. It is no accident that the two dominant and recurring pictures within the book are themselves like this: Moser's tachiste painting of the hero of Solferino, and the Radetzky March itself (Strauss's composition, beautifully described by Roth elsewhere as 'the Marseillaise of conservatism'), so lovingly orchestrated in silver and gold. Both are complex, evolving symbols, repositories of stored value. Their thickness of texture, and their many voices and views accord with the quality of this novel, which offers more time, more space, more amplitude and more coherent thematic organization ('the Spartans among the Austrians'; 'the grandsons') than any of Roth's others.

At the same time, *The Radetzky March* is no *roman-fleuve* or Victorian triple-decker. It has Roth's characteristic zip, his expressionist abruptness, his discontinuities, his fits and starts; '*hurtig*' – 'hasty' – is one of his favourite words. Sights and sounds, colours especially, and music are intensely and vividly there. At many moments, the book has the hallucinatory intensity – aptly enough, considering its mission of describing a vanished civilization – of shapes seen in a fire. Totemic things – boots, sword tassels, glasses of schnapps, physiognomies, shadows, frost, mud, birdsong, curfew and lights-out, coat collars, doorknobs, papyrossa stubs, roulette balls, fountains of cards – seem to be picked out of a surrounding darkness and silence with a blinkered, ghostly, almost claustrophobic acuity: 'He stood in the corridor, full of muddled notions, watching through the black window the endless succession of evanescent fiery serpents spun from the flying sparks of the locomotive, the dense blackness of the forests and the placid stars that studded the arc of the heavens.' The momentary intensity of clocks ticking and bells striking, of footfall, of brief, cropped collocations of colours, of liquids flowing, pervades and repeatedly unsettles what otherwise might appear to be a rather stately novel.

In fact, in the middle of the seemingly intact '*heile Welt*' of the Dual Monarchy, there is a whole drama of destabilization going on. Time and space are handled with great flexibility. Four o'clock at the gendarmerie post may mean utterly different things. Carl Joseph comes into a watch, but prefers to wait for clocks to strike the quarter-hours. The District Commissioner confuses Sundays with weekdays. He falls asleep in his chair, only to 'come round with a start a few minutes later, and feel as though he had been asleep for an eternity'. Valli spends her life and her beauty moving the years as if they were mirrors. The dying Jacques muddles the months. The Emperor – as if Shakespeare had done a Tithonus – wallows in both time and space in a kind of bleary perspicacity: 'He wasn't quite sure how old he was, but when the others were around him, he felt he must be very old. Sometimes he had the feeling that he was drifting away from them, and from the whole world, as though they were all shrinking the longer he looked at them.' The stars are near, far, comforting, not. Vienna is an extension of the court. In the District Commissioner's political imagination, the Dual Monarchy is something as simple and assertive as merely an enlarged version of the Hofburg, with the appropriate wings and extensions; although by the end, 'Austria' is something that still happens once a week, on Sundays. Money is just as bewildering, alcohol, luck, women – 'He felt the rapid alternation of smooth coolness and smooth heat on her skin, those abrupt climatological changes that are among the magical manifestations of love. (Within a single hour, they are capable of piling the characteristics of all four seasons on a single shoulder. They do indeed suspend the laws of time.)' In the moment of catastrophe, at the regiment's centenary celebrations that are incontinently held after only ninety-nine years, in the Shakespearean (again) storm scene when nature is piled on top of history, 'It was only a second or two, but between the lightning and the thunder, a whole eternity seemed to fit.' (Incidentally, ironically, how congruent to

Musil this is; only in *The Man Without Qualities* it is the moment before the catastrophe that is capable of indefinite extension and accommodation, in Roth it is the catastrophe itself.) Space is subject to the same vagaries. Slama's house seems shrunk by the rain. Jacques's curtains hang like aprons in his window. In one of Carl Joseph's crises, his fits of vertiginous inadequacy that stand in for understanding, on his own in Vienna, facing the impending loss of his beloved, he reels and whirls through a crisis like that of geocentric, Ptolemaic astronomy: 'The South was a foreign land somewhere! And lo: there were other countries which were not subject to Emperor Joseph the First, which had armies of their own, with many thousands of their own lieutenants in greater or lesser barracks. In these other countries, the name of the hero of Solferino was without significance. They had their own monarchs. [...] it was just as bewildering as it might be for us to consider that the earth is only one of millions upon millions of heavenly bodies, that there are innumerable other suns in our galaxy, and that each of these suns has its own planets, and that we are therefore relegated to being a very obscure thing indeed, not to say: an insignificant speck of dust!'

This amplification, as I think of it, is one of the hallmarks of *The Radetzky March*. Working in from this outer ring of significance (the significance of one's own insignificance), one may note how much of Austria-Hungary is covered in the book, with Slovenian Sipolje, Moravian W., Galician B. (based on Roth's birthplace of Brody) and the imperial capital all used as settings, as well as references to Laxenburg, Steinhof, Bad Ischl, and the military academy at Mährisch-Weisskirchen (which the young Rilke attended, and Musil); and also how the different seasons and weathers and times of day and night all play memorable roles. It is truly a work of orchestral magnificence and even-handedness. Within that again, one may note how many of the varieties of earthly felicity are contained in it, and how many of the modes of destruction – and how very often they are the same thing: love and friendship, service to king and country, the pleasures of the table, drink and gambling. The one thing almost wholly absent (striking in a work that takes in three generations – but this one is patrilineal; it is in the late, curt sequel, *The Emperor's Tomb*, that a mother–son relationship and marriage are treated) is family, evident really only in truncated or cautionary form, in Demant's history, in the aspirations and worries of Knopfmacher, in the Nechwals and the Stranskys, in the reassuringly banal Captain Lorenz, with his three identical-looking children, and his slovenly penchant for playing pool in his vest. One might equally approach the book by an analysis of its myriad forms of light and colour, by the distribution of fog and clarity, by its many, many images of doubleness and splitting – surely all of them veiled allusions to the Dual Monarchy and the Habsburg double eagle – the whiskers of Franz Joseph and the District Commissioner, the 'two brushes' on the head of Slama, the would-be Commercial Councillor Knopfmacher ('His face seemed about to split in two halves. It was only the grey goatee beard that held it together.'), the eagle and the 'fraternal' vultures, even Chojnicki's sliced loaf that has the appearance of wholeness.

So much of the story is told in such imagery, or in its dramatic, even melodramatic events – battles, woundings, ennoblings, seductions, duels, postings, riots, amours, bankruptcy, espionage, blackmail, withdrawal, war – a systematic, almost a chemical barrage of tests, that there is little scope for 'character'. And indeed, most of the distinction, the authority, the identity of the people in the book is 'positional' not 'personal', to use the valuable terms of the anthropologist Mary Douglas. Who truly finds in themselves the freedom to act, to move even fractionally from where they are put? Not any of the Trottas, following old codes and mistaken paternal dispositions. Not any of their warm or wise friends, Chojnicki or Skovronnek or Demant. Certainly none of the officers or the women. Perhaps, ironically, only the ancient Emperor, in the baggy licence afforded him by his vast age and importance and underratedness, and then only at odd, stolen moments; and his twin and fellow-underpinning, old Jacques.

The people in the book are mostly not even referred to by name, but by designation, rank or occupation. (It is interesting, too, how often Roth has recourse to the German impersonal construction, '*man*', ostensibly the equivalent of the – far more sheepish and less useful – English 'one', but for which I have variously offered the first person, the second person and the third, in an effort to get across this ectoplasmic fluidity of identity.) They put on clothes to fight, to work, to love, to mourn, to be themselves or forget themselves or deceive themselves, to die and to be dead in. *The Radetzky March* is, in a terribly literal sense, 'costume drama'.

It is here that Roth's flat, passive conception of character really triumphs. His men – not even hollow men, but flat men, cardboard models, clothes-horses – are the perfect servants of, ultimately, a hollow empire; able to swell a throng or progress, to look good on parade – effectively, their last hurrah – but not to fight a war. Their separateness, their anonymity, their irrelation is perfect for the future of separate, anonymous, irrelated and irrelevant little statelets into which they will ignorantly or viciously disappear. (The German rump of Austria, post-Versailles, is something at which Roth despaired, and which, notwithstanding his protestation that he 'loved' what remained of his Fatherland 'like a relic', and his subsequent, superstitious devotion to the Habsburgs in exile, he despised, that country of '*Alpentrottel*', 'Alpine cretins'.) *The Radetzky March*, this book that begins with the sun breaking through mist over a battlefield and that ends with the rain pattering gently and indefatigably on the window panes of a café where a bereaved survivor smiles and plays chess – the game of kings, the simulacrum of a battlefield – with himself is an account of a formidable collapse, a deadly loss of scale and illusion.

The popularity of *The Radetzky March* has sometimes been noted with some surprise by critics: it is actually a far bleaker, more unconsoling book than it is taken for, by no means the revanchist or reinstating celebration of a gone order, more the anatomy of a dismantlement. Even Otto Habsburg, who read it, wasn't comforted by it, and, as for Roth himself, while the description of the undeceived Chojnicki may have been self-portraiture, one of the many versions of his paternity that he put into circulation was that his father was a drunken painter. His own 'family' traditions and his personal destiny were mapped out for him by 'Professor' Moser.

Roth was kept alive, first by writers – in the most literal sense by his patron Stefan Zweig (with whom he had a fascinatingly unequal and volatile relationship), and by other friends like the Polish novelist Josef Wittlin (who translated *The Radetzky March* and other novels of Roth's) and Soma Morgenstern; it was no accident that his final collapse was precipitated by the news that another writer friend, Ernst Toller, had hanged himself in New York. Then, after his death, and after the war – actually rather longer after the war than one would like to think – he was figuratively brought back to life – his reputation retrieved – by another novelist, his friend and editor Hermann Kesten, who brought out first a three-volume edition of his novels in 1956 (reviewed by the young Heinrich Böll), then a selection of his letters in 1970, and of the stories in 1973. But for Kesten, we might well have had no Roth. After the writers, it was the turn of the readers. Roth was first recommended to me in 1980 by – it seems possibly symptomatic – a German mathematics student. I first read him in a one-volume compendium of scenes from the books that was all that the Cambridge University German department had of him. (A barbarously unsympathetic context, from which, in fact, Roth emerged quite brilliantly.) Always in academe there was an undercurrent of feeling that Roth was not worthy, somehow sub-literary; when, for instance, some of his manuscripts were offered to Harvard, admittedly quite some time ago, they were turned down on those grounds. The story of his continued publication or renewed publication in the USA and Britain, in the 1980s by Peter Mayer and Jeremy Lewis, and in the 1990s by Robert Weil and Neil Belton, and his reception by Nadine Gordimer, Mavis Gallant, Gabriel Josipovici, James Wood, and very many others, is again attributable to the discernment of these figures as readers. In the generally apathetic, complacent and mistrustful English-speaking world, he is one of very few foreign writers – Lampedusa, Pessoa, Bernhard, Hrabal come to mind – whose books travel by word of mouth among readers, to achieve the stony, predetermined and all too often unloved category of 'classic' – but as living figures.

Michael Hofmann
London, June 2002

PART ONE

# 1

The Trottas were not an old family. Their founder had been ennobled following the battle of Solferino. He was a Slovene. The name of his village – Sipolje – was taken into his title. Fate had singled him out for a particular deed. He subsequently did everything he could to return himself to obscurity. He was an infantry Lieutenant and the commander of a platoon at the battle of Solferino. The battle had been in progress for half an hour or so. Three paces in front of him, he saw the white-clad backs of his men. Their front line was down on one knee, their second stood. They were all in good heart and confident of victory. They had had a good meal, and drunk brandy in honour and at the expense of the Emperor, who had been present on the field of battle since yesterday. Occasionally, a man would fall and leave a gap in the ranks. Trotta would leap into the gap, and fire off the widowed gun of the dead or injured man. Now he closed up the ranks, now he stretched them out again, looking in every direction with hundredfold sharpened eye, listening in every direction with preternaturally acute ear. Amidst the rattling of gunfire, his alert hearing could pick up every occasional, shouted command from his captain, his sharp eye penetrate the grey-blue haze in front of the enemy lines. He never shot without aiming, and his aim was

3

always sure. His men felt his hand and his eye, heard his call and felt secure.

A lull came in the fighting. All down the length of the line came the order: 'Hold your fire!' Here and there came the rattle of a ramrod, or the bang of a tardy, isolated shot. The grey-blue haze between the fronts lifted and the army felt the full noonday heat of a silvery, occluded, stormy sun. Suddenly the Emperor appeared, between the Lieutenant and the front line, with a couple of staff officers. He was in the process of raising a field-glass handed to him by one of his escort, to his eye. Trotta knew what that meant. Even if one assumed that the main body of the enemy forces was busy regrouping, their rearguard was certainly facing the Austrians, and whoever raised a field-glass showed himself a target worthy of a marksman. And no less a one than the youthful Emperor at that. Trotta's heart was in his mouth. Fear of the unimaginable, the boundless catastrophe that would destroy himself, the regiment, the army, the state, the whole world, sent a burning chill through his body. His knees shook. And the ingrained resentment of the lower-ranking officer against the gentlemen of the general staff, who had no idea of the bitter realities of warfare, drove the Lieutenant to the action that wrote his name indelibly in the history of his regiment. With both hands he reached for the monarch's shoulders to pull him down. The Lieutenant probably used a little too much force. The Emperor fell over immediately. His escorts threw themselves at him as he fell. In that instant, a bullet pierced the left shoulder of the Lieutenant, the bullet that had been destined for the heart of the Emperor. As the Emperor got to his feet, the Lieutenant collapsed. All along the front, a confused and irregular fire awoke from rifles abruptly torn from their slumbers. The Emperor, enjoined by his anxious escort to leave this place of danger, still insisted on bending down over the Lieutenant, and, mindful of his imperial duty, asking the unconscious man, who no longer took in anything, what his name might be. A regimental doctor, a medical orderly, and a couple of stretcher-bearers galloped up, heads down and backs bent. The

4

general staff officers pulled the Emperor down, and then flung themselves to the ground. 'Look to the Lieutenant!' the Emperor called to the breathless doctor.

In the meantime, the gunfire had once more abated. And while the cadet replacement officer stood in front of the platoon and announced in clear tones: 'I'm taking over the command!' Franz Joseph and his escort picked themselves up, the medical people carefully strapped the Lieutenant on to the stretcher, and they all departed in the direction of the regimental headquarters, where a snow-white tent housed the nearest dressing station.

Trotta's left collarbone was smashed. The bullet, which had come to rest against his shoulderblade, was removed in the presence of the Supreme Commander-in-Chief, to the sound of unearthly screams from the wounded man, whom pain had roused from unconsciousness.

Four weeks later, Trotta was much better. By the time he returned to his regimental headquarters in southern Hungary, he had been promoted to the rank of captain, awarded the highest military decoration, the Order of Maria Theresa, and ennobled. Henceforth his name was: Captain Joseph Trotta of Sipolje.

It was as if he had received a strange, new, fabricated life in exchange for his own. Every night before going to sleep, and every morning after getting up, he repeated his new name and rank to himself, and stepped in front of the mirror to assure himself that his face still looked the same. Between the clumsy intimacy with which his comrades tried to overcome the gulf that a baffling fate had suddenly created between them, and his own vain attempts to meet the world with the same innocence as heretofore, the ennobled Captain Trotta seemed to lose his equilibrium. He felt as though he had been condemned to spend the rest of his life in borrowed boots on a slippery floor, welcomed by outlandish greetings and the subject of furtive glances. His grandfather had been a simple peasant, his father a sergeant in the Pay Corps, and then a gendarmerie sergeant in the southern marches of the Monarchy. Ever since losing an eye in a fight with Bosnian smugglers, he had lived on his military pension as a watchman in the grounds of Laxenburg Castle, feeding the swans, trimming the hedges, protecting the laburnum in season and later the elderflower from the depredations of lawless hands, and on mild nights, removing the courting couples from the park benches where they had gone to take advantage of the dark. The rank of a common or garden infantry Lieutenant seemed natural and appropriate to the son of a sergeant. But to an ennobled and decorated captain, who went around in the strange, almost eerie aura of imperial favour, as in a golden cloud, his father had suddenly become estranged, and the measured love that the heir felt for the old man seemed to call for different behaviour, new forms between the father and son.

The Captain hadn't seen his father for five years; but even so, once a fortnight, each time the unchanging roster took him to barrack duty, he had written the old man a short letter, in the guard room, by the sparse, flickering light of an official candle, once he'd inspected the sentries, written the hours of their relief, and in the column, 'Other Incidents', entered a clear and energetic 'None', as though to ward off even the remotest possibility of there ever being such a thing. The letters were as formulaic as any military pass or official communication. Written on yellow, fibrous octavo sheets with the greeting 'Dear Father!' on the left, leaving a space of four fingers' breadth at the top of the sheet, and two in the margin, they began with a brief statement of the good health of the writer, continued with the hope of similar on the part of the recipient, and concluded with the unvarying expression, in a paragraph of its own to the bottom right: 'Respectful greetings, your loyal and thankful son, Joseph Trotta, Lieutenant.' Now, even with a different rank and a new roster, how could one possibly alter this accepted form, calculated to last for the whole of a soldier's life, and introduce into the standard sentences unusual communications of circumstances to which one had still to grow accustomed oneself, and whose full import one was yet to grasp? On that quiet evening following his recovery when Captain Trotta first sat down to discharge the duty of correspondence at the table comprehensively notched and scratched by the artistry and the pocket knives of bored men, he saw that he would never be able to get beyond the greeting 'Dear Father!' And he propped his sterile pen against the inkwell, pinched off a bit of the guttering candlewick, as though in the hope that steadier light would inspire him with a happy formulation, and drifted off into memories of childhood in the village, his mother, cadet school. He studied the huge shadows that little things cast against the bare, blue-washed walls, the gleaming curvilinear sabre on its hook by the door, the dark ribbon pushed through the sabre's handguard. He listened to the unabating rain, and its drumming chant on the tin windowsill. And eventually he stood up, having decided to visit his father the following week, after the official audience of thanks with the Emperor, to which he expected to be summoned in the next few days.

A week later, immediately after the audience, which had lasted barely ten minutes, no more than ten minutes of imperial gratitude, ten or a dozen questions read out from a briefing paper to which he had had to respond to with 'Yes, Your Majesty!'s fired off like a volley of rifle shots, he was in the carriage to his father in Laxenburg. He saw the old fellow in his shirtsleeves in the kitchen of his quarters, sitting at the bare, planed-down kitchen table, on which was laid a dark blue handkerchief with red trim, with a large cup of fragrant, steaming coffee on it. His knotty stick of reddish-brown cherrywood was hooked over the table top, swaying slightly. A wrinkly leather tobacco pouch, well filled and half open lay next to the long, charred, yellowing clay pipe. Its tints matched those of his father's mighty white moustache. In the midst of this very plain official household Captain Joseph Trotta of Sipolje appeared like a war god, with a gleaming dress belt, a lacquered helmet that scattered its rays like a black sun, a pair of smooth, burnished riding boots with glittering spurs, two rows of sparkling, almost incandescent buttons on his tunic, and the unearthly glory of the Order of Maria Theresa casting its blessing. Thus the son stood in front of his father, who got up very slowly, as though to cancel the glory of the young man by the slowness of his greeting. Captain Trotta kissed his father's hand, bent down and received a kiss on the forehead and another on the cheek. 'Sit down!' said the old man. The Captain unbuckled part of his splendour, and sat. 'Congratulations!' said the father, in his usual voice, in the stiff German spoken among army Slavs. The consonants growled like minor thunder, and the endings of words had little weights pulling them down. Just five years ago, he had spoken Slovenian to his son, even though the lad understood only a few words of it, and didn't speak any himself. But today the use of his mother tongue would have seemed like an undue intimacy with a son who, by the grace of fate and the Emperor, had moved so far; meanwhile, the Captain never took his eyes off his father's lips, poised to greet the first sound of Slovenian as something familiarly distant and a piece of lost home. 'Congratulations, congratulations!' thundered the Sergeant. 'In my day, it never happened as quickly as that! In my day, we had Radetzky to put us through our paces!' It really is over! thought Captain Trotta. He was cut off from his father by a great weight of military distinction. 'Do you have any raki, Father?' he asked, endeavouring to confirm one last remnant of family solidarity. They drank, touched glasses, drank again, and with each swallow, his father wheezed, disappeared into a protracted fit of coughing, turned purple, spat, slowly recovered himself, and began to tell anecdotes from his own time in service, with the transparent objective of diminishing the career and merits of his son. Finally, the Captain rose, kissed his father's hand, received his father's kiss on brow and cheek, buckled on his sabre, put on his shako, and left – in the certain knowledge that he would never see his father again in this life …

It was indeed the last time. The son continued to write the usual letters to the old man, but there was no other discernible relationship between the two of them: Captain Trotta had been cut adrift from the long line of his Slav peasant forebears. A new line began with him. The round years trundled past like peaceful, equable wheels. In accordance with his rank, Trotta married his colonel's niece, a well-situated party no longer in the first flush of youth, whose father was on the Board of Administration in Western Bohemia; with her he had a son and enjoyed the monotony of a healthy, soldierly existence in a little barracks town. Every morning he rode out to the exercise grounds, and in the afternoons he played chess in the café with the notary; he got to feel at ease in his rank, his social status, his dignity and his fame. He was of middling gifts as an officer, and gave middling proof of the fact in the annual manoeuvres; he was a good husband, wary of other women, uninterested in gambling, gruff but fair-minded in duty, implacably opposed to lying, to unmanly conduct, cowardice, favour-seeking, and all forms of ambition and pretence. He was as straightforward and blameless as his conduct sheet, and only his periodic rages would have shown an observer that the soul of Captain Trotta harboured its share of nocturnal abysses, full of dormant storms and the unknown voices of nameless ancestors.

Captain Trotta did not read books, and he felt quiet pity for his growing son, who was compelled to deal with slate-pencil, slate and sponge, paper and ruler and times-table, and already had the inevitable schoolbooks waiting for him. At this stage, the Captain still assumed that his son would follow him into the army. It never occurred to him that (from then until the end of the family) a Trotta could pursue any other profession. If he had had two, three, four sons (but his wife was infirm, needed doctors and cures, and pregnancy was dangerous to her) they could all have been soldiers, as far as Captain Trotta was concerned. There was talk of a new war; well, he was ready for it. Yes, he was almost certain he had been earmarked for death in battle. His uncomplicated solidity took such a death as the inevitable consequence of military fame. All until one day when, with casual curiosity, he picked up the primer of his son, who was only five and, thanks to his mother's zeal, becoming rather prematurely acquainted with the demands of learning in the person of a tutor. He perused the rhymed morning prayer; unaltered over the decades, he still knew it by heart. He read 'The Four Seasons', 'The Fox and the Hare',

'The King of the Beasts'. He turned to the table of contents, and found a piece entitled 'Franz Joseph I at the Battle of Solferino' that promised to be of particular interest. He began reading, and had to sit down. 'In the battle of Solferino' – thus the narrative began – 'our King and Emperor Franz Joseph I found himself in grave danger.' Why, Trotta himself put in an appearance! But in what a transformation! 'Our monarch,' it said, 'had advanced so far in the heat of the battle that he saw himself ringed by enemy horsemen. In that instant of his direst need, a youthful lieutenant galloped up on a sweating bay mare, swinging his sabre. Whish! how the blows came down on the heads and necks of the foe!' And there was more: 'A lance pierced the breast of the young hero, but only when he had already slain the greater part of the enemy. Shining sabre in his hand, the intrepid young king was easily able to beat off the weakening attackers. The rest of the enemy cavalry were taken prisoner. As for the noble young lieutenant – Joseph von Trotta was his name – he received the highest distinction that our fatherland has to give to its young heroes: the Order of Maria Theresa.'

Book in hand, Captain Trotta went to the little orchard behind the house, where his wife liked to potter on pleasant afternoons, and, with pale lips and low voice, asked her whether she knew of the scandalous piece. She nodded and smiled. 'It's a lie!' yelled the Captain, flinging the book on to the wet earth. 'It's for children!' his wife mildly replied. The Captain turned on his heel. He was shaking with rage, like a reed in a storm. He stalked into the house, his heart fluttering. It was time for his daily chess game. He took the sabre off its hook, slung it round his hips with a furious swivel, and left the house with long angry strides. Anyone seeing him would have thought he was on his way to confront his enemies. After losing a couple of games in the café, still not having said a word, with four deep horizontal creases on his pale, narrow brow under his short stubbly hair, he upset the clattering pieces with a choleric hand, and said to his partner: 'I need your advice!' A pause. 'I've been the victim of a slander,' he went on, looking up into the glinting spectacles of the notary, and it dawned on him that he didn't have the words. He should have taken the primer with him. With that odious item to hand, it would have been considerably easier to explain. 'What sort of slander?' asked the notary. 'I've never served in the cavalry,' Captain Trotta felt obliged to begin, even though he could see it wasn't an ideal way to begin. 'You know the shameless hacks who write those children's books, they say that I came galloping up on a bay mare, a sweating bay mare was what they wrote, to rescue the king.' The notary understood. He knew the piece in question from his own sons' schoolbooks. 'I think you're taking it too seriously, Captain,' he said. 'Bear in mind, it's for children!' Trotta looked at him in alarm. At that moment it seemed to him that the whole world was conspiring against him: the writers of these schoolbooks, the notary, his wife, his son, his house-tutor. 'Historical events,' said the notary, 'are always portrayed differently in the classroom. And I think that's quite right too. Children need examples that they can understand and will remember. They can learn the truth later!' 'The bill!' called the Captain, and stood up. He went to the barracks, caught the duty officer, Lieutenant Amerling, canoodling with a woman in the accounts office, made a personal inspection of the sentries, sent for the company sergeant major, ordered the duty officer to report to him tomorrow, had the company assemble, and ordered weapons drill in the yard. There was bewildered, trembling obedience. Every platoon had one or two men missing; they couldn't be found. Captain Trotta had the roll called. 'Absentees to report to me tomorrow!' he said to the Lieutenant. He drilled the men till they panted. The ramrods clattered, the rifle-straps flew, hot hands smacked against cold metal barrels, the mighty gun-stocks stamped on the soft, stifling ground. 'Load!' ordered the Captain. The air shook with the hollow rattle of blanks. 'Half an hour saluting practice!' commanded the Captain. After ten minutes, he issued new orders. 'Kneel down for prayer!' He listened with relief to the thump of knees on earth, gravel and sand. He was still Captain, still in command of his company. He would show those scribblers.

He didn't go to mess, he didn't even eat, he went to bed. His sleep was deep and dreamless. At officers' report the following morning, he made his curt complaint to the colonel. It was passed along. And so began the martyrdom of Captain Joseph Trotta, the knight of Sipolje, the knight of truth. It took weeks for an acknowledgement to arrive from the War Ministry, saying that the complaint had been forwarded to the Ministry of Culture and Education. Weeks more went by, and then one day the Minister's reply arrived. It read as follows:

Dear, esteemed Captain and Baron!

In reply to your complaint, *re* item # 15 in the series of authorized primers for Austrian elementary schools, as established by the law of 21 July 1864, written and edited by Professors Weidner and Srdcny, the Minister of Education ventures to draw the Captain's attention to the fact that items of historical significance, in particular those concerning the person of His Majesty, the Emperor Franz Joseph, and other members of the Royal Family, are, according to the decree of 21 March 1840, adapted to the comprehension of the pupils and good pedagogical practice. The aforementioned item # 15 was submitted to the Minister in person, and received his personal authorization for use in a school reader. It has long formed part of our educational philosophy to depict heroic actions by our military personnel to the schoolboys and schoolgirls of the Monarchy, in such a way as to render them conformable both to the childish character, and to the imagination and patriotic feeling of the coming genera-tion – not altering the substance of the events depicted, but avoiding a drily factual tone that discourages patriotic feeling and fails to fire the imagination. In consequence of such and similar considerations, the undersigned respectfully urges the addressee to desist from his complaint.

The document was signed by the Education and Culture Minister. The Colonel passed it to Captain Trotta with the fatherly advice, 'I'd let the thing drop if I was you.'

Trotta took the letter and didn't say anything. A week later, via the prescribed channels, he requested an audience with His Majesty, and one morning, three weeks after that, he found himself face to face with His Supreme Commander-in-Chief in the Hofburg.

'Listen, my dear Trotta!' said the Emperor. 'It's a bad business. But we both come out of it looking pretty good. Why don't you drop it!'

'Your Majesty,' the Captain replied, 'the whole thing is a lie!'

'There's a lot of lying goes on,' affirmed His Majesty.

'Your Majesty, I can't,' the Captain blurted out.

The Emperor stepped up to the Captain. The monarch was only slightly taller than Trotta. They looked one another in the eye.

'My Ministers,' began Franz Joseph, 'must know their own business. I have to rely on their judgement. You do understand, my dear Captain Trotta.' And, after a while: 'We'll make it up to you. You'll see!'

The audience was at an end.

His father was still alive. But Trotta didn't drive out to Laxenburg. He returned to barracks, and asked to be discharged from the military.

He was discharged with the rank of Major. He moved to Bohemia, to a small property of his father-in-law's. The imperial favour did not leave him. A week later, he received word that the Emperor had given instructions for five thousand gulden from his private purse to be awarded, for study purposes, to the son of the man who had saved his life. Simultaneously, Trotta was raised to the baronetcy.

Joseph Trotta, the Baron of Sipolje, accepted the imperial gifts as unenthusiastically as if they had been insults. The war against Prussia was fought and lost without him. He was resentful. Already his temples were silvering; his stride slowed, his eye grew dim, his hand heavy, his speech scarce. Even though he was a man in his prime, he seemed to be ageing rapidly. He had been expelled from the paradise of simple faith in Emperor and virtue, truth and justice, and, trapped in silent suffering, he could see that it was guile that underwrote the world, the might of the law, and the greatness of crowned heads. Thanks to the timely expression of the Emperor's wish, item 15 vanished from the schoolbooks of the Monarchy. The name Trotta survived only in the obscure annals of the regiment. The Major lived on as the forgotten bearer of an evanescent fame, not unlike a fleeting shadow projected by a hidden object on to the bright world of the living. On his father-in-law's estate, he pottered around with watering can and gardener's shears, and, just as his father did in the castle grounds at Laxenburg, the Baron trimmed the hedge and mowed the lawn, guarded the laburnum in its season and later the elderflower from the depredations of lawless hands, put in new, freshly sawn fence-posts for old, weathered ones, kept harness and tackle, saddled and bridled his chestnut horses himself, replaced rusty locks on doors and gates, drove carefully carved wooden wedges between sagging hinges, stayed out in the forests for days, shot small game, spent the nights with his forester, and concerned himself with chickens, manure and harvests, fruit trees and trellises, groom and coach-man. He was a miserly and suspicious shopper, drawing coins with long fingers from his dirty leather purse, before hiding it under his shirt again. He became a little Slovenian peasant. Sometimes flashes of his old rage came over him, shaking him like a reed in a storm. Then he would whip the groom and the horse's flanks, slam the doors into the locks he had himself repaired, threaten the labourers with death and destruction, send his dinner plate skimming across the table, growl and refuse to eat. By his side, in her own rooms, there lived his feeble and infirm wife, the boy who saw his father only at mealtimes and submitted his school reports to him twice a year, without eliciting either praise or censure, and his father-in-law, who blithely got through his pension, liked the girls, stayed in town for weeks at a time, and was rather in awe of his son-in-law. A little, old Slovenian peasant, that was Baron Trotta. He still wrote the regular fortnightly letters to his father, late at night with a flickering candle, on yellow octavo sheets, beginning four fingers from the top, two from the side, 'Dear Father!' He didn't often get a reply.

On and off the Baron thought about visiting his father. He felt considerable nostalgia for the cavalry sergeant with his austere poverty, his loose tobacco and his home-distilled raki. But the son worried about the expense, just as his father, his grandfather, his great-grandfather would have done. He felt closer to the pensioner in the Laxenburg Castle now than he had done years before, when he had sat in the blue-washed kitchen of the little official quarters, in the full splendour of his recent ennoblement, and drunk raki with him. He never discussed his origins with his wife. He felt that a bashful pride would come between the daughter of generations of civil servants and a Slovenian cavalry sergeant. So he didn't invite his father to come either.

On a bright day in March, the Baron was clumping over the frozen fields to see his steward, when a servant brought him a letter from the administrator of Laxenburg. The pensioner had passed away peacefully in his sleep at the age of eighty-one. Baron Trotta merely said: 'Tell the Baroness I want my bags packed, I'm going to Vienna tonight!' He carried on to the steward's house, enquired about the seed, discussed the weather, gave instructions for three new ploughs to be ordered, for the vet to come on Monday and the midwife that same day for the maid, who was heavily pregnant, and said in parting, 'My father's died. I'm going to be away in Vienna for three days!' He saluted with a single, casual finger and left.

His bags were packed, the horses were harnessed up; it was an hour to the station. He quickly ate his soup and meat. Then he said to his wife: 'I've finished! My father was a good man. You never met him!' Was that an obituary? A lament? 'You're coming with me!' he said to his terrified son. His wife got up to pack some clothes for the boy. While she was busy upstairs, Trotta said to the little boy: 'You're going to see your grandfather.' The boy trembled and lowered his eyes.

The cavalry sergeant was lying in state when they arrived. Watched over by eight three-foot candles and a couple of fellow pensioners, he lay there on the catafalque in his living room, with his mighty bristling moustache, dressed in a dark blue uniform with three shiny medals on his breast. An Ursuline nun was praying in the corner, by the single, curtained window. The pensioners stood to attention when Trotta entered. He wore his major's uniform with the Maria Theresa Order; he knelt down and his son promptly fell to his knees as well, at the dead man's feet, the mighty bootsoles of the corpse in front of the youthful face. For the first time in his life, Baron Trotta felt a slight stab in his heart. His little eyes were dry. In pious quandariness, he mumbled two or three Lord's Prayers, stood up, bent down over the dead man, kissed the mighty moustache, waved to the invalids, and said to his son: 'Come on.'

'Did you see him?' he asked once they were outside.

'Yes,' said the boy.

'He was just a gendarmerie sergeant,' said the father. 'I saved the Emperor's life at the battle of Solferino – that's what got us the baronetcy.'

The boy said nothing.

The pensioner was buried in the military section of the small cemetery at Laxenburg. Six navy-clad pall-bearers carried the coffin from the chapel to the grave. Major Trotta, in shako and parade uniform, kept his hand on his son's shoulder throughout. The boy sobbed. The sad music of the army band, the unvarying, melancholy droning of the priests, which could be heard each time there was a pause in the music, the gentle waft of incense – all this combined to provoke in the boy a baffling, choking grief. And the rifle salvoes, which a half-platoon loosed off over the grave, shook him with their long and implacable echo. What they were doing was sending soldierly greetings to the spirit of the departed as it flew up to heaven, for evermore clear of this earth.

Father and son rode home. The Baron didn't speak once. Only when they got off the train and boarded the carriage that was waiting for them behind the stationmaster's garden did the Major say: 'He was your grandfather. Don't forget him!'

The Baron returned to his usual occupations. The years rolled on like peaceful, equable, silent wheels. The gendarmerie sergeant's was not the last corpse that the Baron had to bury. After him he buried his father-in-law, then a couple of years later his wife, who died quickly, demurely and without farewell of a sudden bronchial infection. He sent his son to boarding school in Vienna, and decreed that he should never become an active soldier. He lived alone on the estate, in the spacious white house imbued still with the breath of the departed, speaking only to the forester, the steward, the servant and the coachman. The domestics could always feel his rough peasant fists, and his speechless fury hung over them like a yoke over their necks. A fearsome stillness preceded him like a storm. Twice a month he received dutiful letters from his son. Once a month, he replied in a couple of short sentences, on small, scrimped bits of paper, which he tore off the edges of those he had received. Once a year, on 18 August, the Emperor's birthday, he put on his uniform and drove to the nearest garrison town. Twice a year, his son came home on visits, in the Christmas and the summer holidays. On Christmas Eve, the boy was given three hard silver gulden, which he had to sign for, and wasn't allowed to take away with him. That very same evening, they were put away in a little box in the old man's sock drawer. Along with the gulden were his school reports. They spoke of the boy's respectable diligence and his average, but always satisfactory talents. Never was the boy given a toy, never any money, never a book, with the exception of the prescribed school textbooks. He seemed not to feel these privations. He had a tidy, sober and honest mind. His limited imagination desired nothing but to get through his school years as quickly as possible.

He was eighteen on the Christmas Eve when his father announced: 'This year you're not getting three gulden any more!

You can take nine out of your box, if you sign for them. Watch yourself with the girls, most of them are diseased!' And, after a pause: 'I've decided you're going to be a lawyer. You've got two years ahead of you till then. The army's not a pressing thing. They can wait till you're done.'

The boy accepted the nine gulden just as obediently as he accepted his father's wish. He didn't often visit the girls, he chose carefully among them, and by the time he came home for his summer holiday, he still had six gulden. He asked his father if he might bring a friend home with him. 'All right,' said the Major, with some surprise. The friend came without much in the way of luggage, except for a large box of paints, which the master of the house took against. 'Is he a painter then?' asked the old man. 'A very good one!' said Franz, the son. 'He's not to do any of his daubs about the house! Tell him he can paint landscapes if he likes!' The guest painted outdoors, but not landscapes. He painted a portrait of Baron Trotta from memory. Every day at table, he studied the features of the master of the house. 'What's he staring at?' asked the Baron. Both boys blushed and looked at the table-cloth. Even so, the portrait was completed and presented to the old man, framed, at the end of the visit. He examined it carefully, and smiled. He turned it round, as though seeking further clarification on the back, held it up next to the window, then on the other side of the room. He looked at himself in the mirror, compared his reflection with his image, and finally asked: 'Where shall I put it?' It was the first pleasure he had had in many years. 'If your friend is ever short, you can loan him money if you want,' he said quietly to Franz. 'I would like it if you stayed friends!' The portrait was, and was to remain, the only one ever made of the old Trotta. Later, it hung in the living room of his son, and was to preoccupy the imagination of his grandson . . .

But for now, it kept the Major in unusually good spirits for the next several weeks. He tried hanging it now on this wall, now on that; with flattered pleasure he took in the hard, beaky nose, the narrow, pale, moustache-less mouth, the lean cheekbones, which lay like little hills in front of the little black eyes, and the narrow, furrowed brow, under the cropped, bristly, widow's peak. Only now did he come to know his own face; sometimes he gave himself over to silent dialogues with it. It aroused in him quite new thoughts, memories, ungraspable, fleeting shadows of melancholy. He had needed the painting to understand his premature ageing and his deep loneliness; now, from the painted canvas they flowed towards him, his loneliness and his age. Was I always like that? he asked himself. Did I never used to be any different? From time to time, rather aimlessly, he went to the graveyard, visited his wife's grave; he looked at the grey stone and the chalk-white cross, the dates of her birth and death; he calculated that she had died before her time, and he confessed that he could not remember her well. Her hands, for example, he had forgotten. 'Chinese Iron Tonic Wine' he remembered, that was a remedy she had taken for many years. What about her face? He could still summon it up when he closed his eyes; later it disappeared, blurring in a round, reddish haze. He grew milder in his dealings about the house and grounds, was known to pat a horse sometimes, to smile at the cows, to drink the odd glass of schnapps, and one day he wrote his son a few lines outside the normal correspondence times. People began to greet him with a smile, he nodded back with pleasure. Summer came, the holidays brought his son and his friend, the old man drove into town with the pair of them, took them to a pub, drank a couple of glasses of slivovitz, and ordered the young men a big meal.

His son took his law exams, his visits home became more frequent, he looked around the property, he thought he would like to manage it one day and give up his legal career. He told his father. The Major said: 'It's too late for that! You won't be a farmer or a landlord in your lifetime! You'll be a civil servant, and that's that!' It was a foregone conclusion. The son became an officer of state, an Assistant District Commissioner in Silesia. If the name Trotta had disappeared from the officially sanctioned schoolbooks, it was very much present in the confidential files of the political authorities, and the five thousand gulden that had been donated by the grace of the Emperor assured young Trotta of benevolent notice and steady preferment from his unknown superiors. He worked his way up through the grades. A couple of years before he became Chief District Commissioner, the Major died.

He left a rather surprising will. Certain of the fact – he wrote – that his son would never make a good agriculturalist, and hoping that the Trottas, grateful to the Emperor for his continuing favour, would attain rank and station in the service of the state, and make their way in life more happily than he, the testator, he had decided, in memory of his late father, to leave the property he had inherited from his father-in-law, with all its moveable and immoveable goods and chattels, to the Foundation for Military Invalids, requiring of the said foundation only that it arrange for the burial, of the very humblest sort, of the testator, in the same graveyard where his father lay, and if possible, close to his father. The testator asked for a minimum of ceremony. Cash holdings of fifteen thousand florins plus interest, deposited with Efrussi's bank in Vienna, plus the ring, watch and chain belonging to his late mother were to go to the testator's only son, Baron Franz von Trotta and Sipolje.

An army band from Vienna, a company of infantry, a representative of the Knights of the Order of Maria Theresa, representatives of the south Hungarian regiment in which the reticent hero had served, all the pensioners who were still able to march, two officials from the Court and Cabinet Office, and a junior officer carrying the Order of Maria Theresa on a black velvet cushion: these made up the official mourners. Franz, the son, walked apart, small, thin and in black. The band played the same march they had played at his grandfather's funeral. The salvoes discharged on this occasion were louder and left a more lingering echo.

The son had no tears. No one wept for the dead man. Everyone remained dry-eyed and formal. No one spoke at the graveside. Major Baron von Trotta and Sipolje, the knight of truth, was laid beside the gendarmerie sergeant. He was given a plain, military headstone, and alongside name, rank and regiment, the proud sobriquet etched in black, THE HERO OF SOLFERINO.

What was left of the deceased did not amount to much more than that stone, a vanished fame, and the portrait. A peasant walks across his field in springtime, and by summer, all trace of his footsteps has been covered by the wheat he has sown. In that same week, the Kaiserlich und Königlich* Chief District Commissioner Trotta von Sipolje received a letter of condolence from His Majesty, in which the still 'unforgotten services' rendered him by the deceased were referred to twice.

---

*Kaiserlich und Königlich: Imperial and Royal – henceforth K-and-K.

## 2

In all the territory from which the division was drawn, there was no finer military band than that of the Xth Infantry in the small Moravian town of W. The bandleader was one of those old-school Austrian military musicians, whom a good memory and a craving for new variations on old tunes enable to knock out a new march once a month. The marches were as difficult to tell apart as men in uniform. Mostly, they began with a drum roll, contained the *accelerando* of the tattoo and an outbreak of hilarity from the winsome cymbals, and ended with a rumble of thunder from the great side drum – the brief and cheerful storm of a marching tune. What distinguished the bandleader Nechwal from his colleagues was not so much the assiduousness of his composing, as the racy and breezy strictness with which he conducted his music. Some other bandleaders' casual habit of putting the musical adjutant in charge of the first march, and only taking the baton for the second, was in Nechwal's eyes clear evidence of the decline of the Dual Monarchy. As soon as the band members were drawn up in the usual circular formation, and the frail feet of their tiny music stands dug into the cracks of black earth between the cobblestones, there was the bandleader standing in the midst of his musicians, his black ebony baton with its silver head discreetly at the ready.

All their public concerts – they took place under the veranda of the District Commissioner – began with the Radetzky March. Although it was so familiar to all the members of the band that they could have played it in their sleep without a conductor, still the bandleader insisted on reading every note from the score. And, every Sunday, as though he were rehearsing the Radetzky March for the first time, in military and musicianly conscientiousness Nechwal raised his head, his baton and his gaze and aimed all three simultaneously at whichever part of the circle around him most needed his commands. The bitter drums rolled, the sweet flutes warbled, and the winsome cymbals pealed. A pleasant and musing smile came to the faces of the listeners, and the blood quickened in their legs. Even as they stood still, they had the feeling they were marching. Young girls parted their lips and stopped breathing. Mature men looked at the ground and remembered their manoeuvres. Old women sat in the park some distance away, and wobbled their little grey heads. It was summer.

Yes, it was summer. The ancient chestnuts opposite the District Commissioner's house only moved their dense green broad-leaved crowns in the morning and evening. In the daytime, they remained motionless, gave off a bitter scent, and spilled their spacious, cool shade over the road. The skies were never anything other than blue. Invisible larks trilled unremittingly over the silent town. From time to time, a fiacre would trundle over its bumpy cobbles, bearing a stranger on his way from the station to the hotel. Sometimes the hooves of the horses went at a brisk clip, as Herr von Winternigg was driven down the wide avenue, from north to south, from his manor house to his vast hunting grounds. Small, old and pathetic, a yellowed old man under a large, yellow blanket, with a tiny, wizened face, Herr von Winternigg sat in his calèche. Like a pathetic remnant of winter he drove through the plenitude of summer. On silent, bouncy, lofty rubber-tyred wheels, whose delicate brown-lacquered spokes scattered the sunlight, he rolled straight out of bed to his rural idyll. Large dark forests and blond green-clad foresters were already waiting for him. The townspeople greeted him. He did not respond. He rode impassively through a sea of greetings. His black-clad coachman loomed stiffly, his top hat almost brushing the crowns of the chestnuts, his pliant whip stroked the brown backs of the horses, and at certain set, regular intervals there came from his closed mouth a resounding click, louder than the drumming of the hooves, like a tuneful gunshot.

It was the beginning of the holidays. To the fifteen-year-old son of the District Commissioner, Carl Joseph von Trotta, a pupil at the cavalry cadet school in Mährisch-Weisskirchen, his birthplace carried strong associations of summer; it was the home of summer, as much as his own. Christmas and Easter he spent with his uncle. It was only in summer that he got to go home, and his stay always began on a Sunday. That was the will of his father, the District Commissioner Franz von Trotta and Sipolje. Whenever the summer holidays might be slated to begin in the institution, at home they always began on a Sunday. On Sunday, Herr von Trotta and Sipolje did not work. He set aside the entire morning from nine till twelve for his son. Punctually, at ten to nine, a quarter of an hour after early mass, the boy was standing outside his father's door, in his Sunday uniform. At five to nine, Jacques would come down the stairs in his grey livery to announce: 'Young Master, your Papa's on his way.' Carl Joseph straightened his tunic one last time, adjusted his belt, took his cap in his hand, and pressed it, as per regulations, against his hip. His father appeared, the son clicked his heels, the report echoed through the silent old house. The old man opened the door and with a faint gesture ushered his son into the room. As though oblivious of the invitation, the boy remained rooted to the spot. So the father strode through the door and Carl Joseph followed, as far as the threshold. 'Make yourself at home!' the District Commissioner said after a while. Only now did Carl Joseph approach the red plush armchair and sit down, facing his father, knees pressed together, and his cap and white gloves on his knees. Through thin gaps in the green blinds, narrow beams of sunshine fell on the burgundy carpet. A

fly buzzed, the wall clock began to strike. After the nine rings
had echoed away, the District Commissioner began: 'How is
Colonel Marek?' 'Thank you, Father, he's doing well!' 'Still
shaky at geometry?' 'Thank you, Father, a little better!' 'Done
any reading?' 'Yes, Father!' 'How's the riding? Nothing to write
home about last year . . .' 'This year . . .' Carl Joseph began, only
to be immediately cut off. His father had put out his slender hand,
half covered by the round, shiny shirt-cuff. The massy square
golden cuff link sparkled. 'It was nothing to write home about, I
just said. It was –' and the District Commissioner paused, before
adding in a low tone, 'disgraceful!' Father and son didn't speak.
However softly the word 'disgraceful' might have been said, it
lingered in the room. Carl Joseph knew that he had to keep silent
after such a severe rebuke from his father. The judgement had to
be absorbed in its full, crushing weight, it needed to be assimilated
and digested, worked into the heart and mind. Then Carl Joseph
piped up, 'This year, it was much better. The cavalry sergeant
said so himself quite a few times. I was also commended by First
Lieutenant Koppel.' 'Cause for celebration,' growled the District
Commissioner. He shot his cuff by banging it against the edge of
the table. 'Go on!' he said, and lit a cigarette. That was the signal
for the beginning of a new, more genial phase. Carl Joseph put his
cap and gloves on a little desk, stood up and began to relate the
events of the past year. The old man nodded. All at once he said:
'You've shot up all of a sudden, my son! Your voice is breaking! In
love, by any chance?' Carl Joseph blushed. His face burned like a
red paper lantern, bravely he held it up to his father. 'Still waiting,
then!' said the District Commissioner. 'Don't be thrown! Carry
on!' Carl Joseph gulped, his blush paled, suddenly he felt cold.
Slowly, and with many pauses, he made his report. Then he took
his booklist out of his pocket, and handed it to his father. 'Some
solid reading matter there!' said the District Commissioner. 'Now.
Tell me the plot of *Zriny*!' Carl Joseph gave a résumé, act by act.
Then he sat down, tired, pale, his tongue parched.

He shot a covert glance at the clock, it was only half past ten.

There was another hour and a half of his examination still to go. The old man could go on to test him on classical history or German mythology. He was striding about the room now, smoking, his left hand behind his back. The cuff rattled on his right. The stripes of sunlight on the carpet grew in intensity, as they slid towards the window. The sun must be high in the sky already. The church bells began to peal, they clanged into the room as though they were swinging just the other side of the thick blinds. Today the old man only tested him on literature. He spoke at some length about the significance of Grillparzer, and recommended Adalbert Stifter and Ferdinand von Saar as 'light holiday reading'. Then he got back to military subjects, sentry duty, part two of the service regulations, the composition of an army corps, the numbers required to make up a regiment in wartime. Suddenly he asked: 'Define subordination!' 'Subordination is the duty of unconditional obedience,' recited Carl Joseph, 'that is owed by every soldier to his commanding officer, and by . . .' 'Stop!' his father interrupted him, '*and also* by every officer to a superior officer.' Carl Joseph went on, 'When . . .' 'From the moment that,' the old man corrected him. 'From the moment that a command is issued.' Carl Joseph took a deep breath. It struck twelve.

Only now did the holidays really begin. In a quarter of an hour, he would hear the first clattering drum roll of the band leaving barracks. Every Sunday lunchtime they played outside the official residence of the District Commissioner, the representative in this small town of no less a figure than the Emperor himself. Carl Joseph stood concealed on the balcony behind the thick canopy of vine leaves, and received the music as a kind of personal tribute. He felt almost related to the Habsburgs, whose power his father represented and defended, and for whom he would one day go out himself, to fight and to die. He knew the names of all the members of the royal family. He loved them all deeply, with a child's unquestioning devotion, above all the Emperor himself, who was great and kind, lofty and just, infinitely remote and infinitely close, and to no one more than the officers of his army. Ideally, one would die for him to music, and preferably to the music of the Radetzky March. The swift bullets whistled in time about Carl Joseph's head, his gleaming sabre flashed, and with heart and head filled with the gorgeous abruptness of the march, he would sink into its thrumming ecstasy, and a thin scarlet trickle of his blood would run out over the shimmering golds of the cornets, the deep black of the drums and the victorious silver of the cymbals.

Jacques coughed softly behind him. It was time for lunch. Whenever there was a break in the music, he could hear a chink of silver and porcelain from the dining room. It was set back from the balcony by a couple of large rooms, right in the middle of the first floor. During lunch, the music could be heard distantly but clearly enough. If only it played every day. It was useful and good, it twined itself mildly and graciously around the formality of lunch, taking the ceremonial edge off it, and preventing the harsh, abrupt and embarrassing conversations that Father often liked to start. It was possible to be silent, listen and enjoy. The plates had delicate, faded blue-gold rims. Carl Joseph loved them. He thought about them often over the years. About them and the Radetzky March and the paper silhouette of his late mother (whom the boy could no longer remember) and the heavy silver ladle and the fish tureen and the fruit knives with their serrated backs, and the tiny coffee cups and frail coffee spoons that were worn thin as ancient silver coins: all these added up to summer holidays, freedom, home.

He handed Jacques his cloak, cap and gloves, and strode into the dining room. The old man entered it at the same moment, and smiled at his son. Fräulein Hirschwitz, the housekeeper, came in a few moments later, in her grey Sunday silk, head erect, her hair in a heavy bun at her nape, a mighty, crooked brooch like a Tartar scimitar on her bosom. She looked armed and armoured. Carl Joseph dabbed a kiss on her long, bony hand. Jacques moved the chairs. The District Commissioner gave the signal to sit down. Jacques disappeared and returned after a time wearing white gloves, which seemed utterly to transform him. They reflected a further snowy sheen over his pale face, his already white muttonchop whiskers, his white hair. Of all the things that passed for bright in this world, they were certainly the brightest. With these gloves he held a dark tray. On it was a steaming soup tureen. He set it down, carefully, silently and very swiftly in the middle of the table. By custom, it was Fräulein Hirschwitz who served the soup. With amiably outstretched arms, and a grateful smile in their eyes, they took the plates from her. She smiled back. A warm, golden gleam filled their bowls; the soup. Noodle soup. Clear broth, with fine, yellow-gold coiled noodles. Herr von Trotta and Sipolje ate fast, sometimes furiously. It was as though he were demolishing one course after another, with noiseless, rapid, aristocratic aggression, finishing them off like enemies. Fräulein Hirschwitz ate tiny portions at table, and once the meal was finished enjoyed a complete second serving of everything up in her room. Carl Joseph hurriedly and timidly gulped down huge mouthfuls. That way, they all contrived to be finished at the same time. If Herr von Trotta and Sipolje was silent, no one spoke.

The soup was followed by boiled beef with trimmings, from time immemorial the old man's preferred Sunday lunch. The admiring appraisal to which he subjected this dish took up more time than half the meal. The District Commissioner's eye first caressed the thin layer of fat that edged the enormous piece of meat, then the various little side dishes on which the vegetables reposed, the violet lustrous beets, the sober rich-green spinach, the bright, cheerful lettuce, the acrid white horseradish, the flawless ovals of new potatoes swimming in melted butter, suggestive somehow of little toys. He had a curious way with food. It was as though he ate the most important things right away with his eyes. His aesthetic sense consumed the essence of the dishes, as it were, their soul; what remained for mouth and jaws was heavy and irksome and had to be got down as quickly as possible. Certain dishes' beautiful appearance gave the old man as much pleasure as their simplicity. He insisted on so-called 'solid middle-class fare' both from personal preference and by philosophical conviction, which he was pleased to call Spartan. By happy knack he combined the satisfaction of his desires with the performance of his duty. He was a Spartan. But he was also an Austrian.

He set about carving the meat, as he did every Sunday. He shot his cuffs, raised both hands in the air, and applying knife and fork to the joint, he turned to Fräulein Hirschwitz and observed: 'You know, my dear, it's not enough simply to ask the butcher for a tender piece. You need to see how it's cut. Whether it's cut along, or across, I mean. Modern butchers no longer know their craft. They spoil the best meat by cutting it the wrong way. See here, my dear! It's all I can do to rescue it. It's frayed at the edges, it's practically falling apart. As a whole it could probably be called "tender". But the individual pieces will be tough, as you'll see in a moment. As for the condiments, as you Germans would say, I would like my horseradish a little dryer next time. It mustn't lose its edge in the milk. It needs to be prepared afresh, not beforehand. This has been soaking a little too long. A mistake!'

Fräulein Hirschwitz, who had lived in Germany for many years, and always spoke High German – it was to her preference for literary expressions that Herr von Trotta's 'condiments' had been an allusion – nodded slowly and weightily. It evidently cost her no little effort to lift the weight of the knot of hair from her nape and allow her head to make an affirmative motion. In this way, her conscientious amiability acquired something measured, yes, it even seemed to comprise a measure of disagreement. And the District Commissioner felt obliged to add: 'Surely you won't take issue with me over this, my dear?'

He spoke in the nasal Austrian of upper officialdom and nether aristocracy. It sounded a little like the distant jangle of a guitar at night, and the last, soft vibrations of bells as they echoed away; it was a gentle, but precise language, capable of tenderness and malice in the same breath. It accorded with the lean bony face of the speaker and his narrow, hooked nose, where the droning, somewhat plangent consonants seemed to dwell. When the District Commissioner spoke, his nose and mouth seemed more like wind instruments than facial features. His lips were the only part of his face that moved. The dark muttonchop whiskers that Herr von Trotta wore as an extension of his uniform, an emblem of his service to Franz Joseph I and a proof of his belief in a dynastic monarchy, even those whiskers never moved when Herr von Trotta and Sipolje spoke. He sat upright at table, as though holding a pair of reins in his hard hands. When seated, he gave the appearance of standing, and so when he rose, the stature of his rapier-like form was always surprising. He invariably wore dark blue, in summer and winter, on Sundays and weekdays alike; a dark blue tunic and grey striped trousers that he wore tightly around his long legs, and with elastic loops to hold them round his smooth riding boots. Between the second and third courses, he would get up, to 'aid his digestion', as he said. But the effect was more as if he wanted to show his companions at table how a man may get up, stand and walk around, without losing his essential immobility. Jacques tidied away the meat, and caught a flashing look from Fräulein Hirschwitz, telling him to warm up the leftovers for her for later. Herr von Trotta walked with measured tread to the window, drew the curtain aside a little, and returned to the table. At that instant, the cherry dumplings made their entrance on a spacious dish. The District Commissioner took only one, broke it open with a spoon, and said to Fräulein Hirschwitz: 'That, my dear, is the very model of a cherry dumpling. It resists the spoon, and yet will melt on the tongue.' And, turning to Carl Joseph: 'My boy, I would urge you to have two today!' Carl Joseph took two. He gobbled them up in no time, finished moments before his father, and drank a glass of water – there was wine only with dinner – to wash them down into his stomach in case they were still stuck in his throat. He folded up his napkin in time with the old man. They rose. The band outside were playing the Tannhäuser overture. To their sonorous accompaniment, they strode into the drawing room, Fräulein Hirschwitz leading the way. There, Jacques served coffee. They awaited the entrance of Bandleader Nechwal. He appeared, just as his musicians were forming up to march off, in his dark blue parade uniform, with shining sabre and two small, glittering golden harps on his collar. 'Your playing was marvellous,' said Herr von Trotta, as he did every Sunday. 'Really quite exceptional today.' Herr Nechwal bowed. He had lunched an hour ago in the officers' mess, hadn't had time for a black coffee, the taste of the food was still in his mouth, he was desperate for a Virginia. Jacques brought in a box of cigars. The bandleader sucked for a long time on the flame that Carl Joseph steadfastly held up to the long cigar, at grave risk to his fingers. They sat in wide leather armchairs. Herr Nechwal talked about the latest Lehár operetta in Vienna. He was quite a fellow, their bandleader. He went to Vienna twice a month, and Carl Joseph guessed the musician must have the odd secret relating to the great Viennese *demi-monde* lurking in the depths of his soul. He had three children and a wife 'from a humble background', yet he himself stood in the full glare of publicity, quite detached from his family. He enjoyed and liked to tell Jewish jokes with witty merriment. The District Commissioner didn't understand them, didn't laugh at them either, but said: 'Very good, very good!' 'How is your wife?' Herr von Trotta would ask regularly. He had been asking the question for years. He had never met Frau Nechwal, nor did he ever wish to meet the 'wife from a humble background'. On parting, he always said to Herr Nechwal: 'Remember me kindly to your wife, even though we've never met!' And Herr Nechwal promised to convey his regards, and assured him his wife would be very pleased. 'And how are the children?' asked Herr von Trotta, who could never remember if Nechwal had sons or daughters. 'The oldest boy's doing well at school!' replied the bandleader. 'Is he going to be a musician as well?' asked Herr von Trotta, faintly contemptuously. 'No!' replied Herr Nechwal, 'one more year, and he'll be going to cadet school.' 'Ah, an officer!' said the District Commissioner. 'That's the stuff. Infantry?' Herr Nechwal smiled: 'Of course! He's a good lad. He might make the staff one day.' 'I'm sure, I'm sure!' said the District Commissioner. 'Stranger things have happened!' By the following week, he'd have forgotten it all again. To remember a bandleader's children was too much to expect.

Herr Nechwal drank two demitasses of coffee, no more and no less. Reluctantly, he pinched out the final third of his cigar. He had to go, and you couldn't leave with a lit cigar in your hand. 'It really was particularly distinguished today. My regards to your wife. I'm sorry I haven't yet had the pleasure!' said Herr von Trotta and Sipolje. Carl Joseph clicked his heels. He escorted the bandleader to the top of the stairs. Then he returned to the drawing room. He stood in front of his father, and said: 'I'm going for a walk, Papa!' 'Absolutely! Good bracing walk!' said Herr von Trotta, and waved.

Carl Joseph set off. He thought he would walk slowly, he wanted to stroll, to prove to his feet that it was the holidays. Then, when he passed his first soldier, he shaped up, as they say in army parlance, and started to march. He came to the edge of town, the big yellow revenue office, baking gently in the sun. The sweet scent of the fields wafted up to greet him, the rackety larks' song. In the west the blue horizon clarified itself into blue-grey hills, rustic huts with tiled and thatched roofs began to appear, chickens and ducks broke the summery silence with their voices. Stretched out in the brightness of day, the land slept.

Just past the railway embankment stood a gendarmerie post, under the command of a sergeant. Carl Joseph knew him, it was Sergeant Slama. He decided he would knock. He stepped into the baking yard, knocked on the door, tried the bell, no one answered. A window opened. Frau Slama leaned out over the geraniums and called: 'Who is it?' She saw young Trotta, and said: 'Just a moment!' She opened the door; the hall smelled cool and of perfume. Frau Slama had dabbed a drop of scent on to her dress. Carl Joseph tried to imagine the brothels of Vienna. He said: 'Is the Sergeant not at home?' 'He's on duty, Herr von Trotta!' replied his wife. 'But come in, anyway!'

Then Carl Joseph was sitting in the Slamas' front room. It was a low, reddish room, distinctly cool, it felt almost like an icebox; the chairs had upholstered seats, but their arms and backs were brown-stained fretwork foliage that cut into his back. Frau Slama served cool lemonade; she drank dainty little sips, held her little finger at an angle, and crossed her legs. She sat next to Carl Joseph, looking at him, waving a bare stockingless foot that was clad in a red velvet slipper. Carl Joseph looked at the foot, and then at his lemonade. He couldn't look Frau Slama in the eye. His cap was resting on his knees, his knees were pressed together, he sat bolt upright over his lemonade, as though drinking it were part of his duty as a cadet. 'You've not been by for quite some time, Herr von Trotta!' said the sergeant's wife. 'You've shot up! You must be all of fourteen by now.' 'Yes, some time ago.' He thought he would try to leave as quickly as possible. He needed to gulp down his lemonade, make a nice bow, have her say hello to her husband for him, and get out. He looked despairingly at his lemonade, he couldn't get through it. Frau Slama kept topping up his glass. She took out cigarettes. He wasn't allowed to smoke. She lit one for herself, and started to smoke it, coolly, expelling the smoke through her nostrils, waggling her foot. Suddenly, without a word, she took the cap off his knee, and laid it on the table. Then she put her cigarette in his mouth, her hand smelled of smoke and cologne, the light sleeve of her flowered summer frock flashed before his eyes. Politely, he continued to smoke the cigarette, which still had the dampness of her lips on it, and looked at his lemonade. Frau Slama took the cigarette back, jammed it between her teeth and stood behind Carl Joseph. He was scared to look round. All at once, he felt her shimmering sleeves round his neck, and her face pressing down on his hair. He didn't stir. But his heart beat loudly, a great storm broke loose in him, desperately opposed by his frozen body and the stout buttons of his uniform. 'Come on!' whispered Frau Slama. She sat on his lap, kissed him quickly, and looked at him roguishly. A clump of blonde hair fell in her eyes, and she squinted up at it, and tried to blow it out of the way with her lower lip. He began to feel her weight on his legs and, at the same time, fresh strength flooded through him, and tautened the muscles in his thighs and his arms. He embraced the woman and felt the soft coolness of her bosom through the stiff material of his uniform. A little giggle escaped her, it was something between a sob and a trill. There were tears in her eyes. Then she leaned back and, tenderly and methodically, undid one button of his tunic after another. She laid her cool, tender hand on his chest, kissed his mouth for a long time with systematic relish, and suddenly leaped up as though she'd heard a noise. He leaped up himself, she smiled, and slowly, stepping backwards, hands outstretched and head thrown back, with shining eyes, drew him out of the room, pushing the door open with her heel. They slipped into the bedroom.

Helpless, like a prisoner, he watched through half-closed eyelids as she slowly, thoroughly and maternally undressed him. With horror he noticed one item after another of his dress uniform fall limply to the floor, he heard the thud of his shoes and immediately after felt Frau Slama's hand on his foot. From there a further wave of hot and cold feeling travelled up to his chest. He let himself fall. He received the woman like a great soft wave of delight, fire and water.

He awoke. Frau Slama was standing in front of him, handing him his clothes back, item by item; hurriedly he began dressing. She went to the front room, and brought back his cap and gloves. She straightened his tunic, he could feel that she was looking steadily at his face, but he avoided looking back at her. He brought his heels together with a sharp crack, pressed her hand – while keeping his eyes stubbornly on her right shoulder – and went.

A clock was striking seven. The sun was just above the hills, which were now as blue as the sky, and barely distinguishable from blue clouds. A sweet smell came off the trees lining the road. The evening breeze brushed the little grass stalks on the banks either side of the road; they yielded tremblingly to its broad, silent, invisible hand. In the far-off swamps, frogs began their croaking. A young woman was looking out at the road from the open window of a little canary-yellow house. Although Carl Joseph had never seen her before, he saluted her correctly and respectfully. Startled and grateful, she nodded back. He felt as though only now had he taken leave of Frau Slama. The woman standing by the window, unknown and yet familiar, was like a border guard watching the crossing between love and life. After he had saluted her, he felt he was back in the world. He stepped out briskly. At quarter past seven on the dot, he was home, and reported back to his father, pale, to the point and resolute, as a man should be.

The Sergeant was on patrol every other day. Every day he took a bundle of files to the District Commissioner's office. He never saw the District Commissioner's son. Every other day, at four in the afternoon, Carl Joseph marched into the gendarmerie post. He left at seven. The scent he took with him from Frau Slama mingled with the smells of the dry summer evenings and stayed on Carl Joseph's hands day and night. He took care not to come closer to his father than necessary. 'I can smell autumn, can't you?' said the old man one evening. He was half right. Frau Slama always wore mignonette.

## 3

The portrait hung in the District Commissioner's drawing room, facing the windows, and so high up on the wall that the brow and hair were obscured in the mahogany shade of the old beamed ceiling. The grandson's curiosity continually revolved around his grandfather's dim figure and extinguished fame. On quiet afternoons, sometimes – the windows were open, the dark green shadow of the chestnuts in the town park imbued the room with the full, powerful calm of summer, the District Commissioner was leading one of his commissions somewhere out of town, on distant staircases the ghostly shuffle of Jacques could be heard, as he padded around the house in his felt slippers, collecting up shoes, clothes, ashtrays, candelabra or standard lamps to be cleaned – on such afternoons, Carl Joseph would climb up on a chair to take a closer look at the portrait of his grandfather. It disintegrated into numerous deep shadows and bright patches, into brushstrokes and dabs of colour, into a myriad web of painted canvas, into the hard play of dried oil paints. Carl Joseph got down from the chair. The green shadow of the trees played over his grandfather's brown jacket, the brushstrokes and dabs reassembled themselves into the familiar, inscrutable physiognomy, and the eyes recovered their customary remote expression of pondering the dark ceiling. Every year, in the summer holidays, the grandson's silent conversations with his grandfather were resumed. The dead man gave nothing away. The boy learned nothing from him. From year to year, the painting seemed to become dimmer and more otherworldly, as though the hero of Solferino had to die all over again, as though he was gradually taking back all memory of himself, and as though there would one day come a time in which an empty canvas would stare down from the black frame upon his progeny with an even more profound discretion than the portrait.

Down in the yard, in the lee of the wooden balcony, Jacques sat on a stool, in front of a row of polished boots in drill order. Whenever Carl Joseph came home after visiting Frau Slama, he went to Jacques in the yard and perched on a ledge. 'Jacques, tell me about Grandfather!' And Jacques would set down brushes and blacking, and rub his hands together as though to wash away the labour and dirt before beginning to speak of the deceased. And as he always did, and as he had done a score of times already, he began: 'I always got along with him! I was no longer in my first flush of youth when I came into his service, I didn't marry, the deceased wouldn't have liked that at all. He didn't like having women about the place, with the exception of the Baroness, but she passed away quickly, with the consumption. He saved the Emperor's life in the battle of Solferino, but blow me if he ever told a living soul a word about it. That's why they went and wrote THE HERO OF SOLFERINO on his gravestone. He wasn't old when he died, it was in the evening, round about nine o'clock, I think in November. The first snow had just fallen, and in the afternoon he stood out in the yard and said: "Jacques, where have you put the fur-lined boots?" I didn't know where I'd put them, but I replied anyway: "I'll just go and get them, Baron!" "It can wait till the morning!" he said – and in the morning he didn't need them any more. And I never married!' And that was all.

Once (it was in his last school holidays, the following year Carl Joseph was to be passed out), the District Commissioner said goodbye with the following words: 'I hope everything goes well.

You're the grandson of the hero of Solferino. So long as you bear that in mind, nothing will go wrong!' The colonel, the teaching staff and all the non-commissioned officers also bore it in mind, and truly, nothing could go wrong for Carl Joseph. Although not an outstanding rider, mediocre in topography and a total failure at trigonometry, he got through with 'good grades', passed out as a lieutenant, and joined the Xth Dragoons.

Eyes drunk with his own new glory and the formal end-of-year mass, ears still ringing with the Colonel's valedictory address, wearing his sky-blue tunic with gold buttons, a silver munitions pouch with the exalted golden double eagle on the back, a shako with metal chinstrap and horsehair plume in his left hand, scarlet cavalry trousers, highly polished boots, chiming spurs, a sabre with broad hilt at his left hip: that was how Carl Joseph presented himself to his father one hot summer's day. It wasn't a Sunday this time. A lieutenant was welcome even on a weekday. The District Commissioner was sitting in his study. 'Make yourself at home!' he said. He took off his pince-nez, narrowed his eyes, stood up, scrutinized his son, and found everything as it should be. He embraced Carl Joseph, kissing him briskly on both cheeks. 'Sit down!' said the District Commissioner, and pushed the Lieutenant down into an armchair. He himself strode back and forth. He was thinking of an appropriate way to begin. Criticism was not appropriate, and one couldn't begin with an expression of satisfaction. Finally he said, 'You ought to get acquainted with the history of your regiment, and your grandfather's too. I've got to go to Vienna on business for a couple of days, I want you to come with me.' Then he shook the bell. Jacques arrived. 'Fräulein Hirschwitz,' ordered the District Commissioner, 'should have the wine brought up from the cellar today, and, if they can be arranged, boiled beef and cherry dumplings for lunch. Lunch to be served twenty minutes later than usual.' 'Yes, Baron,' said Jacques. He looked at Carl Joseph and whispered: 'My congratulations!' The District Commissioner walked over to the window, the scene was threatening to become mawkish. Behind his back he was aware that his son was shaking hands with Jacques, he heard Jacques scrape his heels together, and murmur something inaudible about the deceased. He didn't turn round until Jacques had left the room.

'Warm, isn't it?' the old man began.

'Yes, Papa!'

'I think we should take the air!'

'Yes, Papa!'

The District Commissioner took his ebony walking stick with the silver handle, rather than the yellow cane he usually took on fine mornings. Also, he pulled on his gloves, rather than carrying them in his left hand. He put on his top hat and strode out of the room, followed by his son. Slowly, and without exchanging a word, the two of them strolled through the summer silence of the town park. The town policeman saluted them, men got up from park benches and greeted them. Next to the dark *gravitas* of the elder man, the jingling colourfulness of the younger one seemed even gaudier and noisier. In the main avenue, where a blonde girl dispensed sodas with raspberry syrup in the shade of a red parasol, the old man stopped and said: 'A cooling drink wouldn't hurt!' He ordered a couple of sodas, unsweetened, and with covert dignity watched the blonde seem to melt yearningly and helplessly into the colourful aura of Carl Joseph. They had their drink and went on. Sometimes the District Commissioner swung his stick a little, occasional expression of an exuberance that knew to keep itself in check. Even though he was just as earnest and taciturn as always, still he seemed to his son almost jolly today. Out of his happy chest there broke from time to time a merry cough that was close to a laugh. When someone greeted him, he raised his hat quickly. There were even moments when he ventured a dashing paradox, such as: 'Politeness can be so burdensome!' He would rather say something controversial than show his joy at the marvelling expressions of passers-by. As they were once more approaching the front gates, he stopped. He turned to face his son, and said: 'When I was younger, I wanted to be a soldier too. Now I'm happy you're not a civil servant!' 'Yes, Papa!' replied Carl Joseph.

There was wine, and the beef and the cherry dumplings were forthcoming as well. Fräulein Hirschwitz came down in her Sunday grey, and at the sight of Carl Joseph dropped the greater part of her severity on the spot. 'It makes me very happy,' she said, 'my felicitations.' 'Felicitations means congratulations,' remarked the District Commissioner. And they began to eat.

'You don't need to rush so!' said the old man. 'If I happen to finish before you, I'll just wait a bit.' Carl Joseph looked up. He understood that his father had known for years how difficult it was for him to keep up. And for the first time he had the feeling he could see through the old man's armour plating, and into his living heart and the tissue of his innermost thoughts. Even though he was now a lieutenant, Carl Joseph blushed. 'Thanks, Papa!' he said. The District Commissioner went on plying his spoon. He seemed not to have heard.

A couple of days later, they boarded the train to Vienna. The son read the newspaper, the father some files. Once, the District Commissioner looked up and said: 'We'll order you another pair of dress trousers, you've only got two.' 'Thank you, Papa!' And they went back to their reading.

When they were only a quarter of an hour or so from Vienna, the father slammed his files shut. Straight away the son laid his newspaper aside. The District Commissioner gazed at the window, and then for a second or two at his son. Suddenly he said: 'You know Sergeant Slama, don't you?' The name struck Carl Joseph's memory, a cry from a distant past. Straight away he pictured the road that led to the gendarmerie post, the low-ceilinged room, the flowered nightgown, the broad and solid bed, and into his nostrils came the waft of meadows and Frau Slama's mignonette. He listened. 'Unfortunately he's become a widower, just this year,' the old man went on. 'Sad. His wife died in childbed. You ought to pay him a visit.'

The compartment suddenly felt insufferable. Carl Joseph tried to loosen his collar. As he racked his brain for something suitable to say, a foolish, hot, childish longing to cry came up in him, choked him; his mouth suddenly felt as dry as if he had drunk nothing for three days. He could feel his father looking at him, and he stared desperately out at the landscape; the destination they were approaching at every moment felt like a sharpening of his torment; he wished he could at least be in the corridor and yet knew that he could not escape his father's look or his news. He mustered what feeble, provisional forces he had, and said: 'I will visit him!'

'I get the impression rail travel doesn't agree with you,' remarked his father.

'No, sir!'

Silent and upright, under attack from a torment that it was beyond him to name, that he had never experienced before, and that seemed to him like a mysterious ailment from somewhere far away, Carl Joseph travelled to their hotel. He was barely able to say: 'Excuse me, Papa!' before locking himself in his room, unpacking his suitcase, and taking out the folder containing a few letters from Frau Slama, still with the envelopes they had come in, with the coded address, Mährisch-Weisskirchen, poste restante. The blue pages were the colour of sky and bore a hint of mignonette, and the delicate, black letters flew across them like an orderly flock of swallows. Letters from the dead Frau Slama! Imbued with the spectral delicacy of which only doomed hands are capable, they seemed to Carl Joseph like a portent of her sudden end, advance greetings from the Beyond. He hadn't yet replied to her last letter. Passing out, the speeches, the goodbyes, the mass, his commission, his new rank and new uniforms; all paled, one might say, into insignificance against the weightless, dark form of the curved letters on the blue ground. His skin still bore traces of the dead woman's caressing hands, and in his own warm hands lay concealed memories of her cool breasts, and with his eyes closed he could see the blissful exhaustion in her love-sated face, her red, parted lips and the white sheen of her teeth, her negligently thrown back arm, the lineaments of peaceful dreams and contented sleep in every line of her body. And now there were worms crawling over her thighs and breasts, and pitiless mould would consume her face. The more strongly the hideous images of corruption came before the eyes of the young man, the more violently they stirred his passion. It seemed to grow out into the baffling limitlessness of those zones into which the dead woman had now departed. I probably wouldn't even have gone to see her again! thought the Lieutenant. I would have forgotten her. Her words were tender, she was like a mother, she loved me, and now she's dead! Clearly, he was responsible for her death. There she lay, across the threshold of his life, a beloved corpse. It was Carl Joseph's first encounter with death. He could not remember his mother. He knew nothing of her beyond the flowers on her grave and one or two photographs. Now Death flashed in front of him like black lightning, striking his innocent pleasure, singeing his youth, and bringing him to the dark boundary that separates the living from the dead. In front of him, it appeared, lay a long life full of sadness. He girded himself to bear it, resolute and pale, as a man ought to be. He packed up the letters. He shut his suitcase. He went out into the corridor, knocked on the door of his father's room, went in, and heard, as through a thick pane of glass, the old man's voice: 'It appears you are somewhat sentimental!' The District Commissioner tied his tie in front of the mirror. He still had some business in the municipal head office, in the police headquarters, and in the Court of Appeal. 'You come with me!' he said.

They drove in a two-horse cab with rubber tyres. The streets seemed gayer than ever to Carl Joseph. The wide gold expanse of the summer afternoon flowed over houses and trees, trams, pedestrians, policemen, green benches, monuments and gardens. They heard the brisk, clicking sound of the hooves on the cobblestones. Young women slipped by like soft bright lights. Soldiers saluted. Shop windows glittered. The mild summer blew through the great city. But all its beauties swung past Carl Joseph's indifferent eyes. His father's words crashed against his ears like surf. The old

man had a hundred changes to report: Trafik* stores that had
moved, new kiosks, extended omnibus lines, altered bus-stops. So
much had been different in his day. But his loyal memory clung
to everything that had vanished, just as it did to everything that
was still the same; tenderly and with unwonted softness his voice
produced tiny treasures from bygone ages, as his bony hand hailed
those places where his youth had once blossomed. Carl Joseph did
not speak. He too had just lost his youth. His love was dead, but
his heart was open to his father's melancholy, and he began to
guess that behind the bony hardness of the District Commissioner
was concealed another man, both enigmatic and familiar, a Trotta,
a descendant of a Slovenian veteran and the extraordinary hero
of Solferino. And the more animated the old man's observations
and exclamations, the quieter and sparser were the son's dutiful
and habitual confirmations; the alert and eager 'Yes, Papa', which
his tongue had been practised in from his early years, sounded
different now – fraternal and natural. The father came to seem
younger, and the son older. They stopped outside government
buildings, and the District Commissioner went in to look up his
early associates, companions of his youth. Brandl had become
police councillor, Smekal was a head of section, Monteschitzky
was now Colonel Monteschitzky, and Hasselbrunner was legation
councillor. They stopped outside shops, ordered a pair of ankle
boots from Reitmeyer in the Tuchlauben, glacé kid for court
balls and audiences, a pair of salon trousers in the Wieden from
Ettlinger, the court and army tailor, and then – as if by miracle –
the District Commissioner chose a solid-silver cigarette case, with
ridged lid, from Schafransky the court jeweller; a luxury which he
had engraved with the following consoling words, IN PERICULO
SECURITAS. DEIN VATER.

They came to the Volksgarten and drank coffee. The round
tables loomed whitely in the dark green shade of the terrace, the
soda siphons bluely against the tablecloths. Whenever the music

---

*Trafik: State monopoly shops selling tobacco, stamps and stationery.

stopped, the jubilant song of the birds was heard. The District Commissioner lifted his head, and as though pulling up a strand of memories, he began, 'This is where I once courted a girl. I wonder how long ago it is now?' He lost himself in silent calculations. Many, many years seemed to have passed since then; Carl Joseph had the feeling it wasn't his father he was sitting with, but some ancestor. 'Mizzi Schinagl! That was her name,' said the old man. In the thick tops of the chestnuts he hunted for the forgotten image of Fräulein Schinagl, as if she'd been a little bird. 'Is she still alive?' asked Carl Joseph, out of politeness and perhaps to obtain a kind of reference point for these bygone times. 'I hope so! In my day, you know, we weren't so sentimental. We said goodbye to girls and to friends as well . . .' Suddenly he stopped. A stranger stood at their table, a man in a wide-brimmed hat and flowing cravat, in a grey and ancient frock coat with floppy tails, with an abundance of hair over his collar, his broad grey face in need of a shave, obviously and at a glance a painter, with all those unnecessarily explicit artistic features that appear unreal and look to have been clipped out of old caricatures. The stranger laid down his folder on their table, and set about offering his works for sale, with that arrogant indifference born of his poverty and his vocation. 'Moser, please!' said Herr von Trotta.

Slowly the painter rolled the heavy lids up from his large bright eyes, gazed at the District Commissioner for a few seconds, put out his hand and said: 'Trotta!' The next instant he was done with his consternation and his gentleness; he slammed his folder down on the table so hard that the glasses shook, and called out three times in succession, 'Thunderation!' as loudly as if he were doing what he was saying, then he looked triumphantly round the neighbouring tables as if expecting of applause, sat down, took off his broad-brimmed hat and tossed it on the gravel next to his chair, nudged the folder off the table with his elbow, calmly referring to it as 'Shite', inclined his head in the direction of the Lieutenant, frowned, leaned back and said: 'So this is your son, Governor?'

'This is Herr Professor Moser, the friend of my youth!' explained the District Commissioner.

'Thunderation, Governor!' repeated Moser. Simultaneously he reached for the tails of a passing waiter, got up and whispered an order, sat down and was silent, his eyes fixed in the direction from which the waiter would come with the drinks. At last a straight-sided water glass stood in front of him, half filled with clear slivovitz; he passed it once or twice under his flaring nostrils, put it to his lips with a mighty movement of his whole arm, as though about to drain a stein of beer at a single draught, and then took a tiny sip, and collected the drops that remained on his lips with the tip of his tongue.

'You're in town for a fortnight, and you haven't paid me a visit!' he began with the stern manner of a superior.

'My dear Moser,' said Herr von Trotta, 'I got here yesterday, and I'm leaving tomorrow.'

The painter looked for a long time into the face of the District Commissioner. Then he lifted the glass to his lips again, and drained it as if it had been water. When he tried to put it back, he missed the saucer, and allowed Carl Joseph to take it from his grasp. 'Thanks!' said the painter, and with his index finger pointing at the Lieutenant, he said: 'Extraordinary resemblance to the hero of Solferino! Just a tad softer! Weaker nose! Soft mouth! Could still change, mind you, in the course of time ...!'

'Professor Moser painted Grandfather's portrait!' old Trotta remarked. Carl Joseph looked at his father and the painter, and in his memory the portrait of his grandfather appeared, in the gloaming under the drawing room ceiling. The relationship between his grandfather and this professor seemed incredible to him; Father's intimacy with Moser scared him, he saw the broad, dirty hand of the stranger fall with a friendly pat on the District Commissioner's striped trousers and he saw the paternal thigh flinch in coy reproach. There was the old man, dignified as ever, leaning or perhaps pressed back by the smell of alcohol breathed at his face and chest, smiling and apparently quite content. 'You ought to get yourself spruced up a bit,' said the painter. 'You've grown mossy! Your father never looked like that.' The District Commissioner stroked his side whiskers and smiled. 'Ah, the old Trotta!' the painter began again.

'The bill!' the District Commissioner suddenly said quietly. 'Excuse us, Moser, we have an appointment.'

The painter remained seated, father and son left the park.

The District Commissioner pushed his arm through his son's. For the first time, Carl Joseph could feel his father's lean arm against his ribs. The paternal hand in its dark grey glacé glove lay there in faintly arched intimacy on his blue uniform sleeve. This was the same hand that, bony and irate, rattled against the stiff cuff, admonishing and threatening, leafed through papers with silent, pointed fingers, pushed a drawer back into a desk with a choleric thrust, withdrew keys so decisively that one supposed the locks would remain shut for all time. This was the hand that drummed on the table edge with ill-concealed impatience if its master didn't get his way, or on the windowpane if there was some embarrassment in the room. This hand raised its lean index finger if anyone in the house had failed to do their duty, it clenched itself into a silent, though never used, fist, wrapped itself tenderly round a brow, carefully plucked off its pince-nez, cupped itself lightly round a wine glass, brought the black Virginia cigar caressingly to the mouth. It was his father's left hand, so long familiar to the son. And yet it was as though he were only now coming to understand that it was his father's hand, the paternal hand. Carl Joseph felt the urge to clasp this hand against his bosom.

'Well, that's Moser for you!' began the District Commissioner, said nothing for a while, sought an apt summing-up, and finally said: 'He could have made something of himself.'

'Yes, Papa!'

'At the time he painted the picture of Grandfather, he was sixteen. We were both of us sixteen! He was my only friend at school! Then he went on to the Academy. Schnapps got him. Even so ...' The District Commissioner was silent, and added, after a minute or two: 'Of all the fellows I've seen again today, he's my only real friend!'

'Yes – Father.'

Joseph had never called him 'Father' before! He hurriedly corrected himself, 'Yes, Papa!'

It grew dark. Evening came down hard on the street.

'Are you cold, Papa?'

'Not a bit of it.'

But the District Commissioner stepped out more briskly. Soon they were near their hotel.

'Governor!' came a cry behind them. The painter Moser must have followed them. They turned round. There he stood, hat in hand, head lowered in humility, as though to undo the effect of his ironic shout. 'Gentlemen, forgive me!' he said. 'I just noticed that I'm clean out of cigarettes!' He produced an open, empty tin case. The District Commissioner pulled out his cigar box. 'I don't smoke cigars!' said the painter.

Carl Joseph held out a packet of cigarettes. Moser fussily put his folder on the pavement in front of him, filled his case, asked for a light, and cupped both hands round the little blue flame. His hands were red and sticky, too big for their wrists, they trembled slightly, they were like useless tools. His nails resembled little flat black shovels, with which he had been grubbing in dirt, colour paste and liquid nicotine. 'So we won't see each other again,' he said, stooping to pick up his folder. 'Never again,' he sobbed. 'I just need to get something from my room,' said Carl Joseph, and he disappeared into the hotel.

He ran up the stairs into his room, leaned out of the window, and fearfully watched his father. He saw the old man pulling out his briefcase, a couple of seconds later the reinvigorated painter put his grisly hand on his shoulder, and then he heard Moser shout: 'All right then, Franz, see you on the third, as usual!' Carl Joseph ran back down the stairs, he felt he had to protect his father; the professor saluted, took a step back, and went with somnambulistic confidence, his head held high, straight across the road, and then waved back one last time from the opposite pavement, before vanishing down a side street. Only, however, to reappear a moment later, cry out, 'Just a minute!' so that it echoed over the quiet street, cross the thoroughfare in a few improbably long and confident bounds, and stand in front of the hotel, as insouciant and well met as if he hadn't just taken his leave moments earlier. And as though he had just clapped eyes on his boyhood friend and his son, he began in a clamorous voice: 'Isn't it sad to meet again under such circumstances! Do you remember how we sat together in the third row? You were no good at Greek, and I always let you crib my work. Be honest, admit it, even in front of your little sprog! Didn't I let you copy my work all the time?' And to Carl Joseph: 'He was a good fellow, but so shy, your father! He wasn't much of a one for the fillies either, I had to encourage him, otherwise he'd never have got in there at all. Be truthful, Trotta! Tell him I set you on the way!'

The District Commissioner smirked but did not say anything. The painter Moser prepared to launch into a major speech. He laid his folder on the pavement, took off his hat, slid one foot forward, and began: 'When I met the old fellow for the first time, it was in the holidays, you remember.' Suddenly he stopped, and felt all his pockets with panic-stricken hands. Sweat stood out on his brow in thick beads. 'I've lost it!' he cried, shaking and trembling. 'I've lost the money!'

At that moment the porter emerged from the hotel doorway. He greeted the District Commissioner and the Lieutenant with a great swing of his gold-braided cap and put on an expression of disfavour. He seemed about to banish the painter Moser from the front of the hotel, where he was causing noise and offence to the guests. Old Trotta reached into his wallet, and the painter fell silent. 'Can you help me out?' asked the father. The Lieutenant said: 'I'll walk the Professor back some of the way. Goodbye, Papa!' The District Commissioner doffed his hat and went into the hotel. The Lieutenant gave the Professor a banknote and followed his father inside. The painter Moser picked up his folder and left the scene with careful, tottering dignity.

Evening had fallen and the hotel lobby was dark. The District Commissioner sat, with his room key in his hand, hat and stick beside him, part of the darkness, in a leather armchair. His son stopped at a respectful distance from him, as though to report that operation Moser had been successfully carried out. The lamps were not yet lit. Out of the darkness came the old man's voice: 'We'll set off tomorrow at a quarter past two.'

'Yes, Papa.'

'Hearing the music reminded me that you ought to call on Bandleader Nechwal. After you've seen Sergeant Slama, of course. Have you any other business in Vienna?'

'Pick up the trousers and the cigarette case.'

'Anything else?'

'Nothing, Papa!'

'Tomorrow I want you to call on your uncle. That's evidently slipped your mind. How many times were you a guest at his house?'

'Twice a year, Papa!'

'Well then! Send him my regards. Tell him I'm sorry I can't make it. What shape is he in now anyway, old Stransky?'

'Very good, when I last saw him.'

The District Commissioner reached for his stick and propped his extended hand on its silver handle, as he often did while standing – suggesting that even when seated a man needed extra support if the conversation happened to turn on Stransky: 'I last saw him nineteen years ago. He was still First Lieutenant then. Already fallen for that Koppelmann woman. Incurable! That episode did for him. In love with a Koppelmann.'

He pronounced the name louder than everything else, and left a caesura between its two parts. 'Of course they didn't have the money to buy him out. Your mother almost persuaded me to stump up half of it.'

'He left the army?'

'Yes, you could say that. He joined the Northern Railways. Made it all the way to railway councillor, so they tell me.'

'Yes, Papa.'

'Well then. And didn't his son become a pharmacist?'

'No, Papa, Alexander's still at school.'

'I see. Has a bit of a limp, or so I've heard, eh?'

'One of his legs is shorter than the other.'

'Well, what do you expect!' crowed the old man, as though Alexander's limp could have been predicted nineteen years ago.

He stood up, the lamps in the lobby flared up and lit his pallor. 'I'd better get some money,' he said. He approached the stairs. 'I'll get it for you, Papa!' said Carl Joseph. 'Thank you!' said the District Commissioner.

'Why don't you try the Rooms of Bacchus,' he said later on, while they were eating their pudding course. 'A new spot! Maybe you'll run into Smekal there.'

'Thank you, Papa! Good night!'

Between eleven and noon the following day, Carl Joseph paid his call on Uncle Stransky. The railway councillor was still in his office; his wife, née Koppelmann, conveyed her warmest greetings to the District Commissioner. Carl Joseph wandered slowly along the Ringstrasse back to the hotel. He turned into the Tuchlauben, asked for the trousers to be sent to the hotel, picked up the cigarette case. The cigarette case was cool, he could feel it against his skin through the thin tunic pocket. He thought of his condolence visit to Sergeant Slama, and resolved not to go inside at any price. My deepest sympathies, Herr Slama! he would say, from out on the porch. The larks trilling invisibly in the blue canopy of sky. The insistent friction of the crickets. A smell of hay, the scent of late acacias, the new buds in the gendarmerie garden. Frau Slama is dead. Kathi. Katharina Luisa on her baptismal certificate. Dead.

They travelled home. The District Commissioner put aside his files, laid his head back against the red velvet bolsters in the corner, and closed his eyes.

For the first time Carl Joseph saw the District Commissioner's head lying horizontally, the flanges of the thin bony nose flaring out, the delicate dimple in the shaved and powdered chin, and the side whiskers calmly spreading their two broad black wings. They were already beginning to silver at the edges, where age had touched them, and the temples as well. One day he will die! thought Carl Joseph. He will die and be buried. I will remain.

They had the compartment all to themselves. The slumbering face of his father lay peacefully against the reddish bolsters. Under the black moustache, the pale bloodless lips were like a single slash; the Adam's apple bulged out in the scrawny throat between the shiny corners of the upright collar, the myriad wrinkled bluish membranes of the closed eyelids trembled continually and faintly, the broad, burgundy tie rose and fell rhythmically, and the hands too were asleep, tucked under the arms folded across his chest. A great calm went out from his resting father. His severity slept peacefully, housed in the silent, vertical pleat between nose and forehead, as a storm sleeps in the deep chasm between two mountain peaks. This furrow was well known, even familiar to Carl Joseph. It graced Grandfather's face too, in the portrait in the drawing room, the very same furrow, choleric ornament of the Trottas, the legacy of the hero of Solferino.

His father opened his eyes: 'How much longer?' 'Two hours, Papa!'

It started raining. It was Wednesday, the visit to Slama was set for Thursday afternoon. It rained on Thursday morning as well. A quarter of an hour after lunch, they were still sitting over coffee in the drawing room, Carl Joseph said: 'I'm going to the Slamas, Papa!'

'Unfortunately he's on his own now!' replied the District Commissioner. 'And four o'clock is the best time to see him.' At that instant two clear peals came from the church tower, the District Commissioner raised his index finger and pointed out of the window in the direction of the bells. Carl Joseph blushed. It appeared that his father, the rain, the bells, people, time and nature were all set on making his task even more difficult. On days when he had gone to visit the living Frau Slama, he had listened for the golden peal of the bells, just as impatient as he was today, but careful not to meet the Sergeant. Those afternoons now seemed to be buried under decades. Death hid them in its shadow, Death stood between then and now, thrusting its whole infinite dark between the past and the present. And yet the golden chime of the hours was still the same, and now, just as then, they were sitting in the drawing room, drinking coffee.

'It's raining,' said Father, as though he had only just noticed it. 'You might want to take the carriage.'

'No, I like walking in the rain, Papa!' What he meant perhaps was: I want to drag out this walk as long as I possibly can. Maybe I would have taken the carriage when she was still alive! It was quiet, the rain was drumming on the windows. The District Commissioner got up: 'I must go across.' He meant to his office. 'I'll see you presently.' He shut the door more softly than was usual for him. Carl Joseph thought his father stayed standing outside the door, listening for a while.

It struck one quarter, then two. Half past two, an hour and a half to go. He went into the corridor, took down his coat, spent a long time arranging the regulation folds on the back, pulled the sword hilt through the slit in the pocket, mechanically put on his cap in front of the mirror, and left the house.

# 4

He walked the familiar road, past the vertical level-crossing barriers, the sleeping yellow revenue building. From there he could already see the lonely gendarmerie post. He walked on. Ten minutes past the gendarmerie post lay the little graveyard with the wooden paling fence. The veil of rain seemed to fall more thickly over the dead. The Lieutenant turned the wet iron handle, and he stepped inside. A bird he couldn't place was singing away; where was it keeping, might it be in a grave? He opened the door of the caretaker's house. An old woman, spectacles perched on her nose, was peeling potatoes. She shook the peels and vegetables from her lap into her bucket, and got to her feet. 'I'd like to visit the grave of Frau Slama!' 'Row fourteen, second from the end. Grave number seven!' the woman shot back, as though she'd long been waiting for the question.

The grave was still fresh: a tiny mound, a small provisional wooden cross, and a wet wreath of glassy violets that evoked bakers' shops and bonbons. 'Katharina Luisa Slama, born such and such, died such and such.' And down there she lay, the fat wriggly worms were just beginning the pleasurable gnawing of her round white breasts. The Lieutenant closed his eyes and took off his cap. The rain caressed his parted hair with damp tenderness. He didn't care about the grave, the crumbling body under this hillock was nothing to do with Frau Slama. She was dead. Dead, in other words unreachable, even when you were standing by her grave. The body that was buried in his memory was closer to him than the corpse under the mound of earth. Carl Joseph put his cap back on and took out his watch. Another half an hour. He left the graveyard.

He arrived at the gendarmerie post, pressed the bell, no one came. The Sergeant wasn't back yet. The rain poured down on the thick vine leaves that grew all over the porch. Carl Joseph walked back and forth, back and forth, lit a cigarette, threw it away immediately; he reminded himself of a sentry. Each time he happened to look at the right-hand window from which Katharina had always greeted him, he turned his head away. He took out his watch, pressed the white button of the doorbell another time, waited.

Four muffled rings came slowly from the clocktower in town. Then the Sergeant appeared. He saluted mechanically, before he'd taken in who was there. More as though to pre-empt any threat from the gendarme than to reply to his greeting, Carl Joseph called out, rather louder than he'd intended, '*Grüss Gott*, Herr Slama!' He stretched out his hand, plunging into the greeting as into an assault; impatiently, as one waits for battle to be joined, he bided the clumsy preparations of the Sergeant, the difficulty with which he pulled off his wet cotton glove, his busy persistence with the process, and his humbly lowered eye. At last, the naked hand lay damp, broad and limp in the Lieutenant's. 'Thank you for the visit, Your Grace!' said the Sergeant, as though the Lieutenant hadn't just arrived, but were in the midst of going. The Sergeant got out his keys. He unlocked the door. A gust of wind lashed the pattering rain against the porch. It was as though it were driving the Lieutenant into the house. The hallway was in half-darkness. Wasn't that a little strip of light, a little iridescent trace of the dead woman? The Sergeant opened the door into the kitchen, the trace was swept away in a flood of light. 'Please take off your coat!' said Slama. He himself still stood in coat and belt.

My sincere condolences! thinks the Lieutenant. I'll quickly say the words and go. Slama already has his arms spread to help Carl Joseph out of his coat. Carl Joseph acquiesces, Slama's hand brushes against the back of the Lieutenant's neck, the shaved short hairs, the very place where Frau Slama used to cross her hands, tender bars of amorous confinement. Now, when, at what exact moment, will I be able to get out my words of condolence? As I walk into the sitting room, or only after we've sat down? Do I have to stand up to say them? It's as though I won't be able to produce a single sound before that silly phrase has been said, a thing I brought with me and carried in my mouth the whole way. It lies on my tongue, heavy and useless, and it tastes bad.

The Sergeant presses down on the door handle, the door to the sitting room is locked. He says, 'Excuse me!' although he's done nothing wrong. He reaches into the pocket of his coat, which he's taken off already – it seems a very long time ago – and rattles the bunch of keys. That door was never locked in Frau Slama's day. So she really isn't there! the Lieutenant finds himself thinking, as though he hadn't come for that very reason, precisely because she wasn't there any more, and he realizes that all along he's been secretly imagining she would be there, sitting in the room and waiting. Well, now there can be no doubt she isn't there. She really is outside, lying in the grave he's just seen.

There's a smell of damp in the sitting room; of the two windows, one is curtained, the other admits the grey day's murky light. 'Please to step inside!' repeats the Sergeant. He's standing directly behind the Lieutenant. 'Thank you!' says Carl Joseph. And he steps inside, and he goes up to the round table, he knows exactly the pattern of the coarse linen cloth that covers it, and the jagged little stain in the middle, the brown varnish and the ornamentation of its grooved feet. Here is the glass cabinet, containing silvered goblets and little china dolls and a yellow clay pig with a slit in its back for coins. 'Would you do me the honour of taking a seat!' murmurs the Sergeant. He's standing behind the chair back, clasping it in his hands, holding it in front of him like a shield. More than four years have passed since Carl Joseph saw him last.

Slama was still in the army then. He wore a shimmering plume of feathers on his black hat, leather bands across his chest, his rifle stock was beside his foot, he stood guard in front of the District Commissioner's office. He was Sergeant Slama, the name and the rank were indivisible, the plume of feathers were as much a part of him as the blond moustache. Now the Sergeant stands there bareheaded, without leather bands and belt; his ribbed uniform has an obvious, greasy sheen across the slight bulge of the belly over the waistband, and it isn't the old Sergeant Slama any more, but Herr Slama, a gendarmerie sergeant on the active list, formerly husband of Frau Slama, now widower and master of his own household. His cropped blond hair, with its centre parting, is like a pair of brushes over the unlined brow with its horizontal reddish crease left by the continuous pressure of the stiff peaked cap. This head is orphaned without a cap or helmet. The face, without the benefit of a shading peak, is a regular oval, filled with cheeks, nose, moustache, and small, blue, stubborn and faithful eyes. He waits for Carl Joseph to sit down, then pushes his chair in, sits himself down and gets out his cigarette case. It has a lid of painted enamel. The Sergeant puts it in the middle of the table, between himself and the Lieutenant, and says: 'Cigarette in order?' Condolence time, thinks Carl Joseph, gets to his feet and says: 'Sincere condolences, Herr Slama!' The Sergeant is sitting, both hands in front of him on the edge of the table, he appears not to have grasped what is happening right away, attempts to smile, stands up too late, just as Carl Joseph is about to sit down again, takes his hands off the table edge and holds them by his side, lowers his head, raises it again, looks at Carl Joseph, as though to ask what he should do now. They both sit down again. It's over. They don't speak. 'She was a good woman, the late Frau Slama!' says the Lieutenant.

The Sergeant is playing with his moustache, and says, a thin end of hair between his fingers: 'She was beautiful, the Baron has seen her himself.' 'Yes, I've seen her, your wife. Did she have an easy death?' 'It took two days. By the time we sent for the doctor, it was too late. Otherwise she would be alive now. I was on night duty. When I got back, she was dead. The wife of the revenue officer over the way, she was with her.' Then, straight away, 'A little raspberry juice in order?'

'Oh, yes please!' says Carl Joseph in a loud tone of voice, as though the raspberry juice would transform the situation, and he watches the Sergeant get up and walk over to the sideboard, and he knows that's not where the raspberry syrup is kept. It's in the white cupboard in the kitchen, behind glass, that's where Frau Slama always got it from. Alertly he follows all the movements of the Sergeant, the short, muscular arms in tight sleeves feeling for the bottle on the top shelf, and then dropping again in disappointment, the feet flattening themselves again after being on tiptoe, and Slama, as though returned from some foreign territory where he has undertaken a somewhat superfluous and sadly unsuccessful expedition, turns back, and, with touching despondency in his shiny blue eyes, reports: 'I'm terribly sorry, sir, I'm unable to find it!'

'Never mind, Herr Slama!' the Lieutenant comforts him.

The Sergeant, either not hearing him, or else under orders from some higher authority that cannot be countermanded by subordinate intervention, leaves the room. We hear him about the kitchen, he comes back with the bottle in his hand, gets the glasses with the pale ornamental rims from the sideboard, puts a jug of water on the table, pours the thick ruby-red liquid from the dark green bottle and once more he says, 'Will your Grace do me the honour?' The Lieutenant pours water from the jug into the raspberry syrup, neither of them speak, it pours in a thick stream from the curved lip of the jug, splashes a little, and is like a small reply to the incessant rain outside, which they can hear throughout. The lonely house, they know, is swathed in it, and it seems to make the two lonely men still lonelier. They are alone. Carl Joseph picks up his glass, the Sergeant does the same, the Lieutenant tastes the sweet, sticky drink. Slama drinks his glass at a draught, he's thirsty, a strange, inexplicable thirst on such a cool day. 'Will the Baron now be joining the Xth Dragoons?' asks

Slama. 'Yes, though I don't know the regiment yet.' 'I know a sergeant there. Accountancy Sergeant Zenower. We were together in the Rifles, then he got himself transferred. A good background, very cultured. I'm sure he'll take the officers' exam. The likes of us, meanwhile, we just stay put. There are no openings in the gendarmerie.' It's raining harder now, the gusts of wind are more violent, it keeps rattling against the window panes. Carl Joseph says: 'Ours is a difficult profession, I mean the military!' The Sergeant bursts into a fit of incomprehensible laughter, it seems to give him extraordinary pleasure that the profession pursued by himself and the Lieutenant is a difficult one. He laughs a little louder than he had meant to. It's obvious from his mouth, which is opened wider than it needs to be in order to laugh, and which stays open when he has done laughing. So, for a moment it appears that for physical reasons alone, the Sergeant is finding it difficult to return to his customary seriousness. Is he really so pleased that he and Carl Joseph are having such a hard road in life? 'The Baron,' he begins, 'is pleased to speak of "our" profession. I would beg him not to take it amiss, but surely what the likes of me are doing is different.' Carl Joseph doesn't know what to say by way of reply. He feels (in an ill-defined way) that the Sergeant has some kind of grudge against him, or maybe against conditions operating in the army and gendarmerie as a whole. They were never taught in cadet school how an officer ought to behave in such a situation. To be on the safe side, then, Carl Joseph just smiles, a smile that stretches his lips and clamps them together like an iron bracket; it makes him look rather more miserly in expressing the mirth that the Sergeant is so liberal with. The raspberry juice that a moment ago tasted so sticky sweet on his tongue, now sends up a bitter, thin taste from the back of his throat, he feels like a cognac to take away the taste. The reddish drawing room appears lower and smaller than otherwise, perhaps so much rain has shrunk it. On the table is the familiar album with its stiff, shiny brass corners. Carl Joseph knows all the pictures in it. Sergeant Slama says: 'Would you permit me?' and he opens the album and holds it in front of the Lieutenant. Here he is in civilian clothes, a young husband by the side of his wife. 'I was a corporal!' he says, a little resentfully, as though to say that even then he would have merited a higher rank. Frau Slama is sitting next to him in a light close-fitting summer dress with a wasp waist like a fragrant suit of armour, with a broad flat white hat perched at an angle on her head. What's this? Has Carl Joseph not seen the picture before? Why does it look so unfamiliar to him today? And so old? And so strange? And so ridiculous too? Yes, he's smiling, as though he were looking at a comic photograph from the olden days, and as though Frau Slama had never been dear and precious to him, and as though she hadn't died just a couple of months ago, but several years. 'She was a very attractive woman. That's quite clear!' he says, no longer out of confusion, as before, but out of honest deceitfulness. We say nice things about a dead woman to her widowed husband when we have come to offer our condolences.

Straight away he feels released, and parted from the dead woman, as though everything, but everything, has been wiped out. It has all just been imagination! He drinks the rest of his raspberry juice, stands, and says: 'Well, I'll leave you now, Herr Slama!' He doesn't wait either, he turns on his heel, the Sergeant has barely had time to get up, already they are both in the hall again, already Carl Joseph is in his coat, slowly and contentedly he slips on his left glove, suddenly he has a little more time, and as he says, 'Goodbye, then, Herr Slama!' he is happy to hear an unwonted arrogance in his voice. Slama stands there, with eyes lowered and perplexed hands that are suddenly empty, as though they've just dropped something they had been holding, and lost it for ever. They shake hands. Does Slama have anything further to say? Never mind! 'Maybe some other time, Lieutenant!' he says finally. Come, he can hardly be serious, Carl Joseph has already forgotten Slama's face. All he sees are the yellow-gold corners of his collar and the three golden brackets on the black sleeve of his gendarmerie tunic. 'Farewell, Sergeant!'

It's still raining gently, inexhaustibly, with occasional sporadic gusts of wind. It's as though it should have been evening long ago, but evening for some reason can't fall. Always this scribbled, wet grey. For the first time in uniform, yes, for the first time he can remember, Carl Joseph has the feeling he has no option but to put up his coat collar. And he gets as far as raising his hands, before he remembers he's in uniform, and then lets them drop. It's as though he's momentarily forgotten his profession. He walks slowly and clankingly over the wet, crunching gravel of the front garden, taking pleasure in his slow pace. He has no need to hurry; it wasn't anything, the whole thing was just a dream. What time is it now? His watch is buried too far under his tunic in his shallow trouser pocket. It would be a shame to unbutton his coat. He is bound to hear the church clock before long anyway.

He opens the garden gate, goes out on the street. 'Baron!' he suddenly hears behind him. The Sergeant – inexplicable how silently he's followed him. Yes, Carl Joseph is startled. He stops, but he can't convince himself to turn round immediately. Maybe the barrel of a pistol is resting right in the hollow of his back, between the regulation pleats of his coat. Gruesome, childish notion! Is he going to have to go through it all again? 'Yes!' he says, still with the casual arrogance, which is like a laborious continuation of his farewell and costs him a lot – and he turns round. The Sergeant is standing in the rain, bareheaded and without a coat, with his wet pair of brushes, and thick drops of water on his smooth, fair brow. He is holding a blue parcel, secured crosswise with silver string. 'This is for you, Baron, sir!' he says, his eyes lowered. 'Please excuse me! The District Commissioner instructed me to do it this way. I tried to deliver it once before. The District Commissioner took a look at it, and told me I was to give it to you personally!' He is silent for a moment, as the rain continues to patter down on the poor, light blue parcel, darkening it up, the parcel can't wait much more. Carl Joseph takes it, buries it in his coat pocket, blushes, thinks for a moment of taking off his right glove, reconsiders, offers the Sergeant his leather-gloved hand, says, 'Thank you,' and quickly walks off.

He can feel the parcel in his pocket. From there, through his hand, along his arm, a mysterious warmth seeps up, and his face reddens further. Now he feels he should undo his collar, much as earlier he had felt he should put it up. The bitter aftertaste of the raspberry juice is back in his mouth. Carl Joseph pulls the parcel out of his pocket. Yes, there's no doubt about it. They are his letters.

Evening should finally come and the rain should stop. A lot of things should be different in the world, maybe the evening sun should send a last ray in this direction. Through the rain, the meadows are exhaling their familiar scent, and the lonely call of an unidentified bird resounds – never been heard here before, it makes it seem like foreign terrain. He hears it strike five, just an hour has passed – no more than a single hour. Shall he walk fast or slowly? Time has a strange, mysterious pace, an hour feels like a year. It strikes quarter past. He has walked a few steps, no more. Carl Joseph begins to walk faster. He crosses the railway tracks, sees the first houses of the town. He walks past the town café, it's the only place that has a modern revolving door. It feels like a good idea to step in, to drink a cognac standing up at the bar, and then to go on. Carl Joseph steps in.

'A cognac, quickly,' he says at the bar. He keeps his cap and coat on; a few customers stand up. There's the clicking of billiard balls and chess pieces. Officers from the local garrison are sitting in shady corners; Carl Joseph doesn't see them and doesn't greet them. Nothing is more urgent than the cognac. He is pale, the ash-blonde cashier gives him a maternal smile from her lofty position, and kindly lays a lump of sugar on the saucer next to the glass. Carl Joseph knocks it back. Right away he orders another. He feels he is doing something forbidden, and he doesn't know why it should be forbidden to drink a couple of cognacs. He's not at cadet school any more, after all. Why is the cashier looking at him with such a peculiar smile? Her navy blue stare is embarrassing to him, and the pencilled black of her eyebrows. He turns away and looks round the bar. There in the corner by the window is his father. Yes, it's the District Commissioner – and what's so strange about that? He comes here every day between five and seven, to read the newspaper and the official digest and to smoke a Virginia. The whole town knows that, it's what he's been doing for thirty years. The District Commissioner sits there; he's looking at his son, and it appears that he's smiling. Carl Joseph takes off his cap and walks over to his father. Old Herr von Trotta looks up quickly from his newspaper, without laying it aside, and says: 'You've been to see Slama?' 'Yes, Papa!' 'He gave you the letters?' 'Yes, Papa!' 'Sit down!' 'Yes, Papa!'

At last, the District Commissioner lays aside the newspaper, props his elbows on the table, turns towards his son, and says: 'She's given you a cheap cognac. I only drink Hennessy.' 'I'll remember, Papa!' 'Not all that often, by the way.' 'Yes, Papa!' 'You still look a bit pale. Take your coat off! Major Kreidl is over there, he's looking this way!' Carl Joseph stands up and bows in the direction of the Major. 'Was he disagreeable, Slama?' 'No, very nice about it!' 'Well then!' Carl Joseph takes off his coat. 'Where've you got the letters?' asks the District Commissioner. The son gets the parcel from his coat pocket. Old Herr von Trotta takes it. He weighs it in his right hand, puts it down again and says: 'A lot of letters!' 'Yes, Papa !'

It's quiet, they hear the clicking of the billiard balls and chess pieces, and outside the rain is pouring down. 'The day after tomorrow you go to join your regiment!' says the District Commissioner, looking over to the window. Suddenly, Carl Joseph feels the bony hand of his father on his right hand. The District Commissioner's hand lies on the Lieutenant's, cool and bony, a tough carapace. Carl Joseph lowers his eyes to the table. He blushes. He says: 'Yes, Papa!'

'Bill, please!' calls the District Commissioner, removing his hand. 'Will you remind the cashier,' he says to the waiter, 'that we only drink Hennessy!'

They walk out through the bar in a perfectly straight diagonal, the father and behind him his son.

There is no more than a mild musical drip from the leaves as they walk slowly through the wet garden to the house. Out of the gate of the District Commissioner's office steps Sergeant Slama, in his helmet, with rifle and fixed bayonet and service book under his arm. '*Grüss Gott*, my dear Slama!' says old Herr von Trotta. 'Nothing to report, eh?'

'Nothing to report, sir!' replies the Sergeant.

# 5

The barracks was to the north of the town. It sat at the end of a wide and well-kept country road that, at the back of the red brick building, began a new life and carried on for miles into the blue countryside. The barracks gave the appearance of having been dropped in the Slav countryside by the royal and imperial army as an emblem of Habsburg power. It even blocked the ancient highway itself, which had become so wide and spacious as a result of centuries of Slav migration. The highway had to go around it. It looped round the barracks. An observer standing on the extreme northern edge of the town, where the houses kept getting smaller and smaller, and finally dwindled into village-like huts, would, on a clear day, be afforded a distant view of the broad, arched, black-and-yellow gate of the barracks, held up in the face of the town like a mighty Habsburg shield, a threat, a protection, or a combination of the two. The regiment was based in Moravia. But its men were not, as one might have expected them to be, Czechs, but Romanians and Ukrainians.

Twice a week, there were exercises on the drill-grounds to the south. Twice a week, the regiment rode through the streets of the little town. The metallic blare of the trumpets interrupted, at regular intervals, the regular clatter of the horses' hooves, and the red trousers of the riders on the sleek, chestnut bodies of their mounts filled the little town with a kind of sanguinary splendour. People stopped by the roadside to watch. The shopkeepers left their shops, the idle patrons of the cafés left their tables, the town policemen their regular posts, and the peasants, who had come from their villages to the marketplace with fresh vegetables, their horses and carts. Only the drivers of the few cabs that waited near the town park remained seated impassively on their boxes. From their elevation, they had an even better view of the spectacle than the people standing by the roadside. And the old horses seemed to greet the dazzling arrival of their younger and healthier fellows with dull equanimity. The cavalry steeds were distant cousins of those drab nags who, for fifteen years, had done nothing but pull cabs to the station and back.

Carl Joseph, Baron von Trotta, was unmoved by the animals. Sometimes he thought he felt the blood of his ancestors in his veins: they had been no horsemen. With the combing harrow in their horny hands, they had set one foot after the other on the earth. They drove the furrowing plough into the juicy sods of ground, and walked with knees bent behind the hefty pair of oxen. They used willow switches to drive their animals, not spurs and whips. With arm aloft, they swung the lightning of the sharpened scythe, and they reaped the blessing they themselves had sown. Grandfather's father had been one of them, a peasant. Sipolje was the name of the village from which the family came. Sipolje: the name had an ancient significance. To the Slovenes of today it hardly meant anything. But Carl Joseph thought he knew the village. He could see it in his mind's eye when he thought about his grandfather's portrait in the gloaming under the drawing room ceiling. It nestled between unfamiliar mountains, under the golden beams of an unfamiliar sun, with wretched huts of mud and straw. A beautiful village, a good village! He would have given his officer's career for it!

Oh, but he was no peasant, he was a baron and a lieutenant of the dragoons! He didn't keep a room in town, like the other fellows. Carl Joseph lived in the barracks. The windows of his room overlooked the yard, facing the privates' accommodation. Every afternoon when he returned to barracks, and the big double gates closed behind him, he had the feeling that they would never open again, that he was trapped. His spurs jingled icily on the bare stone stairs, and his clicking heels echoed on the tarred, brown wooden flooring of the passageways. The whitewashed walls managed to hold on to a little of the light of the parting day and now they let it go, as though insisting in their bareness and miserliness, that the regulation oil lights in the corners not be lit before the final onset of evening; they had prudently saved up the day, so that they could spend it now that it was needed, when it was dark. Carl Joseph lit no lights. With his forehead pressed against the window that ostensibly separated him from the darkness, but that actually represented its familiar, cool, advance guard, he saw into the yellow-lit cosiness of the troops' quarters. He would gladly have swapped places with any one of them. There they sat, half-undressed, in their coarse, yellowish peasant shirts, dangling their feet over the edge of their bunks, singing or talking or playing the harmonica. At this hour of the day – the autumn was already far advanced – an hour after orders, an hour and a half before lights-out, the whole barracks was like a gigantic ship. Carl Joseph even thought he could feel it swaying, as though the miserable yellow oil lamps with their big white mantles were rocking on the swell of some unfamiliar ocean. The men were singing songs in an unfamiliar language, a Slavic language. The old peasants of Sipolje would have understood them! Even Carl Joseph's grandfather might have understood them! His enigmatic portrait hung in the gloaming under the drawing room ceiling. Carl Joseph's memory clung to that portrait, it was the last and only sign that the long and unknown line of his ancestors had left him of themselves. He was their descendant. Ever since joining the regiment, he had felt more like his grandfather's grandson than his father's son; yes, he was more like the son of his eccentric grandfather. They were playing their harmonicas non-stop over there. He could clearly see the movements of their rough brown hands, pushing the tin instrument back and forth against their red mouths, and from time to time a flash of metal. The keening melancholy of the instrument made its way through the closed windows into the black rectangle of the yard and filled the darkness with an inkling of village and wife and child and hearth. Back there they lived in low-ceilinged huts; at night they saw to their wives, and by day they saw to their fields! The snow lay deep and white round their huts in wintertime. In summer, the corn waved deep and yellow round their hips. Peasants they were, peasants! And the Trotta family had lived just like them once! Just like them!

The autumn was already far advanced. When he mounted his horse in the morning, the sun was just surfacing in the east like a bloody orange. And when the exercises began on the water meadows, in the wide, verdant clearing ringed by black firs, the silvery fogs struggled to rise, parted by the regular, violent motions of the dark blue uniforms. Then the sun climbed pale and lugubrious, cool and remote. Its dull silver broke through the black boughs. A frosty shudder, like a cruel comb, passed over the chestnut backs of the horses; and their whinnying could be heard from an adjacent clearing, a mournful cry for home and stables. They had moved on to 'rifle drill'. Carl Joseph was impatient to get back to barracks. He dreaded the quarter of an hour of 'rest' that was invariably called at ten sharp, and the conversations with his comrades, who sometimes assembled in the pub nearby, to have a beer and wait for Colonel Kovacs. Even more embarrassing was the evening at the club. It would be soon. He had to go. The hour of lights-out was fast approaching. Already the dark blue, jingling shadows of the returning men were hurrying through the dark rectangle of the barracks yard. Already Sergeant Reznicek was stepping out of the door, with his yellowish flickering lamp in his hand, and the musicians assembled in the dark. The yellow brass instruments flashed against the deep dark blue of the uniforms. From the stables came the drowsy whinnying of the horses. Up in the sky, the stars sparkled in gold and silver.

There was a knock on the door, Carl Joseph did not stir. It's his man, he'll come in unasked. He'll come in in a moment. He's called Onufri. The time it took you to remember that name! Onufri! Your grandfather would have been familiar with that name.

Onufri came in. Carl Joseph kept his forehead pressed against the glass. Behind him, he heard his man clacking his heels together. Today was Wednesday. Onufri had 'leave'. You had to turn on a light and sign a form. 'Light!' ordered Carl Joseph, without looking round. The men were still playing their harmonicas over there.

Onufri turned on a light. Carl Joseph registered the snap of the switch by the door-jamb. The room behind his back was suddenly very bright. The rectangular darkness was still staring in at the window, and over there was the blinking, cosy light of the privates' quarters. (Electric light was reserved for officers.)

'So where are you off to tonight?' asked Carl Joseph, still staring into the troops' quarters. 'See girl!' said Onufri. It was the first time the Lieutenant had said *du* to him. 'To see any girl in particular?' asked Carl Joseph. 'Katharina!' said Onufri. You could hear him standing 'to attention'. 'At ease!' ordered Carl Joseph. He heard Onufri slide his right foot in front of his left.

Carl Joseph turned round. In front of him stood Onufri, his big horsey teeth shining between his thick red lips. He was incapable of standing 'at ease' without grinning. 'What's she look like, then, your Katharina?' asked Carl Joseph. 'Lieutenant, beg to report, sir, big white breasts!'

'Big white breasts, eh!' The Lieutenant cupped his hands and felt a cool memory of Kathi's breasts. She was dead now, dead!

'The form!' ordered Carl Joseph. Onufri held out the exeat. 'What does she do, Katharina?' asked Carl Joseph. 'In service, with good family!' replied Onufri. And he added happily: 'Big white breasts!' 'Come on, the form!' said Carl Joseph. He took the form, smoothed it out, signed it. 'Go to your Katharina!' said Carl Joseph. Once again, Onufri clacked his heels. 'Dismiss!' ordered Carl Joseph.

He switched the light off. He fumbled for his coat in the dark.

He stepped out into the corridor. At the very instant when he shut the door downstairs, the band began the final bars of lights-out. The stars glinted in the sky. The sentry at the gate saluted. The gate closed behind Carl Joseph's back. The street had a silvery glitter in the moonlight. The yellow lights of the town blinked like fallen stars. His footfall rang out on the newly frozen ground of the autumn night.

Behind his back, he could hear Onufri's footfall. The Lieutenant quickened his step, so as not to be overtaken by his man. But Onufri too quickened his step. So they strode along on the lonely, hard and echoing road, one after another. Obviously, it was what Onufri wanted, to catch up with his lieutenant. Carl Joseph stopped and waited. Onufri stretched in the moonlight; he seemed to grow; he lifted his head towards the stars, as if drawing fresh strength from them for the encounter with his master. He moved his arms jerkily, in the same rhythm as his feet; it was as though he were treading the air with his hands. Three paces in front of Carl Joseph, he stopped, puffed out his chest again, there was a frightful crash of heels, and his hand saluted with five grown-together fingers. Carl Joseph smiled awkwardly. At this point, he thought, anyone else in my position would be able to say something pleasant. It was moving, how Onufri had come after him. He'd never really given him a second look. So long as he hadn't been able to remember the name, he hadn't dared to look him in the eye. It was like having a different man every day. The others talked about their men with solicitousness and expertise, the way they talked about girls, clothes, favourite dishes and horses. When the talk was of servants, Carl Joseph thought of old Jacques at home, old Jacques who had served his grandfather before him. Other than old Jacques, there was no servant in all the world! Now Onufri stood before him on the moonlit road, with mightily puffed out chest, with sparkling buttons, boots polished to a mirroring shine, and in his broad face, a frantic effort to conceal his delight at seeing his lieutenant. 'There now, stand easy!' said Carl Joseph.

He wished he could have said something more. Grandfather would have been able to say something to Jacques. With a crash, Onufri put his right foot in front of his left. His chest remained inflated, the order had had no effect. 'At ease, man!' said Joseph, a little sadly and impatiently. 'Beg to report, sir, am standing at ease!' replied Onufri. 'Does she live a long way away, your girl?' asked Carl Joseph. 'Not far, sir, an hour's march, beg to report, Lieutenant, sir!' No, he couldn't do it. Carl Joseph couldn't come up with any more conversation. This flipness and amiability was making him gag like gristle, he didn't know how to deal with an orderly. Who did he know how to deal with? So much of the time he was tongue-tied, even with his comrades he often didn't know what to say. Why were they always whispering the second he left them, or before he joined them? Why did he cut such a wretched figure on horseback? Oh, he had no illusions about himself! He could see himself as if in a mirror, no one could persuade him otherwise. Behind his back were the secret hissing comments of his comrades. He only understood their jokes once they'd been explained to him, and even then he couldn't laugh; least of all then! But Colonel Kovacs had a soft spot for him. And no doubt he had an impeccable conduct sheet. He was living in the shadow of his grandfather! That was what it was! He was a grandson, the only grandson, of the hero of Solferino. He could feel the dark, enigmatic look of his grandfather boring into his neck. The grandson of the hero of Solferino!

For two minutes Carl Joseph and his orderly Onufri stood facing each other in silence, on the milkily shimmering road. The moon and the stillness made it seem even longer. Onufri never stirred. He stood like a statue, silvered by the moonlight. Suddenly Carl Joseph turned and marched away. Onufri followed, exactly three paces behind. Carl Joseph heard the regular crash of his heavy boots and the iron jingle of his spurs. It was loyalty itself following. Each crash was a fresh, curt, stamped affirmation of loyalty from the man to his officer. Carl Joseph was too afraid to turn round. He wished this dead straight road would suddenly throw off an unexpected, unknown side road, down which he could flee Onufri's insistent presence. The orderly followed in step. The Lieutenant tried in turn to keep step with the boots behind him. He was afraid of disappointing Onufri by a careless change of stride. It was there, in the dependable stamp of the boots, the loyalty of Onufri. Carl Joseph was moved by every new thump. It was as though the clumsy fellow were trying to knock on his master's heart with heavy soles; the helpless tenderness of a spurred and booted bear.

At last they came to the edge of town. Carl Joseph had thought of something he could usefully say on parting. He turned, and said: 'Well, enjoy yourself, Onufri!' And he hurriedly turned down a side street. His fellow's thanks only reached him as a distant echo. He had gone out of his way, and reached the officer's mess ten minutes later. It was on the first floor of one of the better houses on the old Ring. All the windows spilled their light on to the square, as they did every night, and on to its strolling population. It was late, and you had to bob and weave to get through the crowds of promenading burghers and their wives. Every day, it was an indescribable torment to the Lieutenant to turn up among the dark civilians in his jingling gaudiness, to be subjected to curious, resentful and lustful looks, before finally diving into the brightly lit gateway of the mess like some sort of god. This time, he quickly scythed through the strollers. The longish passage took two minutes, two full disgusting minutes! He took the steps two at a time. So long as he didn't meet anyone! Meetings on the stairs were to be avoided: they were ill-omened. Warmth and light and voices gushed out into the hallway. He stepped inside, exchanging greetings. He looked for Colonel Kovacs in his usual corner. Kovacs played dominoes there every night, every night with a different opponent. He was a great afficionado of dominoes, perhaps out of an unreasonable fear of cards. 'Never in my life have I held a card in my hand,' he liked to say. There was a little explosion of contempt in the way he said 'cards'; and by looking at his hands as he did so, he seemed to be seeing in them proof of his unimpugnable character. 'I would urge you to stick to dominoes, gentlemen!' he would sometimes go on to say. 'It's a clean game that teaches moderation.' And occasionally he would hold up one of the little many-eyed black and white stones in the air, like a magical talisman to free sinful card players from their besetting demon.

Tonight, it was Lieutenant Taittinger's turn to be on domino duty. The Colonel's face cast a purplish reflection on the haggard, yellow countenance of the Lieutenant. Carl Joseph stopped in front of the Colonel with a soft jingle of spurs. '*Servus!*'\* said the Colonel, without looking up from the stones. He was an easygoing fellow, Colonel Kovacs. He had settled into his quasi-paternal role many years ago now. Only once a month did he put on a show of temper which he dreaded even more than the regiment did. Any pretext would serve. He roared so loud that the barrack walls and the ancient trees round the water meadow seemed to quake. His purple face paled, even his lips went white, and his riding crop smacked against his boots in a perpetual tremor. He yelled all sorts of incomprehensible stuff, interspersed with the somewhat softer refrain of 'in my regiment', gabbled as if it were one word. Finally, and just as suddenly as he'd begun, he would stop and leave the office, the mess, the training ground, or wherever else he had staged his latest torrential outburst. Yes, everyone knew him, Colonel Kovacs, he was a good sort really! You could rely on the regularity of his rages as on the phases of the moon. Lieutenant Taittinger, who had already had himself transferred twice, and who knew a thing or two about commanding officers, was tireless in affirming to anyone who cared to listen that there was no more good-natured regimental commander in the entire army.

At last, Colonel Kovacs looked up from the board and shook hands with Trotta. 'Eaten already?' he asked. 'Too bad,' he continued, staring into some mysterious distance: 'The schnitzel was quite exceptional today.' 'Exceptional!' he said again, a moment later. He genuinely regretted that Trotta had missed out on the

---

\* *Servus*: An Austrian and Bavarian greeting.

schnitzel. He would have liked to cut it up for the Lieutenant; or at the very least, watch him tuck into it. 'Well, have a pleasant evening anyway!' he said at last, and returned to his dominoes.

There was a lot of commotion at this hour, and it wasn't possible to find a good place anywhere. Lieutenant Taittinger, who had been in charge of the mess from time immemorial, and whose single passion in life was the consumption of pastries, had, over the course of time, managed to recreate the mess in the image of the pastryshop where he spent his afternoons. You could see him sitting there behind the glass door, gloomy and impassive, like a cardboard figure of an officer. He was the shop's best customer, and probably its hungriest. Without its bringing the least animation to his sorrowful expression, he guzzled one plate of sweets after another, took occasional sips from a glass of water, looked impassively through the glass door at the street, nodded appropriately when a passing soldier saluted, and seemed to have nothing at all going on in his great, haggard, sparsely haired skull. He was a mild and extremely indolent officer. Of all his official duties, the only ones in which he took any pleasure were those that involved the mess, the kitchens, the chefs, the orderlies and the wine cellar. His extensive correspondence with vintners and spirits manufacturers kept two secretaries busy. Over the years, he had succeeded in modifying the appearance of the mess till it resembled his beloved pastryshop, with little tables in the corners, and red shades on the lamps.

Carl Joseph took a look around. He was looking for a half-decent place. In between Reserve Ensign Bärenstein von Zaloga, a wealthy lawyer very recently ennobled, and the rosy-pink Lieutenant Kindermann, who came from Germany, was about as safe as one could hope. The Ensign, who, with his middling years and prominent belly, was so ill-suited to his dashing rank that he looked like a civilian in military disguise, and whose face with its little black moustache seemed naked without a pair of pince-nez spectacles, in the context of this mess hall, gave out a kind of dependable dignity. He put Carl Joseph in mind of a family doctor or uncle or suchlike. He was the only one in these two large rooms who was truly seated – all the others were bouncing up and down in their chairs. The only concession, apart from his uniform, that Ensign Dr Bärenstein was prepared to make to the military was to wear a monocle on duty; he actually did wear a pince-nez in civilian life.

Also more restful than the others was Lieutenant Kindermann, no question of that. He was made from some fair, rosy, translucent substance; it almost felt as if you could put your hands through him as through a wispy, sunny, evening mist. Everything he said was gauzy and transparent; it was spun from his being, without in the least bit depleting it. Even the seriousness with which he followed a serious discussion had something sunny and smiling about it. He sat at the table, like a cheerful zero. '*Servus!*' he piped in his squeaky voice, which Colonel Kovacs liked to joke was a wind instrument in the Prussian army. Reserve Ensign Bärenstein rose dutifully but weightily. 'My respects, Lieutenant!' he said. 'Good evening, Doctor!' Carl Joseph only just stopped himself from replying. 'I'm not disturbing you?' he merely asked, and sat down. 'Dr Demant is coming back today,' Bärenstein began, 'I bumped into him this afternoon!' 'Charming fellow,' tootled Kindermann, sounding like an Aeolian harp, after the powerful, forensic baritone of Bärenstein. Kindermann, always quick to compensate for his rather feeble interest in the opposite sex by affecting to pay it particular attention, added, 'And his wife, too – have you met her? Enchanting creature, delightful!' And at the word 'delightful', he raised his hand, and his fingers twirled loosely in the air. 'I knew her in her younger days,' said the Ensign. 'Oh, how interesting,' said Kindermann, blatantly feigning. 'Her father was one of our leading hat manufacturers,' the Ensign went on. It was as though he were reading from a brief. Then the sentence seemed to scare him, and he stopped. The term 'hat manufacturers' sounded too civilian; after all he wasn't in the company of lawyers now. He silently swore to check every one of his sentences before saying it. He certainly owed as much to the cavalry. He tried to catch a look at Trotta, but he was sitting to his left, and Bärenstein wore his monocle in his right eye. The only one he could clearly see was Lieutenant Kindermann, and he didn't mind so much about him. In order to see whether Lieutenant Trotta had been appalled by such a casual reference to a hat manufacturer, Bärenstein got out his cigarette case and offered it to the left, before suddenly remembering that Kindermann was senior, and, turning to his right, quickly saying: 'Pardon me!'

The three of them smoked in silence. Carl Joseph studied the portrait of the Emperor on the opposite wall. There was Franz Joseph in a snow-white general's uniform, with the wide, blood-red sash diagonally across his chest, and the Order of the Golden Fleece round his neck. His large black field-marshal's hat with the thick peacock-green plume of feathers lay next to the Emperor, on a rickety-looking little table. The picture seemed to be very far away, much further than the wall. Carl Joseph remembered how, in his first days with the regiment, the picture had afforded him a certain pride and solace. Then, it had seemed as though the Emperor might step out of the narrow black frame at any moment. But gradually the Commander-in-Chief had acquired the indifferent, heartily familiar expression of his stamps and coins. His painting hung on the wall of the mess room, a strange instance of a sacrifice that a god makes to himself; his eyes – once they had resembled summer holiday skies – now they were just tough blue porcelain. And yet it was still the same Emperor!

Back home, in the District Commissioner's study, there was the same painting. It was in the assembly of the military academy. It was in the Colonel's office in the barracks. Scattered a hundred thousand fold throughout the whole great Empire was Emperor Franz Joseph, as omnipresent among his subjects as God in the world. It was his life that the hero of Solferino had saved. The hero of Solferino had grown old and died. Now he was food for the worms. And his son, Carl Joseph's father, the District Commissioner, he too was becoming an old man. Before long, he too would be food for the worms. Only the Emperor seemed to have grown old very suddenly, on a single day, within the space of one hour; and ever since then, he seemed coffered up in an icy and everlasting old age, like armour of an awe-inspiring crystal. The years could do nothing to him. His eye grew ever bluer and tougher. Even his favour, which he continued to accord the Trotta family, was like a weight of melting ice. Now Carl Joseph shivered under the eye of his emperor. Back home, he remembered, when he had come for the holidays, and when Bandleader Nechwal had drawn up his musicians in the prescribed circle around him on Sunday mornings, he would have been prepared to die a sweet, warm, blissful death for this Emperor. The mission bequeathed by Grandfather had been a living thing then, to save the life of the Emperor. That was what you did if you were a Trotta: you saved the life of the Emperor.

Now he had been with the regiment for barely four months. And all of a sudden it seemed as if the Emperor, unimpregnably cased in his crystal armour, had no more need of the Trottas. Peace had gone on for too long. Death was a remote thing to a young cavalry lieutenant, as remote as the final step of the standard military career. One day you will make it to colonel, and then you will die. But for now, you went to mess every evening, and you looked up at the picture of the Emperor. The longer Lieutenant Trotta gazed at it, the further the Emperor seemed to recede.

'Look!' twittered Lieutenant Kindermann's voice. 'Trotta can't take his eyes off the old man!'

Carl Joseph smiled at Kindermann. Ensign Bärenstein had broken out the dominoes, and was in the process of losing. He felt duty-bound to lose, if he was playing against active officers. In civilian life, he always won. Even among lawyers, he was a feared opponent. But when he joined up for the yearly exercises, he switched off his mind, and tried to be stupid. 'He can't stop losing,' Kindermann said to Trotta. Lieutenant Kindermann was convinced that 'civvies' were inferior beings. They couldn't even win a game of dominoes.

The Colonel was still sitting in his corner with Lieutenant

Taittinger. A few members of the regiment wandered desultorily among the little tables. They didn't dare leave the mess, not while the Colonel was still playing. The gentle grandfather clock whimpered slowly and audibly every quarter-hour, its mournful sound interrupting the clatter of dominoes and chess figures. Sometimes one of the orderlies clicked his heels, went off to the kitchens and returned with a little glass of cognac on a ridiculously large tray. Sometimes someone laughed loudly, and if you looked in the direction of the laughter, you saw four heads leaning together, and you understood that jokes were being told. Those jokes! Those anecdotes where everyone knew right away whether you were laughing because you got it, or because you were eager to please! They sorted out the locals from the outsiders. Whoever didn't get them wasn't from here. And no, Carl Joseph was not the right sort!

He was about to suggest a threesome at dominoes when the door opened, and the orderly, with an exceptionally loud click of the heels, saluted. There was a momentary silence. Colonel Kovacs jumped up out of his chair and turned towards the door. The man who had come in was none other than Regimental Doctor Demant, evidently alarmed to have caused such a stir. The orderly was still standing to attention at his side, clearly bothering him. He motioned to him with his hand, but the fellow took no notice. The doctor's thick spectacles were a little fogged from the damp autumn air outside. He was used to taking them off to clean them when he stepped indoors. Here, he didn't trust himself to do that. It took a while for him to come away from the threshold. 'Well, well, it's the doctor!' cried the Colonel. He yelled at the top of his voice, as though having to make himself heard in the midst of a street celebration. He seemed to believe, the good fellow, that short-sighted people are also hard of hearing, and that their spectacles would work better if their ears took in a little more. The Colonel's voice cleared a passage for itself. The officers got out of the way of it. The handful who had still been sitting at their tables now arose. The regimental doctor shyly slid one foot in front of the other, as if he were walking on ice. His glasses seemed gradually to clear. Greetings rained down upon him from all sides. Not without a little effort he recognized the various gentlemen. He craned forward to scan their expressions, rather in the way one leans forward to read a book. Finally, he came to a halt in front of Colonel Kovacs, and stood there, with chest expanded. He looked rather silly, throwing his otherwise forward-leaning head back on his thin neck, and trying to square his thin, sloping shoulders with a tremendous heave. In the course of his extended sick leave, he had almost been forgotten, he and his unsoldierly bearing with him, and now he was eyed with a certain amount of surprise. The Colonel hastened to put an end to the formalities of welcoming him back. In a voice that made the glasses ring, he roared: 'He's looking well, our doctor!' as though to communicate the fact to the entire army. He slapped Demant on the shoulder, as if to help him regain his natural posture. Actually, he had a bit of a soft spot for the regimental doctor. But by gum, thunderation, the fellow was so unmilitary! If only he'd been a little bit more soldierly, one wouldn't have to look out for him quite so much. By golly, they could have let him have a different doctor, and for this of all regiments! The inner struggle that was going on the whole time between the Colonel's sweet nature and his soldierly principles, all on account of this one damned decent fellow, it was enough to do a man in! This doctor is going to be the end of me! thought the Colonel when he saw the regimental doctor on horseback. One day he had had to ask him to refrain from riding through the town.

Better say something nice to him, he thought agitatedly. The schnitzel was exceptionally good today, swam into his mind. And so he said it. The doctor smiled. The fellow even smiles like a civilian! thought the Colonel. Then suddenly he remembered that there was someone present who hadn't yet met the doctor. Trotta of course! He'd joined the regiment while the doctor had been away. The Colonel thundered: 'Our newest officer, Trotta! You've not met yet, have you?' And Carl Joseph appeared before the regimental doctor.

'The grandson of the hero of Solferino?' enquired Dr Demant. Such familiarity with military history was not expected of him.

'Blow me, he knows everything, the doctor!' shouted the Colonel. 'A veritable bookworm!'

And for the first time in his life, he took such a liking to the dubious term, 'bookworm', that he said it again: 'A bookworm!' in the same caressing tone in which he might have said: 'A dragoon!'

Everyone sat down again, and the evening resumed its customary course. 'Your grandfather,' said the regimental doctor, 'was one of the more remarkable men in the army. Did you know him at all?' 'No, he was before my time,' replied Carl Joseph. 'We have his portrait in the drawing room at home. When I was a boy, I used to spend hours looking at it. His servant, Jacques, is still with us.' 'What sort of portrait is it?' asked the regimental doctor. 'An old schoolfriend of my father painted it,' said Carl Joseph. 'It's a very remarkable picture. It's hanging pretty high up, so when I was little I had to stand on a chair to look at it.'

They were silent for a moment. Then the doctor said: 'My grandfather was an innkeeper; a Jewish innkeeper in Galicia. Are you familiar with Galicia at all?' (Dr Demant was a Jew. All the jokes were about regimental doctors who were Jews. There had been a couple of Jews at cadet school too. They had joined the infantry.)

'Let's go to Resi's! Let's go to Auntie Resi's!' came the call from somewhere.

And everyone repeated: 'To Resi's! We're going to Auntie Resi's!'

'Auntie Resi, here we come!'

Nothing could have been more alarming to Carl Joseph than that chorus. For weeks he had been waiting for it, full of trepidation. He could still remember everything from the previous visit to Frau Horvath's bordello, everything! The mixture of lemonade and camphor they called champagne, the flabby, doughy flesh of the girls, the wallpaper's screaming red and zany yellow, the corridors smelling of cats and mice and lily of the valley, and the heartburn that followed twelve hours afterwards. He had been with the regiment just a week, and it was his first visit to a brothel. 'Bayonet practice!' said Taittinger. He was the ringleader. It was one of the duties of whoever was in charge of the mess, from time immemorial. Pale and haggard, the hilt of his sabre in his arms, with long, thin, jingling strides, he prowled from table to table in Frau Horvath's salon, a creepy instigator of sour joys. Kindermann found the female sex so disagreeable, he almost blacked out when he smelled women. Major Prohaska stood in the toilets, doing his damnedest to push his short, fat fingers down his throat. The silk skirts of Frau Horvath seemed to be rustling all over the house at once. Her large black eyeballs rolled aimlessly and directionlessly around in her wide, mealy face, and her false teeth shimmered in her wide mouth, as yellow and as long as piano keys. From his corner Trautmannsdorf followed her every movement with his tiny, nifty, greenish glances. Finally he got to his feet, and stuffed his hand down the front of Frau Horvath's dress. It looked lost in there, like a white mouse in white mountains. And Pollak, the pianist, sat with bowed back, at the blackly mirroring piano, a slave to music, his celluloid cuffs rattling at his pounding hands, accompanying the tinny piano like scratchy percussion.

Auntie Resi! They were off to Auntie Resi's! The Colonel turned on his heel outside, said: 'Enjoy yourselves, gentlemen!', and in the quiet street, twenty voices chorused back: 'Our respects, Colonel!' and forty spurs jingled together. The regimental doctor Max Demant made a shy attempt similarly to take his leave. 'Do you have to go?' he quietly asked Lieutenant Trotta. 'I expect I do!' Carl Joseph whispered back. And so, without a word, the regimental doctor accompanied him. They were the last in the disorderly rout of officers, clattering through the silent, moony streets of the little town. They didn't speak. Both felt the whispered question and the whispered reply connected them, there was nothing more to be done about that. They were set apart from the rest of the regiment. And they had known one another for barely half an hour.

Suddenly, not knowing why, Carl Joseph said: 'I was in love with a woman by the name of Kathi. She's dead now.'

The regimental doctor stopped and looked directly at the Lieutenant. 'There will be other women in your life,' he said.

And then they went on.

The whistles of late trains could be heard from the distant station, and then the doctor said: 'I want to get away from here, far, far away!'

And then they were standing under Auntie Resi's blue lantern. Lieutenant Taittinger knocked on the barred gate. Someone opened. Within, the piano set up an immediate tinkling: the Radetzky March. The officers marched into the salon. 'Fall out singly,' ordered Taittinger. The naked girls fluttered towards them, like a gaggle of white hens. 'Go with God!' said Prohaska. This time, Trautmannsdorf reached inside Frau Horvath's dress immediately, without even sitting down. He clung on. She had the kitchen and the cellar to see to, she was visibly suffering from the First Lieutenant's attentions, but the rules of hospitality called for a sacrifice. She let herself be seduced. Lieutenant Kindermann turned pale. He was whiter than the powder on the girls' shoulders. Major Prohaska ordered soda water. This was a signal to everyone who knew him that he would go on and get terribly drunk. The water was merely to clear a path for the alcohol, the way streets are cleaned before a parade. 'Is the doctor with us?' he asked aloud. 'There are certain illnesses he can study at source here!' replied Lieutenant Taittinger, haggard and pale as ever, with scholarly earnestness. A blonde had made off with Ensign Bärenstein's monocle. He sat, with twinkling little black eyes, while his brown hairy hands crept all over her like curious animals. Gradually, all had found a place for themselves. On the red sofa, in between the doctor and Carl Joseph, two women sat stiffly, knees together, cowed by the despair on the faces of the two men. When the champagne arrived – brought ceremoniously by the severe-looking housekeeper in a black taffeta dress – Frau Horvath decisively pulled the First Lieutenant's hand out of her cleavage, and put it tidily back on his black trouser leg, the way one might return a borrowed utensil, and stood up, powerful and domineering. She turned out the chandelier, leaving only the little sidelights burning in the corners of the room. In the reddish halflight, the powdered white bodies glowed, the golden stars twinkled, the silver sabres shimmered. One couple after another rose and disappeared. Prohaska, who had long since gone on to cognac, stepped up to the regimental doctor and said: 'You don't seem to have much use for these, do you mind if I take them!' And he took the women and swayed up the stairs, with one either side of him.

So, all at once, they were on their own, Carl Joseph and the doctor. The pianist Pollak was just brushing the keys in the opposite corner of the salon. A very tender waltz dawdled almost shyly across the room. Otherwise it was quiet, and almost domestic, with the clock ticking on the mantelpiece. 'I think we're a bit superfluous here, eh?' said the doctor. He got up, Carl Joseph looked at the clock on the mantel, and got up likewise. It was too dark for him to make out the time, so he went up to the mantelpiece, where he suddenly took a step back. In a bronze, fly-spotted frame was the Commander-in-Chief in miniature, the familiar, ubiquitous portrait of His Majesty, in the snow-white uniform, with the blood-red sash and the Golden Fleece. Something must be done about this, thought the Lieutenant quickly and childishly. Something must be done! He felt how he'd turned pale, and his heart was thumping. He reached for the frame, pushed out the black paper backing, and removed the picture. He folded it up, once, twice, another time, and slipped it into his pocket. He turned round. Behind him stood the regimental doctor, who with his finger indicated the pocket in which Carl Joseph had hidden the imperial portrait. The grandfather would have done exactly the same thing, thought Dr Demant. Carl Joseph blushed. 'Disgusting, isn't it!' he said. 'What do you think about it?'

'Nothing,' replied the doctor. 'I was just thinking of your grandfather!'

'I'm his grandson!' said Carl Joseph. 'I haven't been given the chance of saving his life; more's the pity!'

They put down four silver coins on the table, and left the house of Frau Resi Horvath.

## 6

Dr Max Demant had been with the regiment for three years now. He lived outside the town, on its southern fringe, off the road that led to the two cemeteries, the 'old' cemetery and the 'new' one. The doctor knew the caretakers of both cemeteries well. He would go once or twice a week to pay calls on the dead, those long gone and those not yet forgotten. Sometimes he spent a long time among the graves, and his sabre could be heard clinking softly against a gravestone here or there. Without a doubt, he was an unusual man; a good doctor, so they said, and that already set him apart from the run of army doctors. He kept himself to himself. It was only his official duty that obliged him occasionally (but still more often than he would have wished) to put in an appearance with his comrades. To go by his age and his length of service, he should have made it to medical officer with the rank of captain by now, and no one knew why he hadn't. Maybe he didn't know why himself. 'Some careers are snagged.' That was one of Lieutenant Taittinger's *mots*; he liked to keep the regiment supplied with those as well.

'A career with snags,' the doctor often found himself thinking. 'A life with snags,' he said to Lieutenant Trotta. 'I have a life with snags. If fate had been kind to me, I could have been the assistant to a great Viennese surgeon, and maybe a professor by now.' In the poverty and gloom of his childhood, the great name of the Viennese surgeon had been a rare shaft of glory. Already as a boy, Max Demant had decided to become a doctor. He came from one of the villages in the eastern marches of the Empire. His grandfather had been a devout Jewish innkeeper, and his father, after twelve years with the militia, had become a middle-ranking official in the post office of the nearest border town. Demant remembered his grandfather well. At all hours of the day, he was to be found sitting outside the great gate of his frontier inn. His mighty beard of twirled silver covered his chest, and hung down to his knees. A smell of dung and milk and horses and hay clung to him. He sat outside his inn, like an ancient king among innkeepers. When the peasants returned from the weekly pig market, and stopped outside the inn, the old man stood up, like a mighty mountain in human form. As he was already a little hard of hearing, the little peasants had to shout their wishes up to him through their cupped hands. He merely nodded back. He understood. He granted the wishes of his customers, as if they were personal favours, not paid for in hard, ringing coin. With strong hands, he unharnessed the horses himself, and led them to his stables. Then, while his daughters served brandy and dried, salted peas to the guests in the low, broad bar, he stayed outside and fed the animals, speaking to them in soothing tones. On Saturdays he sat hunched over great holy books. His silver beard covered the lower half of their densely printed pages. If he had known that his grandson would one day stroll through the world in the uniform of an officer, and armed with deadly weapons, he would have cursed his years and the fruit of his loins. Even his son, Dr Demant's father, the middle-ranking official in the post office, was a tenderly tolerated abomination to the old man. The inn, which had been handed down through many generations, would have to be left to his daughters and sons-in-law; while his male heirs seemed destined to remain officials, bookish men, employees and fools for generations to come. For generations to come: that at least wasn't true! The regimental doctor had no children. Nor did he desire any. For his wife . . .

At that point, Dr Demant tended to break off his narrative, and change tack. He thought of his mother: she had lived in continual, desperate need of money. After work, his father sits in the little café. He plays at tarock, and he loses, and he owes for the bill. It is his desire that the boy does four years of middle school and then becomes a state official; in the post office, of course. 'You have all these ideas beyond your station!' he keeps saying to his wife. However disordered his civilian life may be, he keeps the most absurd order in all the paraphernalia he's kept from his army days. His uniform, the uniform of a 'long-serving accountancy sergeant', with gold corners on the cuffs, black trousers and infantry shako, hangs in the cupboard like a human being cut into three pieces but still alive, its gleaming buttons polished every week. And the black, curved sabre with the ribbed handle, also cleaned every week, hangs horizontally above the never-used desk, fixed on two nails, with its casually dangling golden tassel that resembles the closed bud of a dusty sunflower. 'If you hadn't come along,' his father would say to his mother, 'then I'd have done the exam, and I'd be captain in the accountancy corps by now.' On the Emperor's birthday, the post office worker Demant puts on his official uniform, with cocked hat and sword. On that one day of all days, he doesn't play tarock. Every year, on the Emperor's birthday, he makes a resolution to begin a new life and not get into debt. And so he gets drunk. And comes home late at night, stands in the kitchen with drawn sword, and commands an entire regiment. The pots are platoons, the teacups are units, the plates are companies. Simon Demant is a colonel, a colonel in the service of Franz Joseph I. Then the boy's mother, in lace bonnet, pleated nightdress and loose bedjacket, has to climb out of bed, come downstairs, and calm her husband.

One day, the day after the Emperor's birthday, his father suffered a stroke in bed and died. It was a merciful end and a spectacular funeral. All the postmen for miles around followed the coffin. And the dead man was kept alive in the loyal memory of his widow, the model of a husband, fallen in the service of the Emperor and the K-and-K postal service. The two uniforms, that of the non-commissioned officer and that of the postal worker Demant, hung side by side in the closet, and were beautifully kept up by the widow with camphor, clothes brush and brass polish. They looked like mummies, and each time the closet was opened, the son thought he saw his father's body hanging there in duplicate.

He was desperate to become a doctor. He gave private tuition for six measly crowns a month. He went around in gaping boots. When it rained, he left outsize wet footprints on his employers' parquet floors. His flapping boots made his feet seem bigger. And in the end he took his degree. And he qualified as a doctor. The future was still blocked off by poverty, a black wall against which he would shatter. He threw himself, therefore, into the arms of the military. Seven years of board, seven years of clothing, seven years of lodging, seven long years! He became an army doctor. And he remained one.

His thinking couldn't keep pace with his life. Before he had come to any decisions about it, he was already an old man. And he had married Fräulein Eva Knopfmacher.

At this point, Regimental Doctor Demant again broke off his reminiscences. He set off for home.

It was already evening, and, unusually, all the rooms were lit up. 'The old gentleman's here,' reported his man. The old gentleman: that meant Herr Knopfmacher, his father-in-law.

And exactly on cue he stepped out of the bathroom, in a long, fleecy, flower-patterned dressing gown, holding a razor in his hand, with pink, plump, newly shaved and fragrant cheeks. His face seemed about to split in two halves. It was only the grey goatee beard that held it together. 'Max, my dear chap!' said Herr Knopfmacher, carefully setting down the razor on a little table, spreading his arms, and throwing his dressing gown wide open. They embraced with two swift pecks on the cheek and went into the drawing room. 'I'd like a schnapps!' said Herr Knopfmacher. Dr Demant opened the cabinet, looked at the bottles for a while, and then turned. 'I'm no expert,' he said, 'I don't know what you like.' He had had a selection of drinks put together in more or less the fashion in which an uneducated person assembles a library. 'You still not drinking!' said Herr Knopfmacher. 'Have you got slivovitz, arak, rum, cognac, gentian, vodka?' he rattled off, in a way that hardly enhanced his dignity. He stood up. He walked over to the cabinet, his dressing gown flapping, and swiftly pulled out a bottle from the selection.

'I wanted to surprise Eva!' began Herr Knopfmacher. 'And I have to tell you right away, my dear Max, you were gone all afternoon. In your place' – he paused and said again: 'In your place there was a lieutenant here. A dundering fool!'

'You're talking,' replied Max Demant, 'about the only friend I've ever had in the army. Lieutenant Trotta. He's a good chap!'

'A good chap!' repeated his father-in-law. 'Well, I'm a good chap too. And as such, I'd advise you not to leave me alone in the company of a beautiful woman for even an hour, not if you care about her this much.' And with that Knopfmacher pinched thumb and forefinger together, and after a while, he said again: 'This much!' The regimental doctor turned pale. He took off his glasses and spent a long time polishing them. By so doing, he swathed the world around him in a kindly fog, in which his father-in-law in his dressing gown was a large but mercifully indistinct white blotch. And after polishing his glasses, he didn't put them back on right away, but held them in his hand, and spoke into the fog: 'My dear Papa, I have no occasion whatsoever to mistrust Eva or my friend.'

He said it haltingly, the regimental doctor. It sounded to his ears like an utterly alien turn of phrase, something he'd once read, or heard on stage.

He put his glasses back on, and straight away, distinct in girth and outline, old Knopfmacher loomed closer. Correspondingly, the words he had just used seemed to have turned to vapour. There was certainly no truth in them any more. The regimental doctor knew it as much as his father-in-law.

'No occasion whatsoever!' repeated Herr Knopfmacher. 'But I have occasion! I know my daughter! Maybe you don't know your wife! And I know what lieutenants are like! And men in general, come to that! I'm not saying anything against the army. Let's stick to the facts. When my wife, your mother-in-law, was young, I had occasion to know young men – both in and out of uniform. You're a strange lot if you ask me, you –'

He looked for some collective term that would embrace an as yet ill-defined group comprising his son-in-law and other dunderheads. Ideally, he would have liked to say: 'You university people!' Because he himself had grown clever, prosperous and well regarded without having studied. Yes, even now they were in the process of making him a commercial councillor. He unspooled a sweet dream of the future, a dream revolving around charitable donations, large charitable donations, the result of which was ennoblement. And if, for instance, you were to take Hungarian nationality, then the whole thing happened even faster. In Budapest, they didn't believe in putting obstacles in people's way. And incidentally, the ones who did, what were they but the academics, the eggheads, the jobsworths! His own son-in-law was threatening to become an obstacle. If there's the least whiff of scandal around your children, you can kiss your commercial councillorship goodbye! Really, you need to be everywhere at once, to make sure things run smoothly. You even have to attend to the virtue of other people's spouses! 'My dear Max, before it's too late, let me be absolutely straight with you!'

The regimental doctor had no fondness for that expression, he did not want to be told the truth at any price. Oh, he knew his wife just as well as Herr Knopfmacher knew his daughter! But he loved her, what could be done about that! He loved her. In Olmütz, there had been District Commissioner Herdall, in Graz, District Judge Lederer. So long as they weren't his colleagues, the regimental doctor gave thanks to God and his wife. If only he could quit the army. His life was hanging by a thread the whole time. How often as it was he'd been on the point of suggesting to his father-in-law ... He started afresh. 'I know,' he said, 'that Eva is impressionable. Always. Has been for years. She has a frivolous nature, she loves pleasure. Unfortunately. But she will never take it too far,' he stopped and stressed that: 'she will never take it too far!' With that phrase he slaughtered all the doubts that for years had not let him rest. He did away with his own uncertainty, he convinced himself that his wife did not deceive him. 'Of course not!' he said, aloud. He became quite sure of himself: 'Eva's a good woman, in spite of everything!'

'Sure she is!' agreed his father-in-law.

'But this life,' the regimental doctor resumed, 'is hard on us both. The job doesn't satisfy me, as you know. What might I not have become, but for the army? I'd have a brilliant position somewhere out there, and Eva's ambition would be satisfied. Because, unfortunately, she is ambitious!'

'A trait she's inherited from me!' said Herr Knopfmacher, not without satisfaction.

'She's dissatisfied,' the regimental doctor went on, while his father-in-law poured himself another glass, 'she's dissatisfied and she's looking for distraction. I can't blame her for that.'

'You ought to be distracting her yourself!' his father-in-law interrupted.

'I –' Dr Demant was at a loss for words, said nothing for a while, and looked over at the schnapps.

'Have a drink, why don't you!' Herr Knopfmacher exhorted him. And he stood up, fetched a liqueur glass, and filled it; his robe parted, showing his hairy chest and his good-natured belly, which was as rosy as his cheeks. He held the glass up to the lips of his son-in-law. Finally, Max Demant drank.

'There's another thing which may have the effect of forcing me to leave the service. When I joined, my sight was still so-so. But it's got worse with every passing year. And now I can barely ... I'm not able ... I find I can't see anything without my glasses. I ought to make a report of it and leave.'

'Really?' asked Herr Knopfmacher.

'And what . . .'

'What'd I live off?'

His father-in-law crossed his legs, all at once he felt a little chilly; he wrapped his robe around him, and bunched it against his throat. 'Ha,' he said, 'do you really think I can run to that? Since your wedding, I've supported you (I happen to have the figure by heart) to the tune of three hundred crowns a month. But I know, I know! Eva gets through a lot. And if you embark on some new life together, she'll need the same. And so will you, my boy!' He softened. 'Ah, Max, Max, my dear fellow! It's not as easy as it used to be!'

Max said nothing. Herr Knopfmacher, feeling he had rebuffed the assault, allowed his dressing gown to fall open again. He had another drink. It wouldn't go to his head, he knew what he could take. Those fools. And yet even this type of son-in-law was better than the other, that Hermann, Elizabeth's husband. His daughters set him back by six hundred a month. He knew the figures by heart. If the regimental doctor should happen to go blind – he looked at the glinting spectacles. He ought to keep an eye on his wife! Short-sighted or not!

'What's the time ?' he asked, amiably, casually.

'Almost seven o'clock!' said the doctor.

'I'll get dressed!' determined the father-in-law. He stood up, nodded, and swam slowly and with dignity out of the room. The regimental doctor remained behind. After the familiar solitude of the graveyard, the solitude in his own house struck him as enormous, unfamiliar, almost hostile. For the first time in his life, he poured himself a schnapps. It was the first time he'd had a drink. Sort out my life, he thought, I must sort out my life. He resolved to talk to his wife. He went into the corridor. 'Where's my wife?' 'In the bedroom!' said the orderly. Do I knock? the doctor wondered. No! commanded his implacable heart. He opened the door. His wife was standing in front of the mirror, in blue knickers, with a large pink powder puff in her hand. 'Oh!' she screeched, and crossed her arms in front of her bosom. The regimental doctor remained in the doorway. 'Is that you?' said his wife. It was a question, but it sounded like a yawn. 'It's me!' replied the regimental doctor, in a firm voice. Someone else's, he thought. He had his glasses on, but he was speaking into a fog anyway. 'Your father,' he began, 'told me Lieutenant Trotta has been here!'

She turned round. She stood there in her blue knickers, facing her husband, the powder puff in her right hand like a weapon, and said in a light, twittering voice: 'Your friend Trotta's been here! Papa's arrived! Have you seen him yet?'

'That's what brought me!' said the regimental doctor, and he knew immediately that he'd given himself away.

There was silence for a moment.

'Why didn't you knock?' she asked.

'I wanted to surprise you!'

'You startled me!'

'I –' began the regimental doctor. He wanted to say: I'm your husband!

Instead, he said: 'I love you!'

It was true. She stood there in her blue knickers, holding the pink powder puff. And he loved her.

I must be jealous, he thought. He said: 'I don't like it when people come to the house and I'm not told about it!'

'He's such a charming man!' said his wife, and began slowly and thoroughly powdering herself in front of her mirror.

The regimental doctor walked up to his wife, and grabbed her by the shoulders. He looked in the mirror. He saw his brown, hairy hands on her white shoulders. She smiled. He saw it, in the mirror, the glass echo of her smile. 'Be honest!' he begged her. It was as though his hands were kneeling on her shoulders. He knew straight away that she would not be honest. And he repeated: 'Be honest with me, please!' He watched as her deft pale hands fluffed up the blonde hair at her temples. A needless movement: it annoyed him. Her eyes looked at him out of the mirror, a swift, cool, dry, grey look, like a steel dart. I love her, thought the regimental doctor. She torments me, and I love her. He asked: 'Are you cross with me for being gone all afternoon?'

She half turned away from him. Now she sat there, her hips twisted, a lifeless creature, a wax doll in silk underwear. Under the curtain of her long black lashes, her bright eyes were like artificial lightnings made of ice. Her delicate hands were poised on her knickers like white birds stitched on a blue silk ground. And in a low voice that he had never heard before, and that seemed to have been produced mechanically from within her, she said very slowly: 'I never miss you!'

He started pacing to and fro, without looking at her. He knocked a couple of chairs out of the way. He felt as though there were many more things he needed to get out of his way, maybe push back the walls, break through the ceiling with his head, trample the floorboards into the ground with his feet. His spurs jingled softly in his ears, the sound seeming to come from far away, as though someone else was wearing them. A single word was going through his head, swinging back and forth through his brain, without stopping. Over, over, over! A little word. Swift, light as a feather, and heavy as a planet, it flew through his head. His footsteps grew faster and faster as his feet kept pace with the word swinging back and forth in his head. Suddenly he stopped: 'So you don't love me?' he asked. He was sure she wouldn't answer. She won't say anything, he thought. 'No!' she replied: 'No!' She lifted the black fringe of her lashes and looked him up and down with naked, terrifyingly naked eyes, and added: 'You're drunk!' He understood that he had drunk too much.

Contentedly he thought: I am drunk and I'm glad I am. And, in a strange voice, as though it were now his duty not to be himself but to be drunk, he said: 'Ha! Well!' According to his dim notions, those were the words and sounds that a drunken man had to sing out in such moments. And so he sang them. And he did something else besides. He said, very slowly: 'I'll kill you!'

'Kill me!' she twittered back in her old, light, familiar voice. She stood up. She stood up swiftly and supply, with the powder puff in her right hand. The slim, full curve of her silken legs reminded him fleetingly of the limbs of the models in shop windows, the whole woman was a sort of assemblage, put together from little bits and pieces. He didn't love her any more! He didn't love her any more! He was filled with a spitefulness that he himself hated, a rage that had come to him from afar like an unknown enemy and had now taken up residence in his heart. He said aloud what an hour before he had merely thought: 'Sort out my life! I'm going to sort out my life!'

She laughed raucously, as he had never heard her laugh before. A theatrical laugh! he thought. An irresistible urge to prove to her that he was capable of sorting out his life now swelled his muscles, and focused his weak eyes. He said: 'I'm going to leave you in your father's company. I'm going to find Trotta.'

'Go on then! Off you go!' said the woman.

He went. Before leaving the house, he turned back to the drawing room, to drink another schnapps. He was returning, for the first time in his life, to alcohol, as to a trusted friend. He poured himself one glass, a second and a third. He left the house with jingling strides. He walked to the mess. He asked the orderly, 'Where's Lieutenant Trotta?'

Lieutenant Trotta had not come to mess.

The regimental doctor set off down the dead straight road that led to the barracks. The moon was already declining. Its light was still strong and silvery, almost full. Not a breath of air stirred on the road. The thin shadows of the bare chestnut trees either side made a tangled nest on the crest of the road. Dr Demant's footfall sounded hard and frozen. He was on his way to Lieutenant Trotta. He saw from afar, in a sort of bluish white, the mighty barrack walls, he was making straight for them, straight for the enemy citadel. He met the cold, tinny sound of lights-out; Dr Demant marched straight into the frozen metal sounds, and trampled them. Soon, any moment now, Lieutenant Trotta ought to appear. He detached himself, a black pencil stroke, from the mighty whiteness of the barracks, and came towards the doctor. Three more minutes. They stood face to face. The Lieutenant saluted. Dr Demant heard himself, as from an infinite distance, say: 'You were with my wife this afternoon, Lieutenant?'

The question rang back from the glassy blue arc of sky. They'd been calling one another *du* for weeks now. Now they confronted one another like enemies.

'I was with your wife this afternoon, Regimental Doctor!' said the Lieutenant.

Dr Demant went right up to the Lieutenant: 'What is going on between you and my wife, Lieutenant?' The doctor's thick lenses glittered. The regimental doctor had no eyes any more, only glasses.

Carl Joseph didn't say anything. It was as though in all the whole wide world there was no answer to Dr Demant's question. One might have spent decades looking vainly for an answer; as though human speech were exhausted and dried up for all time. His heart beat against his ribs with quick, dry, tough strokes. His tongue cleaved to the roof of his mouth, dry and tough. A horrible cavernous emptiness rushed through his head. It was like confronting some unspecified mortal danger, and at the same time having already been consumed by it. You stood facing an enormous black abyss, and at the same time you had already been engulfed in its blackness. From out of the frozen, glassy distance Dr Demant's words sounded again, dead words, corpses of words: 'Answer me, Lieutenant!'

Nothing. Silence. The stars sparkle, the moon shines. 'Answer me, Lieutenant!' Carl Joseph is being addressed, he must answer. He summons up the pathetic remnants of his strength. Out of the whistling emptiness in his head, a thin, weasely sentence strings itself together. The Lieutenant clacks his heels together (from soldierly instinct, and also in order to hear some, any kind of noise), and the jingle of his spurs solaces him. Then, very quietly, he says: 'There's nothing going on between your wife and me, Regimental Doctor!'

Nothing. Silence. The stars sparkle, the moon shines. Dr

Demant says nothing. He stares at Carl Joseph through dead spectacles. The Lieutenant repeats very softly: 'Nothing at all, Regimental Doctor!' He's gone mad, thinks the Lieutenant. And: It's broken! Something's broken. It's as though he's heard the thin splintering sound of something breaking. A breach of trust, comes to mind, a phrase he read somewhere once. Broken friendship. Yes, that's what this is, a broken friendship.

All of a sudden he understands what the regimental doctor has been to him these past weeks: a friend, his friend! They've seen each other every day. He's gone walking in the cemetery with the regimental doctor, in among the graves. 'There are so many dead,' said the regimental doctor. 'Don't you feel how we live off the dead?' 'I live off my grandfather,' said Trotta. He saw the painting of the hero of Solferino, hanging in the gloaming under the ceiling in his father's house. Yes, there was something fraternal about the regimental doctor, a fraternal spark towards him in Dr Demant's heart. 'My grandfather,' said the regimental doctor, 'was a big old Jew with a silver beard!' Carl Joseph saw the big old Jew with the silvery beard. They were grandsons, both of them were grandsons. When the regimental doctor gets on his horse, he looks a bit silly, smaller, more negligible than he does on foot, the horse carries him on his back like a sack of oats. That's how badly Carl Joseph rides too. He knows. He can imagine himself in a mirror. In the whole regiment there are two officers behind whose backs the rest like to whisper: Dr Demant and the grandson of the hero of Solferino! Two of them in the whole regiment. Two friends.

'Will you give me your word of honour, Lieutenant?' asks the doctor. Without replying, Trotta puts out his hand. The doctor says: 'Thank you!' and shakes it. They walk back down the road together, ten, twenty paces, neither of them says anything.

All at once the regimental doctor begins: 'I don't want you to take it amiss. I've been drinking. My father-in-law's come to stay. He saw you. She doesn't love me. She doesn't love me – can you understand?' 'You're young!' the regimental doctor says again, a while later, as though to say he's wasted his breath. 'You're young!'

'I understand!' says Carl Joseph.

They march along in step, their spurs jingle, their sabres rattle. The lights of the town blink at them, yellow and cosy. Both of them wish that the road might go on for ever. They would like to be marching side by side like this for a long long way. Each of them has something he might have said, but neither of them speaks. A word, a word is quickly said. It isn't said. This is the last time, the Lieutenant thinks, this is the last time we're walking along side by side!

Now they reach the edge of town. The regimental doctor has something else to say before they enter town. 'It's not on account of my wife,' he says. 'She doesn't matter any more! I'm through with her. It's on your account.' He waits for a reply, and knows none will come. 'Never mind, thank you!' he hurriedly says. 'I'm going to mess, just for a while. Will you come?'

No. Lieutenant Trotta won't go to mess today. He turns back. 'Good night!' he says, and he turns back. He returns to barracks.

# 7

Winter came. When the regiment rode out in the mornings, the world was still in darkness. Thin ice crusts on the roads splintered under the horses' hooves. Clouds of grey vapour spilled out of the muzzles of the animals and the mouths of the riders. A dull layer of frost settled on the sheaths of the heavy sabres and the barrels of the light rifles. The little town shrank further. The muffled, frozen shouts of the trumpets could lure none of the usual onlookers to the kerbside any more. Only the cabbies, waiting at the same pick-up point, raised their bearded heads every morning. In the event of a heavy snowfall, they rode out in sleighs. The little bells on the harnesses of their horses tinkled softly, in constant motion because of the restlessness of the freezing beasts. The days resembled one another like snowflakes. The officers of the dragoon regiment were waiting for some extraordinary event to interrupt the monotony of their days. No one knew what sort of event it would be. But this winter seemed to harbour some terrible surprise in its gelid lap. And one day, it burst forth like a bolt of red lightning from the white snow . . .

On that day, Lieutenant Taittinger wasn't sitting on his own as usual, behind the great mirror on the door of the pastryshop. Since early afternoon, he'd been in the little back room, surrounded by his younger comrades. The officers looked strangely haggard and wan. All of them were pale. They drank liqueur constantly, without their faces acquiring any colour. They didn't eat. Only in front of the Lieutenant, as per usual, was there a little mound of sweet things. Yes, it was even possible that he was nibbling more today than he did on other days. Because grief gnawed at his insides, and hollowed him out, and he had to keep himself alive. And so while his bony fingers hoisted one little cake or pastry after another into his wide open mouth, he retold his story, for the fifth time, to his avid ring of listeners: 'Now, as you know, gentlemen, the main thing is absolute discretion with the civilian population! Back when I was in the IXth Dragoons, we had this one chatterbox among us, a reservist wouldn't you know it, and the thing happened with us just as he was joining! So of course, by the time we buried poor Baron Seidl, the whole town knew how he'd suddenly met his death. Gentlemen, I hope we'll manage a more discreet –' he wanted to say 'funeral', but stopped himself, considered for a long time, couldn't come up with a word, looked at the ceiling, and over his head and his listeners' heads there hissed a terrible silence. At last the Lieutenant concluded: '– a more discreet procedure.' He sighed, gulped down a pastry, and drained his glass of water.

They all felt that he had summoned Death. Death floated above them, and they hadn't encountered Death before. They had been born in peacetime, and had become officers by dint of peaceful manoeuvres and exercises. At the time they were still unaware that each of them, without exception, would have an assignation with Death within a couple of years. At the time none of them was able to hear the machinery of the great hidden mills that were already beginning to grind out the Great War. White wintry peace reigned in the little garrison. And a black and red Death fluttered over their heads in the dim little back room. 'I don't understand it!' said one of the young fellows. All of them had already said similar things. 'But I'm telling you for the umpteenth time!' replied Taittinger. 'It all began with the touring company! I don't know what made me go to that particular operetta, what was it again, I've forgotten the name, please someone tell me?' – 'The Tinker!' someone called out. 'Right! Well, it all began with The Tinker! I'm just coming out of the theatre, and in the square I see Trotta standing there all alone in the snow, you see, because I walked out before the end, it's a habit of mine, as you must know! I can never stand to see the end, I know it'll all be happy ever after, I can just tell at the beginning of the third act, and that spoils it for me, so I just walk out of the theatre, as quietly as I can. Anyway, I'd seen the play three times already! So. So there's poor old Trotta standing in the snow all on his own. I say: "The piece was pretty good." And I tell him about Demant's extraordinary behaviour! The way he hardly gives me a glance, leaves his wife on her own in the second act, walks out, and doesn't come back! He could have turned her over to me, but leaving her, just like that, I think that's pretty scandalous, and I say as much to Trotta. "Yes," he says, "I haven't spoken to Demant for a long time . . ."'

'But Trotta and Demant have been inseparable for weeks!' someone called out.

'Of course I know that, and that's what prompted me to tell him about Demant's bizarre behaviour. But I don't like prying in other people's business, and so I ask Trotta if he'd like to accompany me to the pastryshop for a little bite to eat. "No," he says, "I'm meeting someone." So I push off. Now, on that evening of all evenings, the pastryshop happens to close early. That's fate, gentlemen! So – no other option really! – I head for the mess. Tell Tattenbach and whoever else is listening the strange business with Demant, and Trotta waiting to meet someone in the middle of the square. I can hear Tattenbach starting to whistle. "What's all that about?" I ask him. "It's nothing," he says. "Just watch out, I'll say no more: watch out! Trotta and Eva, Trotta and Eva," he croons a couple of times like a cabaret singer, and the name Eva means nothing to me, for all I know he's thinking of Eve from the Garden of Eden, and it's all symbolic and general. See what I mean, gentlemen?'

They all saw, and expressed as much by murmurs and nods. Not only had they understood the story of the Lieutenant, they knew it from beginning to end, if not inside out. And still they asked him to tell it over and over again, because in their secret and foolish heart of hearts, they hoped the Lieutenant's story might somehow come out differently once, and leave a chink of hope for a more favourable outcome. They asked Taittinger again and again. But his story always had the same pattern. Not the tiniest of its sad details ever changed.

'And then?' asked one of them.

'Well, you know the rest!' replied the Lieutenant. 'Just in that instant when we're leaving the mess, Tattenbach, Kindermann and me, who should walk smack into us but Trotta with Frau Demant. "Watch out!" says Tattenbach. "Didn't Trotta tell you he was meeting someone?" "It could just be chance," I reply. And, as we now know, it was just chance. Frau Demant left the theatre on her own. Trotta felt obliged to escort her home. He had to forget about whoever he was meeting. Nothing would have happened, if Demant had turned his wife over to me in the intermission! Nothing!'

'Nothing!' they all chorused.

'The following evening in the mess, Tattenbach's sozzled as always. And the second Demant comes in, he gets up and says: "Well, hello there, doc!" And that's how it began!'

'Downright rude!' two of them said at once.

'Rude, of course it was rude, but the man was sozzled! What do you expect? So I chime in: "Good evening, Regimental Doctor!" And with this authoritative voice I didn't know he had, Demant turns to Tattenbach, and says: "Captain of Horse, I'm Regimental Doctor to you!"

"If I were you I'd stay home and keep watch!" says Tattenbach, and he's holding on to his chair as he says it. It was his name day, you know. Didn't I tell you?'

'No!' they all shouted.

'Well, now you know: it was his name day!' Taittinger repeated.

Greedily they supped the news. It was as though the fact that it was Tattenbach's name day could somehow give the whole lamentable affair a wholly new, unexpected and favourable conclusion. Everyone separately racked their brains as to how to exploit the fact of Tattenbach's name day. And little Sternberg, through whose brain the thoughts passed singly, like stray birds in an empty cloudscape, with no fellows and leaving no trace, burst out with premature jubilation in his voice, 'But then everything's all right! Situation back to normal! It was his name day!'

They all looked at little Count Sternberg, bewildered and uncomforted and yet still prepared to entertain his nonsense. What Sternberg had uttered was extremely foolish, but if you thought hard, couldn't something be made of it, was there no hope, no comfort? Taittinger's hollow laughter immediately plunged them into new consternation. Mouths hanging open, helpless sounds on their silent tongues, eyes staring and sightless, they stopped, mute and dazed, having thought for a moment they had heard words of comfort, or glimpsed a shimmer of hope. All round them was darkness and silence. In all the large, silent, snowed-in, wintry world there was nothing but Taittinger's five-times repeated, unaltering narrative. He resumed: 'Well, then, "I'd sit at home and keep a look out," says Tattenbach. And the doctor, you know how he does it when he's making his rounds, just as if Tattenbach was ill, he gets very close and peers into his face, and he says: "Lieutenant, you're plastered!"'

"I'd keep an eye on my wife," burbles Tattenbach.

"I wouldn't let my wife go round at midnight on the arm of a Lieutenant!"

"You wretch, you're plastered!" says Demant. And, just as I'm getting up, and before I can do a thing to stop it, Tattenbach starts yelling like a madman: "Yid, yid, yid!" Eight times in succession, I had the presence of mind to count.'

'Bravo!' said little Sternberg, and Taittinger nodded his head at him.

'Further,' the Lieutenant went on, 'I had the presence of mind to say: "Orderlies dismiss!" Because there's no point in having those fellows around.'

'Bravo!' called little Sternberg again. And they all nodded approvingly.

They fell silent again. From the kitchen was heard the clattering of dishes, and from the street the tinny jingle of a sleigh. Taittinger popped another pastry in his mouth.

'So this is the upshot!' cried little Sternberg. Taittinger gulped down the rest of his pastry, and said merely: 'Tomorrow morning, twenty past seven!'

Tomorrow, twenty past seven. They know the terms and conditions: pistols at ten paces. Sabres are out of the question for Dr Demant, who is no fencer. Tomorrow morning at seven o'clock the regiment will ride out to exercise on the water meadow. It is barely two hundred steps from the water meadow to the so-called 'green' behind the old castle, where the duel will be fought. Every one of the officers knows that tomorrow morning, before the end of fitness training, he will hear two shots. Already, everyone can hear them, the two shots. Death, with black and red wings, fluttered over their heads.

'The bill!' cried Taittinger. And they left the pastryshop.

It was snowing again. They tramped through the silent, white snow, a silent navy-clad bunch, drifting apart in ones and twos. Each of them was afraid to be on his own; but nor was it possible for them to remain together. They attempted to lose themselves in the alleyways of the little town, only to encounter one another again moments later. The crooked alleyways brought them back together. They were trapped in the small town and in their huge bewilderment. And each time one party approached another, it shrank back, afraid of the other. They waited for it to be supper-time, and at the same time they were afraid of the evening ahead of them in the mess, where even tonight they would not all be present.

They were far from being all present! There was no Tattenbach, no Major Prohaska, no First Lieutenant Zander, no First Lieutenant

Christ, and none of the seconds. Taittinger wasn't eating. He sat at a chess board, playing himself. Nobody spoke. The orderlies stood there, silently and stonily beside the doors, you heard the slow, insistent ticking of the big grandfather clock, and to its left the Commander-in-Chief surveyed his silent officers with his cold, china-blue eyes. No one dared leave alone, nor yet to take another with him. Wherever two or three were seated together, the words dropped heavily and reluctantly from their lips, and between question and answer was a great weight of silence. Everyone could feel the silence on his shoulders.

They were thinking of the absentees, as though they were already dead. All remembered the entrance of Dr Demant only a few days ago, after his long period of sick leave. They saw his faltering stride and his glinting spectacles. They saw Count Tattenbach, his short squat body on his cavalryman's bandy legs, his permanently red face with the cropped white-blond hair parted in the middle, and his small pale red-rimmed eyes. They heard the quiet voice of the doctor, and the rowdy voice of the Captain of Horse. And even though, ever since they had been able to think and to feel, the words honour and death, shoot and duel, death and grave had been at home in them, in their hearts and minds, it seemed unimaginable to them that today they might be parted for ever from the rowdy voice of the Captain of Horse and the gentle voice of the doctor. Each time the mournful bells rang out from the large grandfather clock, the men had the sense that their own final hour had struck. They didn't want to believe their ears, and so they looked up at the wall. No doubt about it: time hadn't stopped. Twenty past seven, twenty past seven, twenty past seven, it hammered in the brains of all those present.

They got up, one after the other, hesitant and bashful; as they left, they felt they were betraying one another. They slunk away almost silently. Their spurs failed to jingle, their swords did not rattle, their boots crept silently over a silent surface. Well before midnight already the mess was deserted. And at a quarter to midnight, First Lieutenant Schlegel and Lieutenant Kindermann reached the barracks where they lived. Up on the first floor, where the officers' quarters were, a single illuminated window cast a yellow rhombus on the rectangular darkness of the courtyard. They both looked up at it at once.

'There's Trotta!' said Kindermann.

'There's Trotta!' repeated Schlegel.

'We ought to look in on him.'

'It would be a bad time!'

They came jingling down the corridor, slowed to a crawl outside Lieutenant Trotta's door, and listened. Within, nothing stirred. First Lieutenant Schlegel put his hand on the doorknob, but didn't turn it. He took his hand off it again, and they continued down the corridor. They nodded to one another, then each went into his own room.

Lieutenant Trotta had failed to hear them. For four hours now, he had been trying to write a detailed letter to his father. He couldn't get past the opening. 'Dear Father,' he began, 'I seem, quite innocently and unwittingly, to have precipitated an affair of honour.' His hand felt heavy. An inert and useless tool, it sat on the paper, gripping the trembling quill. It was the first difficult letter he had ever had to write. It seemed impermissible to the Lieutenant to wait for the matter to be resolved one way or another, and only then write to the District Commissioner. Ever since the unhappy falling out between Tattenbach and Demant, he had put off his account day after day. He simply had to post it today. Before the duel. What would the hero of Solferino have done in his position? Carl Joseph could feel his grandfather's imperious glare at his back. The hero of Solferino urged his grandson to be swift and resolute. You had to write it, immediately, right now. You might even have done well to visit your father. Between the dead hero and the irresolute grandson was Father, the District Commissioner, the guardian of honour, the preserver of the legacy. The blood of the hero of Solferino flowed through the veins of the District Commissioner, red and alive. If you didn't report to Father in timely fashion, it was like trying to keep something concealed from Grandfather.

But in order to write this letter, you would have had to be as strong as Grandfather, as straightforward, as decisive, as close to the peasants of Sipolje. But if you were just his grandson! This letter was a shocking break in the complacent series of unvarying weekly reports that the sons in the Trotta family had always written the fathers. A bloody letter; you had to write it.

The Lieutenant continued:

I had been on a perfectly innocent walk, admittedly almost at midnight, with the wife of our regimental doctor. The situation left me no choice. Comrades saw us together. Captain Tattenbach, who unfortunately is often drunk, made a scurrilous reference to it to the doctor. Tomorrow morning, at twenty past seven, they are fighting a duel with pistols. I shall probably be forced to challenge Tattenbach, if he lives, as I hope he will. Things are hard.

Your faithful son,

Carl Joseph Trotta, Lieutenant

P.S. It may be that I shall have to leave the regiment.

Now the worst was over, thought the Lieutenant. But, as he happened to glance up at the shady ceiling, all at once he saw the exhorting countenance of his grandfather. Next to the hero of Solferino, he thought he saw the white-bearded face of the Jewish innkeeper, whose grandson was the regimental doctor Demant. And he felt the dead calling to the living, and it was as though it were he himself who was stepping up to fight, tomorrow morning at twenty past seven. To fight and die! To die! To fight and die!

On those long-distant Sundays when Carl Joseph had stood on his father's balcony, and Herr Nechwal's band had struck up the Radetzky March, it would have been a trifle, to fight and to die! To the cadet at the K-and-K military academy, Death had been a familiar, albeit a very distant familiar! Tomorrow morning, though, at twenty past seven, Death would await his friend, Dr Demant. And the day after, or in one or two days' time, He would await Lieutenant Carl Joseph von Trotta.

O darkness and dread! To be the occasion of His black arrival and finally to become His victim! And if you weren't His victim yourself, then how many more bodies would lie sprawled in your path? Other people had milestones, but Trotta had gravestones along his route! He was certain that he would never see his friend again, just as he had never seen Katharina again. Never! Under Carl Joseph's eyes, the word stretched into infinity, a dead sea of flat eternity. The little lieutenant clenched his weak white fist against the great black law that trundled the gravestones along and refused to set up any bulwark against the implacable Never, or to light up the eternal darkness. He clenched his fist and walked over to the window, just so as to be able to raise it against the sky. He recalled the night he had last been out with Dr Demant, their walk from the barracks to the town. That was their last walk together, and he had known it then.

Suddenly he felt assailed by a longing for his friend; and by the hope that it might somehow be possible to rescue the doctor! It was twenty past one. Dr Demant had six hours still to live, certainly, six vast hours. This stretch of time now seemed almost as powerful to the Lieutenant as the whole of eternity had only a moment ago. He plunged across the room to his coat hook, buckled on his sabre, raced across the dark rectangle of the yard, past the sentry, ran down the silent road, reached the little town in ten minutes, and a few moments after that, found the only sleigh that was on duty at night, then glided, accompanied by the cheery sound of bells, to the southern edge of town, and the doctor's villa. The house was asleep behind its fence, with all its windows blind. Trotta pushed the bell. Everything remained quiet. He shouted out the name of Dr Demant. Nothing stirred. He waited. He asked the cabbie to crack his whip. No reply anywhere.

If he'd been looking for Count Tattenbach instead, it would have been a simple matter to find him. The night before his duel would almost certainly find him at Resi's, drinking his own health. But it was anyone's guess where Demant was. It was possible that the regimental doctor was walking through the streets of the town. Or maybe he was strolling among the familiar graves, looking for his own. 'Take me to the cemetery!' the Lieutenant ordered the alarmed cabbie. The two cemeteries were both quite close. The sleigh stopped outside the old walls and the locked gate. Trotta climbed down. He walked up to the fence. Following the crazy notion that had brought him here, he cupped his hands in front of his mouth, and facing the graves, called out Dr Demant's name in a voice that seemed strange to him, like a howling from the depths of his heart; and even as he shouted, he believed he was calling to a dead man, and not one of the living; and he was frightened and began to tremble like one of the thin bushes between the graves, that were now being raked by the black winter wind; and the sabre rattled against the Lieutenant's hip.

Sitting up on the box of his sleigh, the cabbie was terrified of his fare. Simple-minded fellow that he was, he felt sure the officer was either a ghost or a madman. But he even felt too afraid of him just to whip his horse and leave him. His teeth chattered, his heart felt as though it were punching a hole in his thick cat fur. 'Please come back, Mr Officer!' he pleaded.

The Lieutenant returned. 'Back into town!' he said. In town, he got out and trotted diligently down the winding lanes and across the tiny squares. The tinny melodies of a music box that started up somewhere in the nocturnal silence, gave him something to aim for; he hurried towards the metallic clang. It was coming through the dimly lit glass door of a pub near to Frau Resi's premises, a bar that was a popular haunt with private soldiers and off limits to officers. The Lieutenant walked up to the brightly lit window and peered over the red curtain into the inside of the bar. He saw the counter and the lean landlord in his shirtsleeves. At one table, three men, also in shirtsleeves, were playing cards, at another was seated a corporal, with a girl at his side. Both of them had glasses of beer in front of them. In the corner was a man on his own, he had a pencil in his hand, he was leaning over a piece of paper; he wrote something down, stopped, sipped from a glass of schnapps, and stared up into space. All at once he pointed his lenses to the window. Only then did Carl Joseph recognize him: it was Dr Demant, in civilian clothes.

Carl Joseph rapped on the glass pane, the landlord came out; the Lieutenant asked him if he would send out the lone man. The regimental doctor came out on the street. 'It's me, Trotta!' said the Lieutenant, holding out his hand. 'You've found me!' said the doctor. He spoke softly, as he always did, but more distinctly than usual, the Lieutenant thought; because in the strangest way, his soft words made themselves heard above the din of the music box. For the first time he stood in front of Trotta in civilian clothes. The familiar voice emerged from the unwonted appearance like a kindly greeting from home. Yes, the voice seemed the more familiar to him, the stranger Demant looked. All the terrors that had bewildered the Lieutenant tonight were dispelled by the voice of his friend, which Carl Joseph hadn't heard for several weeks now, and which he had missed. Yes, he had been missing it; now he understood that. The music stopped. You could hear the night wind howl from time to time, and feel the powdered snow whipping against your face. The Lieutenant took a step closer to the doctor. (He couldn't be close enough to him.) I don't want you to die! he wanted to say to him. He realized that Demant was standing in front of him without his coat, in the snow and wind. If a man's a civilian, it doesn't show right away, he thought. And tenderly he said: 'I don't want you to catch cold!'

Dr Demant's face lit up with the old familiar smile that stretched his lips a little, lifted the black moustache slightly. Carl Joseph went red. It's not possible for him to catch cold any more, he thought. And simultaneously he heard the soft voice of Dr Demant saying: 'I don't have the time to get ill, my dear friend.' He could speak while he smiled. The doctor's words passed straight through the old smile, but it remained intact; it hung in front of his face, a small, sad, white veil. 'But let's go inside anyway!' the doctor went on. He stood, a motionless black shadow in front of the matt illuminated door, casting a second, paler shadow on the snowy pavement. His black hair had a faint silvery dusting of snow on it, lit by the dull gleam that came from the pub. It was like the sheen of the next world on his head, and Trotta was on the point of leaving again. Good night! he would say, and dash off.

'Let's go inside!' repeated the doctor. 'I'll ask them if they can get you in unnoticed!' He went in and left Trotta standing outside. Then he came back out with the landlord. They walked along a passageway and through a courtyard and found themselves in the inn kitchen. 'Do they know you here then?' asked Trotta. 'I come here from time to time,' replied the doctor, 'or rather: quite often!' Carl Joseph looked at the doctor. 'Does that surprise you? I always had my little habits,' said the regimental doctor. – What possessed him to say: had? – thought the Lieutenant; and he remembered from school that there is a tense called the past definite. Had! Why did the regimental doctor say: had?

The landlord brought a table and a couple of chairs into the kitchen, and lit a greenish gas lamp. In the bar, the music box was making its old din again, a medley of marches always linked by the first drum beats of the Radetzky March, muffled by sounds of merriment, but still recognizable. In the greenish gleam that the lampshade cast over the whitewashed walls, the familiar portrait of the Commander-in-Chief in his snow-white uniform appeared in between a couple of enormous reddish copper cauldrons. The Emperor's white tunic was flecked with innumerable flyspots, it looked riddled with shot, and the eyes of Franz Joseph I, which were almost certainly the usual china blue, were dimmed in the shadow of the lampshade. The doctor pointed to the painting. 'A year ago it was in the public bar!' he said. 'Now the landlord doesn't feel like proving he's a loyal subject any more!' The music stopped. In the same instant, a couple of loud strikes on a clock rang out. 'Two o'clock already!' said the Lieutenant. 'Another five hours!' replied the regimental doctor. The landlord brought slivovitz. Twenty past seven, it knelled in the Lieutenant's brain.

He reached for his little glass, raised it high, and said in the steady confident voice of someone trained to issue commands: 'Your health! You must live!'

'To an easy death!' replied the regimental doctor, and drained his glass, while Carl Joseph had merely set his back down on the table.

'This death makes no sense!' the doctor went on. 'It's just as meaningless as my whole life has been!'

'I don't want you to die!' shouted the Lieutenant, and he stamped his feet on the kitchen tiles. 'I don't want to die, and my life is just as meaningless as yours!'

'That's enough!' said Dr Demant. 'You're the grandson of the hero of Solferino. He almost had a meaningless death. Even though it makes a difference whether you go to your death full of conviction as he did, or as doubtfully as the two of us.' He fell silent. 'As the two of us,' he resumed after a while. 'Our grandfathers didn't leave us much strength, not enough strength to live with, but just about enough to die a meaningless death. Ach!' The doctor pushed his glass away, and it was as though he were pushing the whole world away, and his friend with it. 'Ach!' he repeated, 'I'm tired, I've been tired for years! Tomorrow I will die like a hero, a so-called hero, in total opposition to the beliefs of my forefathers and my race, and the will of my grandfather. In one of the old books he read, there is the sentence: "Whoever raises his hand against his fellow man is a murderer." Tomorrow, someone will raise a pistol against me, and I will raise a pistol against him. And that will make me a murderer. But I am short-sighted, I will not aim. It will be my little revenge. Without my glasses, I am blind, completely blind. And I will shoot without being able to see anything! That will be more natural and honest, and appropriate to my nature!'

Lieutenant Trotta couldn't quite follow what the regimental doctor was saying to him. The voice of the doctor was familiar to him, and, once he had got used to the civilian clothes his friend was wearing, so were his face and form. But the thoughts of Dr

Demant reached him from an immeasurable distance, from that immeasurably distant region in which Demant's grandfather, the white-bearded king of the Jewish innkeepers, might have dwelt. Trotta concentrated his mind, as he had done in trigonometry at cadet school, but he understood less and less. He could only feel that his renewed belief in the possibility of pulling everything round was gradually losing strength as his hope slowly cooled to white, substanceless ash, like the fading threads in a singing gas flame. His heart beat as noisily as the hollow tinny ticks of the clock. He didn't understand his friend. Perhaps he had arrived too late. He had much still to say. But his tongue lay heavy in his mouth, there were heavy weights pressing it down. He parted his lips to speak. They were pale, and trembled slightly; it was difficult to close them.

'I think you're running a temperature!' said the regimental doctor, with a return of his bedside manner. He rapped on the table, the landlord arrived with fresh slivovitz glasses. 'You haven't even drunk your first one yet!'

Obediently, Trotta drained his first glass. 'I discovered schnapps too late – shame!' said the doctor. 'You won't believe me: I'm sorry I never drank before.'

The Lieutenant made an enormous effort, raised his head, and stared into the doctor's face for a moment. He raised his second glass, it was heavy, his hand shook, and he spilt a few drops. He drank it down; rage burned inside him, and rose into his head, reddening his face. 'Well, I'll go then!' he said. 'I can't endure your jokes. I was so glad when I found you! I went to your house. I rang the bell. I drove up to the cemetery. I shouted your name at the gates like a lunatic. I ...' He broke off. His quaking lips formed silent words, dumb words, the dumb shadows of dumb sounds. Suddenly his eyes filled with warmth, and a loud groan broke from his chest. He wanted to get up and run away, because he felt so ashamed. I'm crying! he thought, I'm crying! He felt impotent, utterly impotent, faced with the baffling force that was compelling him to cry. He surrendered to it. He surrendered to the pleasure of his impotence. He heard himself groan, and he relished the sound, he felt ashamed of himself, and he relished his shame. He flung himself into the arms of his sweet pain, and, as he sobbed, he kept crying out mechanically: 'I don't, I don't want you to die! I don't want you to die! I don't!'

Dr Demant stood up, walked through the kitchen a couple of times, stopped in front of the portrait of the Commander-in-Chief, began counting the flyspots on the Emperor's tunic, gave up his foolish pastime, went back to Carl Joseph, gently laid his hands on his heaving shoulders, and moved his glinting spectacles till they were just above the Lieutenant's parting. He had already finished with the world, had clever Dr Demant. He had sent his wife to her father in Vienna, packed his man off on holiday, locked up his house. Since the unhappy business had blown up, he had lived in the Golden Bear. He was finished. Ever since he'd broken with the habits of a lifetime and started drinking schnapps, he had even found a hidden meaning in this senseless duel, the quest for Death was the proper end to his mistaken career, yes, and he even sensed a glimmer of the Hereafter, in which he had always believed. Long before the danger in which he presently found himself, he had been acquainted with graves and the death of friends. His childish love of his wife was extinguished. The jealousy that had flared up in his heart only a few weeks before was now just a chilly heap of ashes. The will he had just written was in his jacket pocket, addressed to the Colonel. He had no property to leave, not many people to remember, and so had forgotten nothing. The alcohol made him feel giddy, it was only the waiting that was hard to endure. Twenty past seven, the hour that was tolling fearfully in his comrades' heads, tinkled in his like a little silver bell. For the first time since putting on uniform, he felt light, strong and courageous. He enjoyed the proximity of Death, as a man on the mend might enjoy the proximity of Life. He had finished with everything, he was ready! Then he was standing once more, short-sighted and helpless as ever, in front of his young friend. Yes, there was still youth and friendship and tears that were spilled for him. All at once he felt a kind of yearning for the tawdriness of his life, the disgusting barracks, the hateful uniform, the deadliness of his calls on patients, the reek of the assembled soldiers in their underwear, the routine injections, the carbolic stench of the hospital, the foul moods of his wife, the stifling domesticity of his home, the ash-grey weekdays, the gaping Sundays, the torment of riding lessons, idiotic manoeuvres, and his own unhappiness at so much ghastliness. To the doctor, the sobs and groans of the Lieutenant were like a cry breaking from the living earth, and while he looked for words with which to comfort him, his heart flooded with pity, and love flared up in him with a thousand tongues of fire. Far behind him suddenly lay the indifference in which he had spent the last few days.

Thereupon there were three loud clangs of the clock. Trotta subsided. They heard the triple echo, as it slowly merged with the buzz of the oil lamp. The Lieutenant began in a calm voice: 'You must understand how stupid this whole episode is! I find Taittinger as much of a bore as everyone else does. So I tell him I'm meeting someone, that evening outside the theatre. Then your wife turns up, unaccompanied. I have to escort her. And then just as we're passing the mess, everyone comes out on to the street.'

The doctor took his hands off Trotta's shoulders and commenced his wanderings again. He walked almost in silence, with soft and attentive footfall.

'I have to add,' the Lieutenant went on, 'that I guessed straight away there would be grave consequences. I could barely make small talk to your wife. And then when I was standing in front of your garden, outside your house, the lamp was burning; I remember I could clearly see the line of your footprints going up the garden path to the front door, through the snow, and that gave me the peculiar notion, mad really . . .'

'Yes?' said the doctor, and stopped.

'A bizarre idea: for a brief moment I thought your footprints were like guards or sentries, I can't express it properly, it was as though they were keeping an eye on your wife from down there in the snow.' Dr Demant resumed his seat, looked carefully at Trotta, and slowly said: 'Maybe you're in love with my wife, and don't realize it?'

'I'm not to blame for any of it!' said Trotta.

'No, no, of course you're not to blame!' confirmed the regimental doctor.

'But it always feels as though I am!' said Carl Joseph. 'You remember, I told you about Frau Slama, and all that!' He stopped. Then went on in a whisper: 'I'm scared, I'm scared, everywhere!'

The regimental doctor spread his arms, shrugged his shoulders, and said: 'You're a grandson too!'

At that moment, he wasn't thinking of the Lieutenant's fears. It seemed perfectly possible to him that he might still elude all the threats to himself. Vanish! he thought. Accept dishonour, relegation to the ranks, serve three years as a private, or run away abroad! Not be shot! Already Lieutenant Trotta, grandson of the hero of Solferino, seemed to him like a being from another world, an utter stranger. And he said loudly and scathingly: 'The cretinous stupidity of it! The honour that's invested in the silly tassel hanging on your sabre. You're not permitted to walk a woman home! Can you see how stupid that is? Didn't you rescue him' – he pointed to the portrait of the Emperor – 'from a brothel? Lunacy!' he suddenly shouted, 'bloody lunacy!'

He rapped on the table, the landlord came in with two more glasses. The regimental doctor drank. 'Drink!' he said. Carl Joseph drank. He didn't quite follow what the doctor was saying, but he sensed that Demant was no longer ready to die. The clock ticked off the tinny seconds. Time didn't stop. Twenty past seven, twenty past seven! It would take a miracle if Demant was not to die. And there are no such things as miracles, as the Lieutenant already knew! What if he himself – extraordinary notion – stepped out tomorrow morning at twenty past seven, and said: Gentlemen, Demant has lost his mind in the course of last night, I am taking his place! Ridiculous, not possible, a game! He looked at the doctor once again in his perplexity. Time didn't stop, the clock went on stitching the seconds together. Almost four o'clock: three more hours!

'All right!' the regimental doctor said at last. It sounded as if he had come to a decision, as if he knew just what he was going to do. But he didn't know! His thoughts traced blind and incoherent shapes through the dense fog in his mind. He knew nothing! An abysmal, worthless, stupid, steely, mighty law bound him, sent him bound in chains to a stupid death. He listened for sounds coming from the bar next door. Evidently there was no one there any more, at this late hour. The landlord held the clashing glasses under splashing water, pushed the chairs together, straightened the tables, jingled his keys. Time to go. Maybe the streets, the winter, the night sky, the stars and the snow would have some comfort and advice to offer. He went over to the landlord, paid, and came back all muffled up in his black coat and a broad-brimmed black hat – yet another new guise. He looked ready and armed to Carl Joseph, more ready and armed than he had ever been before, in uniform and cap and sabre.

They walked through the courtyard and back through the passage, back out into the night. The doctor looked up at the sky; from the quiet stars came no advice, they were even colder than the snow round about. The houses were dark, the lanes deaf mutes, the night wind blew the snow to powder, Trotta's spurs clinked softly, the doctor's soles crunched along beside them. They walked fast, as though in a hurry to get somewhere. In their minds, scraps of ideas, of notions, of pictures pursued one another. Their hearts beat like heavy, nimble hammers. Without being aware of it, the regimental doctor led the way; without realizing it, the Lieutenant followed. They approached the Golden Bear. They stood in front of the arched gateway of the hotel. In his mind's eye, Carl Joseph could see Demant's grandfather, the silver-bearded king of the Jewish innkeepers. He would have spent his entire life sitting in front of just such a gate, probably a much bigger one. When the peasants drew up, he would get to his feet. Because he could no longer hear well, the little peasants shouted up their wishes to him, cupping their hands to their mouths. Twenty past seven, twenty past seven rang out again. At twenty past seven, that man's grandson would be dead.

'Dead!' said the Lieutenant aloud. Oh, clever Dr Demant wasn't clever any more! He had been brave and free for a day or two, and it was for nothing; it turned out that he hadn't cleared his decks after all. It's not an easy matter, clearing one's decks! His cleverness, inherited from a long, long line of clever forefathers, was as little able to cope as the simple mind of the Lieutenant, whose ancestors had been the simple peasants of Sipolje. A stupid, steely law left no escape. 'I'm a fool, my friend!' said the doctor. 'I should have left Eva long ago. I don't have the strength to run away from this stupid duel. I will become a hero out of sheer idiocy, bound by the rules of honour and the army. A hero!' He laughed, and his laughter rang out into the night. 'A hero!' he repeated, and stamped back and forth in front of the hotel gates.

Suddenly there rushed through the young, consolation-seeking mind of the Lieutenant a childish hope: they won't shoot at each other at all, and they'll just make it up! Everything will be fine! They will both be transferred to other regiments! And me with them! Silly, laughable, impossible! he thought a moment later. And then he stood quite motionless, lost and despairing, with a bitter head, in front of the doctor who paced to and fro.

How late was it? – He didn't want to look at his watch. Soon the clock would strike. He would wait for that. 'In case we don't see each other again,' said the doctor, paused, and added a few seconds later: 'My advice is, leave the army!' Then he put out his hand: 'Fare well! Go home! I'll manage by myself! *Servus!*' He tugged at the bell-pull. They could hear the jarring bell ringing inside. Steps were heard. The gate was unlocked. Lieutenant Trotta gripped the doctor's hand. In a perfectly ordinary voice, astonishing to himself, he said a perfectly ordinary: '*Servus!*' He hadn't even pulled off his glove. The door fell shut. Already there was no more Dr Demant. As though pulled along by an invisible hand, Lieutenant Trotta walked back the usual way to barracks.

He didn't hear the second-floor window being pushed open above him. The doctor leaned out one last time, saw his friend disappearing round the corner, closed the window again, lit all the lights in the room, went to the washstand, sharpened his razor, tested it on his thumbnail, and lathered up his beard as calmly as he did every morning. He washed. He took his uniform out of the wardrobe. He got dressed, buckled on his sabre, and settled down to wait. He dropped off. He fell into a quiet and dreamless sleep in the big armchair in front of the window.

When he awoke, the sky over the rooftops was already brightening, and a delicate tinge of blue lay over the snow. He waited for the knock. It would be soon. In the distance he could hear the ringing of a sleigh. It drew nearer, and stopped. Then the bell rang. Steps creaked. Spurs jingled. The knock on the door.

Then they were standing in the room, First Lieutenant Christ and Captain Wangert from the infantry regiment with which they shared the barracks. They stayed by the door, the Lieutenant half a step behind the Captain. The regimental doctor looked up at the sky. In a distant echo from his distant childhood there came the quavering voice of his dead grandfather: 'Hearken, O Israel,' said the voice, 'the Lord, our God, is the only God!'

'I'm ready, gentlemen!' said the regimental doctor.

They sat, a little squashed together in the little sleigh; the bells rang out bravely, the chestnut horses lifted their cropped tails and dropped large, yellow steaming balls of dung on to the snow. Suddenly, the regimental doctor, who had been indifferent to animals all his life, felt nostalgia for his mount. It will outlive me! he thought. His expression betrayed no emotion. His companions did not speak.

They stopped about a hundred paces before the clearing, and reached the 'green' on foot. It was already morning, but the sun had not yet risen. The fir trees stood slender, upright and quite still, bearing the snow on their boughs with pride. In the distance cocks crowed back and forth. Tattenbach was talking to his seconds at the top of his voice. The consultant, Dr Mangel, walked back and forth between the two parties. 'Gentlemen!' said a voice. At that moment, Dr Demant took off his spectacles, a little awkwardly as he always did, and laid them carefully on a broad tree-stump. Strange to relate, he could still see the way quite clearly, the place where he was made to stand, the distance between that and the Count, and Tattenbach himself. He waited. Up until the very last moment he was waiting for the fog. But everything remained clear, as if the regimental doctor had never been short-sighted. A voice counted: 'One!' The regimental doctor raised his pistol. He felt brave and free, yes, for the first time in his life, even a little exuberant. He aimed as he had done once as a one-year volunteer at target practice (even then he'd been a wretched shot). I'm not short-sighted at all, he thought, I'll never need my glasses again. In medical terms it was a mystery. The regimental doctor promised to look into ophthalmology. At the very moment in which the name of a famous specialist swam into his mind, the voice counted: 'Two!' The doctor could still see clearly. An anxious bird of a type he could not identify began to twitter, and from faraway he heard the sound of a trumpet. It was just then that the dragoons reached the exercise grounds.

Lieutenant Trotta rode, as he always did, with the second detachment. A dull layer of frost had settled on the sheaths of the heavy sabres and the barrels of the light rifles. The frozen trumpets woke up the sleeping little town. The coachmen, in their thick furs, waiting at their usual positions, raised their bearded faces. When the regiment had reached the water meadows and dismounted, and the troops formed up into double rows for morning exercises, as they always did, Lieutenant Kindermann went up to Carl Joseph and asked: 'Are you ill or something? You look frightful.' And he got out his girlish pocket mirror and held it up to Trotta's face. In the shimmering little rectangle Lieutenant Trotta beheld an ancient face that he knew very well: burning, narrowed black eyes, a large bony beak of a nose, hollow ashen cheeks, a long, pale, bloodless mouth like a long-healed sabre cut, that separated the chin from the moustache. Only the little brown moustache looked unfamiliar to Carl Joseph. Back home, under the ceiling of his father's drawing room, the dimming face of his grandfather was clean-shaven.

'Thanks!' said the Lieutenant. 'I didn't sleep last night.' He left the exercise grounds.

He headed off through the trees, where a path led back on to the wide main road. It was twenty to eight. No shots had been heard. Everything's all right, everything's all right, he said to himself, a miracle must have happened! In ten minutes at the latest, Major Prohaska will come riding up, and then everything will be made known. The sluggish sounds of the little town awakening could be heard, and the long-drawn-out shrill of a locomotive from the station. When the Lieutenant reached the junction of path and road, the Major came clopping along on his chestnut, and Trotta saluted him. 'Morning!' said the Major, and nothing else. The narrow path could not accommodate a rider and a walker abreast. Trotta, therefore, walked along behind the Major. Two minutes or so before the water meadows (the shouts of the non-commissioned officers could already be heard) the Major stopped, half turned in his saddle, and merely said: 'Both of them!' Then, as he rode on, more to himself than to the Lieutenant: 'Couldn't be helped!'

On that particular day, the regiment went back to barracks a good hour earlier than usual. The trumpets sounded as they did every other day. In the afternoon, the duty officers read out the orders, in which Colonel Kovacs noted that Captain of Horse Count Tattenbach and Regimental Doctor Demant had both died a soldier's death for the honour of the regiment.

# 8

In the years before the Great War, at the time the events chronicled in these pages took place, it was not yet a matter of indifference whether a man lived or died. When someone was expunged from the lists of the living, someone else did not immediately step up to take his place, but a gap was left to show where he had been, and those who knew the man who had died or disappeared, well or even less well, fell silent whenever they saw the gap. When a fire happened to consume a particular dwelling in a row of dwellings, the site of the conflagration remained for a long time afterwards. For masons and bricklayers worked slowly and thoughtfully, and when they walked past the ruins, neighbours and passers-by alike recalled the form and the walls of the house that had once stood there. That's how it was then! Everything that grew took long to grow; and everything that ended took a long time to be forgotten. Everything that existed left behind traces of itself, and people then lived by their memories, just as we nowadays live by our capacity to forget, quickly and comprehensively. For a long time afterwards, the feelings of the officers and men of the dragoon regiment, and of the civilian inhabitants of the small town, were shaken and troubled by the deaths of the regimental doctor and Count Tattenbach. The dead men were buried in accordance with the standard military and religious rites. Even though none of their former comrades had breathed a word to anyone outside their own ranks concerning the manner of their deaths, still it seemed somehow to have become known to the general population of the small garrison town that both had fallen victim to the stern sense of honour that prevailed in the regiment. And it was as though, from then on, every one of the remaining officers wore on his face the mark of a near and violent death, and to the shopkeepers and craftsmen of the little town, these strange gentlemen seemed to have become that much more strange. The officers went about like the baffling followers of some remote and cruel godhead, which simultaneously cast them as its colourfully disguised and magnificently decked sacrificial animals. People looked at them and shook their heads. They even felt sorry for them. They have many advantages, so people said. They can walk around with swords, women fall in love with them, and the Emperor looks after them in person, as if they were his own sons. But then, in a trice, before you've even noticed anything, one of them has managed to offend another, and the offence needs to be washed away with red blood! . . .

Those who found themselves spoken of in such terms were indeed not to be envied. Even Captain of Horse Taittinger, of whom word was that he had been involved in a couple of fatal duels in his previous regiments, altered his familiar manner. While the more rowdy and easygoing officers became silent and preoccupied, the habitually silent, lean and sweet-toothed captain of horse was gripped by a strange unrest. He was no longer capable of sitting alone for hours on end behind the glass door of the little sweet shop, eating pastries, or of playing chess or dominoes silently against himself or the Colonel. He was afraid of solitude. He positively clung to the others. If there was no comrade at hand, he would walk into a shop to buy some knick-knack that he didn't really want. He would stay there for a long time, chattering with the shopkeeper about all kinds of silly nonsense, and seemed incapable of leaving the shop; unless, that is, he happened to catch sight of some vague acquaintance outside, in which case he would immediately throw himself upon him instead.

The world was altered beyond recognition. The mess was empty. The officers no longer went on merry expeditions to Frau Resi's premises. The orderlies had very little to do. Whoever ordered himself a schnapps, would see the glass and think to himself that this was the very supply from which Tattenbach had drunk only a couple of days previously. The old anecdotes were still told, but they were no longer met with loud laughter, but at the most with a faint smile. As for Lieutenant Trotta, no one saw anything of him off duty.

It was as though a swift magic hand had washed away every trace of youth from Carl Joseph's face. There was no lieutenant in the whole K-and-K army like him. He had a sense that he ought to perform some special deed or other – but he had absolutely no idea what. It was a foregone conclusion that he would leave the regiment and be assigned to a different one. But he was looking for some demanding task. What he really wanted was some form of expiation. He would never have been able to say so himself, but we can say it on his behalf: it hurt him inexpressibly that he had been a tool in the hand of fate.

Such was his condition when he informed his father of the outcome of the duel, and announced his unavoidable transfer to another regiment. He made no mention of the fact that this change of circumstance allowed him a short period of leave, because he was afraid to show himself to his father. Little did he know the old man. Because, for all that he was the very embodiment of a civil servant, there was little that the District Commissioner did not know about the ways of the military. And, remarkably, he also seemed to sense the griefs and confusions of his son, as was clearly evident from reading between the lines of his reply. The District Commissioner wrote as follows:

Dear Son!
I am grateful to you for your precise statement of the facts,

and for the trust you have placed in me. I was deeply affected to learn of the fate that has befallen your comrades. They died as befits men of honour.

In my day, the practice of duelling was rather more widespread than it is today, and honour meant vastly more than life itself. In my day, I am also tempted to say, officers were made of sterner stuff. My son, you are an officer and the grandson of the hero of Solferino. You will know how to live with the blameless and unwitting role you played in the recent tragic events. Of course you will be sorry to leave your regiment, but bear in mind that in whatever regiment of our armed forces you next serve, you will also be serving our emperor.

Your father

Franz von Trotta

P.S. The fortnight's furlough you are allowed on your transfer you are welcome to spend either under my roof, or, perhaps better still, in your new garrison, to help you adjust a little to your new circumstances.

As above

Lieutenant Trotta felt a little ashamed when he read the letter. His father had sensed everything. In the eyes of the Lieutenant, the figure of the District Commissioner grew to an unbearable scale. Yes, it was almost on a par with that of Grandfather. And if the Lieutenant had been afraid to see the old man before, it was now quite impossible for him to spend the coming furlough under his roof. Later, he thought, later, when I have my regular furlough, thought the Lieutenant, who was made of altogether different stuff than the lieutenants of the District Commissioner's younger days.

'Of course you will be sorry to leave your regiment,' his father had written. Had he written that because he sensed the opposite was true? What was there that Carl Joseph was loath to leave behind? Maybe the window, with the view across the yard into the common soldiers' quarters, the troops themselves, sitting on their beds, the mournful sound of their harmonicas and their singing, those exotic songs that sounded like an accidental echo of similar songs that were sung by the peasants of Sipolje! Maybe I should go to Sipolje, thought the Lieutenant. He walked up to the general staff map that was the only thing he had hanging on his walls. He could have found Sipolje in his sleep. There it was on the extreme southern edge of the Monarchy, the good, quiet village. In the middle of a faintly cross-hatched tan area were the tiny, gossamer-thin, black letters that made up the name Sipolje. And around them were marked a well, a sawmill, a tiny station on a narrow-gauge forest railway, a church and a mosque, a forest plantation, narrow paths through the woods and fields, a scattering of houses. Evening in Sipolje. The women are standing around the fountain in their colourful headscarves, tinted gold by the glowing sunset. The Muslims are kneeling at their evening devotions on the old rugs in the mosque. The tiny locomotive that pulls the narrow-gauge train is jingling its way under the dense green canopy of pines. The sawmill is clattering over the burbling stream. It was a game he was used to playing since cadet school. The familiar images came the moment he shut his eyes. And over it all hung Grandfather's enigmatic expression. There probably weren't any cavalry regiments stationed around there. He would have to switch to the infantry. His mounted comrades felt contempt for foot soldiers, they would feel contemptuous of Trotta when he transferred. His grandfather had been nothing more than a plain captain of infantry. Marching on foot over home soil was almost a return to one's peasant forebears. Heavy-footed, they trod the hard sods, they jabbed the plough into the juicy flesh of the field, they scattered the fruitful seeds with beneficent gestures. No! The Lieutenant had no regrets about leaving this regiment and maybe the cavalry as well! His father would have to give his permission. And then he himself would have to take an infantry course, which might be tedious, but nothing worse.

He had to say his goodbyes. A little soirée in the officers' mess. A round of schnapps. A short address from the Colonel. Hearty handshakes all round. Behind his back they were whispering already. A bottle of champagne. Maybe, who knows, a general decamp to Frau Resi's premises, and a further round of schnapps. Oh, if only the goodbyes were over! He'll take Onufri, his orderly, with him. Learning a whole new name would be far too hard! He'll get out of having to spend the furlough at home. In fact, he'll try to get out of all the demanding and burdensome things attendant on a transfer. Now there was just the hard, hard visit to Dr Demant's widow.

What a visit! Lieutenant Trotta tried to convince himself that Frau Eva Demant would have gone home to her father in Vienna, following the burial of her husband. That would leave him standing outside the villa, ringing the bell for a long time, pointlessly, then getting an address for her in Vienna, and writing a brief, and if possible, kindly note. It's a great relief to learn you can settle the whole thing in writing, particularly if, as the Lieutenant went on to think, you don't have an abundance of courage. If it wasn't for the fact that you constantly felt the dark, enigmatic eyes of Grandfather drilling into your back, my God, what a dismal figure you'd cut, wobbling your way through this arduous thing called life. It was only the thought of the hero of Solferino that gave you backbone. You kept having to resort to Grandfather as if he was a form of Dutch – or Slovene – courage.

And slowly the Lieutenant set off on his difficult visit. It was three in the afternoon. The little shopkeepers stood wretched and frozen outside their shops, waiting for their handful of customers. From the artisans' workshops came industrious and familiar sounds. There was a merry clang of hammering in the blacksmith's, a tinny growl of thunder from the plumber's, a rapid tapping from the cobbler's, a whining of saws from the carpenter's. All the faces and noises in the workshops were familiar to the Lieutenant. He came riding past them twice a day. From his saddle, he could look down over the top of their old blue and white signs. Every day he saw into the low first-floor rooms; the beds and coffee pots, the men in their shirts, the women with their hair loose, flowerpots on the sills, dried fruit and pickled cucumbers lurking in the cupboards.

Then he stood in front of Dr Demant's villa. The gate groaned. He stepped inside. The orderly let him in. The Lieutenant waited. Frau Demant came in. He trembled slightly. He remembered paying his condolences to Sergeant Slama. He could feel that heavy, damp, cold, slack hand in his. He could see the gloomy hallway, and the reddish living room. In his mouth he had the bitter aftertaste of the raspberry juice. So she's not in Vienna, thought the Lieutenant, but only in the instant when he actually saw her in front of him. He was unprepared for her wearing black. It was as though it had taken him till now to grasp that Frau Demant was the regimental doctor's widow. Even the room he now entered wasn't the room he had sat in when his friend had been alive. On the wall, black-bordered now, was a large portrait of the dead man. It kept slipping into the distance, like that of the Emperor in the mess hall, as though it wasn't in front of your eyes and within reach of your hands, but somehow behind the wall, as though seen through a window. 'Thank you for coming!' said Frau Demant. 'I wanted to say goodbye!' replied Trotta. Frau Demant raised her pale face. The Lieutenant saw the pale, grey, beautiful shine of her large eyes. They were directed straight at him, like two rounds of smooth ice. In the wintry gloom of the afternoon, the woman's eyes were the only bright thing. The Lieutenant's eyes fled up to her narrow white forehead and thence to the wall, to the faraway portrait of the dead man. This bit was taking far too long, it was time that Frau Demant offered him a seat. But she said nothing. In the meantime, he could feel the darkness of the evening ahead coming through the window, and he had a childish fear that this house would never be lit. No word or expression came to the Lieutenant's aid. He listened to the quiet breathing of the woman. 'Why are we standing around like this!' she said, finally. 'Let's sit down!' They sat down at the table, facing one another. Carl Joseph sat just as he had done at Sergeant Slama's, with the door behind him. He felt uneasy because of it, as he had then. For no reason, it seemed to open from time to time and shut, all silently. The dusk deepened. Frau Eva Demant's black dress seemed to dissolve in it. Now she was wearing only dusk. Stripped naked, only her white face floated on the dark surface of the evening. The picture of the dead man on the opposite wall had vanished. 'My husband,' said the voice of Frau Demant, through the darkness. The Lieutenant could see the shimmer of her teeth in the dark; they were whiter than her face. Gradually, he was able to make out the smooth rounds of her eyes. 'You were his only friend! Many times he said so! He talked about you so much! If only you knew! I can't get it into my head that he's gone. And' – in a whisper – 'I'm to blame!'

'No, I'm to blame!' said the Lieutenant. His voice sounded loud, rough and unfamiliar to himself. It was no consolation for Demant's widow. 'It's my fault!' he repeated. 'I should have been more careful about which way I took you home. Not straight past the officers' mess.'

The woman started to sob. You saw her pale face leaning ever lower over the table, like a large, white, oval flower slowly sinking. Suddenly white hands appeared either side of it, took receipt of the sliding face, and held it between them. And then, for a time – a minute, another minute – nothing could be heard but the woman's sobbing. An eternity for the Lieutenant. I ought to just get up and go and leave her to cry, he thought. He got up. In a trice, her hands fell back to the table. In a calm voice that seemed to have come from a different throat entirely, she asked: 'Where are you going?'

'Get some light!' said Trotta.

She stood up, walked past him round the table, brushing against him as she did so. He smelled a soft wave of scent; it broke and was gone. The light was harsh; Trotta forced himself to look straight into it. Frau Demant held a hand in front of her eyes. 'Light the lamp over the sideboard,' she ordered. The Lieutenant obeyed. She stood in the doorway, with her hand still shading her eyes. When the small lamp was on under its mild golden yellow shade, she switched out the overhead light. She took down the hand from in front of her eyes, as one might take down a visor. She looked very striking, in her black dress, with her pale face towards Trotta. She was brave and furious. On her cheeks you saw the tiny dried channels where her tears had run. The eyes were as pure as ever.

'Sit down over there on the sofa!' ordered Frau Demant. Carl Joseph sat down. From all sides, subtly and smoothly, the eager cushions slipped towards the Lieutenant, from the armrest, from the corners. He felt that sitting there was dangerous, and he moved determinedly into the corner, rested his hands on the hilt of his sabre, and watched Frau Eva approach him. She looked like the dangerous proprietress of all the cushions and pillows. On the wall to the right hung the portrait of his dead friend. Frau Eva sat down. A harmless little cushion slipped between them. Trotta didn't stir. As always, when he could see no way out of one of the numerous agonizing situations he tended to slip into, he imagined he could leave any time he chose.

'So you're being transferred?' asked Frau Demant.

'I've asked for a transfer!' he said, his eyes on the carpet, his chin on his hands, and his hands cupped around the hilt of his sabre.

'Must you?'

'Yes, I had to!'

'I'm sorry – terribly sorry!'

Frau Demant sat as he did, with her elbows propped on her knees, her chin in her hands, and her eyes on the carpet. She was probably waiting for a word of comfort, some kindly scrap. He was silent. He relished the blissful feeling of avenging his dead friend by an obdurate silence. Tales of dangerous, pretty little murderesses, a popular theme among his comrades, came into his mind. She probably belonged to that dangerous breed of feminine killers. You had to get off their terrain as quickly as you could. He made ready to stand up. At that moment, Frau Demant shifted her position. She took her hands from her chin. With her left hand, she gently and diligently began to stroke the silk braid that ran along the edge of the sofa. Her fingers walked back and forth slowly and rhythmically along the narrow, shining path that led from her to

Lieutenant Trotta. They crept into his view, he wished he had blinkers. The white fingers involved him in a silent but gripping conversation. Cigarette – what a glorious idea! He pulled out his cigarette case, his matches. 'Give me one!' said Frau Demant. He was forced to look her in the face as he lit her cigarette. He thought it was unseemly for her to be smoking, as though nicotine were not permitted to mourners. And the way she took in her first puff, and pursed her lips in a tight round ring from which emerged the delicate blue cloud, that was sinful and . . . indelicate.

'Do you know where you will be transferring to?'

'No,' said the Lieutenant, 'but I want to try and get a long way away from here!'

'A long way? Where, for instance?'

'Maybe to Bosnia!'

'Do you think you'll be happy there?'

'I don't think I can be happy anywhere!'

'I wish you could be!' she said glibly, very glibly, Trotta thought.

She got up, came back with an ashtray, set it on the floor between the Lieutenant and herself, and said: 'So we'll probably never see each other again!'

Never again! The dread words, that boundless dead sea of numb infinity! Never again could you see Katharina, or Dr Demant, or now this woman here! Carl Joseph said: 'No, probably not! Unfortunately!' He thought of adding: I'll never see Max Demant again either! 'Widows should be burned!' one of Taittinger's radical sayings, also sprang to his mind.

The bell rang, and there was some movement in the corridor. 'That'll be my father!' said Frau Demant. And in the same moment Herr Knopfmacher walked in. 'Ah, so there you are, there you are!' He brought acrid snow-smell into the room with him. He opened out a large and beautifully white handkerchief, blew his nose authoritatively, folded the handkerchief carefully back into his inside pocket, like a treasure, put out his hand to the doorframe, and lit the overhead light. Then he walked closer to

Trotta, who had stood up when Knopfmacher had come in, and had now been standing there waiting for him for quite some time, and silently shook his hand. In that pressure, Herr Knopfmacher sought to express all the sadness that could be expressed about the doctor's death. Next he explained to his daughter, gesturing at the main light: 'I'm sorry, I can't stand this spectral illumination!' It was as if he'd tossed a stone at the black-bordered portrait of the dead man.

'My, you do look awful!' Knopfmacher said a moment later, in crowing tones. 'You must have taken it hard, this tragedy, eh?'

'He was my one and only friend!'

'Really,' said Knopfmacher, sat down at the table, and with a smile requested: 'Don't get up, please!' and continued, once the Lieutenant was sitting on the sofa: 'That's exactly what he said of you, when he was still alive, of course. What a calamity!' And he shook his head once or twice, and his full, flushed cheeks wobbled a bit.

Frau Demant pulled a little lace handkerchief from her sleeve, and left the room, holding it pressed to her eyes.

'God knows how she'll ever get over it!' said Knopfmacher. 'Well, I gave her lots of good advice, earlier. Mind you, she didn't want to listen! You see, my dear Lieutenant, it seems to me every career has its perils. But an officer – I hope you don't mind my saying so – an officer really ought not to marry at all. This is between you and me, but I expect he will have told you himself as well, he wanted to leave the army and devote himself to science. And I can't tell you how happy that made me, hearing that. He would certainly have made a first-class doctor. Dear old Max!' Herr Knopfmacher lifted his eyes to the portrait, let them dwell there for a while and concluded his eulogy: 'The potential of the man!'

Frau Demant brought in some of her father's favourite slivovitz.

'You'll have a glass with me, won't you?' asked Knopfmacher, pouring for them both. He carefully carried the little glass over to the sofa himself. The Lieutenant stood up. He felt a bitter taste in his mouth, as once after the raspberry juice. He knocked it back.

'When was the last time you saw him?' asked Knopfmacher.

'The day before,' said the Lieutenant.

'He asked Eva to go to Vienna, there was no hint of anything amiss. She set off in all innocence. And then his farewell letter arrived. And then I knew right away there was nothing to be done!'

'No, there was nothing to be done!'

'There's something anachronistic, if you'll pardon my saying so, about this code of honour! We are in the twentieth century, remember! We have the gramophone, we can telephone people a hundred miles away, and Blériot and some other chaps are even flying through the air! And, well, I don't know if you read the papers or if you're up on politics at all, but there's promise of some major alterations to the constitution. Ever since the universal, secret suffrage has been extended, all sorts of things have been going on, both in this country and in the world at large. Our emperor, may God preserve him, is by no means as old-fashioned as some would have us believe. Of course, there is plenty to be said in favour of the so-called conservative approach too. One should just remember to go forward slowly and cautiously. Don't be in too much of a hurry!'

'I don't know the first thing about politics!' said Trotta.

Knopfmacher felt a certain irritation. He was annoyed with this silly army and its cretinous institutions. His daughter was now a widow, his son-in-law was dead, he had to go and find another one, in civvy street this time, and the promised commercial councillorship was probably lost somewhere in the long grass by now. It was high time to call a halt to this nonsense. Young hotheads like these lieutenant chappies shouldn't be encouraged in the twentieth century. Nations wanted their rights, one man one vote, no more privileges for the aristocracy; social democracy might be a dangerous thing, but it was a useful counter-balance. There's talk about war all the time, but I bet it won't happen. We'll see. These are enlightened times, progressive times. Take England: the King there didn't have any power.

'Of course not!' he said. 'The army's hardly the place for politics. Admittedly,' Knopfmacher nodded in the direction of the portrait, 'he was pretty well up in them.'

'He was a very clever man!' Trotta said quietly.

'There was nothing to be done!' Knopfmacher repeated.

'It seems to me,' said the Lieutenant, and he felt as though some strange wisdom were speaking through him, perhaps from the thick old books of the silver-bearded king of the innkeepers, 'it seems to me he was very clever and very alone!'

He turned pale. He felt the round eyes of Frau Demant upon him. He had better go. There was silence, and nothing more to say.

'We won't be seeing Baron Trotta any more either, Papa! He's being transferred!' said Frau Demant.

'Perhaps you'll drop us the odd line?' asked Knopfmacher.

'You must write!' said Frau Demant.

The Lieutenant stood up. 'Well, all the best!' said Knopfmacher. His hand was big and soft, it felt like warm velvet. Frau Demant went on ahead. The orderly came out to help him into his coat. Frau Demant stood by. Trotta clicked his heels. She said very fast: 'Write to me! I'd like to hear from you.' It was a rushed, warm puff of air, already gone. The orderly opened the door. There were the steps. The fence bulked in front of him; it was just like the time he'd left the Sergeant.

He walked rapidly into town, went into the first café on the way, drank a cognac standing at the bar, then another. 'We drink only Hennessy!' he could hear the District Commissioner say. He hurried towards the barracks.

Outside the door of his room, a blue line against all that white, Onufri was waiting for him. The office orderly had delivered a package for the Lieutenant, on instructions from the Colonel. It lay propped in the corner, thin, wrapped in brown paper. There was a note on the table.

The Lieutenant read:

My dear friend, I'm leaving you my sabre and my watch.
Max Demant.

Trotta unwrapped the sabre. On the hilt hung the smooth silver fob watch of Dr Demant's. It had stopped. It showed ten to twelve. The Lieutenant wound it and held it against his ear. Its delicate, frantic voice ticked consolingly. He prised open the lid with his pocket knife, inquisitive and meddlesome as a small boy. On the inside were marked the initials M.D. He pulled the sabre from its sheath. Directly under the hilt, Dr Demant had incised a few clumsy marks with his pocket knife in the steel. LIVE WELL AND BE FREE! was the legend. The Lieutenant hung the sabre in his wardrobe. He held the portépée in his hand. The metalled silk seemed to trickle between his fingers, like cool golden rain. Trotta shut the wardrobe; he shut a coffin.

He switched off the light, and lay down on his bed fully clothed. The yellow light from the soldiers' quarters swam in the white gloss of the door and bounced off the sparkling brass of the door knob. The mouth harmonica sent up its rough, tremulous sighs, with the bass voices of the men barrelling around it. They were singing the Ukrainian song about the Emperor and the Empress:

> Oh, our Emperor is a brave and valiant man,
> And his wife the Empress is our Queen,
> Among all his horsemen, he's in the van,
> While she stays home and waits for him,
> Oh, she waits for him —
> The Empress waits for the Emperor —

The Empress had been dead many years, but then the Ruthenian peasants didn't know that.

PART TWO

# 9

The Habsburg sun sent its beams as far east as the border with the Russian Tsar. It was the same sun as the one under which the Trotta family had risen to nobility and distinction. The gratitude of Franz Joseph had a long memory, and his favour had a long arm. When one of his favourite sons was in the process of perpetrating some folly, the ministers and civil servants of the Emperor intervened in a timely way, and brought the foolish party to his senses. It would hardly have been appropriate for the only scion of the recently ennobled house of Trotta and Sipolje to serve in the province from which the hero of Solferino had sprung, the grandson of illiterate Slovenian peasants, and the son of a gendarmerie sergeant. His descendant might yet decide to exchange his service with the dragoons for the humbler one with the infantry: in that way, he might be said to be keeping faith with the memory of his grandfather, who had been a simple infantry lieutenant when he had saved the life of the Emperor. But in its wisdom, the K-and-K War Ministry avoided sending a nobleman bearing the name of the village of the founder of the family, into the vicinity of that village. The son of the hero of Solferino, the District Commissioner, was of one mind with the military authorities. He did allow – not without heavy pangs of regret – his son to transfer into the infantry. But he refused to endorse Carl Joseph's desire to move to Slovenia. He himself, the District Commissioner, had never felt any desire to see the home of his fathers. He was an Austrian, a servant and official of the Habsburg monarchy, and his home was the Imperial Palace in Vienna. If he entertained any notion of a political restructuring of this great and varied Empire, then it would have pleased him to see all the Crownlands simply as large and suitably colourful wings and extensions of the Imperial Palace, and all the peoples of the Monarchy as the Habsburgs' faithful servants. He was a District Commissioner with heart and soul. In his district he represented the Habsburg Monarchy. He wore the golden chain, the cocked hat and the sword of office. He had no hankering to drive a plough through the hallowed, ancestral soil of Slovenia. In a letter to his son on the subject, he expressed himself as follows: 'Fate has brought us from being simple border peasants to Austrian subjects. Let us remain so.'

And so it happened that the southern frontier was kept inaccessible to his son Carl Joseph, Baron von Trotta and Sipolje, and he was merely offered the choice between a posting in the interior of the kingdom, and one on its eastern border. He decided in favour of a battalion of Jägers who were stationed no more than two miles from the Russian frontier. Also close by was the orderly Onufri's native village of Burdlaki. For Carl Joseph, the area had the consolation of being the home of the Ukrainian peasants, with their mournful harmonicas and their unforgettable songs: it was a kind of northern sister to Slovenia.

Seventeen hours Lieutenant Trotta sat in the train. In the eighteenth, he reached the most easterly station in the Austrian monarchy. There he alighted. His orderly Onufri accompanied him. The Jäger barracks was in the centre of the little town. Before they set foot in the barracks yard, Onufri crossed himself three times. It was morning. Spring, already well established in the interior of the Empire, had only just arrived here. The laburnum was agleam on the railway sidings. Violets sprang up in the damp forests. Frogs chirruped in the endless swamps. Storks circled over the low thatched roofs of the village huts, looking for the old cart-wheels that were the basis of their summer quarters.

The frontier that ran between Austria and Russia, to the north-east of the kingdom, was at that time a most extraordinary region. Carl Joseph's battalion of Jägers was garrisoned in a town with a population of some ten thousand souls. It had a spacious Ring in the centre of it, the crossing point of its two principal streets. Of these, one went from east to west, the other north to south. One went from the station to the cemetery, the other from the ruined castle to the steam-mill. Of the ten thousand inhabitants, roughly a third lived by various handiwork and crafts. A further third scratched a living from the soil. And the rest were engaged in a kind of trade.

I say: a kind of trade – for neither the commodities that were traded nor the commercial practices that were followed quite corresponded to the ideas of trade that were held in the civilized world. The traders of that region tended to live more from chance than foresight, more from an inscrutable Fate than any rational calculation, and every trader was prepared at any time to take up whatever goods Fate happened to deal him, and even, if God failed to provide him with any, then to invent some for himself. In fact, the lives of these traders were a mystery. They had no premises. They had no names. They had no credit. But they had an acute and miraculous sixth sense for any obscure or mysterious source of money. They lived off the work of others, but they also created work for others. They were modest. They lived every bit as wretchedly as if they were living from the work of their own hands. But it was the work of others. Always in transit, always on the move, with quick speech and a clear understanding, they would have been equipped to conquer half the world, if they had understood the world at all. But they did not. Because they lived far away from it, between east and west, jammed in between night and day, a kind of living ghost that was sprung from the night and went about in the daytime.

Did I say they lived as though 'jammed in'? The nature of their

139

homeland never gave them that sensation. Nature had set an endless and impressive horizon around these frontier people, and put them in the midst of green forests and blue hills. And even when they walked in the shade of dark pine forests, they could reckon themselves favoured by God, if the intensity of their daily struggle to provide bread for their wives and children allowed them still to feel God's great goodness. But the reason they were walking in the pine forests was only to acquire wood to sell to buyers in the towns, for the approaching winter. For, among other things, they also traded in wood. And they traded in corals for the peasant women in the surrounding villages, and for the peasant women who lived on the other side of the border, on Russian territory. They traded in feathers, in horsehair, in tobacco, in silver bars, in jewels, in Chinese tea, in exotic fruits, in horses and cattle, in hens and eggs, in fish and vegetables, in jute and wool, in butter and cheese, in forests and property, in Italian marble and in human hair from China used for the manufacture of wigs, in silkworms and in silk, in textiles from Manchester, in lace from Brussels and galoshes from Moscow, in Viennese linens and Bohemian lead. Not one of the wares in which this world is so rich was either so marvellous or so ordinary as to be beyond the ken of these traders and dealers. What they were unable to get hold of or to sell in accordance with the prevailing laws, they would obtain and sell in violation of every law, swiftly and secretly, boldly and slyly, with cunning and with calculation. Yes, some of them even traded in human beings, in live human beings. They dispatched deserters from the Russian army to the United States, and young peasant girls to Argentina and Brazil. They had shares in shipping agencies and foreign brothels. And in spite of all that, their profits were minuscule, and they had no conception of the wide and lavish margins on which a man can really live. Their senses, honed and practised in the finding of money, and their hands as capable of striking gold from railway ballast, as others' hands were of striking sparks, proved incapable of bringing rejoicing to their hearts or health to their bodies. The people of this area were swamp-bred.

Because the swamps lay eerily spread out over the entire breadth of the countryside, either side of the main road, with their frogs and fever bacteria and treacherous grass, that, to an ignorant traveller, unfamiliar with the country, could be a terrible lure to a terrible death. Many died, without anyone ever hearing their last cries. But everyone who was born there was acquainted with the treacherousness of the swamps, and a lot of that treacherousness was with them, in their own veins. In spring and in summer, the air was filled with the incessant fat chirruping of frogs. Under the canopy of the sky, there was an equally fat trilling of skylarks. It was like a never-ending dialogue between sky and swamp.

Among the traders already mentioned there were many who were Jews. By some freak of nature, perhaps an obscure inheritance from the mythical Khasars, many of these frontier Jews had red hair. The hair flamed on their heads. Their beards were like conflagrations. The backs of their nimble hands were sown with stiff red bristles like tiny spears. And from their ears there sprouted a soft reddish wool like the flames from whatever furnaces might be burning inside their heads.

Any strangers who came to this part of the world were slowly but irresistibly doomed. No one was a match for the swamp. No one could stand up to the border. At that time, the important people in Vienna and Petersburg were already making their preparations for the Great War. The people on the border felt it coming before anyone else did; not just because they were used to sensing things early, but also because every day they could read the signs of the impending catastrophe with their own eyes. Also, they profited from these preparations. Some lived off espionage and counter-espionage, accepting Austrian gulden from the Austrian police, and Russian roubles from the Russians. And in the tedious swampy remoteness of the garrison, from time to time an officer would fall prey to despair, cards, debts, and sinister contacts. The cemeteries of the border garrisons held the bodies of many weak young men.

But there too, the soldiers drilled as they did in all the other garrisons the length and breadth of the Empire. Every day, the Jäger battalion marched back to barracks with grey mud on their boots. Major Zoglauer rode up ahead. Lieutenant Trotta led the second platoon of the first company. The tempo in which they marched was set by a broad, mannerly signal from the horn player, not the exuberant fanfare that arrayed, interrupted and played around the hooftaps of the dragoons' mounts. Carl Joseph was now on foot, and he imagined he felt better for it. All around him, the nailed boots of the Jägers crunched on the jagged little ballast pebbles that, repeatedly, as often as once a week in spring-time, were sacrificed to the swampy tracks on the insistence of the military authorities. All those stones, those millions of stones, were swallowed up by the insatiable road. And ever new, victori-ous, silver-grey, shining layers of mud were churned up from the depths, ate up the stones and cement, and smacked together over the stamping boots of the soldiers.

The barracks was just behind the town park. Left of it was the District Court, and opposite was the District Commissioner's office, behind whose dignified and somewhat dilapidated masonry were the two churches, one Roman Catholic, one Greek Orthodox, while to the right of the barracks was the secondary school. The town was tiny, no more than twenty minutes' walk from one end to the other. Its important buildings were pressed up against each other like troublesome neighbours. For their evening stroll, people made tours of the circular park like prisoners in a prison yard. It was a good half-hour's march to the station. The Jäger officers' mess was accommodated in two small rooms in a private house. Most of the fellows ate in the station restaurant. Carl Joseph did too. He was perfectly willing to march through the smacking mud if there was a station at the other end. It was the last of all the stations in the Monarchy, but even so: it too boasted a couple of sets of shining rails which led directly to the heart of the Empire. It too had bright, cheerful, glassy signals (a faint echo of a mother's calls), and an incessantly ticking telegraph, on which the beautiful confused voices of a distant lost world were busily tapped out, as if by a clattering sewing machine. This station too had a porter, and this porter swung a jangling bell, and the bell signified: departure, all aboard! Once a day, at exactly noon, the porter swung his bell for the train that headed west, towards Cracow, Oderberg, all points to Vienna. A dear train, a good train! It stopped there almost as long as it took to eat lunch, alongside the first-class dining room where the officers sat. Not until coffee was served did the locomotive whistle. The grey steam condensed against the windows. By the time it began to trickle down the panes in beads and runnels of moisture, the train would be gone. You drank your coffee, and headed back in a slow disconsolate pack through the silvery grey mud. Even generals on tours of inspection tended to steer clear of the place. They didn't come, no one came. In the one and only hotel in the town, where most of the Jäger officers had settled as long-term tenants, it was only twice a year that the rich hop-traders came, from Nuremberg and Prague and Zatec. When they had pulled off their mysterious deals, they called for music and played cards in the town's only café, which belonged to the hotel.

From his room on the second storey of Brodnitzer's hotel, Carl Joseph could overlook the whole town. He could see the gables of the District Court, the little white turret of the District Commissioner's office, the yellow and black flag flying over the barracks, the doubled cross of the Greek Orthodox church, the weathervane over the town hall, and all the dark grey shingle roofs of the little single-storey houses. Brodnitzer's hotel was the tallest building in town. It was a landmark, as much as the church, the town hall and the other public buildings. The streets had no names and the little houses no numbers, and anyone looking for a particular place had to follow whatever proximate directions he was offered. This fellow lived behind the church, that one opposite the town gaol, a third past the District Court. It was just like living in a village. And the secrets of the people in the low houses, under the dark grey shingle roofs, behind the small, square windows and the wooden doors, seeped out through cracks and gaps, into the muddy lanes and even into the large inaccessible yard of the barracks. This man had been deceived by his wife, and that one had sold his daughter to a Russian captain; here was someone who sold bad eggs, and there someone else who lived from smuggling; this man had done time in prison, and that one only avoided it by the skin of his teeth; another lent money to the officers, and his neighbour creamed off a third of the profits. Carl Joseph's comrades, mainly from middle-class backgrounds and of German descent, had lived in this garrison town for many years and had grown accustomed to the place and its strange habits. Cut adrift from the ways of home, from their German mother tongue, which here had degenerated into a kind of militarese, exposed to the endless drabness of the swamps, they had fallen prey to games of chance, and the powerful schnapps that was produced locally, which went by the name of 'ninety-proof'. From the positions of harmless mediocrity they had advanced to, thanks to cadet school and an unvarying training, they slithered into this doomy stretch of land, which felt the chill breath of the great enemy empire of the Tsar. Russia was less than ten miles away. Officers from the Russian border regiment were not infrequent visitors, in their long sand-yellow or dove-grey greatcoats, with massy silver and gold epaulettes on their broad shoulders, and mirroring galoshes pulled over their shiny boots in all weathers. The respective garrisons even kept up reciprocal comradely relations. Sometimes it was the Austrians who crossed the border in little canvas-topped baggage carts, to watch the riding skills of the Cossacks and to drink Russian schnapps. Over in the Russian border town the schnapps barrels stood on the edge of the wooden pavements, guarded by troops with rifles and three-sided bayonets. With the arrival of evening, the barrels were trundled through the rickety streets, steered by the boots of the Cossacks, in the direction of the Russian mess, and a quiet splashing and gurgling gave at least an indication of their contents to the townsfolk. There the Tsar's officers gave the officers of His Apostolic Majesty a lesson in Russian hospitality. And none of the Tsar's officers, and none of the officers of His Apostolic Majesty knew then that over the glass bumpers from which they drank Death had already crossed his bony invisible hands.

In the wide plains that lay between the border forests of Russia and Austria, sotnias of Cossacks galloped about, uniformed winds in military order, mounted on the short, nippy horses of their native steppes, brandishing their lances over their lofty fur caps like long-stalked lightnings, pretty lightnings with pretty pennants. On the soft, springy, swampy soil, the drumming of hooves was almost inaudible. The earth responded with no more than a damp sigh to the impacts of the flying hooves. The virid green grass scarcely bent. It was as though the Cossacks were floating above the landscape. And when they galloped along the sandy yellow road, a great, shining, fine-grained column of golden dust went up, sparkling in the sun, spreading, and then sinking in myriad little clouds. The guests sat on rough wooden benches. The motion of the riders was almost too fast for the eyesight of the spectators. With their strong yellow horsey teeth, the Cossacks picked up their red and blue handkerchiefs off the ground while galloping at full tilt, their bodies seeming suddenly to slump under the bellies of their steeds while their legs in their shining boots continued to squeeze the flanks of the animals. Others threw their lances far up into the air, where they twirled and turned and obediently fell back into the raised fists of the rider; like living falcons they returned to their master's hands. Others again leaped, their bodies pressed flat against their horses' backs, the mouths of man and horse side by side in brotherly fashion, through astonishingly small hoops of iron, no bigger than a cooper would use for an average barrel. The horses put out all four feet. Their manes lifted like wings, their tails stood upright like rudders, their fine heads were like the trim bows of a speedy vessel. Others again would leap over twenty barrels that were laid on the ground one after the other. Here, the horses would whinny before they began their run-up. The rider came hurtling up from an infinite distance away, first he was nothing but a tiny grey spot, then, in racing speed, a line, a body, a rider, and then an enormous chimera-like hybrid of man and horse, a flying cyclops, who, having made the leap, would stand a hundred paces from the barrels, perfectly still, a monument of some inanimate substance. Others yet, while flying along like arrows (and themselves, the archers, looking like arrows), loosed off arrows at flying targets, great round white butts held by riders riding parallel to them: the archers galloped, shot and hit. Not a few tumbled off their mounts. Their comrades coming after them whistled over their bodies, not a hoof brushed them. There were riders who had a horse running along beside them, and leaped between saddles at a gallop, returned to their original saddle, suddenly back to the accompanying horse, and finally, with both hands clutching a saddle apiece, and their legs trailing between the horses' bodies, they pulled up with a jerk at a pre-arranged place, both horses stopping dead, so that they looked as if they'd been cast out of bronze. These Cossack riding displays were not the only ones in the border territory between the Monarchy and Russia. Also based in the town was a regiment of dragoons. The very closest of bonds between the officers of the Jäger battalion, the dragoons and the gentlemen of the Russian border regiments were created and maintained by one Count Chojnicki, one of the wealthiest Polish landowners in the region. Count Wojciech Chojnicki, related to the Ledochowskis and the Potockis, an in-law of the Sternbergs, friend of the Thuns, man of the world, forty years old but of no discernible age, Captain of Horse with the reserve, a fast-living and melancholy bachelor, was a lover of horses, of alcohol, of society, of frivolity and also of seriousness. He spent his winters in large cities and in the casinos of the Riviera. Like a migrating bird he would return to his ancestral homeland the moment the laburnum came into flower on the railway embankments. He brought with him a slightly scented whiff of the great world outside, and of romance and adventure. He was one of those people who can have no enemies, but no true friends either, only companions, accomplices and the indifferent. With his bright, clever, slightly protuberant eyes, his shiny, bald

pate, his little blond moustache, his narrow shoulders, his exces-
sively long legs, Chojnicki won the affection of everyone whose
path he crossed or happened to cross. He shuttled between his two
houses, reverently referred to as the 'old' and the 'new' castle by
the populace. The so-called 'old castle' was an extensive, somewhat dilapidated hunting pavilion, which, for inexplicable reasons
of his own, the Count was loath to have renovated. The 'new
castle' was a spacious, two-storey villa, whose upstairs was constantly occupied by curious and occasionally alarming strangers.
These were the 'poor relations' of the Count. Even with the most
acute scrutiny of his family history, it would have been beyond
him to establish the degree of these guests' relatedness to him. It
had, over time, become the thing to do, to visit the 'new castle' as
a distant cousin of Chojnicki's, and spend the summer there. Well
fed and rested, sometimes even fitted out with a new wardrobe by
the Count's local tailor, the visitors would return to wherever they
had sprung from the moment the maize was harvested and the first
migrations of starlings became audible at night. The master of the
house seemed to be perfectly and equally oblivious to the arrival,
the presence and the departure of his guests. He had merely
decreed, once and for all, that his Jewish estate manager check that
they were in fact relatives, keep an eye on their consumption, and
make sure that they left before the beginning of winter. The house
had two entrances. While the Count and such visitors as were not
related to him used the front entrance, his relatives had to make a
long detour through the orchard, and come and go through a little
gate in the garden wall. Apart from that, though, the unbidden
ones could please themselves.

Twice a week, on Mondays and Thursdays, Count Chojnicki
held little 'soirées', and once a month his so-called 'parties'. For the
'soirées' six of the rooms were lit and made ready for the guests,
for the parties twelve. On the occasion of the 'petites soirées', the
staff served without gloves and in an ochre livery; but on 'party'
nights, the servants wore white gloves and brick-red coats with
black velvet collars and silver buttons. The evenings always began

with vermouth and sherry. Then they moved on to Burgundy and Bordeaux. Then champagne was brought. And that was followed by cognac. They concluded, in apt tribute to the *genius loci*, with the local spirit, the ninety-proof.

The aristocratic officers of the exclusive dragoons regiment and the predominantly middle-class officers of the Jägers formed lifelong emotional ties at Count Chojnicki's. Dawning summer days peeping through the broad arched windows of the castle beheld a colourful confusion of infantry and cavalry uniforms. The sleepers snored under a golden sun. At a little before five in the morning, a gaggle of despairing orderlies would come running to the castle to waken their gentlemen, because it was at six that the regiments went out to drill. The master of the house, who was never exhausted by drinking, would have long since been in his little hunting pavilion. There he fiddled about with peculiar glass tubes, burners and bits of equipment. The rumour went around that the Count was engaged in trying to manufacture gold. And he really did give the appearance of being embarked on some hare-brained alchemical scheme or other. Even if he was unsuccessful at making gold, he did at least know how to win it at roulette. From time to time he would intimate that he had inherited a dependable 'system' from some mysterious, now long-dead gambler.

For many years he had been a delegate at the Reichstag, regularly returned by his district, seeing off all comers with a combination of money, violence and cunning; a favourite with the government and a despiser of the parliamentary body to which he belonged. He had never made a speech, never even heckled. Illusionless, mocking, fearless and self-assured, Chojnicki would tell all and sundry that the Emperor was a senile idiot, the government a bunch of morons, the Upper House an assembly of credulous and pathetic nitwits, the state authorities corrupt, villainous and lazy. Austrians of German stock crooned waltzes in their cups, Hungarians stank, Czechs were born to clean shoes, Ruthenians treacherously disguised Russians, Croats and Slovenes, whom he called 'stoats and ravens', were broom-makers and

chestnut-roasters, and Poles, of whom he himself was one, for-
nicators, barbers and fashion-photographers. Whenever he came
home from Vienna, or wherever else in the wide world he'd been
disporting himself, he would deliver a lugubrious lecture, which
would go roughly as follows: 'This empire's had it. As soon as the
Emperor says goodnight, we'll break up into a hundred pieces.
The Balkans will be more powerful than we will. All the peoples
will set up their own dirty little statelets, and even the Jews will
proclaim a King in Palestine. Vienna stinks of the sweat of democrats, I can't stand to be on the Ringstrasse any more. Ever since
they got their red flags, the workers have stopped working. The
mayor of Vienna is a churchgoing janitor. The clergy's desperate to
ingratiate itself with the people, you can hear the sermon in Czech
if you please. In the Burgtheater, they put on Jewish garbage, and
they ennoble one Hungarian toilet-manufacturer a week. I tell
you, gentlemen, unless we start shooting, it's all up. In our lifetime, I tell you.'

Those who listened to the Count laughed and refilled their
glasses. They didn't get it. There was shooting, from time to
time, especially round election time, to make sure that the likes
of Count Chojnicki were duly returned, and to prove that the
world couldn't end just like that. The Emperor was still alive.
There was an heir to the throne in place. The army drilled and
dazzled in all the proper colours. The peoples loved the dynasty
and worshipped it in their various national costumes. Chojnicki
was pulling their leg.

Lieutenant Trotta, however, more sensitive than his comrades,
sadder than them, and with the constant echo in his heart of the
dark, rushing wings of death, which he had now already twice
encountered: Lieutenant Trotta occasionally felt the prophetic
force of his gloomy speeches.

# 10

Once a week, when he had barrack duty, Lieutenant Trotta sent one of his unvarying reports to the District Commissioner. There was no electric light in the barracks. The guardrooms were lit by the same old official regulation candles as in the days of the hero of Solferino. Now they were called 'Apollo candles', and they were made of soft, snow-white stearin, with tightly woven wicks and a steady flame. The Lieutenant's letters gave nothing away of his changed circumstances, or of the unusual conditions that obtained near the border. The District Commissioner, for his part, was careful not to ask any questions. His replies, which he mailed off to his son every fourth Sunday were just as unchanging as the letters of the Lieutenant.

Every morning, old Jacques would carry the post into the room where, for many years now, the District Commissioner had been in the habit of taking his breakfast. It was a somewhat remote room, not used during the day. The window, which faced east, admitted all mornings, such as they were, bright, dull, warm, chilly or wet; winter and summer, it was kept open during breakfast. In the winter, the District Commissioner kept his legs warmly wrapped in a rug, and the table was moved close to a wide stove, with a warm fire crackling away, which old Jacques had lit half an hour earlier. On 15 April every year, Jacques stopped lighting the stove. On 15 April every year, regardless of the weather, the District Commissioner took up his summer constitutionals. At six o'clock, the barber's apprentice, himself unshaven and still half asleep, arrived in Trotta's bedroom. By six fifteen the District Commissioner's chin lay smooth and powdered between the faintly silvered wings of his whiskers. His bald skull had been massaged and faintly reddened with a few drops of cologne, and all the superfluous little hairs growing either from the nostrils or from his ears, and a few that occasionally trained themselves to grow up his neck, past the high collar, had been removed without trace. Then the District Commissioner reached for his light cane and his grey top hat and made for the town park. He wore a white waistcoat with grey buttons that went all the way up, and a dove-grey morning coat. His tight trousers, uncreased, were pulled down over his narrow, pointed riding boots of softest kid's leather, without toecaps or stitching, by means of dark grey elastic loops. At this time the streets were still deserted. The municipal sprinkling wagon, drawn by a couple of chestnut dray horses, came clattering along the bumpy cobbles. The driver on his high box dropped his whip the moment he saw the District Commissioner, looped the traces round the brake handle, and doffed his cap so far that it touched his knees. He was the only man in the little town, yes, in the whole area, whom Herr Trotta greeted with a cheery, even exuberant wave. At the entrance to the town park, the communal policeman saluted him. To him, Herr Trotta gave a hearty '*Grüss Gott!*' without, however, moving his hand. Thereupon he went along to the blonde proprietress of the soda booth, where he lifted his grey top hat a little, drank a cup of soda water to help the digestion, took a coin out of his waistcoat pocket, without removing his grey gloves, and went on his way. Bakers, chimneysweeps, greengrocers and butchers passed him. Everyone greeted him. The District Commissioner replied by touching his index finger softly to his hat brim. It was only to the apothecary Kronauer, another devotee of early walks and a borough councillor to boot, that Herr von Trotta took off his hat. Sometimes he would say: 'Good morning, apothecary!' stop, and enquire: 'How is everything?' 'Excellent!' the apothecary replied. 'Very good!' observed the District Commissioner, doffed his hat once more, and went on his way.

He was never back before eight o'clock. Sometimes he encountered the postman in the passage or on the stairs. Then he would go and wait in his office for a little while. For he loved to find the morning post already there beside the tray with breakfast. He quite categorically refused to see anyone, never mind speak to them, during breakfast. It was just about in order for old Jacques to pop in on a winter morning, to see how the fire was doing, or in summer, to shut the window, if it happened to be raining too hard. Fräulein Hirschwitz, though, was beyond the pale. Any time before one o'clock the sight of her was repugnant to the District Commissioner.

One day, it was the end of May, Herr von Trotta returned home from his walk at five past eight. The postman should have been and gone long ago. Herr von Trotta sat down at the table in his breakfast room. Today, as ever, there was his 'three minute' egg in its silver eggcup. The honey was liquid gold, the fresh rolls smelled of fire and yeast as they did on every other day; the butter, nestled on an enormous dark green leaf, was a gleamy yellow, and the coffee steamed in its gold-rimmed china. It was all there. Or at least it was Herr von Trotta's initial impression that it was all there. But straight away, he got up, put down his napkin, and looked over the table once more. The post was not in its usual place. So far as the District Commissioner could remember, not a single day had ever gone by without at least one item of official correspondence. Herr von Trotta's first reaction was to walk over to the open window, as though to confirm that the world was still there outside. Yes, the old chestnuts in the park still wore their dense green crowns. Within them, the birds were making their invisible racket as they did every morning. And the milk cart that often stopped outside the District Commissioner's residence at this time, it was standing there quite serenely, as if today were a day like any other. So outside nothing has changed, the District Commissioner concluded. Was it possible that there was no post? Was it possible that Jacques had forgotten it? Herr von Trotta shook the table bell. Its silver chime scurried through the silent house. Nobody answered. He gave it another shake. At last there was a knock. He was astonished, appalled, mortified, when he saw his housekeeper, Fräulein Hirschwitz, enter.

She was wearing a kind of morning armour that he had never seen her in before. A large apron of dark blue oilcloth wrapped her from top to toe and a white bonnet sat squarely on her head, showing her large ears, with their soft, broad, fleshy lobes. She seemed extremely repellent to Herr von Trotta – he couldn't abide the smell of oilcloth.

'Poor show!' he said, ignoring her greeting. 'Where's Jacques?'

'Jacques is discommoded today.'

'Discommoded?' repeated the District Commissioner, who didn't immediately understand. 'You mean he's sick?' he went on to ask.

'He's running a temperature!' said Fräulein Hirschwitz.

'Thank you,' said Herr von Trotta, and waved her away. He took his seat at the table. He drank the coffee, nothing more. He left the egg, the honey, the butter and the rolls on the tray. All he knew was that Jacques had been taken ill, and wasn't able to take up the post. But why had Jacques been taken ill? He had always been as healthy as – as the post, for instance. If that had suddenly stopped delivering letters, that would have been no more surprising. The District Commissioner himself was never ill. If you were ill, it meant you were going to die. Illness was nothing but an attempt on the part of nature to get people used to the idea of dying. Epidemic diseases – the cholera that had been a scourge in Herr von Trotta's youth – could be defeated by some individuals here and there. But other illnesses that snuck up on you more individually, they had your number, whatever names they went by. Doctors – the District Commissioner called them 'quacks' – claimed they could cure you; but that was only to keep themselves in a job. There might be exceptions, people who survived an illness, but so far as Herr von Trotta could remember, there were no such in his closer or his wider acquaintance.

He gave the bell another shake. 'I want my post,' he said to Fräulein Hirschwitz, 'but please get someone else to take it up to me! By the way, what's wrong with Jacques?'

'He has a temperature!' said Fräulein Hirschwitz. 'He will have caught a chill!'

'You mean he's got a cold? In May?!'

'He's not as young as he was!'

'Send for Dr Sribny!'

Sribny was the local doctor. He held a surgery in the District Commissioner's offices between nine and twelve. He would be there soon. In the opinion of the District Commissioner, he was an 'honest fellow'.

The beadle brought the post. The District Commissioner merely looked at the envelopes, handed them back and instructed the man to leave them in the office. He stood by the window, feeling quite astonished at the degree of unawareness that the world at large displayed of the changes in his household. Today he had neither breakfasted nor read his post. Jacques was laid low by some mysterious ailment. And life outside was going on as normal.

Very slowly, taken up with several unclear lines of thought at once, Herr von Trotta made his way to his office, twenty minutes later than usual he sat down at his desk. His assistant came in with his report. There had been another meeting of Czech workers yesterday. A Sokol* celebration had been announced, delegates from 'Slavic states' – that meant Russia and Serbia, but they were never referred to by name in official communications – were expected as early as tomorrow. And the German-speaking social democrats were acting up as well. In the yarn factory, a worker

---

* Sokol: A gymnastic-cum-nationalist-separatist society initially founded in Prague in 1862 but rapidly spreading throughout the empire.

had been beaten up by his fellows, apparently and according to the report of spies, for refusing to join the Reds. All this distressed the District Commissioner, pained him, offended him, wounded him. Everything that was undertaken by dissident sections of the populace to weaken the state, to offend directly or indirectly the Emperor, to make the law yet feebler than it already was, to disturb the peace, to offend against decency, to mock dignity, to set up Czech schools, to have opposition delegates elected: all these were actions undertaken against himself, the District Commissioner, in person. To begin with, he had merely despised the nations who wanted self-determination and the people who were clamouring for 'more rights'. By and by, however, he had begun to hate them, the carpenters, the arsonists, the soap box orators. He ordered his deputy to break up on the spot any assembly that showed any signs of passing any 'resolutions'. Of all the words that had lately come into currency this was the one he hated most; perhaps because it was only one little letter away from the most deleterious of all words, which was 'revolution'. That he wouldn't hear of. It did not exist anywhere in his personal or official vocabulary; and if he ever happened in a report submitted to him by some inferior, say, to come across the term 'revolutionary agitator' for one of those active social democrats, then he would cross out the words in red and replace them with 'suspicious individual'. Perhaps there were revolutionaries to be found somewhere in the Monarchy: in Herr von Trotta's district there were none.

'Will you send Sergeant Slama along to me after lunch!' Herr von Trotta said to his deputy. 'I want the gendarmerie reinforced for these Sokols or whatever they are. Write a report to the District Council, I want to see it tomorrow. It's possible we'll have to liaise with the military authorities. In any case, the gendarmerie are to be placed on heightened alert from tomorrow. And I want to see an excerpt of the relevant parts of the latest ministerial decrees concerning the state of alert.'

'Very well, sir!'

'All right. Has Dr Sribny been in yet?'

'He was called to see Jacques right away.'

'Tell him I want to see him.'

The District Commissioner read no more files that day. Back in the tranquil years when he had started to settle into the district, there hadn't been any separatists, any social democrats, and relatively few 'suspicious individuals'. And with the slow passage of the years, the proliferation of such, their spreading influence and the dangers associated with them had barely been perceptible. The District Commissioner had the sense that it was only Jacques's illness that had alerted him to the hideous changes that were afoot – as though the Death that might be squatting at the old retainer's bedside were threatening others as well. If Jacques dies, the District Commissioner thought, then in a sense the hero of Solferino will die all over again, and perhaps – and here Herr von Trotta's heart stopped for an instant – the man whose life the hero of Solferino had saved. Oh, it wasn't just Jacques who had fallen ill today! The letters lay unopened on the desk of the District Commissioner: who could say what might be contained in them! Under the eyes of the authorities and the gendarmerie those Sokols were multiplying in the interior of the kingdom. Those Sokols, which the District Commissioner thought of as 'Sokolites', as though to transform them from a sizeable grouping among the Slav peoples into a sort of insignificant splinter, claimed to be gymnasts, interested only in strengthening their muscles. In reality, they were spies or rebels in the Tsar's employ. Only yesterday he had read in the paper that the German students in Prague were in the habit of singing the 'Watch on the Rhine', that hymn of the Prussians, those ancestral enemies of Austria who were now supposedly allies of Austria. On whom could you rely? The District Commissioner shuddered. And, for the first time since he'd begun working in this office, he walked up to the window, on an unequivocally warm spring day, and shut it. At that moment, the district general practitioner walked in, and Herr von Trotta asked him how old Jacques was doing. Dr Sribny said: 'If it develops into pneumonia, he won't make it. He's very old.

He's got a temperature of forty already. He's asked to see a priest.' The District Commissioner leaned down over the table. He was afraid Dr Sribny might detect some change in his expression, and he could feel something in his expression changing. He pulled open the desk drawer, got out his cigars, and offered one to the doctor. He motioned to the armchair. They both smoked. 'So you don't hold out much hope?' Herr von Trotta asked finally. 'Very little, truth to tell!' replied the doctor. 'At his age –' He didn't finish the sentence, and looked up at the District Commissioner, as though to see whether he was significantly younger than the servant. 'But he's never been ill!' said the District Commissioner, and it was as though that were an extenuating circumstance, and the doctor were an appeal court who would decide about his life. 'I know, I know,' said the doctor. 'That happens. How old is he?' The District Commissioner thought a while and said: 'I should say seventy-eight to eighty, something like that.' 'Yes,' said Dr Sribny, 'that's what I thought. Or rather: that's what I started to think today. But as long as someone's running around, you can't help thinking he'll go on for ever!'

Thereupon the district doctor got up to go on with his work. Herr von Trotta wrote: 'Am in Jacques's apartment!' on a piece of paper, put a paperweight over it, and went out in the courtyard.

He had never been inside Jacques's apartment. It was a little tiny house built against the back wall of the courtyard, with a little tiny roof and a chimney that was much too big for it. It had three walls of yellowish brick, and a brown door in the middle. You walked into the kitchen, and then through a glass door into the living room. Jacques's pet canary was standing on the roof of his wire cage, beside the window with the slightly too short white curtains, that made it seem as though the window had grown. The planed kitchen table was pushed back against the wall. Over it hung a kerosene lamp with a round mirror and a light-intensifier. A framed picture of the Virgin was on the table, propped against the wall, the way people sometimes have portraits of their relatives. Jacques was in bed, with his head against the wall with the window, under a white mass of pillows and sheets. He thought it was the priest who had come, and gave a deep sigh of relief, as though he were now on his way to Grace. 'Oh, Baron!' he said a moment later. The District Commissioner went up to the old man. His own grandfather, the gendarmerie sergeant, had lain in state in a similar room once, in the pensioners' quarters in Laxenburg. The District Commissioner could still see the yellow gleam of the tall white candles in the dim, shrouded room, and the outsize boot-soles of the ceremonially clad corpse seemed to loom in his face. Was it Jacques's turn now? The old man propped himself up on his elbows. He was wearing a knitted nightcap of dark blue wool, his silver hair glimmered through the stitches. His clean-shaven face, bony and fever-flushed, was like tinted ivory. The District Commissioner sat down on a chair beside the bed, and said: 'Well, the doctor's just said it's not too serious! Nothing more than a head cold!' 'Yes, Baron!' replied Jacques, making a feeble effort to bring his heels together under the bedclothes. He sat up in bed. 'Pardon me!' he added. 'I think tomorrow it'll be all over!' 'Certainly, in a few days at the most!' 'I'm waiting for the priest, Baron!' 'Yes, yes,' said Herr von Trotta, 'I'm sure he's coming. There's plenty of time till then!' 'But he's on his way!' replied Jacques, his voice sounding as though he could see him with his own eyes. 'He's on his way,' he went on, and suddenly he seemed no longer to be aware that the District Commissioner was sitting beside him. 'When the late lamented Baron died,' he went on, 'we none of us suspected any-thing. In the morning, or was it the day before still, he went into the courtyard and said: "Jacques, where are the boots?" Yes, that was the day before. Then the winter began, and a very cold one it was too. I think I'll manage to hang on until winter. It's not all that long to go now, I just need to be patient. It's July now, so July, June, April, May, August, November, and by Christmas I think I can company dismiss, by the right, quick march!' He stopped, and with his large, shining blue eyes, he looked straight through the District Commissioner as if through a sheet of glass.

Gently, Herr von Trotta tried to push the old fellow back into the pillows, but Jacques stiffened his body and wouldn't yield. His head was trembling, and his dark blue nightcap was trembling uncontrollably as well. Tiny beads of sweat glistened on his lofty, bony, yellow brow. The District Commissioner wiped them off with his handkerchief from time to time, but new ones kept appearing. He took old Jacques's hand, looked at the dry, flaky, reddish skin on the back of the hand, and the strong thumb that stood out a long way. Then he carefully laid the hand back on the covers, went back to his office, instructed the beadle to have the priest and a Sister of Mercy sent for, and told Fräulein Hirschwitz to sit with Jacques until they arrived; then he took receipt of his hat, stick and gloves, and strode off into the park, to the astonishment of all who beheld him at this unusual hour.

Before long, though, he left the deep shade of the chestnuts and returned home. As he approached the door, he heard the tinkling of the priest with the Last Sacrament. He doffed his hat and stood, with head bowed, in front of his house. Some of the passers-by stopped similarly. Then the priest left the house. A few people waited for the District Commissioner to disappear into the entry, watched him curiously, and heard from the beadle that Jacques was dying. The whole town knew Jacques. And they gave Jacques, who was leaving them, a few moments of respectful silence.

The District Commissioner strode through the courtyard, and straight into the room of the dying man. He carefully looked out a place in the dark kitchen for his hat, stick and gloves, and finally stowed them all on the kitchen shelves, in among the pots and dishes. He shooed away Fräulein Hirschwitz and sat down on the bedside. The sun was now so high in the sky that it brightened the whole of the wide courtyard, and shone through the window into Jacques's room. The short white curtain hung in front of the window like a sunny, cheerful little apron. The canary was twittering away brightly and without cease; the bare, smooth floorboards had a yellowish shine in the sun; a wide silver sunbeam fell across the foot of the bed, the bottom of the white coverlet was now of an intense, unearthly whiteness, and the sunbeam started climbing up the wall against which the bed was stood. From time to time a gentle breeze stirred the few old trees planted along the courtyard wall, that were probably as old as Jacques if not older, and had sheltered him in their shadow every day of his life. The breeze blew, the crowns of the trees rustled, and Jacques seemed to feel it. Because he stood up and said: 'Excuse me, Baron, the window please!' The District Commissioner lifted the window latch, and straight away the blithe maying sounds of the yard came into the little room. You could hear the soughing of the trees, the soft puff of air, the rowdy buzz of the glittering blue-green flies and the trilling of the larks up in their blue endlessness. The canary flew out, but only really to demonstrate that he was still capable of flight. For he returned a moment later, perched on the windowsill, and started singing twice as volubly. It was a cheerful world, inside and out. And Jacques leaned out of bed and listened without moving; the little beads of sweat shone on his hard forehead, and his thin lips slowly parted. At first he merely smiled silently. Then he pinched his eyes shut, his lean, flushed cheeks creased round his cheekbones; now he looked like an old rascal, and a thin giggle came from him. He was laughing. He laughed and laughed; the pillows shook faintly, even the bed frame creaked a little. The District Commissioner was chortling too. Yes, Death was coming for old Jacques like a pretty girl in spring, and Jacques opened his old mouth, and showed him the few yellowed teeth he had. He lifted his hand, pointed at the window, and, still giggling, shook his head. 'A beautiful day!' observed the District Commissioner. 'There he is, there he is!' said Jacques. 'On a white horse, dressed all in white, but why's he riding so slowly? See, see how slowly he's riding! *Grüss Gott! Grüss Gott!* Won't you come closer? Come on! Come on! A beautiful day, wouldn't you agree?' He pulled his hand back, turned to the District Commissioner and said: 'My, how slowly he's riding! That's because he's come from yonder! He's been dead a long time, and he's no longer accustomed to riding on stones like here! Yes, that was once! D'you remember what he looked like? I want to see the painting. Do you suppose he's greatly altered? Will you bring me the picture, please, Baron, bring it to me here! Please let me have a look at it, Baron!'

The District Commissioner understood immediately that he was talking about the portrait of the hero of Solferino. He obediently left the room. He even took the stairs two at a time, strode into the drawing room, climbed on to a chair, and lifted the picture of the hero of Solferino off its hook. It was a little dusty; he blew on it, and wiped it with the handkerchief he had just used to dry the dying man's brow. All the while, the District Commissioner was still chortling away to himself. He was cheerful. It was a long time since he'd last felt so cheerful. He walked quickly, the big painting under his arm, across the courtyard. He went up to Jacques's bed. Jacques examined the picture for a long time, pointed his finger at the face, wobbled it around, and finally said: 'Put it in the sun!' The District Commissioner obeyed. He held the painting in the strip of sunlight at the foot of the bed, Jacques sat up and said: 'Yes, that's his spit and image all right!' and he lay back down in the pillows.

The District Commissioner put the picture on the table, next to the Virgin, and returned to the bed. 'I'm heading up there soon myself!' said Jacques smiling, and pointing up at the ceiling. 'You've plenty of time till then!' replied the District Commissioner. 'No, no!' said Jacques, laughing happily. 'I've had my time. Now I'm heading up. Go and see how old I am. I've forgotten.' 'Where shall I look it up?' 'Down there!' said Jacques, pointing at the bed frame. There was a drawer there. The District Commissioner pulled it out. He saw a tidy parcel wrapped in brown paper, and next to it a round tin with a bleached picture of a shepherdess in a white wig, which he remembered was one of those sweet tins from his boyhood that some of his comrades found under their Christmas trees. 'There's the little book!' said Jacques. It was his army service book. The District Commissioner put on his pince-nez and read: 'Franz Xaver Joseph Kromichl.' 'Is that your book?' Herr von Trotta asked. 'Of course it is!' said Jacques. 'But it says your name's Franz Xaver Joseph?' 'I expect that's right!' 'So why do you go by Jacques then?' 'Those were his orders!' 'I see,' said Herr von Trotta, and read the year of his birth. 'That makes you eighty-two in August!' 'What are we today?' '19 May!' 'So how long is it till August?' 'Three months!' 'Well,' said Jacques, very calmly, lying back down in the pillows. 'I won't live to see that then!'

'Open the tin!' said Jacques, and the District Commissioner opened it. 'There's Saint Antony and Saint George,' Jacques went on. 'You can keep them. And then there's a bit of fever-root. You give that to your son, to Carl Joseph. Give him my best! He can use it, because it's swampy over where he is. And now shut the window. I want to sleep!'

It was now noon. The bed was swimming in bright sunshine. The big flies clung to the windows without moving, and the canary had stopped singing, and was nibbling at his sugar. The town hall clock struck twelve times, and its golden echo died away in the courtyard. Jacques was breathing quietly. The District Commissioner walked over to the dining room.

'I don't want lunch!' he said to Fräulein Hirschwitz. He looked around the dining room. This place, here, was where Jacques had always stood with the tray, he had walked up to the table like this, this was how he carried the tray. Herr von Trotta couldn't eat anything today. He went down into the courtyard, and sat down on a bench against the wall, under the brown beams of the overhanging roof, to wait for the Sister of Mercy to come. 'He's asleep now!' he said to her as she arrived. A soft breeze blew by from time to time. The shadow of the eaves slowly grew longer and broader. Flies buzzed round the District Commissioner's whiskers. From time to time, he swatted at them with his hand, and his cuff rattled. For the first time ever since he'd been in the Emperor's service, he did nothing at all on a regulation weekday. He had never felt the need to have a holiday. This was the first day off that he had ever had. Old Jacques was on his mind the whole time, but in spite of that he felt cheerful. Old Jacques was dying, but it was as though he were celebrating some great event, and that gave the District

Commissioner the occasion for this holiday. All at once he heard the Sister of Mercy step outside. She said that Jacques, with his temperature gone, and apparently in full command of his senses, had got out of bed, and was just getting dressed. And a moment later, the District Commissioner did indeed catch sight of the old fellow in the window. He had laid out brush, soap and razor on the windowsill, as he did every morning when he was well, had looped the hand mirror on the window latch, and was just in the process of shaving himself. Jacques opened the window, and with his normal, healthy voice, he called out: 'I'm feeling fine, Baron, I'm completely restored, please forgive me, I hope you haven't been inconvenienced at all!'

'Well, then everything's all right! I'm pleased, extremely pleased. Now you'll begin a new life as Franz Xaver Joseph!' 'I'd sooner stick with Jacques!'

Delighted, but also a little perplexed at this unexpected turn of things, Herr von Trotta went back to his bench, asked the Sister of Mercy to remain a while just in case, and asked her if she'd ever known such a dramatic improvement in the case of anyone of comparable age. The sister, looking down at her rosary, and pulling the answer with her fingers from the beads, replied that cure and illness, be they slow or rapid, lie entirely in God's hands; and His Will had many times already brought back the dying from the brink. A more scientific answer would have pleased the District Commissioner better. And he decided to ask the doctor for his opinion tomorrow. He went to his office for the moment, feeling a great load had been taken off his shoulders but also profoundly and inexplicably disquieted. He wasn't able to work. To Sergeant Slama, who had been waiting for him a long time, he gave instructions concerning the Sokol celebrations, but without sounding particularly stern or emphatic. All the perils facing the District of W. and the Monarchy suddenly seemed much less acute to Herr von Trotta than they had that morning. He dismissed the sergeant, only to recall him a moment later: 'Listen, Slama, have you ever heard the like, only this morning old Jacques looks as though he's on his deathbed, and now it seems he's as fit as a fiddle again!'

No, Sergeant Slama had never heard of such a thing. And in response to the question from the District Commissioner whether he would accompany him to see the old man, Slama replied certainly. And they went down to the courtyard together.

They came upon Jacques seated on his stool, a row of pairs of boots in front of him in military order, brush in hand, and spitting away into the wooden box of blacking. He tried to get up when the District Commissioner stood in front of him, but couldn't do it in time, and felt Herr von Trotta's hands pressing down upon his shoulders. He cheerily saluted the Sergeant with the shoe brush. The District Commissioner sat down on the bench, the Sergeant leaned his rifle against the wall, and sat down as well, at a respectful distance; Jacques remained on his stool, polishing the boots, albeit more slowly and less energetically than usual. The Sister of Mercy was inside, praying.

'It's just occurred to me,' said Jacques, 'that I said *du* to the Baron today! I just remembered that!'

'Never mind that, Jacques!' said Herr von Trotta. 'You were feverish!'

'Yes, I think it was the corpse speaking in me. And, Sergeant, you ought to have me locked up for personation. My name's actually Franz Xaver Joseph! But I'd still like it if it said Jacques on my tombstone. My savings book is in there with my army service book, there's a bit in it to pay for the funeral and a mass, and I'd like to be Jacques again, if it's all one to you!'

'I'm sure that won't be a problem!' said the District Commissioner. 'There's plenty of time!'

The Sergeant laughed loudly, and wiped his brow.

Jacques had cleaned all the boots. He was shivering a little; he went inside, and came out in his winter fur that he wore in summer too if it was raining, and sat down on his stool again. The canary followed him, fluttering above his silvered head, looked for somewhere to alight, and then settled on the clothes-rack that had a couple of carpets hanging from it, and began to warble. Its song awoke hundreds of sparrows in the crowns of the two or three trees in the courtyard, and for a few minutes the air was filled with a bedlam of jolly twittering and whistling. Jacques lifted his head, and listened, with a measure of pride, to the voice of his champion as it saw off the competition. The District Commissioner smiled. The Sergeant laughed, with his handkerchief in front of his mouth, and Jacques giggled. Even the Sister interrupted her praying, and smiled through the window. The golden rays of the afternoon sun were already on the wooden eaves, and playing in the crowns of the green trees. Midges, soft round clouds of them, set up their drowsy evening dance, and from time to time a heavy May-bug droned past the little group, headed straight for the trees and disaster, in all probability the open beak of one of the sparrows. The wind had got up a little. The birds fell silent. The sky in front of them had turned a deep blue, and the fluffy white clouds were rosy.

'It's your bedtime!' said Herr von Trotta to Jacques.

'I just need to take the picture back upstairs!' murmured the old man, and he went and fetched the portrait of the hero of Solferino and disappeared up the dark staircase. The Sergeant watched him go, and said: 'Extraordinary!'

'Yes, quite extraordinary!' agreed Herr von Trotta.

Jacques returned, and approached the bench. Without a word, and rather surprisingly he sat down between the District Commissioner and the Sergeant, opened his mouth, took a deep breath, and before they had even turned to him, his old neck had slumped against the backrest, his hands dropped on to the bench, his fur opened, his legs stuck out stiffly, and the curled toes of his slippers were pointing up in the air. A swift gust blew through the courtyard. The reddish clouds sailed on into the sunset. The sun itself had disappeared behind the wall. The District Commissioner held the silver head of his servant with his left hand, and with his right felt for the heart. The Sergeant was up on his feet in alarm, his black cap lying on the ground. The Sister of Mercy came running out. She took the old man's hand, held it between her fingers for a while, then laid it gently on the fur, and crossed herself. She looked silently at the Sergeant. He understood, and clasped Jacques under the arms. She took him by the legs. They carried him into the little room, laid him on his bed, folded his hands together and entwined a rosary around them, and set the picture of the Virgin at his head. They knelt down beside his bed, and the District Commissioner prayed. It was a long time since he had last prayed. A prayer came to him from the buried depths of his childhood, a prayer for the salvation of dead relatives, and he spoke it in a whisper. Then he stood up, looked down at his trousers, brushed the dirt off his knees, and strode out, followed by the Sergeant.

'That's how I'd like to die when the time comes, my dear Slama!' he said, instead of the usual '*Grüss Gott!*' and he went up to the drawing room. He wrote the instructions for the lying-in and the burial of his servant on a large sheet of official foolscap, carefully, like a master of ceremonies, item by item, with headings and sub-headings. He set off to the cemetery the next morning to select a grave, bought a gravestone, and dictated the words: 'Here dwells in God Franz Xaver Joseph Kromichl, familiarly Jacques, an old servant and a faithful friend,' and he ordered a first-class funeral, with four black stallions and eight pallbearers. Three days later he followed the coffin on foot, as the only mourner, followed at a fitting distance by Sergeant Slama and a few others who went along because they had known Jacques, and especially because they saw Herr von Trotta there on foot. And so it happened that a respectable number of people accompanied the old Franz Xaver Joseph Kromichl, known to everyone familiarly as Jacques, to his final resting place.

From then on, the District Commissioner felt his house was different, empty, no longer home. He no longer saw the post next to his breakfast tray, and he was reluctant to give the beadle any more instructions. He no longer shook any of his little silver bells, and when he sometimes distractedly reached out his hand for one of them, he would merely stroke it. In the afternoon sometimes, he would listen and think he heard old Jacques's ghostly footfall on the stairs. Sometimes he would go into the little room where Jacques had lived, to pass the canary a bit of sugar between the bars of its cage.

One day – it was shortly before the Sokol celebrations, and his presence in the office was not unimportant – he made a surprising decision.

What it was, we will tell you in the next chapter.

# 11

The District Commissioner decided to pay a visit to his son in the faraway border garrison. For a man like Herr von Trotta, this was not a straightforward undertaking. He had some unusual ideas about the eastern marches of the Monarchy. Two of his schoolfriends had been transferred, following the revelation of embarrassing shortcomings in office, to that remote Crownland, where, no doubt, the wild Siberian winds could be heard howling. There bears and wolves and even worse dangers like lice and bed-bugs threatened the civilized Austrian. The Ruthenian peasants made sacrifices to heathen gods, and the Jews waged an incessant campaign of rapine against anything that was not nailed down. Herr von Trotta packed his old service revolver. Not that he was alarmed at the prospect of such adventures, you understand, rather he experienced the blissful feelings he had had as a boy long ago, when he and his old friend Moser had gone out hunting in the dark forests of his father's estate or to the cemetery at midnight. He said an unemotional farewell to Fräulein Hirschwitz, with the vague and daring hope that he might never see her again. He took himself to the station. The clerk behind the counter said: 'Oh, a long journey at last! I hope you enjoy your trip!' The station-master bustled out on to the platform. 'Are you going on official business?' he enquired. And the District Commissioner, in the sort of jovial mood in which he didn't mind being mysterious, replied: 'If you like, Stationmaster! In a manner of speaking, you could say it was "official"!' 'Are you going to stay longer?' 'If I can manage it!' The District Commissioner stood by the window, and waved. He took a cheerful leave of his district. He didn't even think about going back. He read through the list of stops again in the gazetteer. 'Change trains in Oderberg!' he reminded himself. He compared the actual and notional arrival and departure times, and checked his pocket watch against the station clocks he passed. Unexpectedly, every irregularity pleased, even refreshed him. In Oderberg he let the first train leave without him. Feeling a lively curiosity, looking about him in all directions, he sauntered along the platforms, through the various waiting rooms, and even a little way into the town. Once back at the station, he pretended he had been delayed, and complained to the porter: 'My train left without me!' He was disappointed that the porter was not more surprised. He now had to change trains again, in Cracow. So much the better. If it hadn't been for the fact that he'd told Carl Joseph when to expect him, and if that 'dead and alive place' had boasted two trains a day instead of one, he would gladly have broken his journey again, to see a little more of the world. Still, a good part of it presented itself to him through the window. Spring accompanied him all the way. He arrived in the afternoon. Calm and alert he climbed down from the steps with that 'suppleness of stride' that the newspapers used to single out for mention in the old Emperor, and which had gradually been copied by a number of elderly civil servants. Because there was in the Monarchy at that time a very distinct, now completely forgotten way of stepping down from railway trains and carriages, of entering restaurants, platforms and private houses, of approaching friends and relatives; a type of stride that was perhaps also determined by the tight trousers of the elderly gentlemen, and by the elasticated trouser loops that many of them liked to wear over their boots. It was with this particular walk, then, that Herr von Trotta left his railway carriage. He embraced his son, who was standing in front of the carriage door. Herr von Trotta was the only traveller to emerge from the first- or second-class carriages on that day. A few holidaymakers and railwaymen and Jews in their long, black flapping kaftans emerged from the third-class carriage. Everyone looked at the father and son. The District Commissioner hurried into the waiting room. There he kissed Carl Joseph on the forehead. At the bar, he called for two cognacs. On the wall behind the rows of bottles, hung the mirror. As they drank, father and son inspected their faces. 'Is it the mirror,' asked Herr von Trotta, 'or do you really look as bad as that?' And have you really gone so grey? Carl Joseph felt like asking. Because he saw a lot of silver glimmering in his father's dark whiskers and on his temples. 'Let's have a look at you!' the District Commissioner went on. 'No, that's not the mirror's fault! Being stationed here must be doing that to you! Is it hard?' The District Commissioner was forced to see that his son didn't look the way a young lieutenant ought to look. Maybe he's ill, thought Herr von Trotta. The only other illnesses, apart from those that killed you, were those awful diseases that were apparently quite common among officers. 'Are you sure you're allowed to drink cognac?' he asked, attempting in a roundabout fashion to establish the truth. 'Yes of course, Papa,' said the Lieutenant. He could still hear the voice that had tested him all those years ago, on those quiet Sunday mornings, the nasal tones of officialdom, the strict, always slightly disbelieving and questing voice that would nail any lie at source. 'Are you happy in the infantry?' 'Very happy, Papa!' 'What about your horse?' 'I took it with me, Papa!' 'Do you ride often?' 'Not that much, Papa!' 'Don't you enjoy it then?' 'No, Papa, I never did!' 'Stop the "Papa" stuff,' said Herr von Trotta suddenly. 'You're old enough! And I'm on holiday!'

They rode into town. 'Well, I certainly don't see any bright lights!' said the District Commissioner. 'What do you do for fun here?'

'A lot!' said Carl Joseph. 'We go to Count Chojnicki's. Everyone does. You'll meet him. I like him a lot.'

'Would he be your first proper friend then?'

'There was Regimental Doctor Max Demant. He was,' replied Carl Joseph. 'Here's your room, Papa!' said the Lieutenant. 'The whole gang of us live here, and it's sometimes a bit noisy at night. But there's no other hotel. And I told them to keep it down while you're here!'

'There's no need, really no need!' said the District Commissioner.

He pulled a round tin out of his suitcase, opened it and showed it to Carl Joseph. 'This is some kind of root – said to be good against swamp fever. It's from Jacques!'

'How's he getting on?'

'Oh, he's already gone on!' The District Commissioner pointed to the ceiling. 'Gone on!' repeated the Lieutenant. The District Commissioner had the impression it was an old man speaking. His son probably had a lot of secrets. The father didn't know them. You said: father and son, but there were many years between them, great chains of hills! You didn't know more about Carl Joseph than you did about any other lieutenant. He'd joined the cavalry, and later transferred to the infantry. He wore the green cuffs of the Jägers instead of the red ones of the dragoons. Well, and? That was about the size of it! And now you were getting on. You didn't quite belong entirely to your work, or to your duties! You also belonged to Jacques and to Carl Joseph. You carried that rock-hard wizened bit of root from one to the other.

Still leaning over his suitcase, the District Commissioner opened his mouth. He talked into the suitcase, as into an open grave. But he didn't say, as he had wanted to say: I love you, my boy! but: 'He had a very easy death. It was a real May evening, and all the birds were singing. D'you remember his canary? He was the noisiest of the whole bunch of them. Jacques polished all the boots in the house. And then he died, in the yard, on the bench. Slama was there as well. He had a temperature only that morning. He sends you his best.'

Then the District Commissioner looked up from his suitcase,

and looked his son in the eye. 'I wouldn't mind a death like that myself one day!'

The Lieutenant went into his room, and placed the bit of fever-root in the top drawer of his chest of drawers, next to Katharina's letters and Max Demant's sabre. He took out the doctor's watch. To his eye, the frail second hand was going round the tiny circle faster than any he had ever seen, and its ticking was noisier than he had ever heard a watch tick. The hands were going nowhere, their ticking was meaningless. Before long, I'll be able to hear the ticking of Papa's fob watch, when he leaves it to me. My room will have the portrait of the hero of Solferino hanging on the wall, and Max Demant's sabre, and some memento of Papa's. And it will all be buried with me. I'm the last of the Trottas! He was sufficiently young to derive a bittersweet feeling of delight from his sadness, and a kind of painful dignity from his conviction that he would be the last. From the nearby swamps came the deafening waves of frogs' croaking. The declining sun dipped the room's walls and furniture in red. He heard a light wagonet approach, the nimble trot of hooves on the dusty street. The conveyance stopped, a straw-coloured britshka, the summer conveyance of Count Chojnicki. Three times his cracking whip interrupted the song of the frogs.

Count Chojnicki was curious. No other passion than curiosity sent him out into the world, drew him to the tables of the great gaming halls, sequestered him behind the walls of his old hunting pavilion, sat him down on the parliamentarians' benches, deter-mined that he would return home every spring, compelled him to throw his regular parties, and prevented him from cutting his own throat. It was curiosity that kept him alive. He was insatiably curious. Lieutenant Trotta had told him that his father, the District Commissioner, was coming; and, even though Chojnicki knew probably a dozen commissioners or so, and more fathers of lieu-tenants than you could shake a stick at, he was nevertheless eager to meet District Commissioner Trotta. 'I'm a friend of your son's,' said Chojnicki. 'You're a guest of mine. Your son will have told you! I've seen yoú before somewhere, it seems to me. Do you by any chance know Dr Svoboda at the Ministry of Trade?' 'We went to school together!' 'Well then, that's it!' exclaimed Chojnicki. 'Svoboda's a good friend of mine. Perhaps getting a little calcified these days! But a hell of a fine fellow! Do you mind if I make a personal observation? You remind me of Franz Joseph.'

There was silence for a moment. The Emperor's name had never passed the District Commissioner's lips. On formal occasions, one said: His Majesty. In daily life, one said: the Emperor. But Chojnicki said: Franz Joseph, as he had just said: Svoboda. 'Yes, you remind me of Franz Joseph,' repeated Chojnicki.

They drove off. Either side of them was the racket of the endless frog choir, and the endless expanse of blue-green swamp. The evening swam towards them in violet and gold. They heard the soft rolling of the wheels on the soft sand of the track, and the sharp creaking of the axles. Chojnicki stopped in front of the little hunting pavilion.

It backed on to the dark edge of the pine forest. It was separated from the narrow road by a small garden and an ornamental stone wall. The hedges that bordered the short garden path had not been trimmed for some time; here and there, they sprawled untidily across the path, their branches grew towards each other, and left no space for two people to walk abreast. Therefore, the three men came down the path in single file, followed, obediently, by the horse, drawing the little wagonet after it. It seemed well acquainted with this path; perhaps it thought it was a person as well, and lived in the pavilion. Behind the hedges on either side thistles flourished, guarded by the wide dark green faces of coltsfoot. On the right was a broken stone pillar, all that was left of some tower, it seemed. Like an immense broken tooth the stone jutted out of the front garden towards the sky, adorned with dark green splotches of moss and delicate black cracks. The massive wooden door had the Chojnickis' coat of arms on it, a blue shield divided into three, with three golden deer whose antlers had grown together into a solid tangle. Chojnicki lit some lamps. They found themselves standing in a wide, low-ceilinged room. The last glimmer of day was falling through cracks in the green blinds. A table under one of the lamps was set with plates, bottles, china dishes and silver. 'I've ventured to have a little snack prepared for you!' said Chojnicki. He filled three little glasses with the crystal-clear ninety-proof, held out two of them to his guests, and raised the third himself. They drank. The District Commissioner was a little confused as he put his glass back on the table. The pavilion was mysterious, but the dishes seemed real enough and the District Commissioner's appetite was greater than his confusion. A brown liver pâté, studded with coal-black truffles, was presented in a glittering round of ice crystals. A tender breast of roast pheasant loomed all by itself on a snow-white dish, attended by a retinue of green, red, white and yellow vegetables, each in its own blue-and-gold-rimmed bowl with the family crest. In a wide-necked crystal jar were millions upon millions of little grey-black caviar eggs, surrounded by yellow-gold slices of lemon. And round pink wheels of ham, guarded by a large, three-tined silver fork, lined up dutifully on a longish dish, in the company of fat red-cheeked radishes that were reminiscent of fresh-faced village girls. Broad, heavy slabs of carp and slender slippery pike had been boiled, baked or steeped in a sweet and sour onion marinade, and now lay on glass, silver and china. Round loaves, black, brown and white, rested – like babies in cradles – in plain baskets of rustic weave, the slices artfully pressed together so that the loaves looked whole. Between the various dishes stood squat, paunchy bottles and tall, slender four- and six-sided crystal decanters and also smooth round ones; bottles long- and short-necked; with labels and without; and all followed by a regiment of glasses of every different shape and size.

They helped themselves and began to eat.

To the District Commissioner, this unusual way of having a 'snack' and the unusual hour constituted an extremely pleasant indication of the exceptional customs of this border region. In the old Dual Monarchy, even such spartan characters as Herr von Trotta liked their pleasures as much as the rest of them. A lot of time had flown by since the day the District Commissioner had eaten his last exceptional meal. The occasion then had been the dinner for Prince M., who had been awarded a prestigious posting to the newly occupied regions of Bosnia and Herzegovina, partly on the strength of his celebrated abilities as a linguist, and partly because of his alleged gift for 'the taming of wild peoples'. Yes, and on that evening the District Commissioner had done himself proud! And that day, along with a few other days of feasting and drinking, had etched itself in his memory just as deeply as those other days, when he had received a commendation from the Ministry, or been promoted, first to assistant district commissioner, and then to chief district commissioner. He tasted the excellence of the food with his eyes as much as others did with their palates. His eyes travelled across the laden table, taking delight and lingering pleasurably here and there. He had almost succeeded in forgetting the mysterious, even somewhat intimidating surroundings. They ate. They drank from the various bottles. And the District Commissioner praised everything, saying, as he went from one thing to the next, 'marvellous' and 'exquisite'. Slowly his countenance began to redden. And the wings of his side whiskers were in continual motion.

'The reason I've asked you here, gentlemen,' said Chojnicki, 'is that we wouldn't have remained undisturbed in the "new castle". There my door is, so to speak, always open, and all my friends can come when they please. This is usually the place where I work.'

'You work?' asked the District Commissioner. 'Yes,' said Chojnicki, 'I work. I work for the fun of it. I continue the tradition of my forefathers, though I must admit, I'm not as serious about it as even my grandfather still was. The peasants of this region thought of him as a magician, and they may have been right. They think I'm one too, but I know they're wrong. So far, I haven't been able to make a grain!'

'A grain?' asked the District Commissioner, 'a grain of what?' 'Of gold, of course!' said Chojnicki, as if it were glaringly obvious what he was talking about.

'I have a certain aptitude for chemistry,' he went on, 'something that runs in our family. Along these walls, you will have noticed, is an array of the very oldest and the very newest equipment.' He pointed to the walls. The District Commissioner saw six rows of wooden shelves along each wall. They were freighted with mortars and pestles, little and not so little paper bags, glass retorts of the kind they used to have in old-fashioned chemist's shops, curious glass balloons full of coloured liquids, lights, gas burners and tubes.

'Curious, curious, very curious indeed!' said Herr von Trotta. 'And I myself,' Chojnicki went on, 'am not able to say whether or not I'm serious about it. Yes, sometimes I feel enthusiastic when I come here in the mornings, and I browse in my grandfather's formulae, and I experiment; then I laugh at myself and leave. And then I come back and I try again.' 'Curious, curious!' repeated the District Commissioner. 'No more curious,' said the Count, 'than whatever else I might turn my hand to. What about becoming Minister of Education and Science? Someone thought I should do that. Or shall I be Head of Section at the Interior Ministry instead? Again, I've been put forward for that. Or shall I go to Court, into the office of the Comptroller of the Household? That was another possibility, Franz Joseph knows me, and —'

The District Commissioner slid his chair back a couple of inches. To hear Chojnicki refer to the Emperor in such a casual way, as if he were one of those laughable delegates who had been returned to Parliament since the introduction of direct, universal, secret suffrage, or, as if, to put another construction on it, he were already dead and a figure in the history of the fatherland — it cut the District Commissioner to the quick. Chojnicki corrected himself: 'His Majesty knows me!'

The District Commissioner moved his chair back up to the table and asked: 'And why — forgive me! — would it be just as foolish to serve the Fatherland as it would be to make gold?'

'Because the Fatherland no longer exists.'

'I'm afraid I don't understand!' said Herr von Trotta.

'I thought you mightn't understand!' said Chojnicki. 'The fact is we're all dead!'

It was very quiet. The last dim light of the day was long gone.

Through the thin gaps in the blinds, you could have sighted a sprinkling of stars already out. The fat rackety song of the frogs had been replaced by the softer metallic tones of the nocturnal field crickets. From time to time you heard the harsh cry of the cuckoo. The District Commissioner, put in a strange, almost charmed state by the alcohol, by the striking surroundings, and the unusual speeches of his host, sneaked glances at his son, merely in order to glimpse someone who was dear and familiar to him. But even Carl-Joseph no longer seemed that. Maybe Chojnicki had been right, and they had all gone on: the Fatherland, the District Commissioner and his son! With a supreme effort, Herr von Trotta managed to put the question: 'I don't understand! What do you mean the Monarchy doesn't exist any more?'

'Of course, taken literally,' Chojnicki replied, 'it still exists. We still have an army' – he nodded at the Lieutenant – 'and we have an officialdom' – with a nod back at the District Commissioner. 'But it's falling apart as we speak. As we speak, it's falling apart, it's already fallen apart! An old man with not long to go, a head cold could finish him off, he keeps his throne by the simple miracle that he's still able to sit on it. But how much longer, how much longer? The age doesn't want us any more! This age wants to establish autonomous nation states! People have stopped believing in God. Nationalism is the new religion. People don't go to church. They go to nationalist meetings. The Monarchy, our monarchy is founded on faith and devotion: on the belief that God has chosen the Habsburgs to reign over a certain number of Christian peoples. Our emperor is like a worldlier pope, his full title is His Royal and Imperial Apostolic Majesty, there is no other apostolic majesty anywhere, and no other royal family in Europe is as dependent on the grace of God and the people's belief in that grace. The German Kaiser will still rule if God deserts him; by the grace of the nation, it would then be. But the Emperor of

Austria-Hungary may not be deserted by God. And now God has deserted him!'

The District Commissioner got to his feet. Never would he have believed that there was someone capable of saying God had deserted the Emperor. And yet it seemed to him, who all his life had been happy to leave the affairs of Heaven in the hands of theologians, while being of the opinion that church, mass, Ascension, clergy and the Almighty were all institutions of the Monarchy, it seemed to him that the Count's pronouncement explained all the confusion he had experienced in the last few weeks, particularly since Jacques's death. Of course, God must have abandoned the old Emperor! The District Commissioner took a few steps, and the old floorboards creaked under his feet. He walked over to the window, and through the gaps in the blinds he saw slices of the dark blue night outside. All the processes of nature and all the events of ordinary daily life suddenly were touched by a menacing and unfathomable significance. The whispering chorus of crickets was unfathomable, unfathomable the blinking of the stars, the velvety blue of the night, and to the District Commissioner his own trip to the frontier was unfathomable and his being a guest of this count. He returned to the table and rubbed one of his whiskers, as he did when he was a little bewildered. A little bewildered! Never in his life had he been so utterly bewildered as he was now!

There was a full glass in front of him. He drank it down. 'Well then,' he said, 'so you're telling me that we, we're ...' 'We're lost,' Chojnicki put in. 'Yes, we're lost, you and your son and I. We are, as I say, among the last people in a world where God still extends His Grace to monarchs, and where madmen like myself make gold. Listen! Look!' And Chojnicki stood up and walked over to the door, turned a switch, and lights came on in the great chandelier overhead. 'You see!' said Chojnicki, 'this is the age of electricity, not alchemy. And chemistry too, of course! Have you heard of the stuff? Nitroglycerine,' the Count pronounced it very carefully, saying each syllable distinctly. 'Nitroglycerine!' he said again. 'Not gold! In Franz Joseph's palace, they still burn candles most of the time! You understand? Electricity and nitroglycerine will be the end of us. You'll see, it won't be long now, it won't be long at all!'

The shine of the electric bulbs set up a series of red, green and blue, delicately and more stoutly vibrating reflections in the glass tubes on the shelves. Carl Joseph sat there silent and pale. He had been drinking the whole time. The District Commissioner looked at the Lieutenant. He thought of his friend, the painter Moser. And since he had been drinking himself, old Herr von Trotta, he saw, as in a very far off mirror, a pale reflection of his drunken son under the green trees of the Volksgarten, with a floppy hat on his head, a big folder under his arm, and it was as though the Count's gift for predicting the broad outlines of the future had transferred itself to the District Commissioner, and allowed him to see what lay in store for his son and heir. Half empty and sad were the plates and dishes, the bottles and glasses. The light sparkled magically in the glass tubing round the walls. A couple of bewhiskered old servants, who might have been brothers to Emperor Franz Joseph and to the District Commissioner, came in and started to clear the table. From time to time the harsh cry of the cuckoo broke on the crickets' continuo like a hammer blow. Chojnicki held up a bottle. 'You must drink this, it's the local product' – that was how he described the schnapps – 'there's just a little bit left in the bottle!' And they drank the rest of the 'local product'. The District Commissioner pulled out his watch, but couldn't quite make out the time. It was as though the hands were whirling round the white face of the watch, as though there were a hundred of them instead of the normal two. And instead of twelve digits, there were twelve times twelve! Because the figures huddled as close together as the minute strokes. It could be nine o'clock, or it could be midnight. 'Ten o'clock!' said Chojnicki.

The bewhiskered servants took the guests gently by the elbows and led them outside, to where Chojnicki's big carriage was waiting. The sky was very near, a good, familiar, earthly bulb of familiar blue glass, it lay covering the earth, close enough to touch.

The stone pillar, for instance, to the right of the pavilion, seemed to be touching it. The stars had been punched into the close heavens by human hands like pins in a map. From time to time the entire blue night revolved around the District Commissioner, rocked gently and came to a stop. The frogs croaked in the endless swamps. It smelled damp, of rain, grass. The coachman in his black cloak loomed over the ghostly white horses that were pulling the black carriage. They whinnied, and their hooves, soft as cats' paws, scraped at the damp sandy ground.

The coachman clicked his tongue, and they were off.

They drove out the way they had come, then turned into a broad gravelled avenue of birches and came to the lanterns that announced 'the new castle'. The silver birch trunks seemed to give off more light than the lanterns. The sturdy rubber tyres of the carriage rolled smoothly and with a low rumble over the stones; far louder was the crisp strike of the swift horses' hooves. The carriage was wide and comfortable. You sat back in it as on a sofa. Lieutenant Trotta was asleep. He was seated beside his father. His pale face was almost horizontal on the cushioned headrest, the breeze fanned it through the open window. From time to time one of the lanterns lit it up. Then Chojnicki, who was sitting facing his guests, would see the Lieutenant's half-open bloodless lips, and his hard, hooked bony nose. 'He's a sound sleeper!' he said to the District Commissioner. It was as though the Lieutenant had two fathers. The District Commissioner was sobering up in the night air, but a vague fear was still lurking in his heart. He could see the world coming to an end, and it was his world. Alive, or to all appearances still alive, Chojnicki sat opposite him, even knocking against his shin with his knee from time to time, but still somehow unearthly. The old service revolver that Herr von Trotta had brought with him pressed in his back pocket. What was the point of taking a revolver! There were no bears or wolves in the border region! There was just the end of the world!

The carriage stopped in front of the arched wooden gate. The coachman cracked his whip. The two wings of the gate opened, and the greys walked up the slight incline with measured tread. From every window on the front elevation, yellow light spilled out on to the gravel, and on to the lawns either side of the drive. Voices, a piano. No question, this was one of the 'parties'.

People had already eaten. The footmen were running around with large glasses of brilliantly coloured liqueurs. The guests were dancing, playing whist and tarock, there was someone holding forth to a group of people who weren't listening. A few went reeling through the rooms, one or two were asleep in a corner somewhere. Only men were dancing together. The black dress tunics of the dragoons pressed against the blue of the Jägers. On Count Chojnicki's orders, the rooms of 'the new castle' were lit only by candles. Fat snow-white and wax-yellow candles sprouted from mighty silver candlesticks that were stood on stone pediments or promontories, or held by footmen who were relieved every half hour. Their little flames quivered occasionally in the night air that came in through the open windows. Each time the piano was still for a moment or two, you could hear the night-ingale sounding, the crickets rustling, and from time to time the little tears of wax splashing down on to the silver. The District Commissioner went looking for his son. A sudden panic chased the old man through the suite of rooms. His son – where was he keeping? Neither among the dancers, nor among those drunkenly staggering about, nor among the players, nor among the calmer, older set who were holding conversations in little nooks. The Lieutenant was sitting all alone in a distant room. A big, paunchy bottle stood by his feet, faithful but now half empty. Next to the slender, crumpled figure of the drinker it looked solid and powerful, almost as though it could swallow him up. The District Commissioner stood in front of the Lieutenant, nudging the bottle with the pointed toes of his boots. The son saw two fathers, more, they were multiplying every second. He felt oppressed by them; if there were that many of them, there was no point in his paying all of them the respect owed to one of them by getting up. There was no point, so the Lieutenant remained in his peculiar posture, which was a combination of sitting, lying and cowering. The District Commissioner did not move. His brain was working very fast, it threw up a thousand memories all at once. For instance he saw Carl Joseph as a cadet on the summer Sundays when he had come into the study, his snow-white gloves and black cadet cap on his knees, answering every question with clear voice and obedient young eyes. The District Commissioner saw the newly promoted cavalry lieutenant stride into the same room, now in blue and gold and crimson. This young man, however, was now a very long way from old Herr von Trotta. What was this drunken lieutenant of the Jägers to him? Why did it hurt him so much to see him?

Lieutenant Trotta did not budge. He could remember that his father had recently arrived, and he understood that it wasn't this father, but a whole bunch of fathers that were standing in front of him. But he was unable to recall either why his father had come today, or why he was multiplying so extremely, or yet why he, the Lieutenant, was unable to stand up.

In the course of the last several weeks, Lieutenant Trotta had acquired a taste for the ninety-proof. It didn't go to your head, it just, as its aficionados like to say, 'went to your feet'. At first, it produced a pleasant sensation of warmth in your chest. The blood started rolling through your veins a little faster, and queasiness and a desire to vomit were replaced by hunger. Then you drank another ninety-proof. If it was a chilly grey morning, you went bravely out to meet it, as good-humoured as if it were a sunny and happy day. During the break you ate a little snack with the others in the frontier bar, near the woods where the Jägers exercised, and you drank another ninety-proof. It ran down your throat like liquid fire. You were barely aware of having eaten anything. You went back to barracks, got changed, and headed out to the station for lunch. Although it was a long trek, you weren't at all hungry. And so you drank another ninety-proof. You finally had something to eat, and felt sleepy right away. So you had an espresso, with another ninety-proof to follow. In short: in the course of a boring day, there was never an occasion not to have one. On the contrary, there were afternoons and evenings when it was imperative to drink schnapps.

Because life was so simple, once you'd had a drink! That was the miraculous thing about this frontier! It made life difficult for a sober man – but who could stay sober?! Once he'd had a drink, Lieutenant Trotta saw in all his comrades, superiors and juniors, good old friends. He felt so much at home in the little town, it was as though he'd been born and grown up there. He would set foot in the tiny little general stores that had burrowed their way into the walls of the bazaar, narrow, dark and twisting, like hamster runs stuffed full of all kinds of goods, and offering the most useless objects: fake corals, cheap mirrors, horrible soap, combs of aspen wood, and woven dogleads – purely and simply because he gave in to the appeals of the red-haired traders. He smiled at everyone, the peasant women with their colourful headscarves and their big raffia baskets under their arms, the tricked-out daughters of the Jews, the officials in the District Commissioner's office, and the teachers at the secondary school. A broad stream of kindness and friendliness flowed through this little world. Merry greetings were offered to the Lieutenant by all these people. And there was no awkwardness any more. No awkwardness in the service, or away from it. Everything was tied up promptly and easily. You understood Onufri's mother tongue. Sometimes you got out into one of the outlying villages, and you asked the peasants the way, and they answered in that foreign language. And you understood what they said. You no longer rode. You lent out your horse to comrades: good horsemen, who knew its worth. In a word: you were content. Only, Lieutenant Trotta didn't know that his walk was becoming unsteady, that there were stains on his tunic, that his trousers didn't have a crease, that there were buttons missing on his shirt, that the colour of his skin was yellow at night and ashen in the mornings, and that the look in his eyes was unfocused and apathetic. He didn't gamble – and that was the only thing that eased Major Zoglauer's concerns about him. Everyone had times in their lives when they had to drink. Never mind, it'll pass!

Schnapps was cheap. What did for most of them were their debts. Trotta was no sloppier than the others in the way he discharged his duties. Unlike some of them, he didn't get into trouble. On the contrary, he grew milder and gentler, the more he drank. In time, he'll get married and sober up, thought the Major. He has protectors in some pretty elevated circles. He'll make his way up the ladder. There's general staff material there, if he puts his mind to it.

Herr von Trotta perched on the edge of the sofa next to his son, and wondered what to say. He wasn't really used to talking to drunks. 'You ought,' he began, after a long pause for thought, 'you ought really to be a bit careful with schnapps! I myself, I've never drunk more than my thirst.' The Lieutenant made an enormous effort to get out of his half-cowering, half-sprawling position into a respectably upright one. In vain. He looked at the old man – thank God there was just one of them now – having to perch on the edge of the sofa, and, propping his hands on his knees, he asked: 'What did you just say, Papa?' 'You ought to be careful with schnapps!' repeated the District Commissioner. 'Why?' asked the Lieutenant. 'What do you mean?' asked Herr von Trotta, slightly comforted in that his son seemed sufficiently clear-headed to grasp what had been said to him. 'Schnapps will destroy you, you remember Moser, don't you?' 'Moser, Moser,' said Carl Joseph. 'Of course! But he's quite right! I remember him. He painted the picture of Grandfather!' 'Had you forgotten?' asked Herr von Trotta, very softly. 'No, I haven't forgotten,' replied the Lieutenant, 'I've always thought about that picture. I'm not strong enough for that picture. The dead! I can't forget the dead! Father, I can't forget anything! Oh, Father!'

Herr von Trotta sat beside his son in bewilderment, he couldn't quite understand what he was saying, but he sensed that it was more than drunkenness that was speaking in the young man. He felt that here was a cry for help from the Lieutenant, and he was unable to help! He had come to this frontier region in search of a little help himself. For he was all alone in this world. And now this world was ending! Jacques was in the ground, he was alone, he wanted to see his son once more, and his son was alone too, and because he was younger, perhaps that much closer to the end of the world. How simple the world always appeared to be, thought the District Commissioner. For every situation, there was a prescribed attitude. When the boy came home for the holidays, you gave him a test. When he became a lieutenant, you congratulated him. When he wrote his dutiful letters that said so little, you wrote him a couple of measured sentences back. But what did you do when your son was drunk? When he cried 'Father'? Or when something in him cried 'Father'?

He saw Chojnicki walk in, and he stood up more suddenly than was his style. 'There's a telegram for you!' said Chojnicki. 'The hotel porter brought it.' It was an official telegram. It summoned Herr von Trotta back home. 'Sadly, they're calling you back already!' said Chojnicki. 'It'll be to do with the Sokols.' 'Yes, that's the probable cause,' said Herr von Trotta. 'There are going to be some disturbances!' He knew now that he was too feeble to do anything about any disturbances. He was very tired. Only a couple of years till he could retire! And at that moment he suddenly thought he might retire sooner rather than later. He could look after Carl Joseph; a fitting task for an ageing father.

Chojnicki said: 'It's not easy to do anything about disturbances with your hands tied, the way they are in this dratted monarchy. If you have a couple of the ringleaders arrested, then the freemasons, the deputies, the nationalist spokesmen and the newspapers will pile into you, and you'll have to set them free. If you have the Sokol dissolved – you'll get a ticking off from the authorities. Autonomy! Just wait! Here, in my district, every public disorder ends with shooting. Yes, as long as I live here, I'm the government candidate and I'll be returned. Purely because this province is far enough away from the offices of those filthy newspapers where they hatch all their rotten new schemes!'

He went up to Carl Joseph, and, with the emphasis and the weight of a man who's used to dealing with drunks, said: 'Your

Papa has to go home!' Carl Joseph understood right away. He was even able to get to his feet. With a glazed expression, he looked in the direction of his father.

'I'm sorry, Father!'

'I'm a little concerned about him!' the District Commissioner said to Chojnicki.

'Rightly so!' replied Chojnicki. 'He needs to get away from here. When he gets some holiday, I'll take him out and try to show him a bit of the world. Then he won't feel like coming back here. Maybe he'll fall in love –'

'I'll never fall in love,' said Carl Joseph very slowly.

They drove back to the hotel.

On the way back, only one word fell between them, one single word: 'Father!' said Carl Joseph, and nothing more.

The District Commissioner awoke very late the following morning, the trumpets were already sounding for the return of the battalion. The train left in two hours' time. Carl Joseph came in. There was Chojnicki's whiplash signal. The District Commissioner was lunching in the station restaurant, at the table of the Jäger officers.

An immensely long time had gone by since he'd left his district of W. With difficulty he remembered that he'd boarded the train only two days ago. He sat at the long, horseshoe-shaped table, the only civilian there apart from Count Chojnicki, in the company of the brightly clad officers, dark and lean, under the mural of Franz Joseph I, showing the familiar, universally circulated portrait of the Supreme Commander-in-Chief in his snow-white field-marshal's tunic and crimson sash. Just a foot below the Emperor's white whiskers and almost aligned with them, were the dark, barely greying wings of Trotta's whiskers. The junior officers, sitting at the two ends of the horseshoe, detected the resemblance between His Apostolic Majesty and his servant. From where he was sitting, Lieutenant Trotta could also compare the Emperor's face with that of his father. And for a few brief seconds the Lieutenant had the impression that the portrait on the wall was that of his somewhat aged father, while the man actually sitting at the table was a slightly younger version of the Emperor in civilian clothes. And Emperor and Father alike grew strange and distant to him.

The District Commissioner, meanwhile, sent a despondent, enquiring look around the table, over the downy and almost hairless faces of the youngest officers, and the moustached faces of the older ones. Next to him sat Major Zoglauer. Oh, how Herr von Trotta would have liked to confide his worries about Carl Joseph in him! But there was no time. The train was already being made ready outside the window.

The District Commissioner was quite cowed. From all sides, they were drinking to his health, to his trip home, and to the successful accomplishment of the tasks that there awaited him. He smiled back in every direction, stood up, clinked glasses with some of them, and his head was weighed down with worries, and his heart was oppressed by gloomy forebodings. What an immensely long time had passed since his departure from the district of W.! Yes, the District Commissioner had set off cheerfully and exuberantly into this precarious region to see his dear son. And now he was leaving there lonely, leaving his lonely son, leaving this frontier, where the end of the world could clearly be seen coming, as one might see a storm brewing over the edge of a city, while its streets are still basking innocently under a cloudless sky. Already the jingle of the porter's bell. Already the whistle of the locomotive. Already the condensation of the wet steam from the train, beading in fine grey pearls against the restaurant windows. Already lunch was over, and the company stood. The 'whole battalion' accompanied Herr von Trotta out on to the platform. Herr von Trotta desired to say something markworthy, but nothing came to him. He shot a tender look in the direction of his son. Straight away, he felt afraid someone would see it, and he lowered his eyes. He thanked Chojnicki. He doffed the dignified, grey top hat that he wore on trips. He held his hat in his left hand and threw his right round his son's shoulders. He kissed him on both cheeks. And although he wanted to say: Don't upset me. I love you, my boy! he merely said: 'Chin up!' Because the Trottas were reticent men.

And now he climbed aboard, the District Commissioner. He stood by the window. His hand rested on the open window, in its dark grey kid glove.

His bald head shone. Once more, his troubled eye sought out Carl Joseph's face. 'Next time you come, District Commissioner,' said the perennially cheerful Captain Wagner, 'next time you'll find a proper little Monte Carlo awaits you!' 'How so?' asked the District Commissioner. 'We're starting a casino!' Wagner gave back. And before Herr von Trotta could summon his son, to warn him urgently against such a 'Monte Carlo', the locomotive whistled, the couplings clanked together, and the train slipped away. The District Commissioner waved his grey glove. The officers all saluted. Only Carl Joseph didn't stir.

On the way back, he walked with Captain Wagner. 'It'll be a great little casino!' enthused the Captain. 'A veritable gaming hall! God Almighty! How long is it since I last saw roulette! You know, the way the ball rolls, I love it so much, and the noise it makes! I'm so pleased!' And it wasn't just Captain Wagner who was looking forward to the opening of the new gaming hall. They were all waiting. For years, the frontier garrison had been waiting for the gaming hall that Kapturak would set up.

Kapturak arrived a week after the District Commissioner left. Probably his arrival would have attracted much more notice had it not coincided with that of a certain lady, who, instead, captured everyone's attention.

# 12

On the frontiers of the Austro-Hungarian Monarchy there were at that time many men of Kapturak's sort. All round the old Empire they started to circle like those cowardly black birds that can see someone dying from an enormous distance. With black and impatient wing-flaps, they wait for his life to end. With pointed beaks they jab at their prey. No one knows where they come from, or where they're bound. They are the feathered brothers of mysterious Death, his heralds, his companions and his camp-followers.

Kapturak is a short, unobtrusive fellow. Rumours whiz around him, fly ahead of him on his complicated routes, and follow the barely perceptible traces of his passage. He lives in the frontier tavern. He is in touch with agents of the South American shipping companies that each year move thousands of Russian deserters on their steamships to a harsh new homeland. He likes to gamble, and drinks little. He is not without a certain mournful gaiety. He claims to have become involved in the trade in people on the other side of the border first, and then, after the identification and punishment of a ring of corrupt officials and soldiers, to have abandoned home, wife and children, for fear of being sent to Siberia. And, in reply to the question as to what he proposes to do with himself here, Kapturak replies, curtly but with a smile: 'Business.'

The owner of the hotel where the officers put up, a certain Brodnitzer, who came originally from Silesia and had wound up in the border region no one knows why, opened his gaming hall. He put up a big notice in the window of his café. He announced that games of all kinds would be played, that every night a band would 'perform' until the small hours, and that 'celebrated night club chanteuses' had been engaged. The 'upgrading' of the establishment began with the concerts of the band, which consisted of eight local musicians. Later, the so-called 'Mariahilf Nightingale' arrived, a flaxen-haired girl from Oderberg. She sang Lehár waltzes, and the risqué number: 'In the morning after a night of love . . .', and, as an encore: 'Under my little dress I wear sheer silk, with little rosy pleats . . .' In this way, Brodnitzer heightened expectation among his clientele. And it transpired that as well as various large and small card tables, he had also set up a little roulette table in a shady, curtained nook. Captain Wagner told everyone, and drummed up enthusiasm. To the men, who had served on the frontier for many years, the little ball (and many of them had never seen roulette in their lives before) appeared one of those magical things in the world, with the help of which a man might come by beautiful women, costly horses and rich castles, and all at the same time. How could the little ball be disobliging? They all had had miserable institutional boyhoods, tough adolescent years in the military academy, grim years on duty at the frontier. They were waiting for war. Instead of which there had been one partial mobilization against Serbia, from which they had returned without fanfare, to the familiar prospects of a pedestrian career. Manoeuvres, duty, mess, mess, duty, manoeuvres! They had never heard the clattering little ball before, and so they knew that this was fortune, now circulating in their midst (yes, even theirs), and poised to land on this man or that as early as tomorrow. Strangers sat there; pale, rich and taciturn gentlemen who had never been seen before. One day, Captain Wagner won five hundred crowns. The next day he had paid off his debts. That month for the first time in many months, he was paid his salary in full, all three thirds of it. Admittedly, Lieutenants Schnabel and Gründler were down a hundred crowns apiece. So what, tomorrow they might win a thousand! ...

When the little white ball began to spin like a milky ring orbiting the black and red squares, and when the black and red squares themselves blended into a single ring of indeterminate colour, then the hearts of the officers began to flutter, and in their heads there was a strange whooshing, as though there was a little ball spinning in each of their brains, and their eyes went black, red, black, red. Their knees shook, even though they were sitting down. Their eyes flew off in desperate pursuit of the ball, but they never managed to catch it in flight. Following some laws peculiar to itself, it eventually began to stagger, drunk from its spinning, and came to rest in one of the numbered chambers. Everyone groaned. Even those who had lost felt somehow relieved. The following morning they told each other about it. And a great giddiness came over all of them. More and more officers went to the gaming room. For inscrutable reasons, the strange newcomers did too. It was they who fed the game, filled the bank, pulled big banknotes from their wallets, golden ducats, watches and chains from their waistcoat pockets, and rings from their fingers. All the rooms in the hotel were occupied. The sleepy cabs that had always used to wait in line before, with yawning coachmen on the box, and bony mares in harness, like waxwork models in the panopticum: they too bestirred themselves, and behold: the wheels could turn and the bony mares clattered from the station to the hotel, from the hotel to the border and back into the little town. The morose traders had a smile. Their dark shops appeared brighter, their wares more colourful, and night after night the 'Mariahilf Nightingale' sang. And, as though her singing had awoken a sisterhood, other girls, strangers, nicely done up, new girls came to the café. The tables were pushed aside, and they danced to the waltzes of Lehár. The world was transformed.

Yes indeed, the whole world! In other places, peculiar posters appeared the like of which had never been seen before in the locality. In every one of the local languages they called upon the workers in the brush factory to lay down their labour. The manufacture of brushes is the only industry there is for miles. The workers are poor peasants. Some of them live by chopping wood in winter, and by helping with the harvest in the autumn. In summer they all report to the brush factory. Others are drawn from among the poorer Jews. They can't reckon and can't trade, and they have never learned a craft either. Far and wide, for a radius of perhaps twenty miles, it's the only factory there is.

The production of bristles was associated with awkward and expensive legal requirements with which the factory-owners were reluctant to comply. The workers ought to be given face masks to keep off dust and germs, they ought to work in large bright rooms, the rubbish should be burned twice a day, and if a worker started to cough, another should be taken on in his stead. Because, sooner or later, all those who worked on the cleaning of bristles would begin to cough blood. The factory was a ramshackle old structure with small windows, a slate roof in bad repair, and a wildly sprouting willow hedge as a sort of fence; it stood on a dreadful piece of waste ground where from time immemorial rubbish had been thrown, dead cats and rats were left to decompose, tin plates and cans rusted away, and broken earthenware nestled among gaping shoes. Beyond, the fields stretched out in all directions, full of the golden benediction of corn, thrilling to the incessant song of crickets, forever echoing to the cheerful noise of frogs. Outside the little grey windows where the workers sat, endlessly combing out knotted thickets of bristles with iron combs, and gulping down dry clouds of dust, the swallows darted by, the iridescent summer flies danced, cabbage white and coloured butterflies drifted past, and through the open patches of the roof came the triumphant song of the larks. The workers, who had arrived only a few months before from the freedom of the villages where they had been born and raised in the sweet smell of hay, in the cold smell of snow, in the acrid fume of dung, in the deafening racket of birdsong, in the whole richly varied blessing of nature: the workers saw through the grey dust clouds to swallow, butterfly and mosquito dance, and felt homesick. When the larks trilled, they grew restless. They had not known before that their health was protected by law; that the Monarchy afforded them a parliament; and that among the deputies to that parliament were some who were themselves workers. Strangers came, who wrote out placards, organized public meetings, explained the constitution along with some of the injustices it contained, read aloud from newspapers and addressed them in all the local languages. They were louder than the larks and the frogs: and the workers went on strike.

It was the first strike the region had seen. The political authorities were alarmed. For decades they had done nothing more than organize rather casual censuses, celebrate the Emperor's birthday, take part in the annual recruiting drives, and send identical-sounding reports to the government. Occasionally, they would arrest a Russophile Ukrainian here, an Orthodox priest there, Jews caught smuggling cigarettes, spies. For decades, the region had been known for providing bristles; they were sent from there to the broom-making factories of Moravia, or Bohemia or Silesia, from where the finished brooms were re-imported. For years, the workers had been coughing; they coughed blood, they fell ill, and they died in hospital. But they didn't strike. Now, all the gendarmerie posts in the wider area had to be co-ordinated, and a report sent to the government. They in turn would get in touch with the army. And the army high command would inform the respective garrison commanders.

The younger officers were of the belief that 'the people', which is to say the lowest-ranking civilian population, were demanding to be put on an equal footing with officials, noblemen and commercial councillors. And that couldn't possibly be accepted, if one wanted to avoid a revolution. No one wanted a revolution of course; so one had to shoot before things got out of hand.

Major Zoglauer held a short address in which all this was spelled out. Admittedly, a war is much pleasanter in every way. You're an officer, not a gendarme or a policeman. But for the present, there isn't a war to be had. Orders are orders. If the worst comes to the worst, you will have to advance with fixed bayonets, and give the order to 'Fire!' Orders are orders! Which isn't to say you can't go into Brodnitzer's café, and win yourself an awful lot of money. One day, Captain Wagner lost an awful lot of money. A stranger, ex-dragoons, with a sonorous name, a landowner in Silesia, won on two evenings in a row, and on the third received a telegram calling him home. It came to two thousand crowns, a bagatelle for a cavalryman. No bagatelle for a captain of the Jägers! You could have cadged it off Chojnicki, except that you already owed him three hundred.

Brodnitzer said: 'Captain, will you allow my signature to stand for you!'

'Fine,' said the Captain, 'but who will give that much for your signature?'

Brodnitzer thought about it for a while, and then said, 'Herr Kapturak!'

Kapturak turned up and said, 'So. I gather two thousand crowns are involved. Will I see them again?'

'I've no idea!'

'A lot of money, Captain!'

'I'll get it back!' replied the Captain.

'How, in what instalments? You know you're only allowed to set aside a third of your salary. Moreover, your colleagues are all in a similar position. I don't see how I can do it!'

'Herr Brodnitzer . . .,' began the Captain.

'Herr Brodnitzer,' retorted Kapturak, as though Brodnitzer were not present in front of him, 'Herr Brodnitzer owes me a lot of money as well. I could advance the sum in question if one of your comrades, who isn't yet involved, would come in. Someone like Lieutenant Trotta, for instance. He's joined you from the cavalry, he owns a horse!'

'Right,' said the Captain, 'I'll have a word with him.' And he ran upstairs to wake Lieutenant Trotta.

They stood together in the long, dark, narrow hotel passageway. 'Hurry up and sign!' whispered the Captain. 'They're waiting. It'll look as if you're reluctant or something!' Trotta signed.

'Come down right away!' said Wagner, 'I'll be waiting for you!'

There was a little door at the back of the room, by which long-term residents of the hotel could enter the café, and there Carl Joseph stopped. He had not been in Brodnitzer's recently opened gaming saloon before. A dark green ribbed silk curtain was draped around the roulette table. Captain Wagner drew it aside and slipped into a different world. Carl Joseph could hear the soft, velvety buzzing of the little ball. He didn't dare raise the curtain. At the other end of the café, next to the street entrance, was a stage, and up on the stage the indefatigable 'Mariahilf Nightingale' was sashaying away. Play was in progress at the card tables. The cards fell with a smack on the fake marble surface. People gave incomprehensible cries. They looked as though they were in uniform, because they were all in white shirtsleeves; a seated regiment of players. Their jackets hung over the backs of their chairs. Their empty sleeves swayed in a weak ghostly manner with every movement they made. Over their heads hung a dense storm cloud of cigarette smoke. The tiny tips of cigarettes glowed a silvery red in the grey haze, and kept sending fresh supplies of blue to nourish the thick pall above. And underneath the visible layer of smoke, there seemed to be another one, of noise, a roaring, growling, buzzing cloud. If you closed your eyes, you might think a vast clamorous swarm of locusts had been set loose over the seated men.

Captain Wagner emerged through the curtain, looking completely transformed. His eyes were sunk in purple hollows. His brown moustache dangled ill-disciplinedly over his mouth, half of it bizarrely looking shorter than the other, and on his chin were reddish bristles, a fertile little field of tiny spears. 'Where are you, Trotta?' called the Captain, even though he was standing chest to chest with the Lieutenant. 'Lost two hundred!' he cried. 'That bloody red! Out of luck at damned roulette. Better try elsewhere!' And he hauled Trotta off to the card tables.

Kapturak and Brodnitzer rose to their feet. 'Win?' enquired Kapturak, who could see that the Captain had lost. 'No, lost, lost!' roared the Captain.

'Shame, shame!' said Kapturak. 'But look at me: how many times I've won and lost! I've lost everything I had! Won it all back! Don't stay with the same game! Be sure you don't stay with the same game! That's the secret!'

Captain Wagner put up his jacket collar. The customary ruddy brownness returned to his face. His moustache seemed to even itself out. He clapped Trotta on the back. 'You've never held a card in your hand before!'

Trotta watches Kapturak pull a deck of shiny new playing cards from his pocket, and lay it cautiously on the table, so as not to hurt the colourful face of whatever card is on the bottom. He strokes the pile with his deft fingers. The backs of the cards shine like smooth green mirrors. In their subtle curvature they reflect the overhead lights. Some cards seem to pick themselves up, stand upright on their sharp narrow edges, only to lie down again, now on their backs, now on their bellies, pile up in a heap, which in turn sheds its leaves with a soft rattle, lets the black and red faces rush by in a brief colourful storm, reconfigures itself and drops on to the table, broken up into smaller heaps. From these, individual cards detach themselves, move tenderly closer, each covering half the other's back, forming eventually into a circle reminiscent of a strangely reversed and flattened artichoke, then fly back into line, and assemble into their deck once more. All the cards obey the silent commands of the fingers. Captain Wagner follows this appetizer with hungry eyes.

How he loved cards! Sometimes the ones he summoned came to him, sometimes they fled him. He loved it when his crazed desires went galloping after them and finally, in the end, forced them to turn back. Sometimes, admittedly, the runaways were faster, and the Captain's desires were forced to go home exhausted. Over the years, the Captain had evolved a rather inscrutable and dauntingly complicated plan of campaign, in which no possible way of coercing fortune was left out of account: neither wheedling nor threatening nor ambushing nor impassioned prayer nor amorous luring. At one point the poor Captain, desperate for a heart, had to feign despair and secretly assure the coy beauty that if she didn't come to him soon, he would kill himself that very day; at another, it seemed more prudent to keep his dignity and pretend that the longed-for darling was a matter of complete indifference to him. To win a third time he had to shuffle the cards himself, with his left hand, a knack he had forced himself to learn by force of iron will and many hours of practice; a fourth time it was more helpful to sit on the right of the banker. Most of the time, admittedly, he combined several methods at once, or alternated so rapidly between them that even his fellow players couldn't keep up with him. That was important. 'Let's change places!' was something the Captain might propose perfectly innocently. And if he thought he saw a comprehending smirk on the face of his fellow players, he laughed and added: 'You're mistaken! This isn't being superstitious! The light's in my eyes here!' If his fellow players learned about the strategic tricks of the Captain, then their hands would inform the cards of what he was up to. The cards would get wind of his plan and have time to make their escape. And so, the moment he sat down at the card table, the Captain started working as busily as an entire general staff. And while his brain performed with superhuman effort, fires and chills, hopes and agonies, glee and bitterness shook his heart. He fought, he struggled, he suffered atrociously. From the moment they had started playing roulette here, he had got to work on cunning battle plans to implement against the tricky ball. (He must have known that it was harder to defeat than the playing cards.)

His usual game was baccarat, even though it was not only banned, but even held in scorn. But then what good to him were games that made you reckon odds and think — think and reckon sensibly – when his speculations tended to the incalculable and the inexplicable numen, sometimes actually revealed it and occasionally even forced it into submission? No! He wanted to take on the riddles of fortune directly, and solve them! So he sat down to baccarat. And won. He had three nines and three eights in succession, while Trotta was dealt a bunch of knaves and kings, and Kapturak a pair of fours and fives. And then Captain Wagner got above himself. Even though it was one of his principles not to show Lady Luck that he was sure of her, he suddenly trebled his stake. He hoped he'd make up his debt today. And there began his misfortune. The Captain lost, and Trotta had never stopped losing anyway. By the end, Kapturak won five hundred crowns. The Captain was forced to sign another IOU.

Wagner and Trotta got up. They started mixing cognac with ninety-proof, and then mixed that with Okocimer beer. Captain Wagner was ashamed of his defeat, just like a general who loses a battle after he's invited a friend to share in his triumph. The Lieutenant shared in the Captain's shame. They both knew they were incapable of looking the other in the eye without alcohol. They drank slowly, in small steady sips.

'Here's to you!' said the Captain. 'To you!' said Trotta.

Each time they drank to each other, they looked bravely at one another, and proved to each other that they were capable of meeting their disaster with equanimity. Then all at once the Lieutenant felt that the Captain, his best friend, was the saddest man in the world, and he started crying bitterly. 'Why are you crying?' asked the Captain, with trembling lips. 'Over you, over you!' said Trotta, 'my poor friend!' Self-pity – sometimes silent, sometimes loquacious – consumed them both.

An old plan surfaced in Captain Wagner's memory. It revolved around Trotta's horse, on which he rode out every day, which he had come to love, and which he had originally thought of buying himself. Then he had gone on to think that if he had as much money as the horse was likely to cost, he could win a fortune with it at baccarat, and buy himself a whole string of horses. That made him think of taking the horse off the Lieutenant's hands, not purchasing it outright, but putting it in hock, gambling with the money and then buying it back with his winnings. Was that unethical? Who would be hurt by that? How long would it take? A couple of hours of playing, and he'd have that much! The best way to win was sitting down and playing without fear, without worrying about the odds at all. Oh, if he could only play, one single time, like an independent man of wealth. Once! The Captain cursed his army pay. It was so mean, it didn't allow him to play 'like a human being'.

Now as they sat there side by side in the plenitude of their feeling, oblivious of the world around them, and convinced that the world had forgotten them, the Captain finally felt able to put it to his friend: 'Sell me your horse!' 'I'll give it to you!' said Trotta, moved. You're not allowed to sell a present, not even temporarily, thought the Captain, and he said: 'No, sell it to me!' 'Take it!' Trotta begged him. 'No, I'll pay you for it!' insisted the Captain.

They argued back and forth for a few minutes. Then the Captain stood up, swayed slightly and shouted: 'I order you to sell it to me!' 'Yes, sir!' Trotta replied mechanically. 'But I've got no money!' mumbled the Captain, sat down again and was as tender-hearted as before. 'Never mind! I'll give it to you.' 'No, that's just what I don't want! I don't want to buy it any more either. I just want the money!'

'Then I can sell it to someone else!' said Trotta. He glowed with pleasure at having had such an unusual idea.

'Brilliant!' exclaimed the Captain. 'But who to?' 'Chojnicki, for example!' 'Absolutely brilliant!' repeated the Captain. 'I owe him five hundred crowns!' 'Then I'll take on your debt!' said Trotta.

Because he has been drinking, his heart is full of sympathy for the Captain. His poor comrade needs to be rescued! He is in great danger. He is dear and close to him, good Captain Wagner. Besides which, the Lieutenant thinks it is absolutely essential at this time to say something kindly and comforting and perhaps even magnificent, and to do something helpful. Magnanimity, friendship, and the desire to appear strong and helpful flow together in his heart, like three warm streams. Trotta stands up. The morning is at hand. Only a few lamps are still burning, pale already against the pallor of the day now breaking through the blinds. Except for Herr Brodnitzer and his one waiter there's no one left in the bar now. Tables and chairs are standing around in desultory fashion, facing the stage on which the 'Mariahilf Nightingale' had skipped about in the course of the night. All the detritus lying around suggests terrible scenes of sudden departure, as though, surprised by some danger, the guests had all left at once in a noisy rout. Long cardboard cigarette-holders are littered over the floor alongside short cigar butts. They are what's left of Russian papyrossas and Austrian cigars, and they betray the fact that foreign visitors have been drinking and gaming here with the locals.

'The bill!' cries the Captain. He embraces the Lieutenant, presses him long and fervently to his chest. 'Go with God!' he says, the tears welling up in his eyes.

Out on the street, it was already morning, the morning was already there, the morning of a small town in the east, full of the fragrance of chestnut candles, lilacs just coming into bloom, and fresh sour black rye loaves being carried outside by bakers in great baskets. The birds were squabbling, it was an endless ocean of twittering, the air was a sonorous ocean. A pale translucent sky lay, taut and near, above the grey skewed shingle roofs of the little houses. The peasants' tiny carts rolled softly and slowly and still a little sleepily down the dusty road, scattering straws, chaff and dry tufts of last year's hay. The sun rose rapidly in the blank eastern sky. Lieutenant Trotta walked straight into it, slightly sobered up by the mild wind that preceded the day, and full of his proud plan to rescue his brother officer. It wasn't easy to sell the horse without asking the District Commissioner for permission. But it was for friendship's sake! Nor was it easy – what was easy in this life for Lieutenant Trotta! – to offer Chojnicki the horse. But the more difficult the undertaking, the more vigorously and decisively Trotta marched out to meet it. The clock was striking already. Trotta arrived at the entrance to the 'new castle' just as Chojnicki, booted and whip in hand, was getting into his britshka. He noticed the illusory ruddiness and freshness (the drinker's rouge) on the Lieutenant's drawn and unshaven face. It overlay his true pallor like the glow of a red light on a white tablecloth. He's going to the dogs! thought Chojnicki.

'I've got a proposition for you!' said Trotta. 'Do you want my horse?' The question shocked him. All at once, he found it hard to go on.

'You're not a keen rider, I know that, you left the cavalry, but ... so you don't like looking after the animal and you don't care to make use of it, all right ... But you might regret it.'

'No!' said Trotta. He wanted everything out in the open. 'I need money.'

The Lieutenant felt ashamed. There was nothing dishonourable, contemptible or dubious about borrowing money from Chojnicki. But even so, Carl Joseph had the impression that with this first loan, he was embarking on a new phase of his life, for which he ought really to have had his father's permission. He felt ashamed. He said, 'Not to beat about the bush: I gave my word on a comrade's behalf. A lot of money. On top of that, he's lost a little bit more last night. I can't possibly borrow. Yes,' the Lieutenant repeated, 'it's simply impossible. The man in question already owes you.'

'But he's no business of yours then!' said Chojnicki. 'His debt to me doesn't concern you. You'll pay me back soon enough. It's a bagatelle! Listen, I'm wealthy, I'm what they call a wealthy man. Money is nothing to me. It's as if you asked me for a glass of schnapps, it's no different. Come along, what's all this fuss! Look,' Chojnicki stretched out his hand towards the horizon, and described a semi-circle with it, 'all these woods are mine. It's utterly without significance, just so you don't feel any pang of conscience. I'm grateful to anyone who will relieve me of some of it. No, ridiculous, it doesn't matter, it's silly to waste more words over it. What about this: I'll buy your horse, and you keep it for a year. Then, if you don't change your mind, it'll belong to me.'

Clearly, Chojnicki is getting impatient. Also, the battalion is moving out soon. The sun is climbing higher all the time. It's day.

Trotta hurried back to barracks. In half an hour's time, the battalion would be drawn up. He had no time to get shaved. Major Zoglauer would arrive at about eleven. (He didn't like unshaven platoon commanders. The only thing that still mattered to him after the years of frontier duty was 'immaculate turnout whilst on duty'.) Well, it was too late! He ran into the barracks. At least he'd sobered up. He ran into Captain Wagner in front of the assembled company. 'It's all fixed!' he said under his breath, and he stood in front of his platoon. And gave the order: 'In double rows, by the right. March!' His sabre glittered. The trumpets blew. The battalion moved out.

Captain Wagner stumped up for the so-called 'refreshments' in the frontier bar. There was half an hour, enough time to get two or three glasses of ninety-proof down you. Captain Wagner understood exactly that the mastery of his own destiny was almost within reach. He could direct it all by himself! This afternoon he'd have two thousand, five hundred crowns! He'd use fifteen hundred of them for repayment right away, and sit down, all calm and easy like a rich man, to play a few rounds of baccarat! He'd take the bank! He'd shuffle the cards himself! Left-handed, don't forget! Or maybe he'd only repay a thousand for now, and sit down, all calm and easy like a rich man, to play, and with five hundred for roulette, and a thousand for baccarat! That would be better yet! 'On my tab please – Captain Wagner!' he called out in the direction of the bar. And they stood up, their break was over, next up were the 'field exercises'.

Happily, Major Zoglauer didn't stay for longer than half an hour today. Captain Wagner handed over the command to First Lieutenant Zander, and galloped off to Brodnitzer's. He enquired whether there would be players to make up a game this afternoon, four-ish. Absolutely, no problem! Everything was looking incredibly promising! Even the so-called 'house-spirits', those invisible beings that Captain Wagner could sense in every gaming room, and with whom he sometimes held inaudible conversations – and even then in a sort of coded jargon he'd devised over the years – even the house-spirits here were full of benevolence towards Wagner today. In order to put them in a still better frame of mind, or perhaps prevent them changing, Wagner decided that for once he would have lunch in Brodnitzer's café, and not budge from here till Trotta came along. He stayed. A little before three in the afternoon, the first gamblers arrived. Captain Wagner started to quake. What if Trotta left him in the lurch and didn't bring the money till, say, tomorrow? Then maybe all his chances were done for. Maybe he'd never meet with another day like today! The gods were favourable, and it was a Thursday. Whereas on Friday! Appealing to Lady Luck on a Friday was a bit like asking the regimental doctor to take drill! The more time passed, the more irritably Captain Wagner thought about the delinquent Lieutenant Trotta. The young rascal wasn't coming. And he'd gone to such trouble to leave the exercise grounds early, he'd foregone his normal lunch in the station restaurant, negotiated extensively with the house-spirits, and done everything to hold on to this propitious Thursday! And now he was left in the lurch. The hand on the clock edged forward incessantly, and Trotta wasn't coming, wasn't coming, wasn't coming!

But no! Here he is! The door opens, and Wagner's eyes shine! He doesn't even shake hands with Trotta! His fingers are trembling. Every finger like an impatient thief. The very next moment, they are clutching a lovely crackling envelope. 'Have a seat!' orders the Captain. 'I'll be back in half an hour at the very outside!' And he disappeared behind the green curtain.

The half an hour passed, then an hour, then another hour. It was evening already, the lamps were lit. Slowly Captain Wagner approached. The only recognizable thing about him was his uniform, and even that was altered. The buttons gaped open, the black celluloid neck band protruded through the collar, the sabre handle was under the tunic, the pockets were stretched, and cigarette ash was sprinkled over the blouson. The Captain's parting was wrecked, his brown hair dishevelled, and under the ruffled moustache the lips gaped open. The Captain whispered, 'The lot!' and he slumped down.

There was nothing they could say to each other. Once or twice, Trotta tried to put a question. Wagner with out-thrust hand and, as it were, out-thrust eyes, motioned him to be quiet. Then he got up. He straightened his uniform. He saw that his life had lost any point it might have had. He was going to put an end to it. 'Farewell!' he said formally and walked out.

But outside, a kindly, summery evening fanned him with a myriad stars and a hundred scents. It had to be easier not to gamble any more than not to be alive any more. And he gave himself his word of honour that he would never gamble again. Sooner die than ever touch a card again. Ever! Ever was a long time, perhaps needlessly long. So: No gambling before 31 August! Then one might reconsider! Word of honour, Captain Wagner!

And with freshly salved conscience, proud of his firmness of purpose, and happy to have saved his own life, Captain Wagner walks round to Chojnicki's. Chojnicki meets him at the door. He's known the Captain long enough to tell at a glance that Wagner's lost heavily and has once again taken a vow not to gamble. And he calls out: 'Where have you left Trotta?'

'Haven't seen him!'

'The lot?'

The Captain lowers his head, looks at his toecaps and says: 'I've given my word of honour ...'

'Very good!' says Chojnicki, 'it's about time!'

He has decided to relieve Lieutenant Trotta of his friendship with that crazy Wagner. Get him out of here! thinks Chojnicki. To begin with, send him off on holiday for a few days, with Valli! And he drives into town.

'Yes!' says Trotta, unhesitatingly. He's afraid of Vienna and he's afraid of going there in the company of a woman. But he has to do it. He feels that particular clutching sensation that comes over him before every change in his circumstances. He feels he's facing a new threat, the biggest danger there can be, namely the one he's been longing for. He doesn't dare ask who the woman is. Faces of strange women, blue eyes, brown eyes, black eyes, blonde hair, black hair, hips, breasts, thighs, women he might have brushed past once, as a boy, as a lad; all floating past him quickly, all in a rush, a wonderful, delicate stream of strange women. He smells their scent; he feels their cool, firm, soft knees; already his shoulders feel the yoke of bare arms, and at his neck is the bar of clasped fingers.

There is a fear of carnality that is itself carnal, just as a certain fear of death may be deadly. This fear now gripped Lieutenant Trotta.

## 13

Frau von Taussig was beautiful and no longer young. The daughter of a stationmaster, the widow of a Master of Horse by the name of Eichberg who had died young, she had married again a few years ago, this time a recently ennobled Herr Taussig, a rich manufacturer in poor health. He suffered from a mild, so-called cyclical disorder. His fits occurred with great regularity at six-month intervals. He could feel their onset weeks in advance. Then he would check into the sanatorium on Lake Constance where pampered madmen from wealthy families were carefully and expensively treated, and the orderlies were as tender as midwives. Shortly before one of his episodes, and on the advice of one of those garrulous and fashionable doctors who prescribe 'finer feelings' to their patients just as readily as old-fashioned general practition-ers used to prescribe rhubarb or castor oil, Herr von Taussig had married the widow of his friend Eichberg. He duly had his 'finer feelings', but his next episode came on with even greater speed and violence. In the course of her brief marriage to Herr von Eichberg, his wife had made many friends, and following the death of her husband, had turned down several perfectly sincere proposals of marriage. Her extramarital affairs were hushed up, out of respect for the lady. The morals of the times were, as we know, severe. But exceptions were made, often with alacrity. This was one of a hand-ful of aristocratic principles, according to which ordinary citizens were second-class people, but the occasional middle-class officer was made personal equerry to the Emperor; according to which Jews were barred from claiming high honours, but the odd Jew was ennobled, and hobnobbed with archdukes; according to which women were expected to be first chaste and then faithful, but this or that particular woman was afforded a cavalry officer's licence to love. (All these principles we like to call hypocritical today, because we are so much more unyielding, implacable and deadly earnest.)

The only one of the widow's close friends not to make her an offer of marriage was Chojnicki. The world in which it would have been worth living was doomed. The world that would follow did not merit any decent inhabitants. So there was no sense in loving durably, in marrying and begetting heirs. With his sad, pale blue, prominent eyes, Chojnicki looked at the widow and said: 'I'm sorry, but I don't want to marry you!' With those words he ended his visit of condolence.

And so the widow married the periodically demented Taussig. She needed money, and he was less trouble than a baby. As soon as an attack was over, he would summon her. She came, permitted him a kiss, and took him off home. 'Till our next joyful reunion!' Herr von Taussig called out to the doctor who had escorted him as far as the barrier to the locked ward. 'À bientôt!' said his wife. (She loved it when her husband was away ill.) And they drove home.

It was ten years since she had last visited Chojnicki; not yet married to Taussig, she was as beautiful then as she was today, and a whole ten years younger. She hadn't returned home unac-companied that time, either. A lieutenant, young and melancholy like this one, had escorted her. He was called Ewald, and he was an Uhlan. (There had been Uhlans stationed here then.) It would have been the first true grief of her life to return home on her own; and it would have been a disappointment even if it had been, say, a first lieutenant. She didn't feel nearly old enough for more senior charges. In another ten years – perhaps.

But age drew nearer with cruel and silent tread, and oftentimes in treacherous disguise. She counted the days that ran past her, and each morning the delicate wrinkles – the hair-fine mesh that old age had spun overnight round her innocently sleeping eyes. All the while her heart remained the heart of a sixteen-year-old girl. Blessed with everlasting youth, it dwelt within an ageing body, a beautiful secret in a crumbling castle. Every young man whom Frau von Taussig received in her arms was the long-awaited guest. To her chagrin, he didn't go in beyond the antechamber. She didn't live; all she did was wait! One after the other, she watched them go, with troubled, dissatisfied, embittered expressions. Gradually, she got used to seeing men come and go, the race of infantile giants, like foolish oversized insects, at once fleeting and ponderous; an army of crass idiots who tried to flap their leaden wings; warriors who imagined themselves victorious when they were held in contempt, possessors when they were laughed at, gourmets when they had barely had a taste; a horde of barbarians that you nevertheless spent all your time waiting for. Maybe, maybe, one individual might just arise out of the confused and undistinguished mass of them, light and shining, a prince with blessed hands. But he didn't come! You waited, and he didn't come! You were growing old, and he didn't come! Frau von Taussig set up barriers of young men like dams against encroaching age. Afraid of her own illusionless vision, she walked into every one of her so-called adventures with eyes tightly shut. And with her own needs, she transfigured the foolish men for her use. Unfortunately, they failed to notice. And they were not in the least transfigured.

She ran the rule over Lieutenant Trotta. He looks old for his years, she thought: he's been through some sad experience, and failed to learn from it. He won't be a passionate lover, but maybe not superficial either. He is already so unhappy than one can only make him happy.

The following morning, Trotta was given three days' furlough 'for family reasons'. At one in the afternoon, he said goodbye to his comrades in the station dining room. Envied and cheered on, he and Frau von Taussig climbed into a first-class compartment, for which he had admittedly had to pay a surcharge.

As night fell, he became as frightened of the dark as a child; and he left the compartment to smoke, or rather claiming he needed to smoke. He stood in the corridor, full of muddled notions, watching through the black window the endless succession of evanescent fiery serpents spun from the flying sparks of the locomotive, the dense blackness of the forests and the placid stars that studded the arc of the heavens. Quietly he slid the door aside and tiptoed back into the compartment. 'Maybe we should have taken a sleeping car,' the woman remarked unexpectedly, dismayingly even, from the darkness. 'You need to smoke all the time! Well, you can smoke in here as well!' So she still wasn't asleep. The match lit up her face. It lay whitely, framed by tangled black hair, on the dark red cushions. Yes, maybe they should have taken a sleeping car. The cigarette glowed redly in the darkness. They were just going over a bridge, the clattering of the wheels was briefly louder. 'Bridges!' said the woman. 'I'm always afraid they might collapse!' Yes, thought the Lieutenant, let them! It seemed to him that his only choice was between a sudden catastrophe and a more gradual one. He sat perfectly still, facing the woman, watched the lights of the passing stations sporadically illuminate the compartment, and Frau von Taussig's face grow yet paler. He was incapable of uttering a word. Having failed to talk to her, he thought he would have to kiss her. He kept putting off the kiss. After the next station, he told himself. All at once, the woman put out her hand, felt for the bolt on the compartment door, and clicked it shut. Trotta bent down over her hand.

Frau von Taussig loved the Lieutenant with the same passion she had evinced for Lieutenant Ewald ten years previously, on the same piece of track, at the same time of day, and, who knows, perhaps in the same compartment. But for now that Uhlan was wiped away, as his predecessors and successors were too. Desire came cascading over memory, and washed away all traces. Frau von Taussig's first name was Valerie, and she went by the petname of Valli. That name, whispered to her in various intimate situations over the years, sounded new to her in this intimate situation. This young man was just christening her, she was a little girl again (as new as her name). Even so, merely from force of habit, she found herself saying ruefully that she was 'much older' than he was: a remark she always risked with her young men, out of a kind of dashing carefulness. The remark, incidentally, was the prelude to a further wave of caresses. All the tendernesses she knew and had once bestowed upon this man or that, she now fetched out once more. Next – how familiar, sadly, was the sequence of events! – there would be the inevitable plea from the man not to talk about age or time. She knew how little such pleas were worth – and she still believed them anyway. She waited. But Lieutenant Trotta didn't speak, evidently an unusually shy young man. She was afraid his silence might be a judgement on her; so she cautiously began: 'How much older do you think I am than you?' He was puzzled. What could you say to such a question, what did it matter? He felt the rapid alternation of smooth coolness and smooth heat on her skin, those abrupt climatological changes that are among the magical manifestations of love. (Within a single hour, they are capable of piling the characteristics of all four seasons on a single shoulder. They do indeed suspend the laws of time.) 'I'm old enough to be your mother!' the woman whispered. 'Guess how old I am?' 'I don't know!' said the unhappy fellow. 'Forty-one!' said Frau Valli. She had just had her forty-second birthday. But some women are prevented by nature from telling the truth; that same nature that prevents them from ever getting any older. Frau von Taussig was perhaps too proud to steal three years. But to take away just one miserable year couldn't really be accounted a theft.

'You're lying!' he said at last, with great vehemence born out of politeness. And in a new upsurge of gratitude she threw her arms around him. The white lights of the stations ran past the window, lit up the compartment, lit up her pale face, and seemed to strip her white shoulder anew. The Lieutenant lay across her breast like a baby. She felt a blissful, beneficent, maternal pang. Maternal love coursed into her arms, and gave her fresh strength. She wanted to be good to her lover as if to her own child; as though the womb had borne him, into which she now received him. 'My child, my child!' she kept saying. She was no longer afraid of old age. Yes, for the first time she blessed the years that kept her from the Lieutenant. When the morning, a sparkling early summer morning, broke through the window of the moving compartment, she fearlessly showed the Lieutenant her face unprepared for day. She was, however, counting on a little help from the dawn's redness. Because the window where she was sitting just happened to be facing east.

To Lieutenant Trotta, the world was changed. That suggested to him that he had just encountered love, or rather: his own notion of what it was. In fact, he merely felt gratitude. He was a satisfied child. 'We'll stay together when we're in Vienna, won't we?' – 'Dear child, dear child!' she kept thinking. She gazed at him, full of maternal pride, as though giving him credit for virtues he didn't possess, but which, like a mother, she attributed to him.

She prepared an endless round of little treats. It happened that their arrival coincided with the feast of Corpus Christi. She would get hold of a couple of seats on the grandstand. With him, she will watch the colourful procession, which, like all Austrian women of every social rank at that time, she adored.

She got them seats on the grandstand. The cheerful pomp of the parade projected its warm and rejuvenating glow on her. From her youth, she'd been familiar – as familiar, probably, as the master of ceremonies – with all the phases, parts and rules governing the Corpus Christi procession, in the way that old habituees of opera boxes remember all the scenes of their favourite operas. Her pleasure was in no way diminished, quite the opposite, by her intimate knowledge of the proceedings. Carl Joseph relived his boyhood dreams of heroism as he had thrilled listening to the Radetzky March in the holidays at home on his father's balcony. The whole majesty and power of the old Empire filed past beneath his eyes. The Lieutenant thought of his grandfather, the hero of Solferino, and of the unshakeable patriotism of his father, like a stout little rock among the mighty peaks of Habsburg power. He thought of his own sacred duty to die for the Emperor, at any moment, at sea, on land, and in the air too, anywhere at all. The phrases of the oath he had given once or twice mechanically came to life. They arose, one word rose after another, each of them a waving banner.

The china-blue eyes of the Supreme Commander, gone cold on so many reproductions on so many walls in the Empire, filled with new fatherly devotion and looked out at the grandson of the hero of Solferino like a whole blue sky. The pale blue trousers of the infantry shone. The coffee-brown artillery filed by with all the seriousness befitting the discipline of ballistics. The blood-red fezzes on the heads of the pale blue Bosnians burned in the sun like little bonfires of joy, lit by Islam to the Honour of His Apostolic Majesty. In black lacquered carriages sat the gold-decked Knights of the Golden Fleece, and the grave red-cheeked councillors. After them, billowing like majestic storms, restraining their impetuosity around the Emperor, came the horsehair crests of the Life Guards Infantry. Finally, led in by the crashing sounds of the beating to arms came the terrestrial but still apostolic army cherubim sing-ing the K-and-K anthem, the 'Gott erhalte', 'God preserve, God protect', over the standing crowds, the marching soldiers, the gently trotting horses, and the silently rolling carriages. It floated over all their heads, a sky of melody, a canopy of black and yellow notes. The Lieutenant's heart stopped, and at the same time it beat fiercely – a medical anomaly. In amongst the slow chords of the anthem, individual huzzahs fluttered out like little white flags surrounded by large banners with coats of arms on them. A Lipizzaner grey came tripping along, with the majestic coquetterie of the celebrated Lipizzaner breed, who received their training in the royal and imperial stud. It was followed by the drumming hooves of half a squadron of dragoons, a little thunder on parade. The black and golden helmets glinted in the sun. The calls of the brassy fanfares rang out, their voices like jolly reminders: Look out, look out, here comes the old Emperor!

And there was the Emperor: eight snow-white horses drew his carriage. Mounted on the horses, in gold-embroidered black coats and with powdered wigs were the lackeys. One might have taken them for gods, but they were only the servants of demigods. Either side of the carriage stood a couple of Hungarian Life Guards with black and yellow panther skins draped over their shoulders. They resembled the guardians on the walls of Jerusalem, the holy city whose king Emperor Franz Joseph was. The Emperor wore the snow-white coat that was familiar from all the portraits scattered throughout the Monarchy, and a mighty green bunch of parrot feathers on his hat. The feathers riffled slightly in the breeze. The Emperor smiled in all directions. On his ancient face the smile was like a little sun he had made himself. The bells rang out from St Stephen's, greetings from the church of Rome, offered to the Holy Roman Emperor of the German nation. The old Emperor climbed down from the carriage with the supple elastic stride that was so widely famed in the newspapers, and walked into the church like a common man; he walked to church, the Holy Roman Emperor of the German nation, the bells ringing in his ears.

No lieutenant of the Royal and Imperial Army would have been capable of looking on unmoved. And Carl Joseph was one of the most impressionable of lieutenants. He watched the golden gleam that was spread by the procession, and he didn't hear the grim wing-flap of the vultures. Because the vultures were already circling above the Habsburg double eagle, its fraternal foes.

No, the world wasn't doomed, whatever Chojnicki said, you could see with your own eyes how alive it was! The inhabitants of this city, cheerful subjects of His Apostolic Majesty, members virtually of his household, thronged the entire Ringstrasse. The whole city was just an extended court. In the arcades of the ancient palaces stood the liveried porters with their staffs of office, mighty gods among the lackeys. Black coaches on lofty, rubber-tyred wheels with delicate spokes were parked outside the gates. The horses stroked the paving stones with their cautious hooves. High officials in cocked hats, gold collars and narrow swords were making their way back from the procession, dignified and sweaty. Schoolgirls in white dresses, flowers in their hair and candles in their hands, were walking home, jammed in between ceremonious parents, like incarnations of their slightly distracted and somewhat overpowered souls. Over the pale hats of pale ladies, led out by their beaux as if on leashes, arced the delicate canopies of parasols. Blue, brown, black, gold- and silver-embroidered uniforms moved like rare specimens of trees and plants, escaped from some southern garden, and now striving for some distant homeland. The anthracite fire of top hats shone over eager red faces. Colourful sashes, civic rainbows, spanned broad bosoms, waistcoats and bellies. Then in two columns the Life Guards streamed across the Ringstrasse in their white angels' cloaks with red linings and white tufts of feathers, glittering halberds in their fists, and the trams, the fiacres, and even the automobiles stopped for them, as for familiar historical ghosts. On crossroads and corners, fat, tenaproned flower-sellers (the urban counterpart to fairies) watered their shining bunches of flowers from dark green watering cans, blessed passing lovers with smiling eyes, tied little bunches of lily of the valley, and all the while their old tongues prattled away. The golden helmets of the firemen, on their way to the show, sparkled like twinkling reminders of danger and catastrophe. The air was heavy with lilac and hawthorn. The sounds of the city were still not loud enough to drown out the piping of the blackbirds in the gardens and the trilling of the larks in the air. It all was poured out over Lieutenant Trotta. He sat in a coach beside his lady friend, he loved her, and he was driving, or so it appeared to him, through the first good day of his life.

And it really was as though his life were only now beginning. He learned to drink wine in the same way as he had the ninetyproof at the border. He ate with his mistress in the renowned restaurant whose manageress was as dignified as an empress, whose premises were as serene and worshipful as a temple, noble as a castle, and peaceful as a country hut. Here excellencies ate at the same tables for years, and the waiters who served them resembled them, so that it looked as though guests and waiters might change places after a certain time had elapsed. And everyone referred to everyone else by their first name like brothers; and yet they greeted each other with the punctilio of noblemen. They were au fait with the young and the old, the good horsemen and the indifferent, the lovers and the gamblers, the suave, the ambitious, the favourites, the latest of a long line of – proverbial, sanctioned and reverenced – imbeciles, and the clever chaps of whom great things were expected. Nothing was audible beyond a delicate tinkling of well-bred forks and spoons, and the smiled *sotto voce* of the diners, audible only to the party for whom it is intended, though the informed party at the next table will have no difficulty in guessing its import. The white tablecloths gave out a peaceful sheen, a restrained version of daylight came in through the high covered windows, the wine flowed from the bottles with a tender purr, and whoever wanted anything from the waiter needed only raise their eyes. Because in this civilized silence the movement of an eyebrow was like a shout elsewhere.

Yes, and that was how it began, the thing he thought of as 'life', and which may indeed have been life at that time: driving along in a well-sprung carriage through the dense aromas of a well-advanced spring, at the side of a woman who loved him. Every one of her tender glances seemed to reinforce his youthful belief that he was an outstanding man of many qualities, and, more, an 'outstanding officer' in the sense those words were given in the army. He remembered that practically all his life he had been sad and shy and one might almost say resentful. But looking at himself now, he didn't understand why he had ever been sad, shy and resentful. He had been upset by the proximity of death. But even his melancholy reflections on Katharina and on Max Demant now afforded him pleasure. As he saw it, he had been through hard times. He thoroughly deserved the tender glances of a beautiful woman. Still, he couldn't help looking at her fearfully from time to time. Was it anything more than a whim of hers to take him along like a little boy, and show him a good time for a few days?

That was not to be borne. He was, no question of that, an outstanding individual, and whoever loved him would have to love him entirely, honestly and to death, as poor Katharina had done. And who could say how many men this beautiful woman thought of while supposing or claiming she loved only him?! Was he jealous? Certainly, he was jealous! And powerless too, as he realized a moment later. Jealous and without any possibility of staying on here or driving on with this woman, keeping her with him as long as he pleased, exploring her and winning her for himself. Yes, he was a poor little Lieutenant on an allowance of fifty crowns a month from his father, and debts . . .

'Do you gamble in your barracks?' Frau von Taussig suddenly asked.

'The others do,' he said. 'Captain Wagner, for instance. He's made some enormous losses!'

'What about you?'

'Never!' said the Lieutenant. In that instant he knew how to acquire power. He rebelled against his mediocre lot. Something in him cried out for distinction. If he had become a civil servant, he might have been able to put to use some of the intellectual qualities he was sure he possessed, and make a career for himself. But what was an officer in peacetime?! What had the hero of Solferino achieved even in war, by his heroic act?!

'You really must avoid gambling!' said Frau von Taussig. 'You don't look like someone who's lucky with money!'

He felt offended. Straight away he was gripped by the desire to prove he was lucky, lucky in everything! He started hatching secret plans for today, for right now, for tonight. His embraces were only a first instalment on future embraces, rehearsals for a love that he wanted to give on the morrow, as a man not just of outstanding deserts, but of power. He kept an eye on the time, and was thinking up some excuse to leave before it got too late. Frau Valli sent him away herself. 'It's getting late, you'd better go!' 'Till tomorrow morning!' 'Tomorrow morning!'

The hotel porter told him of a nearby casino. The Lieutenant was welcomed with brisk politeness. He spotted a couple of senior officers and froze to attention in front of them. They waved to him casually, staring at him in bafflement, as though not even capable of grasping that they were being treated militarily; as though they had long ceased to be part of the army, and were merely still going around in uniform; and as though this greenhorn awoke in them a remote memory of a remote time in which they had been officers. They were at a different, perhaps a more secretive stage of their lives, and only their clothes and their stars connected them to their ordinary daily existence, which would resume tomorrow at first light. The Lieutenant reckoned up his money; it came to a hundred and fifty crowns. He put fifty of them in his pocket, as he had seen Captain Wagner do, and the rest in his cigarette case. For a while he observed at one of the two roulette tables without putting any money down: he didn't trust himself at cards, having too little understanding of them. He was both calm and astonished at his calm. He watched as the piles of red, white and blue tokens shrank and grew, and moved this way and that. It never occurred to him that he had come to watch them all land up in front of him. Finally he decided to sit down, and he felt it was no more than his duty. He won. He staked half his winnings, and won again. He didn't bet by colours and he didn't bet by numbers. He put his tokens somewhere or other, with equanimity. He won. He staked all his winnings. He won a fourth time. A major motioned to him. Trotta stood up. The Major: 'This is your first time here. You've won a thousand crowns. You'd better go now.' 'Yes, sir!' said Trotta, and he obediently went. When he cashed in his chips, he regretted having obeyed the Major. He was annoyed with himself for being so full of obedience. Why did he allow himself to be sent packing like that? And why didn't he have the courage to return? He left feeling dissatisfied with himself and unhappy with his first experience of winning.

It was late already and so quiet that you could hear the footfall of people in adjacent streets. In the strip of sky between a narrow lane's tall buildings, the stars blinked remotely and peacefully. A dark form turned the corner and approached the Lieutenant. It was swaying; a drunk, no question. The Lieutenant knew who it was right away. It was the painter Moser, on his normal nocturnal beat through the streets of the city, with his folder of pictures and his floppy hat. He touched a finger to its brim, and started to offer them. 'I've got girls here in all sorts of positions!' Carl Joseph stopped. He thought it was Fate personally sending him the painter Moser. He didn't know that, for the last several years, running into the Professor in one of these downtown streets at this time of night was a racing certainty. He took the fifty crowns he'd kept in his pocket and gave them to the old man. He did it as though someone had silently told him to; as though following a command. Just like him, he thought, just like him, he's quite happy, he's absolutely right! His own feeling alarmed him. He looked for reasons why the painter Moser should be right, could find none, felt still more alarmed, and already he felt a thirst for alcohol, a drinker's thirst, which is a thirst of the soul and the body. Suddenly you see as little as a short-sighted person, you have the feeble hearing of the deaf. You need a drink, right away. The Lieutenant turned back, caught up with the painter Moser and asked him: 'Where can we get a drink?'

There was an all-night bar not far from the Wollzeile. They had slivovitz there, unfortunately it was only about three-quarters the strength of the ninety-proof. The Lieutenant and the painter sat down and drank. Gradually it dawned on Trotta that he was far from being the master of his destiny, and far from being an exceptional man with many good qualities. Rather, he was poor and miserable and cast down about his obedience to a major who had prevented him from winning hundreds of thousands. No! He wasn't born to be lucky! Frau von Taussig and the Major in the casino and all the rest of them, everyone in fact, just laughed at him. Only this man here, the painter Moser (he could certainly call him a friend) was honest, upright and true. He should make himself known to him. This outstanding man was his father's oldest and only friend. He shouldn't be ashamed of him. He had painted Grandfather's portrait! The Lieutenant took a deep breath, in order to draw courage from the air, and said: 'We've known each other a long time, did you realize?' The painter Moser craned his neck, there was a flash of eyes under the bushy eyebrows, and he asked: 'We've – known each other? Personally, you mean? Because of course you know my work as a painter! I'm widely known as a painter. Otherwise, though, I'm sorry to say I think you're mistaken! Or?' – Moser looked downcast – 'is it possible to mistake me?'

'My name is Trotta!' said the Lieutenant.

The painter Moser looked at the Lieutenant with glassy, sightless eyes and reached out his hand. Then a thunderous sob broke from him. He pulled the Lieutenant halfway across the table, leaning across to him, and there, over the middle of the table, they kissed each other fraternally and long.

'What's he doing now, your father?' asked the Professor. 'Is he still doing the same job? Or is he a governor by now? Haven't heard from him in ages! A while ago I ran into him in the Volksgarten, he gave me some money, he wasn't alone then, he had his son with him, that fellow – hang on, that must be you.'

'Yes, that was me,' said the Lieutenant. 'It's a long time ago now, a very long time.'

He remembered the shock he had felt then at the sight of the sticky red hand on his father's leg. 'I must beg your forgiveness, yes, your forgiveness!' said the Lieutenant. 'I behaved shoddily to you then, I was shoddy to you! Please forgive me, my dear friend!'

'Yes, it was shoddy of you!' Moser agreed. 'I'll forgive you! Not another word about it! Where are you living? I'll walk you!' They were shutting the bar. Arm in arm they staggered through the silent lanes. 'This is where I'm staying,' muttered the painter. 'Here's my address! Look me up tomorrow, my boy!' And he gave the Lieutenant one of the rather vulgar business cards that he doled out to strangers in cafés.

## 14

The day the Lieutenant had to return to his garrison was a sad day and, as it happened, rather a grey one as well. He walked back through the streets where the procession had passed a couple of days before. In those days, thought the Lieutenant (in those days, he thought), he had briefly been proud of himself and his career. But today the thought of his return walked along at his side like a guard escorting a prisoner. For the first time, Lieutenant Trotta found himself rebelling against the army rules that governed his life. He had obeyed ever since he'd been a small boy. Now he didn't want to obey any more. He hardly knew what freedom was; but he felt it must be different from a holiday, in roughly the same way a war is different from a manoeuvre. The comparison occurred to him because he was a soldier (and because to a soldier war is freedom). It occurred to him that the munitions you needed for freedom was money. The sum he had on his person was like the blanks you fired during manoeuvres. What could he call his own? Could he even afford freedom? Had his grandfather, the hero of Solferino, left a fortune? Would he ever inherit it from his father? Never previously had he had such thoughts. Now they flocked to him like a crowd of strange birds, built themselves nests in his brain, and there fluttered about restlessly. Now he heard all the bewildering clamour of the big wide world. Since yesterday he'd known that this year Chojnicki planned to leave home earlier than usual, and travel south later that same week, with his mistress. And he felt jealous of his friend, a jealousy that was doubly shameful. He was on his way to the north-east frontier. But his mistress and his friend were headed South. And that 'South', which up to that moment had been a neutral geographical term, shimmered with all the iridescent colour of an unknown paradise. The South was a foreign land somewhere! And lo: there were other countries which were not subject to Emperor Franz Joseph, which had armies of their own, with many thousands of their own lieutenants in greater or lesser barracks. In these other countries, the name of the hero of Solferino was without significance. They had their own monarchs. And these monarchs had their own people to rescue them from mortal danger. It was bewildering in the extreme to follow these thoughts; for a lieutenant in the Monarchy it was just as bewildering as it might be for us to consider that the earth is only one of millions upon millions of heavenly bodies, that there are innumerable other suns in our galaxy, and that each of these suns has its own planets, and that we therefore are relegated to being a very obscure thing indeed, not to say: an insignificant speck of dust!

The Lieutenant still had seven hundred crowns of his winnings. He hadn't dared to visit another casino; and not only out of fear of the unknown major, who might have been sent there by the city commandant to keep an eye on younger officers, but also for fear of the memory of his abject flight. Oh! Of course he knew that, at the least look or gesture from a superior officer, he would leave any casino on the spot a hundred times over. And like a sickly child, he lost himself pleasantly in the painful knowledge that he was incapable of compelling fortune. He felt inordinately sorry for himself. And just then it was good for him to feel sorry for himself. He drank a few glasses of schnapps. And straight away he felt at home in his incapacity. And then, like a man entering a prison or a monastery, the money he had on him

seemed oppressive and unnecessary to the Lieutenant. He decided
to spend it all at once. He walked into the shop where his father
had bought him the silver cigarette case, and he bought a pearl
necklace for his girlfriend. With a bunch of flowers in his hand,
the pearls in his pocket, and an utterly glum expression on his face,
he appeared before Frau von Taussig. 'I brought you something,'
he said, as though to say: I've stolen something for you! He felt
he was miscast, playing this part of a playboy. And only in the
instant when he had his present in his hand, did he see that it was
rather extravagant, humiliating to himself, and possibly offensive
to someone who was after all a rich woman. 'Please forgive me!'
he said. 'I wanted to get you some little token – but –' And that
was all he was able to say. And he blushed and lowered his eyes.

Oh, Lieutenant Trotta, he didn't understand women who could
see the approach of old age! He didn't know that to them every
present is a magical gift that will rejuvenate them, and that their
wise and yearning eyes see things differently! Anyway, Frau von
Taussig adored his helplessness, and the more evident his youthful-
ness, the younger she became! And so, clever and wild, she flung
her arms round his neck, kissed him like her child, wept because
she was to lose him, laughed because she still had him, and also
a little bit because the pearls were so beautiful, and said, through
a violent splendid torrent of tears: 'My darling, darling boy!' She
regretted it straight away, because the words made her older than
she felt just then. Happily, a moment later, she noticed that he
was as proud to have been called that as if it were a distinction
bestowed upon him by the Commander-in-Chief in person. She
thought, he's still too young to know how old I am! . . .

But, in order to destroy, to eliminate her true age, to drown it
in the sea of her passion, she gripped the Lieutenant by the shoulders, his warm, tender bones already confusing her hands, and
pulled him across to the sofa. She fell upon him with her furious
desire to be young. Passion burst from her in violent arcs of flame,
and tethered the Lieutenant and pulled him down. Her eyes
blinked up in dazed gratitude at the young face above hers. The

very sight of him made her younger. And her desire to be for ever young was as great as her desire to love. For a while she thought she would never have enough of this lieutenant. A moment later, admittedly, she was saying: 'A shame you have to leave today! . . .'

'Will I never see you again?' he asked piteously, every bit the young lover.

'Wait for me, I'll be back!' And: 'Don't deceive me!' she added hurriedly, with the older woman's fear of her lover's youth and possible infidelity.

'I love only you!' replied the honest voice of a young man, to whom nothing is as important as fidelity.

And that was their leavetaking.

Lieutenant Trotta drove to the station, arrived much too early, and had to wait.

He felt as though he was already on his way. Every further minute he might have spent in the city would have been a torment, maybe even a humiliation. He took the edge off his own plight by persuading himself that he had to leave a little earlier than he actually did. At last he was able to board his train. He fell into a happy, almost uninterrupted sleep, and woke just before the border.

Waiting for him was his orderly Onufri, who told him that the town was in turmoil. The brush workers were demonstrating, and the garrison had been placed on alert.

Now Lieutenant Trotta realized why Chojnicki was leaving so early. He was heading 'South' with Frau von Taussig! While he himself was like a feeble detainee, unable to turn round on the spot, and get on the next train back!

There were no cabs waiting outside the station today. Lieutenant Trotta was forced to walk. Onufri walked behind him, carrying his grip. The little shops of the little town were closed. Iron bars bolted the wooden doors and window shutters of the low houses. Gendarmes patrolled with fixed bayonets. There was no sound to be heard, except the familiar croaking of the frogs in the swamp. The dust that the sandy soil of the region continually produced was hurled by the wind in great handfuls over roofs, walls, pile fences, wooden pavements and occasional willow trees. Hundreds of years' worth of dust seemed to lie over this forgotten world. There was no one in the streets, you had the impression that behind their barred doors and windows they had all met with a sudden death. There was a redoubled watch outside the barracks. As of yesterday, all the officers were quartered there, and Brodnitzer's hotel was empty. Lieutenant Trotta reported back to Major Zoglauer. His commanding officer told him that the trip seemed to have done him good. By the lights of a man who had been serving on the border for more than ten years, a trip could do nothing else. And, as though it were some perfectly routine matter, the Major informed the Lieutenant that a platoon of Jägers was to go out tomorrow morning early, and take up a position on the road opposite the brush factory, ready to put down with armed force if necessary any 'threat to national security' on the part of the workers. It was actually a small matter, and there was every reason to suppose that the gendarmes on their own would be sufficient to keep order; they needed to keep a cool head and not intervene prematurely; it was, finally, a decision for the civil political authorities whether the Jägers would be called upon or not; this was certainly not to the liking of any officer; how could you take your orders from a district commissioner, after all? But in the end, this ticklish duty represented a kind of distinction for the youngest lieutenant in the battalion; plus the fact that none of the other gentlemen were recently returned from furlough, and the elementary rules of decency and good comradeship would have allowed for nothing else and so . . .

'Yes, sir!' said the Lieutenant, and he dismissed.

He could have no complaints against Major Zoglauer. When he might have ordered him, he had almost begged the grandson of the hero of Solferino. And the grandson of the hero of Solferino had just had the most glorious and unexpected furlough. And now Fate had thrown this political demonstration his way. That was why he had returned to the border. He thought he knew now that a particular sort of canny and calculating Fate had first given him his furlough, only to go on to destroy him. The others were sitting in the canteen; they hailed him with an excessive delight that was more to do with their desire to hear 'a bit of news' than their feelings for the returnee, and they duly all enquired how 'it' had been. Only Captain Wagner said: 'Once tomorrow's over, he can talk about it then.' And at that, they all fell silent.

'What if I get killed tomorrow?' Lieutenant Trotta said to Captain Wagner.

'Faugh!' replied the Captain. 'A horrible death. Horrible business altogether! I feel sorry for the poor buggers really. Maybe they're right!'

It hadn't occurred to Lieutenant Trotta that they were poor buggers, and that they might be right. The Captain's remarks seemed just to him now, and he no longer doubted that they were poor buggers. So he knocked back a couple of glasses of ninety-proof, and said: 'Well, I just won't have any shooting then! And no advancing with fixed bayonet either! The gendarmes can look after themselves for all I care!'

'You'll do whatever you're told! You know that!'

No! At that moment, Carl Joseph did not know it. And very quickly he got into that state where he thought himself capable of all kinds of things. Insubordination, cashiered, triumphant resurrection as a professional gambler. He didn't want any more bodies crossing his path! 'Get out of the army!' had been Dr Max Demant's advice to him. The Lieutenant had been feeble for long enough! Instead of leaving the army, he had got himself transferred to the border. And now it was all about to come to an end. You couldn't allow them to turn you into a sort of glorified watchman tomorrow! Maybe the day after, you'll be on traffic duty and responsible for giving directions to visitors! Ridiculous, this playing at soldiers in peacetime! There will never be a war! You'll rot away in the canteens! But not Lieutenant Trotta: maybe this time next week, he'll be sitting somewhere in the 'South'!

All of which he said to Captain Wagner, aloud and with

vehemence. A couple of the others gathered round and listened. There were some who weren't out for war. Most would have been quite content, if they'd had slightly better pay, slightly more comfortable garrisons, and slightly improved prospects for promotion. Some thought Trotta odd, and even a little sinister. He was someone's protégé. He was just back from a wonderful furlough. So? And now he didn't want to move out tomorrow?

Lieutenant Trotta could feel a hostile silence all around. For the first time since he'd been in the army, he decided to challenge his comrades. And, knowing what would be guaranteed to hurt them the most, he said: 'I don't know, maybe I'll get myself put through staff school!' Of course, why wouldn't he, the other officers thought to themselves. He had come from the cavalry, let him go on to staff school. He would get himself put through the exams and become general out of turn, at an age when the likes of them would just have become captain and be allowed to put on spurs. It couldn't hurt him to go out to tomorrow's kerfuffle!

Since it was the army that controlled the timetable, he had to move out very early the next morning. It grabbed hold of time, and put it down in the place where, militarily speaking, it belonged. Even though the 'threat to national security' was not expected till lunchtime, eight o'clock found Lieutenant Trotta marching along the wide, dusty main road. Behind the even, tidy pyramids of rifles, which looked at once peaceful and dangerous, the soldiers lounged and stood and wandered around. Larks sang, crickets chirped, mosquitoes buzzed. Away in the distant fields, you could see the brightly coloured kerchiefs of the peasant women. They were singing. And sometimes the soldiers who had been born in this region replied to them with the same songs. They would have known what to do in the fields! But they didn't understand what they were waiting for here. Was it war already? Were they going to die this afternoon?

There was a little village bar nearby. Lieutenant Trotta went there to drink a ninety-proof. The low-ceilinged public bar was crowded. The Lieutenant realized that here were the workers who would assemble outside the factory at noon. Everyone fell silent when he walked in, jangling and fearsomely girded. He stood at the bar. Slowly, terribly slowly, the landlord fetched bottles and glasses. The silence thickened behind Trotta's back, a massive mountain of silence. He knocked his drink back. He felt them all waiting for him to be gone again. He would have liked to tell them that it wasn't his fault, that there was nothing he could do. But he was capable neither of speaking nor of leaving. He didn't want to appear intimidated, and he drank several more glasses of schnapps. Still they were silent. Maybe they were signalling to each other behind his back. He didn't turn round. Finally he left the pub, and had the feeling of having to force his way past a hard boulder of silence, a hundred pairs of eyes stuck in his neck like darts.

When he had returned to his platoon, it seemed a good idea to give orders to fall in at once, even though it was only ten in the morning. He was bored, and he had learned that a troop of men become demoralized by boredom, and that even rifle exercises have some ethical value. In no time, the platoon were on their feet in front of him, formed up into two ranks, and it struck him suddenly, and probably for the first time in his military career, that these men with their drilled precision were dead parts of dead machines that didn't produce anything. The whole platoon stood there impassively, all the men held their breath. But Lieutenant Trotta, who had just felt the violent and meaning silence of the workers behind his back in the bar, realized that there were at least two types of silence. And maybe, he went on to think, there were more than that, just as there were many types of sound. Nobody had commanded the workers to fall in when he walked into the bar. And yet they had gone silent. And from their silence came a sinister and noiseless loathing, just as at times the electric humidity of an impending storm comes from low and taciturn clouds.

Lieutenant Trotta strained his ears. But the dead silence of his motionless platoon emanated nothing. It was just one stony face after another. Most of them reminded him a bit of his orderly

Onufri. They had wide thick-lipped mouths they could barely close, and narrow, flashing, expressionless eyes. And, standing there in front of his platoon, under the shimmery blue canopy of the early summer day, amidst the singing of the larks around him, the chirping of the crickets, the buzzing of the mosquitoes, and still hearing the dead silence of his men more clearly than all the voices of the day, just then the unhappy Lieutenant Trotta felt for certain that this was not the place for him. Where else? he asked himself, while the platoon waited for further commands from him. Where do I belong? Not with those men sitting in the bar! In Sipolje? With my forefathers? With a plough in my hand instead of a sword? And the Lieutenant left his men standing frozen to attention.

'At ease!' he finally ordered. 'Rifles on the ground! Dismiss!'

And all was as before. The soldiers lay sprawled behind the pyramids of rifles. From distant fields came the singing of the peasant women. And the soldiers sang their songs back to them.

The gendarmes came marching up from the direction of the town, three reinforced files, accompanied by District Mayor Horak. Lieutenant Trotta knew him. He was a good dancer, a Pole from Silesia, a combination of smoothness and doughtiness. Even though you didn't know his father, still he contrived to put you in mind of him. A postman. Today, he was in uniform, as per regulation, black and green with violet trim, and he was carrying his sword. His short, blond moustache had a wheaty shimmer, and the powder on his plump and rosy cheeks could be smelled some way off. He was as cheerful as the day of a parade. 'My instructions are,' he told Lieutenant Trotta, 'to have the rally broken up immediately. Are you ready, Lieutenant?' He positioned his gendarmes all round the dismal factory yard where the rally was to take place. Lieutenant Trotta said 'Yes!' and turned his back on him.

He waited. He would have liked another ninety-proof, but he couldn't get away to the bar any more. He saw the sergeant, corporal and the lance corporal all disappear into it, and return again. He lay down on the grass by the side of the road and waited. The day grew ever fuller, the sun climbed higher, and the singing of the peasant women in the distant fields came to a stop. It seemed to Lieutenant Trotta that an immeasurably long time had passed since his return from Vienna. All he could see from those remote days was the woman, probably off in the 'South' by now, who had left him. Betrayed him, he thought. So there he was lying by the side of the road, waiting – not for the enemy, but for some demonstrators.

There they were. They were coming from the direction of the bar. They were singing, pushing a song ahead of them that the Lieutenant had never heard. It hadn't been much heard in the region. It was the 'Internationale', and it was being sung in three different languages. District Mayor Horak knew it, for professional reasons. Lieutenant Trotta couldn't make out a word of it. But the tune struck him as the musical equivalent of that silence he had earlier felt at his back. A little pompous agitation came over the sleek district mayor. He ran from one gendarme to the next. Pencil and pad in his hand. Once more, Trotta gave the order to fall in. And, like a cloud fallen to earth, the dense crowd of demonstrators moved past the grim-faced double barrier of Jägers. The Lieutenant had a sudden premonition of the end of the world. He remembered the colour and splendour of the procession at Corpus Christi, and for a moment the grey cloud of rebels seemed to be hurtling against the imperial procession. For a split second, the Lieutenant was endowed with a lofty visionary power; and he saw the epochs rolling one against the other like two boulders, and himself, the Lieutenant, being crushed between the pair of them.

His platoon shouldered arms, while over yonder, lifted up by invisible hands, the head and shoulders of a man appeared over the dense, dark and turbulent mass of people. From that moment forth, the floating body formed almost the exact centre of the circle. His hands reached up into the sky. Incomprehensible sounds were uttered from his mouth. The crowd roared back. Next to the Lieutenant, notebook and pencil in hand, stood Mayor Horak. All at once, he clapped his notebook shut, and slowly, between two gleaming policemen, he strode towards the crowd on the opposite side of the street.

'In the name of the law!' he called out. His high voice was heard above the speaker's. The assembly was officially dissolved.

For a second there was silence. Then there was a massed shout from the whole crowd. Next to the faces appeared the white fists of the men, every face flanked by a couple of white fists. The gendarmes closed ranks, and formed a cordon. The next moment, the crescent-shaped mass of people was surging forward. They ran yelling towards the gendarmes.

'Fix bayonets!' ordered Trotta. He drew his sabre. He didn't see the way it flashed in the sunlight, sending a fleeting, playful and provocative reflection over to the shady side of the street, where the people had assembled. The knobs of the gendarmes' helmets and the points of their bayonets had suddenly been swallowed up by the crowd. 'To the factory!' ordered Trotta. 'Platoon, march!' The Jägers moved forward, to be greeted by dark lumps of iron, brown boards and white rocks; there was a whistling and whirring, a puffing and humming. Light as a weasel, Horak ran alongside the Lieutenant, whispering: 'Tell them to shoot, Lieutenant, for heaven's sake!'

'Platoon, halt!' ordered Trotta, and, 'Fire!'

The Jägers loosed off the first salvo, as Major Zoglauer had specified, into the air. It was followed by complete silence. For a moment, one could hear all the peaceable sounds of the summer noontide. And one could feel the generous warmth of the sun through the dust stirred up by the soldiers and the crowd, and also through the slowly dissipating scorched smell of ammunition. All at once, the high wail of a woman's voice rent the midday air. And since some in the crowd evidently believed she had been hit by a bullet, they began again to throw whatever they had to hand at the troops. And a handful of throwers were followed by more, and finally by all of them. A few Jägers in the front rank had already slumped to the ground, and while Lieutenant Trotta stood there indecisively, with his sabre in his right hand, and groping for his pistol holster with his left, he heard the whisper of Horak at his side: 'Shoot! For God's sake, shoot!' In the space of a single second, hundreds of incomplete thoughts and notions raced through Lieutenant Trotta's excited brain, some of them simultaneously, and a muddle of voices in his breast told him now to have sympathy, now to be ruthless, reminding him what his grandfather would have done in this situation, threatened him with death in the next instant, and at the same time presented his death as the only possible and desirable outcome for this fight. He had an impression of someone raising his hand, from within him a voice he didn't know repeated the order to 'Fire!' and he just managed to notice that this time the rifles were levelled at the crowd. A second later, that was all he knew. For part of the crowd that had originally been put to flight, or had given the appearance of fleeing, had, it now seemed, merely taken a circuitous route round, and was now charging at the Jägers from behind, so that Lieutenant Trotta's platoon was caught between two enemies. Even as the Jägers were loosing off their second salvo, their necks and backs were assailed by stones and nailed planks. Struck on the head by one of these, Lieutenant Trotta fell to the ground unconscious. The now leaderless Jägers fired indiscriminately at their attackers on all sides, and forced them back. The whole thing lasted perhaps three minutes. When they formed up in their double rows again, under their non-commissioned officer, the dusty highway was littered with wounded soldiers and workers, and it took a long time for the ambulance wagons to arrive. Lieutenant Trotta was taken to the little garrison hospital, where he was diagnosed with a broken skull and left collarbone, and a possibility of brain fever. An evidently meaningless coincidence had given the grandson of the hero of Solferino the broken collarbone. (Incidentally, no one alive, with the possible exception of the Emperor, could have known that the Trottas owed their rise to the hero of Solferino's collarbone.)

Three days later, the brain fever did indeed set in. And the District Commissioner would certainly have been notified, had the Lieutenant not urgently beseeched the Major, once he had come to on his first day in hospital, on no account to inform his father of the events. The Lieutenant had lapsed back into unconsciousness, and there was even reason to fear for his life; but nevertheless the Major decided to wait it out. And so it came about that the District Commissioner didn't get to hear about the insurrection at the border and the unhappy role played by his son, until two weeks later. He learned of it from the newspapers, who had it courtesy of some opposition politicians. For the opposition was determined to blame the army, the Jäger battalion, and specifically Lieutenant Trotta, who had given the orders to fire, for the casualties, the widows and the orphans. And the Lieutenant was now threatened with a type of investigation, which is to say: a formal commission of inquiry designed to mollify the politicians, composed of War Ministry officials, and used by them as an occasion to rehabilitate and ultimately even to honour the accused. The District Commissioner, however, was in no way relieved. He even sent a couple of wires to his son, and one to Major Zoglauer. The Lieutenant was by now on the mend. He was still immobilized in bed, but his life was no longer in danger. He wrote a brief account of the events, and sent it to his father. His own condition didn't worry him. What he thought about was that once more he had left dead people on his path, and he was determined to leave the army at last. Preoccupied as he was, it would have been impossible for him to see and speak to his father, however much he yearned to do so. He felt a sort of homesickness for his father, while knowing at the same time that his father was no longer home. The army was no longer his profession. And however much he abominated the sequence of actions that had caused him to fetch up in hospital, still, he welcomed his infirmity because it put off the need to take decisive action. He abandoned himself to the sorry smell of carbolic, the bleak whiteness of the walls and sheets, the pain, the changing of dressings, the firm and motherly gentleness of the nurses, and the boring visits from his perennially cheerful comrades. He read a couple of books that his father had once recommended to him – he hadn't read anything since his cadet school days – and every line reminded him of his father and the quiet Sunday mornings in summer, and of Jacques, Bandleader Nechwal and the Radetzky March.

There visited him one day Captain Wagner, sat at his bedside a long time, said a word here and a word there, stood up, sat down again. Finally, with a sigh, he pulled a bond from his jacket, and asked Trotta to sign it. It was for one thousand five hundred crowns. Kapturak had specifically asked for Trotta's guarantee. Captain Wagner became very animated, told some rigmarole about some racehorse that he wanted to buy cheaply and race in Baden, tossed in one or two more anecdotes and suddenly left. Two days later, the head doctor, worried and pale-looking, appeared at Trotta's bedside and told him Captain Wagner was dead. He had shot himself in the frontier woods. He left a note to all his comrades and fond greetings to Lieutenant Trotta.

The Lieutenant didn't give another thought to the bond and the consequences of his signature. He lapsed into fever. He dreamed – and, dreaming, babbled – about being called by the dead, and that it was time for him now to quit the earth. Old Jacques, Max Demant, Captain Wagner and the unknown dead workers all stood in a row, calling to him. Between him and them there was an empty roulette wheel, on which the ball, though moved by no human hand, spun without cease.

His fever lasted for two weeks. A welcome pretext for the military authorities to put off the investigation a little longer, and to remind various political bodies that the army had suffered its share of losses, that the political authorities in the frontier town bore some responsibility, and that the gendarmerie should have been reinforced sooner. A vast file was opened on the case of Lieutenant Trotta, and the file grew and grew, and every office in every department sprinkled a little more ink over it, the way you water flowers to make them grow, until finally the whole affair was brought to the attention of the imperial War Office, because a particularly attentive senior auditor had discovered that the

Lieutenant was the grandson of the erstwhile hero of Solferino, who had stood in some now rather obscure but certainly close relation to the Supreme Commander-in-Chief; higher authorities might well therefore take some interest in this particular lieutenant; and so it would be advisable to wait before setting up the investigation of the case.

Which was why, one morning at seven o'clock, the Emperor, newly returned from Bad Ischl, came to be concerned with a certain Carl Joseph Baron Trotta and Sipolje. And since the Emperor, though refreshed by his sojourn at Bad Ischl, was an old man, he was unable to account for the fact that the name Trotta was somehow connected in his mind to the battle of Solferino, and he left his desk and walked up and down his plain study with his old man's short steps, up and down, up and down, until his old manservant wondered at it and knocked on the door.

'Come in!' said the Emperor. And, seeing his manservant: 'What time's Montenuovo coming?'

'Eight o'clock, Your Majesty!'

That was half an hour away. And the Emperor felt he couldn't bear this state of his for such a long time. Why, why was it that the name of Trotta reminded him of Solferino? And why could he not remember the connection? Was he already so old? Ever since getting back from Ischl, he'd been preoccupied with the question of his age, because it suddenly struck him as rather odd that you needed to subtract the year of your birth from the current year to calculate your age, but that the years always began with the month of January, while his birthday was on 18 August! Why didn't the year begin in August! Even if he'd happened to be born on 18 January then it wouldn't have mattered so much! But this way, you could never be certain whether you were eighty-two and in your eighty-third year, or eighty-three and in your eighty-fourth! And the Emperor didn't like to ask. Everyone was so busy anyway, and in the end it didn't really matter if you were a year older or a year younger, and even if you were younger, it still didn't help you remember why that wretched Trotta reminded you of Solferino.

The Comptroller of the Household would know. But he wasn't due till eight o'clock. Still, perhaps his manservant would know?

And the Emperor stopped on his skippy walk, and asked his servant, 'I say: Does the name "Trotta" mean anything to you?'

The Emperor had intended to say *du* to his manservant, as he often did, but this was a question of global historical importance, and he felt duty-bound to respect anyone to whom he was turning for information on such historical events. 'Trotta!' said the Emperor's manservant. 'Trotta!'

He was old himself, the manservant, and he had a very dim recollection of a page in his school reader headed: 'The Battle of Solferino'. And suddenly memory beamed across his face like a sun. 'Trotta!' he cried, 'Trotta! That was the man who saved Your Majesty's life!'

The Emperor went up to his desk. Through the open study window came the jubilation of the matutinal birds of Schönbrunn. It seemed to the Emperor that he was young again, and he heard the clattering of rifles, and he felt himself seized by the shoulder and pulled to the ground. And all at once, the name Trotta seemed very familiar to him, as familiar as Solferino.

'Ah, yes,' said the Emperor holding up his hand in acknowledgement, and wrote on the margin of the Trotta file: 'To be settled favourably!'

Then he got up again, and went over to the window. The birds were jubilant; and the old man smiled at them, quite as if he could see them.

## 15

The Emperor was an old man. He was the oldest emperor in the world. All round him, Death was drawing his circles, mowing and mowing. Already the whole field was bare, and only the Emperor, like a forgotten silver stalk, still stood and waited. His hard and bright eyes had been looking confusedly into a confused distance for many years. The curve of his skull was as bare as a desert. His whiskers were as white as a pair of snowy wings. The creases in his face were a tangled shrubbery where the decades lived. His body was lean, his back slightly stooped. At home he walked around with short pattering little steps. But as soon as he set foot on the street outside, he tried to make his thighs sinewy, his knees supple, his feet light, his back straight. He filled his eyes with an unnatural goodness, and with the true quality of imperial eyes: that of appearing to look at anyone who looked at the Emperor, and to greet anyone who greeted him. But in reality, the faces fluttered and flew past him, and his eyes remained fixed on the fine line that marks the border between life and death, the line of the horizon, which the eyes of old people always see, even when there are houses or forests or mountains obscuring it from sight. People believed Franz Joseph knew less than they did, because he was so much older than they were. But it was possible that he knew more. He saw the sun go down on his kingdom, but he didn't say anything. He knew he would die even before it went down. Sometimes he feigned ignorance, and was glad to be enlightened about things he understood perfectly well. For with the cunning of small children and the old, he loved to mislead people. And he was glad of the vanity with which they kept trying to prove to themselves how much cleverer they were. He hid his cleverness in simplicity: for it is not right for an emperor to be as clever as his ministers. He would rather appear simple than too clever. When he went hunting, he knew very well that they set the quarry in front of his rifle, and, though he might have been able to shoot at another, he shot only what had been driven in front of him. Because it's not right for an old emperor to show that he can see through a deception, and that he can shoot better than a forester. When they told him a fairy story, he made as if he believed it. Because it's not right for an emperor to catch someone telling a lie. If they smiled when his back was turned, he pretended not to know. Because it's not right for an emperor to know that there are people smiling about him; the smiles are of no consequence, as long as he doesn't interest himself in them. If he had a temperature and everyone around him was trembling, and his personal physician denied there was anything the matter with him, the Emperor said: 'That's all right then!' even though he knew he had a temperature. Because an emperor isn't there to prove a doctor's lying. And anyway he knew that the hour of his death was not yet come. He had lived through many feverish nights that his doctors knew nothing about. Because he was ill sometimes, and no one was aware of it. And on other occasions, when he was well, and they said he was ill, then he pretended that he was ill. Where people took him to be kindly, he was actually indifferent. And where they said he was cold, he felt a pang in his heart. He had lived long enough to know the folly of telling the truth. He left people in error, and he had still less belief in the continued existence of his world than the jokers all over his great empire who poked fun at him. But it's not done for an emperor to measure himself against jokers and smart alecs. And so the Emperor held his peace.

Although he had recovered, and his physician was pleased with his pulse rate and his lungs and his breathing, he had had a catarrh since yesterday. It didn't occur to him to draw anyone's attention to it. He might be prevented from attending the autumn manoeuvres on the eastern frontier, and he wanted to watch the manoeuvres again at least once more in his life, if only for a day. The action of the man who had saved his life, and whose name he had forgotten again, had put him in mind of Solferino. He didn't like wars (he knew they ended in defeat), but he loved the army, war games, uniforms, rifle drill, parades, marches past and company exercises. It sometimes upset him that officers were allowed to wear caps with higher peaks than his own, and pleats and patent leather shoes, and absurdly high collars on their tunics. Quite a few of them were even clean-shaven. Not all that long ago, he had run into a clean-shaven militia officer on the street, and that had spoiled his whole day. But when he went out to see them, they remembered what was right and what was merely foppish. Sometimes he would give someone a dressing-down. Because in the army, everything was right for an emperor, in the army even the Emperor was a soldier. Oh! He loved the blare of trumpets, even though he had to pretend it was the tactical plans that interested him. And though he knew perfectly well that God had put him on his throne, from time to time he would still feel irked that he wasn't an officer in the front line, and he bore a grudge against his general staff. He remembered how, after the battle of Solferino, he had yelled at the disorderly troops like a sergeant and straightened them out. He was convinced – but to whom could he ever say so! – that ten good sergeants were worth more than twenty general-staffers. He longed for manoeuvres!

He decided, therefore, that he would keep quiet about his catarrh, and make as little use as possible of his handkerchief. No one was to know in advance, he wanted to take the manoeuvres by surprise, and the whole region, by simply turning up there. He looked forward to the despair of the civil authorities, when they saw that their security precautions were inadequate. He wasn't scared. He knew perfectly that the hour of his death was not yet come. He terrorized them all. They tried to talk him out of it. He wasn't having it. One day, he boarded the royal train and trundled east.

In the village of Z., not more than ten miles from the Russian frontier, he was billeted in an old castle. The Emperor would rather have stayed in one of the huts where his officers were put up. It was years since he'd had his last taste of a soldier's life. Once, only once, namely in that unhappy Italian campaign, he'd seen a real live flea in his bed, but he hadn't told anyone about it. Because he was an emperor, and an emperor doesn't talk about insects. That had been his view, even then.

They shut the windows in his bedroom. At night – he couldn't sleep, while all around slept those who were supposed to be guarding him – the Emperor got out of bed in his long, rumpled nightgown, and softly, softly, so as not to wake anyone, he opened the high, narrow side window. He stood there for a while, breathing in the cool air of the autumnal night, watching the stars in the deep blue sky, and the reddish campfires of the soldiers. He had once read a book about himself, which had the sentence in it: 'Franz Joseph I is no romantic.' They say in their books, thought the old man, that I'm no romantic. But I love campfires. He would have loved to be an ordinary lieutenant, and young. Maybe I'm no romantic, he thought, but I'd give anything to be young! If I'm not mistaken, the Emperor mused further, I was just eighteen when I came to the throne. When I came to the throne – the phrase seemed terribly daring to the Emperor, just then he was finding it difficult to take himself for the Emperor at all. But of course! It was all in the book that had been presented to him, with the usual respectful dedication. There could be no doubt but that he was Franz Joseph I! Outside his window hung the endless, deep blue, starry sky. The land around was flat and deep. They had told him his windows were facing north-east. So he was looking towards Russia. The border couldn't of course be seen. But at that moment Emperor Franz Joseph would have liked to see the border of his empire. His empire! He smiled. The night was blue and round and deep and full of stars. The Emperor stood by the window, old and thin, in a white nightshirt, and he seemed very tiny to himself in front of the illimitable night. The least of his soldiers on watch outside the tents was mightier than he was. The least of them! And he was the Supreme Commander-in-Chief! Every one of his soldiers swore an oath of allegiance by Almighty God to Emperor Franz Joseph I.

He was a monarch by the Grace of God, and he believed in Almighty God. Behind the gold-spangled blue of the heavens the Almighty was hiding – unimaginable! They were His stars that were glittering in the sky, and His sky that hung over the earth, and one piece of this earth, namely the Monarchy of Austria-Hungary, he had apportioned to Franz Joseph I, who was a skinny old man, standing in front of an open window, half-afraid of being caught by his guards at any moment. The crickets chirruped. Their song, as endless as the night, awoke the same awe in the Emperor as the stars. Sometimes the Emperor had the sense that it was the stars themselves that were singing. He shivered mildly. But he was afraid too to close the window, it might not be as easy as opening it. His hands shook. He thought he must have been here before sometime, watching manoeuvres, many years ago. Even this bed-room now seemed to have something distantly familiar about it. But he had no idea whether it was ten years, or twenty, or still more that had elapsed since then. He felt as though he was adrift on a sea of time – not heading for anywhere, just bobbing about on the surface, often pushed back to rocks he had probably encountered before. One day, he was bound to go under. He felt a sneeze coming on. Yes, his catarrh! Nothing stirred in the anteroom. Cautiously he shut the window, and pattered back to bed on his bare bony feet. The image of the curved, starry expanse of heaven accompanied him. He kept it behind his closed eyes. And so he fell asleep, canopied by the night, as if he were sleeping in the open.

He awoke, as he always did when he was 'in the field' (as he liked to refer to manoeuvres), punctually, at four o'clock. There was a footman in the room already. And behind the door, he knew, were his equerries. Yes, it was time to start the day. All day, he would have hardly an hour to himself. Luckily, he had outwitted the lot of them in the night just past, and had spent fully a quarter of an hour standing by the open window. He thought back to his cannily stolen pleasure, and smiled. He giggled at the servant, and at the lackey who just walked into the room and froze, terrified by the Emperor's giggle, by His Majesty's braces, which he had never seen before in his life, by the still wild-looking, somewhat tangled whiskers, between which the giggling was wheezing in and out like a soft, tired old bird, by the yellow complexion of the Emperor, and his bald head which was flaking. He couldn't even tell whether he ought to smile along with the old man or wait in silence. All at once, the Emperor began to whistle. He really did purse his lips, the wings of his dundrearies moved a little closer together, and the Emperor whistled a tune, a familiar, if somewhat distorted tune. It sounded like a tiny shepherd's flute. And the Emperor said: 'That's the tune Hojos keeps whistling. I'd love to know the name of it!' But neither of them, neither the servant nor the equerry could help; and a little while later, when he was washing, the Emperor had forgotten the tune again.

It was a daunting day. Franz Joseph looked at the piece of paper where his engagements were listed, hour by hour. The only church in the town was Greek Orthodox. So first a Roman Catholic priest will read mass, then a Greek Orthodox one. He found liturgical ceremonies terribly draining. He had the feeling of having to pull himself together in God's presence, as before some superior. And he was already so old! He could have made it a little easier for me! thought the Emperor. But God is even older than I am, and His ways are just as mysterious to me as mine may be to the men in my army! And where would it end, if every inferior were able to criticize his superiors! Through the high arched window, the Emperor watched God's sun climb. He crossed himself, and knelt down. He had watched the sun rise every single day for time immemorial. All his life, he was up before dawn, the way a soldier gets up before his commander. He had known all sorts of dawns; the happy, flaring dawns of summer, and the dim, slow, tardy ones of winter. He didn't remember dates, the days and months and years when good fortune or catastrophe had befallen him; but he could remember the mornings that had ushered in every significant day of his life. And he knew that one morning had been bright, and another dull. And every morning, he had crossed himself and knelt down, just as some trees spread their leaves to the sun every morning, no matter whether the day is one bringing with it storm, or the woodman's axe, or a lethal freeze late in spring, or peace and warmth and life.

The Emperor got to his feet. His barber came. The same time every day, he thrust out his chin, and his whiskers were trimmed and brushed. The cool metal of the scissors tickled around his ears and nostrils. Sometimes it made the Emperor sneeze. Today he was sitting in front of a small, oval mirror, and with wry amusement he followed the movements of the barber's skinny hands. With every little hair that fell, every stroke of the razor, and every sweep of the comb or brush, the barber leaped back, and gasped: 'Majesty!' with trembling lips. The Emperor didn't catch the word. He only saw that the barber's lips were in continual motion, didn't dare ask, and finally concluded the fellow was a bit nervous. 'What's your name?' asked the Emperor. The barber – he already had a corporal's rank, even though he'd been with the militia for just six months, since he served his colonel impeccably, and enjoyed the goodwill of his superiors – leaped as far back as the door this time. He did so elegantly, as his occupation demanded, but also somewhat militarily; it was a leap, and a bow and a standing to attention practically simultaneously, and the Emperor nodded approvingly. 'Hartenstein!' yelled the barber. 'Why d'you keep jumping around like that?' asked Franz Joseph. But he received no reply. The Corporal once more hesitantly approached the Emperor and with nimble hands finished the work. He wished he could

be very far away, back in camp. 'Stay a while!' said the Emperor.
'So you're a corporal! Have you been serving long?' 'Half a year,
so please Your Majesty!' whispered the barber. 'Well, now! And
already a corporal? In my day,' said the Emperor, quite as if it
had been a veteran speaking, 'it used to take a lot longer than
that! But you're a fine-looking soldier. Do you mean to stay in
the army?' – Barber Hartenstein had a wife and child and a nice
little business in Olmütz, and had already tried a couple of times
to feign arthritis, to get an early discharge. But he couldn't say no
to the Emperor. 'Yes, Your Majesty!' he said, and he knew at that
moment that he'd made a mess of his entire life. 'Well, that's good.
You're a sergeant now! But don't you be so nervous!'

There. Now the Emperor had made someone happy. He was
pleased. He was pleased. He was pleased. He had done a wonderful
thing for that Hartenstein. Now the day might begin. His carriage was already waiting. They drove slowly up the hill on top
of which stood the Greek Orthodox church. Its golden doubled
cross sparkled in the morning sun. Army bands played the 'Gott
erhalte'. The Emperor got out and walked into the church. He
knelt down in front of the altar, moved his lips, but didn't pray. He
was still thinking about the barber. The Almighty couldn't bestow
such sudden favours upon his Emperor as the Emperor could upon
a corporal, and that was a pity. King of Jerusalem: that was the
highest rank that God had to offer a crowned head. And Franz
Joseph was already King of Jerusalem. Pity, thought the Emperor.
Someone whispered to him that the Jews in the village were still
waiting for him. They'd been completely forgotten. Oh dear, the
Jews as well, thought the Emperor. All right! Have them come!
But they'd better hurry. Otherwise he'd be late for the battle.

The Greek priest finished the mass with great dispatch. Once
again, the bands struck up 'Gott erhalte'. The Emperor left the
church. It was nine o'clock. The battle was at twenty past. Franz
Joseph decided he would mount his horse now, and not get in
the carriage again. He could greet those Jews on horseback just
as well. He had the carriage drive back, and he rode to meet the

Jews. At the edge of the village, where the broad highway began that led to his billet, and to the designated battlefield as well, they surged towards him, a swarthy cloud. Like a field full of strange black grain in the wind, the community of Jews bowed before the Emperor. He saw their bent backs from the saddle. Then he rode nearer, and could make out the long, silver-white, coal-black and fire-red beards that were moving in the mild autumnal breeze, and the long, bony noses that seemed to be looking for something on the ground. The Emperor, in his blue cloak, sat on his white horse. His whiskers shone in the silvery autumnal sun. From the fields round about rose white tufts of mist. The leader of the Jews surged up to the Emperor, an old man with a waving beard in the black-striped prayer coat of the Jews. The Emperor was riding at a trot. The feet of the old Jew grew slower and slower. Finally he seemed to be standing in one place, and still to be moving. Franz Joseph shivered slightly. He stopped, so abruptly as to make his horse rear. He dismounted. His retinue followed suit. He walked. His highly polished boots became coated with the dust of the road, their narrow seams clogged with heavy grey dung. The black rout of Jews surged towards him.

Their backs rose and fell. Their coal-black, fire-red and silver-white beards billowed in the breeze. The elder stopped three paces before the Emperor. He carried a large purple roll of the Torah in his arms, ornamented with a golden crown whose bell was tinkling softly. Then the Jew held up the Torah to the Emperor. And his overgrown, toothless mouth began to mumble in an incomprehensible language the blessing that Jews have to speak when they see an emperor. Franz Joseph inclined his head. Above his black cap, it was a fine, silvered, Indian summer, the wild ducks were hooting in the air, a cock crowed in a faraway farmyard. Other than that, it was perfectly silent. From the rout of Jews an indistinct muttering arose. Their backs bent still further. The silvery blue sky stretched across the earth, without a cloud, without end. 'Blessed art thou!' said the Jew to the Emperor. 'Thou shalt not witness the end of the world!' I know, thought Franz Joseph.

He shook hands with the old man. He turned. He mounted his white horse.

He turned left and trotted across the hard crusts of the autumn fields, followed by his retinue. The words that Captain of Horse Kaunitz addressed to his companion next to him were carried to the Emperor on the wind: 'I didn't understand a syllable of what that Jew was saying!' The Emperor turned in his saddle and said: 'Never you mind, Kaunitz, he was talking to me!' and he rode on.

He didn't understand what the manoeuvres were about. He only knew that the 'Reds' were fighting the 'Blues'. He asked to have it explained to him. 'I see,' he kept saying, 'I see.' He liked giving the impression of trying to understand, and failing. The fools! he thought. He shook his head at them. But they thought his head was shaking because he was old. 'I see,' the Emperor kept repeating, 'I see.' The exercise was fairly well advanced. The Blues' left flank, at present a mile and a half behind the village of Z., had been on the retreat for the past couple of days, under pressure from the Red cavalry. Their centre was occupying the area around P., hilly ground, difficult to attack, easy to defend, but also liable to be cut off – and that was presently what the Reds were endeavouring to do: to sever the Blues' left and right wings from their centre. While the left wing was withdrawing, however, the right was holding firm, in fact it was advancing slowly, and gave every indication of extending so far as to give the impression that it meant to outflank the enemy. It was, in the opinion of the Emperor, a pretty humdrum situation. If he'd been in command of the Reds, he would have lured the Blues' advancing wing on by continued withdrawal, and tied down its vanguard, so that before long a weak point would have been identified between it and the centre. But the Emperor said nothing. He was distracted by the monstrous appearance of Colonel Lugatti, a Triestine and a dandy of a sort that, in the unshakeable opinion of Franz Joseph, only Italians could be, who wore his coat-collar cut high, higher even than tunic collars were allowed to be, and, in order to show his rank, had left that repulsively high collar open in the most coquettish way. 'Would you mind telling me, Colonel,' asked the Emperor, 'where you have your coats made? In Milan? I'm afraid to say I've quite forgotten the names of the tailors there.' Staff Colonel Lugatti clicked his heels together and did his coat up. 'One might take you for a lieutenant now,' said Franz Joseph. 'You look so dashing!' And he set spurs to his horse, and galloped over to the hill, where, just as in pictures of historic battles, the generals were watching. He was determined that if the whole thing went on for too long, he would have the 'battle' called off, because he wanted to see the march past. Franz Ferdinand was different. He liked to take sides, began to issue commands, and of course always came out on top. Where was the general who had ever bested the heir to the throne? The Emperor's old, pale blue eyes took in the faces around him. What a vain lot! he thought. Even a couple of years ago, he would have lost his temper with them. Not any more, not any more! He wasn't quite sure how old he was, but when the others were around him, he felt he must be very old. Sometimes he had the feeling that he was drifting away from them and from the whole world, as though they were all shrinking the longer he looked at them. The things they said reached his ears from a vast distance, and then bounced away meaninglessly. And if one or other of them had some bit of bad news, he could see how hard they tried to break it to him gently. Oh, they didn't know he could take everything! The great sorrows were already at home in his breast, and new sorrows joined them like long-lost brothers. He no longer got so angry. He no longer felt so happy. He no longer suffered so keenly. In the end he did call off the 'hostilities', and it was time for the march past. They formed up on the endless plains, the regiments of all the various branches, regrettably in field-grey (another one of those new-fanglednesses that the Emperor didn't care for). But even so, the blood-red of the cavalry trousers scorched over the dry yellow of the stubble fields, and broke from the infantry grey like fire from clouds. The narrow matt lightning of sabres flashed against the single and double lines of marching men, the red crosses on white ground glowed behind the machine-gun emplacements. Like old war gods on their heavy waggons, the artillerymen trundled up, and the beautiful bay and chestnut horses reared up in proud and strong subservience. Through his field glasses, Franz Joseph observed the movements of every single platoon; for a few minutes he felt proud of his army and for a few minutes he also felt regret for its loss. Because he could already see it defeated and broken up, distributed among the many peoples of his great empire. He could see the great golden sun of the Habsburgs sinking, smashing on the bottom of the universe, crumbling into various littler suns, which would shine as independent bodies to independent nations. They've just had enough of my rule, thought the old man. And there's nothing to be done about that! he added fatalistically. Because he was an Austrian ...

Then, to the consternation of all his commanders, he made his way down from the hill, and began to inspect the stationary regiments, almost platoon by platoon. From time to time, he walked between ranks, examined the new knapsacks and bread bags, occasionally he would pull out a can of something and ask what was in it, occasionally he would peer into a rigid face and ask it questions about home and family and work, barely taking in what was said in reply, and sometimes he would put out his old hand and pat a lieutenant on the back. In this way, he came to the battalion of Jägers with which Trotta was serving.

Trotta had been out of hospital for just four weeks. He stood before his platoon, pale, thin and apathetic. But as the Emperor came nearer, he began to notice and to regret his apathy. He had the sense that he was failing in his duty. The army meant nothing to him. The Commander-in-Chief meant nothing to him. Lieutenant Trotta was like a man who had lost not only his home, but also his homesickness, his nostalgia for that home. He felt pity for the white-bearded old man who was coming ever nearer, curiously taking knapsacks, bread bags and cans in his hands and turning them over. The Lieutenant could have wished himself back in that state of exaltation that had always taken him in the ceremonial hours of his army career – on summer Sundays at home, at every previous parade, when he had gained his commission, and even just a few months ago, at the Corpus Christi procession in Vienna. Now, nothing stirred in Lieutenant Trotta. As he stood barely five paces from his Emperor, nothing stirred in his out-thrust chest except pity for an old man. Major Zoglauer barked out the appropriate phrases. For some reason, the Emperor took against him. Franz Joseph had the suspicion that something was amiss in the battalion that this man commanded, and he thought he would take a closer look at it. He gazed intently into the unmoving faces, pointed to Carl Joseph, and asked: 'Is he ill?'

Major Zoglauer reported on what had happened to Lieutenant Trotta. The name had a familiar, and also a vaguely irksome ring to Franz Joseph's ear, and in his memory the incident surfaced as it had been reported in the files, and behind that incident there stirred a recollection of the long-forgotten battle of Solferino. He could still see the Captain at that ridiculous audience, passionately pleading for the removal of a piece in a patriotic primer. It was piece number fifteen. The Emperor remembered the number with the delight that trivial evidence of his 'good memory' never failed to afford him. His mood brightened visibly. Major Zoglauer didn't seem such a bad fellow any more. 'I remember your father very well!' said the Emperor to Trotta. 'He was a very modest man, the hero of Solferino!' 'Your Majesty,' replied the Lieutenant, 'that was my grandfather!'

The Emperor reeled, as though knocked backwards by the colossal time that had suddenly thrust its bulk between the young man and himself. Well, well! He could remember the number of the piece in the primer, but not the vast number of years he had put behind him. 'Ah!' he said, 'so that was your grandfather! Well, well! And your father's a colonel or something?' 'He's District Commissioner in W.' 'Well, well!' repeated Franz Joseph. 'I'll make a note of it!' he added: an apology of a sort for the mistake he had made.

He stood a while longer in front of the Lieutenant, but he

saw neither Trotta nor any of the others. He no longer felt like inspecting the ranks, but he probably had to, lest people notice how much his own age had shocked him. His eyes were once more fixed on the distance, as they generally were, where the edges of infinity had come a little closer. He failed to notice, therefore, that a crystalline drop had appeared on the end of his nose, and that everyone was staring in helpless fascination at this drop, which finally, finally, fell into the thick, silver moustache and there disappeared from view.

And then everyone felt relieved. And the march past could begin.

PART THREE

## 16

Various important changes were afoot in the life and household of the District Commissioner. He registered them with surprise and a little annoyance. Subtle indications, though they seemed momentous enough to him, gave him to understand that the world about him was changing, and he remembered Chojnicki's prophesies, and wondered if it was coming to an end. He was looking for a new manservant. He was recommended a fair few young and obviously sound candidates with unblemished credentials, men who had served their full three years in the army, and a few who had even achieved promotion to lance corporal. He took one or other of them into his household 'for a trial period'. But none of them made the grade. Their names might be Karl, Franz, Alexander, Joseph, Alois, Christoph or something else. But the District Commissioner tried to call each of them 'Jacques'. Even the real Jacques had been called something else originally, and had taken on his name and proudly worn it a whole lifetime in the way that a famous poet might assume the *nom de plume* under which he had written his deathless verses. It turned out, however, that after not many days the Aloises, Alexanders, Josephs and the rest of them were unwilling to answer to the great name of Jacques, and the District Commissioner took this rebelliousness not only as a breach of discipline and natural order, but as an offence against the memory of the departed. What? They didn't want to be called Jacques?! Those layabouts without merit or experience, intelligence or discipline?! For the late Jacques lived on in the memory of the District Commissioner as a servant of exemplary qualities, as the ideal of a human being, even. Even more than the refractoriness of these would-be successors, Herr von Trotta was puzzled by the irresponsibility of the various parties who had given favourable reports of such lamentable characters. If it was even possible that a certain specimen by the name of Alexander Cak – a man whose name he vowed never to forget, a name that lent itself to being pronounced with a certain venom, so that it sounded as though that Cak had already been executed when the District Commissioner so much as named him: if it was possible, then, that this Cak fellow belonged to the Social Democratic Party and still had managed to become a lance corporal in his regiment, then one could only shake one's head not just at the regiment in question, but at the entire army. And in the opinion of the District Commissioner, the army was the only remaining institution in the Monarchy that was still trustworthy! The District Commissioner gained the impression that all of a sudden the world was made up entirely of Czechs: a nation he took to be rebellious, stubborn and stupid, and on top of everything else probably responsible for the invention of nationalism. As far as he was concerned, there were plenty of peoples, but no nations. Moreover there was now a spate of barely comprehensible decrees and orders from the government, concerning kid-gloved treatment of the 'national minorities', one of Herr von Trotta's least favoured expressions. To his mind, 'national minorities' was nothing more than the collective form for 'revolutionary individuals'. Yes, he was surrounded by revolutionary individuals. He had even formed the impression that they were multiplying preternaturally, in a way that human beings generally didn't. It had become evident to the District Commissioner that 'loyal subjects' were becoming increasingly infertile and having smaller and smaller families, as the census statistics confirmed, when he consulted them from time to time. He could not keep from himself the ghastly thought that Providence itself was displeased with the Monarchy, and as a practising if not very devout Christian, he inclined ever more to the belief that God Himself was punishing the Emperor for something. In fact, he was coming to entertain some rather startling notions altogether. The dignity that had been his from the very day he had become District Commissioner had aged him anyway. Even when his whiskers had still been quite black, it would not have occurred to anyone to take Herr von Trotta for a youthful person. But only now did the people in his little town start saying to one another that the District Commissioner was getting on. He had had to set aside various habits of his. For instance, since the death of the late lamented Jacques, and his return from his son's garrison on the frontier, he had stopped going for his constitutionals before breakfast, for fear that one of the rapid succession of dubious individuals whom he had working for him, might have forgotten to lay the post on his breakfast table, or even to open the window. He hated his housekeeper. He had always hated her, but had still managed to speak to her from time to time. Ever since old Jacques had stopped serving, the District Commissioner refrained from all conversation at table. For in reality, his spiteful observations had always been meant for Jacques; in a sense they had been suing for the old servant's approval. But now that the old fellow was no more, Herr von Trotta understood that – like an actor who knows he has a long-standing and regular admirer of his art in the stalls – he had only ever spoken for Jacques's benefit. And if the District Commissioner had always been in the habit of bolting his food, now he was ready to leave the table after the first bite. It seemed sinful to him to enjoy his boiled beef while the worms were gnawing at old Jacques in the grave. And, while he did from time to time direct his glances upwards, in the hope and the innately pious feeling that the deceased might be in Heaven, looking down upon him, the District Commissioner never managed to see anything beyond the familiar ceiling of the room; because he had left the simplicities of belief behind him, and his senses no longer obeyed the instructions of his heart. Oh, it was a shame.

On occasion, on quite ordinary days, the District Commissioner even forgot to go to work. And it sometimes happened that, say on a Thursday morning, he would put on his black frock coat to go to church. Once outside, he would realize from various unquestionably unsabbatical signs that it was not a Sunday, and he would turn back and get into his ordinary weekday suit. And conversely: on some Sundays, he forgot to go to church, and still stayed in bed longer than usual and only remembered when Bandleader Nechwal and his players turned up outside, that it was a Sunday. As on every Sunday, there was boiled beef with vegetables. And Bandleader Nechwal came up for coffee. They sat in the drawing room. They smoked their Virginias. Bandleader Nechwal had aged as well. He was due to retire soon. He no longer went to Vienna quite so frequently, and, after many years, the jokes he told seemed profoundly familiar to the District Commissioner. He still didn't understand them, but he recognized them, like people he often saw though he didn't know their names. 'How are the family?' asked Herr von Trotta. 'Very well, thank you!' replied the bandleader.

'Your lady wife?' 'She's fine, thank you!' 'The children?' (the District Commissioner still didn't know whether Bandleader Nechwal had sons or daughters, and therefore, after twenty years, still asked cautiously after 'the children'). 'My eldest has been made Lieutenant!' replied Nechwal. 'Infantry, I expect?' asked Herr von Trotta, as he usually did, and a second later, he remembered that his own son was with the Jägers, and not with the cavalry any more. 'Yes, in the infantry!' said Nechwal. 'He's due to visit me soon. I'd like to present him to you, if I may!' 'By all means, by all means, I'd be delighted!' said the District Commissioner. One day, Nechwal junior turned up. He was serving with the Deutschmeisters, had received his commission only a year ago, and, in Herr von Trotta's opinion looked 'like a musician'. 'Just like his father,' said the District Commissioner, 'your spit and image,' even though the young Nechwal resembled his mother more than he did the bandleader. 'Just like a musician': by that, the District Commissioner was referring to a certain bold insouciance in the Lieutenant's expression, the tiny, blond, turned-up moustache that looked like a horizontal curly bracket under the short, broad nose, the minuscule, perfectly formed china doll's ears, and the tidy, sun-bleached, centre-parted hair. 'He looks a good lad!' Herr von Trotta said to Herr Nechwal. 'Are you happy where you are?' he asked the young man. 'To be perfectly honest, District Commissioner, sir,' replied the bandleader's son, 'it's a bit dull!' 'Dull?' asked Herr von Trotta, 'Vienna?' 'Yes,' said young Nechwal, 'it's dull! You see, sir, at least if you're serving in a small garrison, you don't realize you've got no money!' The District Commissioner was offended. He thought it wasn't proper to discuss money, and he suspected that young Nechwal might be alluding to the rather better-off Carl Joseph. 'Well, my son may be serving on the frontier,' said Herr von Trotta, 'but he's always managed to get by pretty well. Even when he was in the cavalry.' He stressed the word. For the first time, it occasioned him a little awkwardness that Carl Joseph had left the Uhlans. You didn't get Nechwal's sort in the cavalry! And the idea that this son of a bandleader might imagine himself to be comparable to young Trotta caused the District Commissioner almost physical pain. He decided to interrogate the 'musician'. There was a whiff of treason about this boy, with his now decidedly 'Czech' nose. 'Do you enjoy the service?' asked the District Commissioner. 'To be perfectly honest,' said Lieutenant Nechwal, 'I could imagine a better career!' 'A better career? Really? In what way?' 'Just more practical!' said young Nechwal. 'Oh – is fighting for the fatherland not practical?' asked Herr von Trotta, 'always assuming one is practically inclined to begin with?' It was clear that he was giving an ironic twist to the word 'practical'. 'But we're not even fighting,' replied the Lieutenant. 'And if we ever get to fighting, maybe it won't be practical.' 'Why ever not?' asked the District Commissioner. 'Because we're certainly going to lose,' said Nechwal, the Lieutenant. 'Times have changed,' he added – rather offensively, as Herr von Trotta thought. He blinked his little eyes shut so that they almost disappeared entirely, and in a way that struck the District Commissioner as perfectly repulsive he retracted his upper lip to expose his gums, and his moustache rubbed against his nose, making it look like the broad muzzle of some kind of animal, in Herr von Trotta's opinion. What a revolting character, thought the District Commissioner. 'These are different times,' repeated young Nechwal. 'All the different nationalities won't stay together much longer!' 'I see,' said the District Commissioner, 'and what makes you so sure of that, Lieutenant?' And straight away the District Commissioner realized that his scorn was hollow, and he felt like a veteran brandishing his harmless sabre against an enemy. 'Everybody knows,' said the youth, 'and it's what everybody says too!' 'They say so too?' repeated Herr von Trotta. 'Your comrades say so?' 'Yes, they say so!'

The District Commissioner didn't speak. It suddenly seemed to him as if he were on a high mountain, facing Lieutenant Nechwal in a deep valley. Lieutenant Nechwal was so small! But even though he was so small, and standing so low down, he was right. And the world was not what it had been. It was at an end. And it was in the disposition of these things that, barely an hour before its end, the valleys and the young and the fools would all be in the right, while the mountains and the old and the wise would all be in the wrong. The District Commissioner was silent. It was a summer Sunday afternoon. A filtered golden sunshine came pouring through the yellow blinds in the drawing room. The clock ticked. The flies buzzed. The District Commissioner recalled the day when his son Carl Joseph had come home in the uniform of a cavalry lieutenant. How much time had passed since that day? A couple of years, no more! But the District Commissioner had the sense that in those years things had happened thick and fast. It was as if the sun had risen and gone down twice a day; and every week had had a couple of Sundays in it and every month sixty days!

And the years had been double years. And Herr von Trotta felt he had been deceived by time, even though it had given him double helpings; and it was as though eternity had given him false double years, in place of genuine single years. And, while he despised the Lieutenant who was facing him, so deep in his vale of misery, he distrusted the mountain on which he himself was standing. Oh, he was experiencing an injustice! Injustice! Injustice! And for the first time in his life, the District Commissioner felt he was the victim of an injustice.

He longed to see Dr Skovronnek, the man with whom he had been playing chess every afternoon for the past several months now. For these regular games of chess were another one of the changes that had taken place in the District Commissioner's life. He had known Dr Skovronnek for a long time, just as he'd known other regulars at the café, no more and no less. One afternoon had found them sitting facing one another. Each of them half hidden behind an open newspaper. As on a given cue, both had laid their newspapers aside simultaneously, and their eyes had met. At the very same instant, both suddenly realized they'd been reading the same article. It was an article about a summer fair in Hitzing, where a butcher by the name of Alois Schinagl, thanks to his supernatural greed, had become the Champion Eater of Pork Hocks and been awarded the Gold Medal at the All-Hitzing Public Eating Contest. And the eyes of the two men said, each to the other: We're quite fond of pork hocks ourselves, but the idea of giving a gold medal for something like that is a crazy bit of newfangledness! Whether there can be love at first sight is something of which experts are rightly sceptical. But that there can be friendship at first sight, friendship between elderly men, of that there can be no doubt. Dr Skovronnek looked at the District Commissioner over the tops of his rimless oval spectacles, and at the very same moment the District Commissioner took off his pince-nez. He gestured invitingly with it. And Dr Skovronnek approached the table of the District Commissioner.

'Do you play chess?' asked Dr Skovronnek.

'With pleasure!' said the District Commissioner.

There was no need for them to make times to see each other. They met every afternoon at the same hour. They arrived together. In their daily routines it seemed there was a complete accord. They hardly spoke during their games of chess. Over the small chess board, their bony fingers sometimes ran into one another like people in a small square, and then shrank back and went home. But however fleeting these collisions were: it was as though the fingers had eyes and ears, and so they understood everything about one another, and about the men of whom they were a part. And after the District Commissioner and Dr Skovronnek had bumped hands a few times over the chess board, it seemed to both of them that they had known each other for many years, and that they had no secrets one from another. And so one day, gentle conversations began to garnish their games, and over their hands, which long since had been intimate with each other, the men began to exchange remarks about the weather, the world, politics and people. An estimable chap! the District Commissioner thought about Dr Skovronnek. Extraordinarily fine man! Dr Skovronnek thought about the District Commissioner.

Most of the time, Dr Skovronnek was unoccupied. He worked for just four months a year as the spa doctor in Franzensbad, and his entire understanding of the world stemmed from the confessions of his female patients there; because the women would tell him everything they thought was troubling them, and there was nothing in the world that did not trouble them. Their health suffered as much from their husband's work as from their neglect, from the 'difficult times for everyone', from inflation, from political crises, from the constant threat of war, from their husbands' newspaper subscriptions, their own idleness, the faithlessness of their lovers, from men's indifference – but also from their rampant jealousy. In this way, Dr Skovronnek came to know the various classes and the way they lived, their kitchens and their bedrooms, their desires and passions and follies. And since he didn't believe everything the women told him, but only maybe three-quarters of it, he acquired in time an outstanding knowledge of the world, which was more valuable than his medical training. Even when he spoke to men, his lips had the sceptical and yet ready smile of a man who never knows what he will hear next. A defensive kindness shone on his small wincing face. And his fondness of people matched his low opinion of them.

Did Herr von Trotta's simple soul guess something of the deep cunning of Dr Skovronnek's? At any rate, here was the first person since his boyhood friend Moser for whom the District Commissioner began to feel trust and respect. 'Have you been living in our town for a long time, doctor?' he asked. 'From my birth,' replied Skovronnek. 'Pity', said the District Commissioner, 'pity we only got to know each other so late.' 'I've known you for a long time, District Commissioner,' said Dr Skovronnek. 'I've watched you from time to time!' replied Herr von Trotta. 'Your son was here once!' said Skovronnek. 'It was a few years ago now.' 'Yes, yes, I remember,' said the District Commissioner. He recalled the afternoon when Carl Joseph had come in with his letters to the late Frau Slama. It was summertime. It had been raining. The boy had drunk a bad cognac, standing at the bar. 'He's got himself transferred,' said Herr von Trotta. 'He's with the Jägers now, on the border, in B.' 'And he makes you proud?' Skovronnek asked. He had meant to say 'worried'. 'Yes, I suppose he does! Yes!' replied the District Commissioner. He stood up quickly, and left Dr Skovronnek.

For some time now, he had been contemplating making a clean breast of everything to Dr Skovronnek. He was growing old, he needed someone to talk to. Every afternoon, the District Commissioner resolved that today would be the day he would talk to Dr Skovronnek. But he didn't manage to say the word that would have initiated a confidential talk between them. Dr Skovronnek awaited it daily. He sensed that the time had come for the District Commissioner to make his confession. For several weeks, the District Commissioner had been going around with a letter from his son in his breast pocket. Herr von Trotta owed him a reply, but he couldn't do it. And in the meantime, the letter was getting heavier all the time, it was like a lead weight in his pocket. Before long, the District Commissioner could feel it pressing against his old heart. What Carl Joseph had written was that he was thinking of leaving the army. Yes, the opening sentence of the letter read: 'I am considering leaving the army.' When the District Commissioner read that sentence, he stopped reading, and cast his eye down to the signature, to assure himself that the letter actually was from Carl Joseph. Then Herr von Trotta laid aside the pince-nez that he used for reading, and the letter with it. He rested. He was sitting in his office. The official correspondence was not yet opened. There might be all manner of urgent and important news there. But everything related to his work seemed, after Carl Joseph's reflections, to have been dealt with already, and badly. For the District Commissioner, it was the first time that the performance of his official duties came after something that concerned him personally. And, however humble and dutiful a servant of the state he was: his son's wondering whether to leave the army hit Herr von Trotta as hard as if he had received an official communiqué from the K-and-K army that it was minded to seek its own dissolution. Everything, everything in the whole world had lost its meaning. The end of the world was at hand! And when the District Commissioner decided, nevertheless, to read the official correspondence, he felt as if he were fulfilling some futile, anonymous and heroic duty, like a telephonist, as it were, on a sinking ship.

Only fully an hour later, did he return to his son's letter. Carl Joseph was asking for his agreement with the proposed step. And the District Commissioner wrote as follows:

My dear son!
I am shaken by your letter. I will give you my final decision as soon as I am able.
Your Father

Carl Joseph hadn't written back since. Yes, he had broken off the regular series of his communications, and the District Commissioner had had no word from him for some time. He waited every morning, the old man, and he knew he was waiting in vain. And it felt, not as though the expected letter had failed to arrive, but as though the expected and dreaded silence came punctually every morning. His son was silent. But the father heard his silence. It was as though the son revoked his duty of filial obedience to the old man every day. And the longer Carl Joseph's missives failed to come, the harder it was for the District Commissioner to write his promised reply. And while it had seemed perfectly self-evident to him at first that he would forbid the boy to leave the army, after a time Herr von Trotta came to believe that he no longer had the right to forbid anything. He was rather discouraged, the District Commissioner. His whiskers were turning silver. His temples were already completely white. Sometimes his head would droop, and his chin and the two wings of his whiskers came to rest against his starched shirt. He would suddenly go to sleep like that, in his armchair, come round with a start a few minutes later, and feel as though he had been asleep for an eternity. His scrupulously accurate sense of the hours was gradually going astray, ever since he had given up this or that of his former habits. Because it had been precisely for the maintenance of these habits that the hours and the days had served, and now they were like empty vessels that could no longer be filled, and about which one no longer needed to worry. It was only for his afternoon chess games with Dr Skovronnek that the District Commissioner was still punctual.

One day, he had an unexpected visitor. He was sitting in his office, over some papers, when the familiar rowdy voice of his boyhood friend Moser reached his ears, and the vain efforts of the beadle to turn the Professor away. The District Commissioner rang his bell, and had the Professor come in. '*Grüss Gott*, Governor!' said Moser. With his wide-brimmed hat, his folder, and no coat, Moser didn't look like someone who has just got off the train, but rather as if he'd just walked across the street. The District Commissioner had the terrifying thought that Moser might have come to take up residence in W. The Professor first went over to the door and turned the key and said: 'Just so that we're not interrupted, *mon cher*! It might hurt your career!' Then, with long, slow strides he rounded the desk, embraced the District Commissioner and pressed a smacking kiss on his bald head. Whereupon he sank down in the armchair next to the desk, dropped his folder and hat on the ground in front of him, and did not speak.

Herr von Trotta did not speak either. He knew now why Moser had come. He hadn't sent him any money for three months. 'I'm sorry!' said Herr von Trotta. 'I want to make it up right away! Please forgive me! I've had a lot on my mind lately!' 'I can imagine!' replied Moser. 'Your son must set you back quite a bit. I see him in Vienna every other week! Seems to be having a good time, the Lieutenant.'

The District Commissioner got to his feet. He clutched at his heart. He felt Carl Joseph's letter in his pocket. He walked over to the window. With his back to Moser, he gazed at the old chestnuts in the park opposite and asked: 'Have you talked to him?'

'We always have a little glass together when we meet,' said Moser, 'he's a very generous fellow, your son!'

'I see! He's generous, is he?' echoed Herr von Trotta.

He walked quickly back to his desk, pulled open a drawer, riffled through some banknotes, took out a few, and gave them to the painter. Moser put the money in his hat, between the ripped lining and the felt, and got up. 'Just a minute!' said the District Commissioner. He went to the door, unlocked it, and said to the beadle: 'Will you see the Professor to the station, please. He's going back to Vienna. The train leaves in an hour.' 'At your service,' said Moser, with a bow. The District Commissioner waited for a couple of minutes. Then he took his hat and cane and went to the café.

He was a little late. Dr Skovronnek was already seated at the table, with the chess pieces laid out in front of him on the board. Herr von Trotta sat down. 'Black or white, District Commissioner?' asked Skovronnek. 'I'm not playing today!' said the District Commissioner. He ordered a cognac, knocked it back, and began: 'Doctor, there is something I would like to burden you with!'

'By all means!' said Skovronnek.

'It's about my son,' the District Commissioner began. And in his slow, official, slightly drawling voice, he talked about his concerns, quite as though he were discussing official business with a governor. He presented his concerns as principal and subsidiary concerns, as it were. And, point by point, with little spaces between the paragraphs, he told Dr Skovronnek the story of his father, himself and his son. By the time he had finished, all the clients had left the café, and the greenish gaslights had been lit in the gaming room, where their monotonous drone buzzed over the empty tables.

'Well! And so that's how it is!' concluded the District Commissioner.

There was a long silence between the two men. The District Commissioner didn't dare look at Dr Skovronnek. And Dr Skovronnek didn't dare look at the District Commissioner. They faced each other with lowered eyes, as though each had caught the other red-handed in some criminal act. Finally, Skovronnek said, 'Do you think a woman is involved? What other reason might your son have for spending so much time in Vienna?'

It wouldn't have occurred to the District Commissioner to think of a woman. It was such an obvious idea, it seemed incredible to him that he hadn't thought of it himself right away. Then everything he had ever heard – and it wasn't very much – concerning the deleterious influence of women on young men, crashed into his brain, at the same time freeing his heart. If it was only a woman who had prompted Carl Joseph to think of leaving the army, well, the damage wasn't yet undone, but at least one could see where the evil was coming from, and the end of the world was no longer a question of anonymous, dark, secret forces against which one was powerless. A woman! he thought. No! He didn't know anything about any woman! And, in his official style, he said, 'Nothing has come to my ears regarding any person of the opposite sex!'

'Person of the opposite sex, eh!' echoed Skovronnek, and he smiled: 'Well, it could be a lady too.'

'So you think,' Herr von Trotta said, 'my son is contemplating marriage?'

'Not necessarily,' said Skovronnek. 'There are other things one can do with ladies than marry them.'

He understood that the District Commissioner's was one of those simple natures that could do with being put through school again. And he decided he would treat the District Commissioner like a child that's just learning its own mother tongue. And he said: 'Let's leave the ladies out of it for the moment, District Commissioner! It doesn't matter! For whatever reason, your son doesn't want to remain in the army. I can understand that!'

'You understand that?'

'Of course I do, District Commissioner! If he thinks about it at all, a young officer in our army can't possibly be content with his profession. He must needs be yearning for war. And he knows that war would spell the end for our monarchy.'

'The end of our monarchy?'

'Yes, the end, District Commissioner! I'm afraid so! Let your son do as he pleases. Perhaps he would be better suited to a different career!'

'A different career!' echoed Herr von Trotta.

'A different career!' he repeated. They were silent for a long time. Then, for the third time, the District Commissioner said: 'A different career!'

He tried to get accustomed to the phrase, but it remained as unspeakably alien to him as, for instance, 'revolutionary' or 'national minorities'. And then the District Commissioner felt he wouldn't have long to wait for the end of the world. He banged the table with his bony fist, making his round cuffs rattle and the greenish lamp overhead sway slightly, and he asked, 'What sort of career, Doctor?'

'There might,' said Dr Skovronnek, 'be an opening for him on the railways!'

The District Commissioner had a vision of his son in a conductor's uniform, with a gadget for punching holes in tickets in his hand. The expression 'an opening for him on the railways' made his heart wilt. He shuddered.

'You think so?'

'It's the best I can do!' said Dr Skovronnek.

And, as the District Commissioner now got to his feet, Dr Skovronnek also rose and said: 'I'll walk you back!'

They walked through the park. It was raining. The District Commissioner didn't open his umbrella. Here and there, heavy drops landed on his shoulders and his stiff hat from the dense crowns of the trees. It was dark and quiet. Each time they passed one of the occasional lamps that hid their silver heads in the green foliage, both men inclined their heads. And when they stood at the exit to the park, they both briefly hesitated. And Dr Skovronnek said suddenly: 'Goodbye, District Commissioner!' And Herr von Trotta crossed the street alone, to the broad arched entrance to his residence.

Encountering his housekeeper on the stairs, he said: 'I'm not hungry tonight!' and he hurriedly walked on. He felt like taking the stairs two at a time, but felt ashamed of himself and went into his office at his usual dignified pace. For the first time in his tenure of the commissionership, he was in the office of an evening. He lit the green table lamp, which he usually only did on winter afternoons. The windows were open. The rain rattled against the metal windowsills. Herr von Trotta took a piece of yellowish foolscap from the drawer and wrote:

Dear Son!

On mature reflection, I have decided to leave the responsibility for your future with you. All I ask is that you inform me of your decision.

Your Father

Herr von Trotta remained seated over his letter for a long time. He read over the few sentences he had written. They sounded like a will to him. Never previously would it have occurred to him to take himself more seriously as a father than as a civil servant. But, now that he was renouncing his authority over his son, it seemed to him that his entire life had lost its meaning, and that, really, he ought to stop being a civil servant as well. What he was doing was in no way dishonourable. But he felt as though he were cursing himself. He left the office, letter in hand, and went to the drawing room. There he lit every single light in the room, the standard lamp in the corner and the ceiling light, and stood in front of the portrait of the hero of Solferino. He could not see his father's face clearly. The painting broke up into a hundred little oily flecks of light and colour, the mouth was a pale red slash and the eyes two black shards of coal. The District Commissioner climbed up on to a chair (not since his boyhood had he stood up on a chair), craned his neck, stood on tiptoe, held the pince-nez in front of his eyes, and was only just able to make out Moser's signature in the lower right-hand corner. He climbed awkwardly back down, suppressing a sigh, and backed away across the room to the opposite wall, collided painfully with the edge of the table, and started examining the painting from a distance. He turned off the ceiling light. And in the deep gloom, he thought he could see a sheen of animation come over his father's face. Now it seemed to come nearer, now it withdrew again, to disappear beyond the wall, staring into the room through an open window immeasurably far away. A deep fatigue came over Herr von Trotta. He sat down in an armchair, moved it so that it was directly facing the painting, and unbuttoned his waistcoat. He listened to the rain, the drops falling more infrequently now as the shower relented, beating against the window panes with a tough and occasional clatter, and the wind rustling in the old chestnut trees in the park across the street. He closed his eyes. And he fell asleep, the letter in its envelope in his hand, and his hand dangling from the arm-rest of the chair.

When he awoke, daylight was already streaming through the three large, arched windows. The District Commissioner opened his eyes on the portrait of the hero of Solferino, and then he felt the letter in his hand, saw the address, read the name of his son, and sighing, stood up. His shirt front was rumpled, his broad burgundy tie with its white spots was skewed, and on his striped trousers, Herr von Trotta saw, for the first time since he had put on trousers, upsetting horizontal creases. He looked at himself in the mirror a while. And he saw that his whiskers were ruffled, and that a few pathetic grey hairs were twined across his bald head, and that his beetling eyebrows were every which way, as though a small storm had passed over them. The District Commissioner looked at his watch. And, seeing as the barber was due soon, he hurriedly got undressed and slipped into bed, to give the impression of its being a normal morning. But he kept the letter in his hand. And held on to it while he was lathered and shaved, and later on, while he was washing, the letter lay on the edge of the little washtable where the ewer stood. Only when Herr von Trotta sat down to breakfast did he hand the letter to the beadle, with the instruction to have it posted along with the next batch of official mail.

And then, as he did every day, he went up to work. No one could have told that Herr von Trotta had lost his faith. The care with which he accomplished his work that day was no less than it was on every other day. Only it was care of a completely different kind. It was care of the hands, of the eyes, even of the pince-nez. Herr von Trotta was like a virtuoso in whom the fire has gone out, whose soul has become empty and mute, and whose fingers produce the correct sounds by virtue of a cold efficiency they have acquired over the years, thanks to a dead memory that inheres in them. But, as I say, nobody noticed. And in the afternoon, as usual, came Sergeant Slama. And Herr von Trotta asked him: 'Tell me, my dear Slama, did you ever remarry?' He didn't know himself what prompted him to ask the question, and why the private life of the gendarme should suddenly be of concern to him. 'No, Baron!' said Slama. 'And I won't marry again either!' 'You're quite right!' said Herr von Trotta. But he didn't know why the sergeant should be right in his decision not to remarry.

The hour came for his daily visit to the café, and so he went along there. The chess board was already out on the table. Dr Skovronnek walked in with him, and they sat down together. 'Black or white, District Commissioner?' asked the doctor, as he did every day. 'I don't mind!' said the District Commissioner. And they started their game. Herr von Trotta played carefully, almost intently today, and he won. 'You're getting to be a real grand master!' said Skovronnek. The District Commissioner felt flattered by the compliment. 'Perhaps I could have been one!' he replied. And he thought it would have been better, that anything would have been better.

'By the way, I've written to my son,' he said after a while. 'He can do what he likes!'

'I think that's right!' said Dr Skovronnek. 'You can't bear responsibility for another human being! No one should do that.'

'My father was responsible for me,' said the District Commissioner, 'and my grandfather was for my father.'

'Things were different then,' replied Skovronnek. 'Today not even the Emperor can be responsible for the Monarchy. Yes, it even looks as though God doesn't want to be responsible for the world any more. It was easier then! Every stone was in its place. The roads of life were properly paved. There were stout roofs on the walls of the houses. Whereas today, District Commissioner, today the stones are lying all over the roads, and in dangerous heaps some of them, and the roofs are full of holes, and the rain falls into the houses, and it's up to the individual what road he walks, and what house he lives in. When your late father told you you wouldn't be a farmer but a civil servant, he was right. And you were an exemplary civil servant. But when you told your son he was to be a soldier, you were wrong. And he's not an exemplary soldier!'

'I suppose not!' agreed Herr von Trotta.

'And that's why you should let things go, let everything please itself! If my children disobey me, I just try to keep a modicum of dignity. It's all you can do. I look at them sometimes when they're asleep. Their faces look strange to me, almost unrecognizable, and I see that they are strangers, from a time that's yet to come and that I won't live to see. They're still so young, my children! One of them is eight, the other ten, and when they're asleep, they have round rosy faces. And yet there's cruelty in those sleeping faces. Sometimes I think it's the cruelty of their time, the future, that comes over them. I don't want to live to see that time!'

'I suppose not!' said the District Commissioner.

They played another game, but this time Herr von Trotta lost. 'It seems I won't be a grand master after all!' he remarked mildly, at ease with his faults. Today, too, it had got late; the greenish gaslights, the voices of silence, were already humming, and the café was empty. Once again, they walked back through the park together. Today, it was a fine evening, and they met other good-humoured promenaders. They talked about what a wet summer it had been, and how dry last winter had been and how cold the coming one promised to be. Skovronnek walked the District Commissioner back to the residence. 'You were right to send your letter, District Commissioner!' he said.

'I suppose so!' agreed Herr von Trotta.

He went into the dining room, and quickly and silently ate his half a roast chicken with salad. The housekeeper threw him fearful, covert glances. Ever since Jacques's death, she had served him herself. She left the room before he did, with a failed curtsy, just like the one she had made thirty years previously, to her head-master. The District Commissioner waved her away as one might shoo away a fly. Then he got up and went to bed. He felt tired and almost ill; the past night was like a distant dream in his memory, but as a present terror in his body.

He fell asleep peacefully; he thought he had got through the worst of it. He didn't know, old Herr von Trotta, that Fate was spinning more sorrow for him while he slept. He was old and tired, and Death was already waiting for him, but Life wasn't done with him yet. Like a cruel host, it detained him at its table, because he hadn't yet tasted all the bitterness that had been prepared for him.

17

No, the District Commissioner hadn't yet supped his fill of bitterness! Carl Joseph received his father's letter too late, that is to say, at a time when he had long since decided not to open or write any more letters. In any case, Frau von Taussig communicated by telegraph. Like swift little swallows, her telegrams arrived every other week to summon him. And Carl Joseph dashed across to his wardrobe, pulled out his grey civilian suit – his better, more vital, secret life – and changed into it. Straight away he felt at ease in the world for which he was headed and forgot about his military life. The replacement for Captain Wagner was Captain Jedlicek from the First Jägers, a 'stout fellow' in every sense, of enormous physical dimensions, broad, cheerful and gentle as most giants are, and very amenable to suggestion. What a man! The moment he arrived, everyone knew that he would be able to cope with the swampland, and that he was stronger than the frontier. There was someone to depend on! He violated every military regulation, but not just that – it was as though he annihilated them! He could have invented and established a completely new rule book, and got it accepted: that was the sort of man he looked to be! He needed lots of money, but he was also awash with it. His comrades gave him loans, signed chits for him, pawned their rings and their watches, wrote letters to their fathers and their aunts for him. Not that he was exactly popular! Popularity would have meant they were close to him, and he seemed not to desire any closeness. For physical reasons alone, it would have been difficult; his size, his breadth, his weight seemed to rebuff them all, so his cheerfulness went unchallenged. 'Just go!' he said to Lieutenant Trotta. 'I'll bear the responsibility!' He bore the responsibility, and he was well able to bear it too. And he needed money every week. He got it from Kapturak. Lieutenant Trotta needed money for himself as well. It seemed not on to arrive at Frau von Taussig's without any. It would have been like entering an armed camp without weapons. Sheer folly! And he gradually increased his requirements, and raised the sums he took with him, and still he returned from every visit down to his very last crown, and each time he promised himself he would take more the next time. Sometimes he tried to account for the money he got through. But he could never remember the individual expenses, and sometimes he couldn't do the simple addition. He couldn't do figures. His little notebooks told a tale of desperate attempts to keep order. Endless columns of figures were drawn up on every page. But they became muddled and confused, he lost his grip on them, they added themselves up and misled him with their wrong totals, they galloped away under his very eyes, to return a moment later subtly altered and impossible to recognize. He wasn't even able to keep track of his debts. The interest payments he didn't understand. What he lent others was dwarfed by what he owed, as a hill is dwarfed by a mountain. He didn't understand how Kapturak worked it out. And if he doubted Kapturak's honesty, then he had much more reason to doubt his own ability to deal with figures. Numbers bored him. And with the courage of desperation and helplessness he gave up, once and for all, every attempt to calculate.

Six thousand crowns was what he owed to Kapturak and Brodnitzer. Even to his own sketchy understanding of numbers, this was an enormous sum, in comparison to his monthly salary. (And he regularly had a third taken off that.) And yet he had gradually become accustomed to the figure 6000, as to a hugely powerful but very old enemy. Yes, in good times he could be persuaded that the number was getting smaller and losing strength. In bad times, however, it appeared to be growing and getting stronger.

He went to see Frau von Taussig. For weeks now, he had been undertaking these brief secret visits, these sinful pilgrimages, to Frau von Taussig. Like simple believers to whom a pilgrimage is a pleasure, a distraction, and sometimes even a revelation, Lieutenant Trotta associated the object of his pilgrimage with its site, with his own perpetual longing for an unfettered life (as he imagined it to be), with the civilian clothes he put on, and with the lure of the forbidden. He loved these trips of his. He loved the ten minutes' drive to the station in the closed carriage, unremarked, as he imagined, by anyone. He loved the few borrowed hundred crown notes in his breast pocket, which today and tomorrow were his alone, and which didn't proclaim that they had been borrowed and were already beginning to swell and to grow in Kapturak's account books. He loved the civilian anonymity with which he passed through the Nordbahnhof in Vienna and left it behind. No one recognized him. Officers and men passed him. He didn't salute and he wasn't saluted. Sometimes, automatically, he raised his hand to salute. Quickly he remembered his civilian clothes, and he lowered it again. His waistcoat, for instance, was a source of childlike glee to Lieutenant Trotta. He tried putting his hands in all its various pockets, whose use he of course didn't understand. With a dandy's fingers, he stroked the knot of the tie he wore above it, the only one he owned – it was a gift from Frau von Taussig – and which, even after innumerable efforts, he couldn't manage to tie properly. The dimmest detective would have spotted Lieutenant Trotta for what he was – an officer in civvies – at a glance.

Frau von Taussig was standing on the platform of the Nordbahnhof. Twenty years ago – she thought it was fifteen, because she had been denying her age for so long now, that she

275

had become convinced that time in her life had come to a stop – twenty years ago, she had also been waiting at the Nordbahnhof, also for a lieutenant, in that case a cavalryman. On the platform, she felt she was at a fount of youth. She plunged into the acrid coal fumes, the whistles and steam of the shunting locomotives, the busy ringing of the signals. She was wearing a short travelling veil. She had the feeling such veils had been in fashion fifteen years ago. She was wrong: it was actually twenty-five years – not even twenty! How she loved waiting on station platforms. She loved the moment when the train rolled in, and she spotted Trotta's ridiculous little dark green Alpine hat in the window of the compartment, and his dear, puzzled young face. (She tended to make Lieutenant Trotta younger as well, and more puzzled and more foolish, just as she made herself.) The moment the Lieutenant stepped off the lowest step, she threw her arms open, just as she had done twenty, or as she would have it, fifteen years ago. And from her face of today there emerged the young, rosy, unlined face that had been hers twenty, or as she would have it, fifteen years ago, a girlish face, sweet and slightly flushed. Round her neck, where a couple of parallel creases were already being dug in the skin, she was wearing the thin, childish gold chain that, twenty, or as she would have it, fifteen years ago, had been her only jewellery. And, just as she had done twenty, or as she would have it, fifteen years ago, she drove with the Lieutenant to one of those small hotels where clandestine loves flower, in rented, wretched, creaking and altogether paradisal beds. It was a time for strolls. For passionate quarter-hours in the fresh green of the Vienna Woods, small, abrupt storms of the blood. For evenings in the red velvet gloaming of boxes at the opera, behind drawn curtains. For certain caresses, familiar but still surprising caresses, for which the experienced and yet ever-susceptible flesh was waiting. The ears knew the music they had heard many times, but the eyes knew only parts of the scenery. For when Frau von Taussig had gone to the opera, it had always been behind drawn curtains, or with eyes closed. The blandishments born of the music, and passed on to the man's hands, she felt, by the orchestra, arrived on her skin, cool and burning at once, familiarly intimate and forever youthful sisters, presents she had often received before, but had forgotten and supposed she had merely dreamed them. The discreet restaurants opened their portals. The discreet suppers commenced, at corner tables, where the wine she drank seemed to grow, ripened by the love which shone steadily in the dark. And then it was a time for farewells, one last embrace in the afternoon, to the urgent, ticking accompaniment of the watch lying on the bedside table, and filled already with the anticipation of the next meeting; the rush to catch the train; the very last kiss on the running board, and the hope, abandoned only at the very last moment, that she might come too.

Tired, but sated on all the sweets that love and the world had to offer, Lieutenant Trotta returned to his garrison town. His man Onufri had his uniform all ready. Trotta changed into it in the back room of the restaurant, and drove to the barracks. He went to the company office. All quiet, no incidents to report. Captain Jedlicek was cheerful, happy, stout and healthy as ever. Lieutenant Trotta felt relieved and a tiny bit disappointed as well. In a secret corner of his heart he had hoped for some disaster which would have made it impossible for him to continue in the army. He was all ready to turn on his heel and go back to Vienna. But there hadn't been anything like that. And so he had to spend the next twelve days here, locked up within the four walls of the barrack yard, in the bleak little alleyways of the town. He glanced round at the targets painted on the walls of the yard. Little blue men, peppered with bullets and repainted, they looked to the Lieutenant like wicked imps, the evil spirits of the barracks, themselves brandishing the weapons with which they were hit, no longer targets but dangerous marksmen. As soon as he got to Brodnitzer's hotel, entered his bare room, threw himself on his iron bed, he made the resolution not to come back from his next furlough.

He was incapable of doing any such thing, and he knew it. In fact, he was waiting for a spectacular piece of luck, that one day would fall into his hands and free him for all time: from the army and from the necessity to leave it voluntarily. The only thing he could do was stop writing letters to his father, and not open the few letters addressed to him by the District Commissioner; later maybe, when things were different . . .

The next twelve days rolled by. He opened his wardrobe, looked at his civilian suit, and waited for the telegram to come.

It always came at this time, at dusk, in the hour before nightfall, like a bird returning to its nest. Today, though, it didn't come, not even once night had fallen. In a spirit of denial, the Lieutenant refused to switch on any light. Awake and fully dressed he lay on his bed. All the familiar sounds of spring came wafting in through the open window: the deep basses of the frogs and, above them, their higher, milder brother, the song of the crickets, in between the distant call of the nocturnal jays and the songs of the lads and lasses from the border village. At last the telegram came. It told the Lieutenant that he couldn't come this time. Frau von Taussig had gone to visit her husband. She wanted to return soon, but couldn't say when. The message ended with 'thousand kisses'. The figure offended the Lieutenant. She shouldn't have been so miserly, he thought. Why couldn't she have telegraphed hundred thousand! It occurred to him that he owed six thousand crowns. Compared to that, a thousand kisses was a pretty measly figure. He got up to close the open door of the wardrobe. There it hung, clean and straight, a well-pressed corpse, charcoal-grey, civilian, Trotta at liberty. He shut the door on it. A coffin: buried! buried!

The Lieutenant opened the door on to the corridor. Onufri was always sitting there, either silently or humming softly to himself or with the harmonica to his lips, cupping his hands over the instrument to hush the notes. Sometimes Onufri would be sitting on a chair. Sometimes he squatted down against the door-jamb. He should have left the army a year ago. He was staying on of his own free will. His native village of Burdlaki was near. Whenever the Lieutenant went away, he went to his village. He took a staff of cherrywood, a white handkerchief embroidered with blue flowers, filled the handkerchief with God knows what, tied the bundle to an end of the stick, escorted the Lieutenant to the station, waited for the train to leave, stood on the platform in a rigid salute, even if Trotta wasn't looking out of his compartment window, and then set off to Burdlaki, through the swamps, along the narrow path where the willows grew, the only safe way where there was no risk of going under. Onufri was always back in time to meet Trotta's train. And he sat outside Trotta's door, silently, or humming softly to himself or playing the harmonica in his cupped hands.

The Lieutenant opened the door on to the corridor. 'You can't go to Burdlaki this time! I'm not going anywhere!' 'Very good, Lieutenant!' Onufri stood, rigidly saluting, in the white corridor, a straight, dark blue line. 'You stay here!' Trotta repeated; he thought Onufri hadn't understood.

But Onufri just said: 'Very good!' once more. And, as though to prove that he understood more than he was told, he went downstairs and returned with a bottle of ninety-proof.

Trotta drank. The bare room became cosier. The naked bulb on its woven flex swaying in the night wind, moths fluttering around it, set off pretty, fugitive shimmerings in the brown polished surface of the table. Gradually too, Trotta's disappointment was replaced by a sweet melancholy. He made a pact with his sadness. Everything in the world was as sad as it could be, and at the very heart of this wretched world was the Lieutenant. It was for him that the frogs were bruiting so piteously tonight, and the pain-filled crickets were wailing on his behalf. It was for him that the spring night was filled with such a sweet and easy sadness, for him that the stars were positioned so unattainably high in the sky, and it was to him alone that their light blinked so longingly and vainly. The unending pain of the world fitted itself to Trotta's hurt. He suffered in total harmony with the grieving world. Behind the deep blue bowl of the sky, God Himself was gazing down upon him with sympathy. Trotta opened his wardrobe again. There he hung, the free Trotta, dead and gone now. Beside him glinted the sabre of his dead friend Max Demant. In his suitcase lay old Jacques's memento, the rock-hard piece of root, next to the letters of the late Frau

Slama. And on the windowsill lay no fewer than three unopened letters from his father, who might himself be dead by now! Oh! Lieutenant Trotta wasn't just unhappy and sorry for himself, he was also bad, a thoroughly bad character! Carl Joseph went back to the table, poured himself another glass, and knocked it back. Outside in the corridor, Onufri was just beginning on another tune, the well-known song, 'Oh, our Emperor . . .' Trotta had forgotten the first few words of the Ukrainian version: '*Oj nasch cisar, cisarewa*'. He hadn't managed to learn the local language. Not only did he have a thoroughly bad character, he had a tired and empty head as well. In short, his whole life was in ruins! His chest heaved, the tears welled up at the back of his throat, soon to rise to his eyes. He drank another glass to make it easier for them. At last, they broke from his eyes. He laid his arms on the table, his head on his arms, and started sobbing helplessly. He cried like that for a quarter of an hour. He didn't hear Onufri stop his playing and knock on the door. Not until it fell shut did he lift his head. And saw Kapturak.

He managed to stem his tears and ask angrily: 'How did you get in here?'

Kapturak stood, cap in hand, close to the door; he was only slightly taller than the handle. His yellow-grey face was smiling. He was dressed in grey. His shoes were grey canvas. Their rims were coated with the grey, fresh, shining mud of the unpaved streets of this part of the world. A few grey curls detached themselves from his tiny skull. 'Good evening!' he said, with a little bow. His shadow flashed up on the white door, and collapsed again. 'Where's my man?' asked Trotta, 'and what do you want?'

'You did not go to Vienna!' began Kapturak.

'I never go to Vienna,' said Trotta.

'You have not wanted money this week!' said Kapturak. 'I have expected your visit. I had some questions. I have just been to see Captain Jedlicek. He is not there.'

'So he's not there,' echoed Trotta with a shrug.

'Yes,' said Kapturak. 'He is not there, something has happened to him.'

Trotta registered that something had happened to Captain Jedlicek. But he didn't ask what. Firstly, he wasn't curious. (Today, at least, he wasn't curious.) Secondly, it seemed to him that an enormous amount had happened to him, too much really, and that he couldn't afford to be interested in anyone else much. Thirdly, he wasn't in the mood to listen to one of Kapturak's stories. He was furious at Kapturak's presence. Only he didn't have the strength to do anything about the little man. A very remote memory of the six thousand crowns he owed his visitor kept surfacing in him; an embarrassing memory: he kept trying to force it down. That sum, as he quietly endeavoured to convince himself, is nothing whatever to do with his presence here now. There are two different people: the one I owe money to, who isn't here, and the other one who's standing in my room and wants to tell me some cock and bull story about Jedlicek. He stared at Kapturak. For a few moments, the Lieutenant had the impression that his guest was dissolving into and then reassembling himself out of flecks of grey fog. Trotta waited till Kapturak was fully back together again. It took some effort to take advantage of the moment; because there was every chance that the little grey man would start to melt away again and dissolve. Kapturak took a step forward, as though understanding that he was not clearly visible to the Lieutenant, and he repeated, a little louder, 'Something has happened to the Captain!'

'All right then, tell me what's happened to him?' Trotta mumbled, as though in a dream.

Kapturak took another step closer to the table and whispered, through cupped hands, in a way that turned his whisper into a hiss: 'He's been arrested and taken away. On suspicion of espionage.'

At that word, the Lieutenant got to his feet. Now he stood there, propping both hands on the table. He could hardly feel his legs. It was as though he was supported on his hands. He almost dug into the table with them. 'I don't want to hear any more from you,' he said. 'Go away!'

'Unfortunately not possible, unfortunately!' said Kapturak.

He was now standing close to the table, next to Trotta. He lowered his head, as though making some embarrassing confession, and said: 'I must insist on a partial repayment!'

'Tomorrow!' said Trotta.

'Tomorrow!' echoed Kapturak. 'Tomorrow is perhaps not possible! You see, such surprises every day. I have lost a fortune on the Captain. Who can say whether I ever see him again. You are his friend!'

'What did you say?' asked Trotta. He took his hands off the table, and suddenly stood solidly on his feet. He understood suddenly that Kapturak had said something monstrous, even though it was true; and that the only reason it appeared monstrous was because it was true. At the same time the Lieutenant remembered the only hour of his life in which he had been dangerous to other people. He wanted now to be armed as he was then, with pistol and sabre, and his platoon behind him. The danger posed by the little grey man today was much greater than that of those several hundred people then. And in order to make up for his utter helplessness, Trotta tried to fill his heart with a factitious rage. He clenched his fists; he had never done that before, he felt that he was incapable of being threatening, at the most he might mimic someone being threatening. A blue vein swelled on his forehead, his face reddened, the blood climbed to his eyes too, and his gaze went rigid. He succeeded in looking extremely dangerous. Kapturak shrank back.

'What's that you said?' repeated the Lieutenant.

'Nothing!' said Kapturak.

'Repeat what you just said!' ordered Trotta.

'Nothing!' replied Kapturak.

He threatened to dissolve once more into flecks of grey fog. And Lieutenant Trotta was gripped by panic that the little man might have the ghost's gift of breaking up into little pieces, and reassembling himself again. And an irresistible desire to test the corporality of Kapturak flared up in Lieutenant Trotta, like the unquenchable curiosity of a scientist. Behind him on the bedpost hung the sabre, his weapon, representing his honour as a man and a soldier, and in this instance also, curiously, a magical tool able to solve the riddle of unstable ghosts. And, as though magnetically drawn towards it, he took a backward leap, gazing all the while at the continually dissolving and hardening Kapturak, seized the weapon with his left hand, in a trice drew the blade with his right, and as Kapturak sprang towards the door, dropping his cap, which fell to the ground just in front of his grey shoes, Trotta followed him waving his sabre. And, not knowing what he was doing, the Lieutenant pressed the point of the blade against the chest of the grey ghost, felt down the length of the steel the resistance of clothes and flesh, and sighed with relief, because at last it seemed proven to him that Kapturak was human – and yet he was incapable of sinking the blade into him. It all only took a moment.

But in that moment, Lieutenant Trotta was able to see and smell everything that lived in the world, the voices of night, the stars in the sky, the light of the lamp, the objects in the room, and his own form as though it were somewhere outside himself, the dance of the mosquitoes round the light, the damp exhalations of the swamp, and the cool breath of the night wind. All at once, Kapturak spread his arms wide. His bony little hands clawed round the door-jambs. His balding head with its scattering of grey curling hairs slumped on to his shoulder. At the same time he pushed one foot in front of the other, and coiled his ridiculous grey shoes into a knot. And behind him, on the white door, Lieutenant Trotta's staring eyes all at once beheld the reeling shadow of a black cross.

Trotta's hand shook, and he dropped the sword. It fell with a soft, plaintive clatter. At the same moment, Kapturak dropped his arms. His head slipped off his shoulder, and toppled forward against his chest. His eyes were tight shut. His lips trembled. His whole body was trembling. There was silence. You could hear the moaning of the mosquitoes round the lamp, and beyond the window, the frogs, the crickets, and the sporadic barking of a dog. Lieutenant Trotta reeled. He turned round. 'Sit down!' he said, pointing to the only chair in the room.

'Yes,' said Kapturak, 'I need to sit down!'

He strode briskly over to the table, as briskly, so it seemed to Trotta, as though nothing had happened. He nudged the sabre aside with his toe, then stooped to pick it up. As if he had been entrusted with tidying up the room, holding the bare sword between finger and thumb, he walked across to the table where the sheath lay, and without looking at the Lieutenant, he put it back, and hung it round the bedpost again. Then he circled the table again, and sat down facing the standing Trotta. Only now did he seem to look at him. 'Just stay a moment,' he said, 'I want to settle my nerves.' The Lieutenant did not speak.

'I would like my money back this time next week,' Kapturak went on. 'I don't want to do business with you any more. The total sum is seven thousand two hundred and fifty crowns. I should also tell you that Herr Brodnitzer is standing behind the door, and has witnessed this whole exchange. As you know, this year Count Chojnicki is coming back later than usual, if he comes back at all. And now I want to go, Lieutenant!'

He got up, went to the door, stooped, picked up his cap, and took one more look back. The door closed behind him.

The Lieutenant was now completely sober. Even so, the whole thing felt like a dream to him. He opened the door. Onufri was sitting on his chair as always, even though it was probably very late. Trotta looked at his watch. It was half past nine. 'Why aren't you asleep yet?' 'Because of visitor!' replied Onufri. 'Did you hear everything?' 'Everything!' said Onufri. 'Has Brodnitzer been here?' 'Yes!' affirmed Onufri.

There could no longer be any doubt, everything that Lieutenant Trotta thought had happened, had actually happened. So he would have to report the whole thing in the morning. His comrades were still out. He went from door to door, their rooms were all unoccupied. They must all be sitting in the mess, chewing over the dreadful business with Captain Jedlicek, the Jedlicek affair. He would be court-martialled, stripped of his rank, and shot. Trotta buckled on his sabre, took his cap, and went downstairs.

He had to warn his comrades. He patrolled back and forth outside the hotel. More important, strangely, than the scene he had just been through with Kapturak was the business with the Captain. He thought he could see the fingerprints of a sinister power on it, it seemed an extraordinary coincidence that Frau von Taussig had to go and visit her husband today of all days, and by and by he was able to see all the grim events of his life in a grim pattern, and all in the hands of some vastly powerful, hate-filled, invisible string-puller, whose aim it was to destroy the Lieutenant. It was quite obvious, it was, as people say, as clear as day, that Lieutenant Trotta, the grandson of the hero of Solferino, was partly bringing about the doom of others, partly being pulled under by those who were themselves going down, and, in any case, that he was one of those unhappy beings on whom an evil power had cast its evil eye. He walked back and forth in the quiet lane, his footfall echoed in front of the lit and curtained windows of the café, where there was music playing, where cards were smacked down on the table, and where, in place of the old 'nightingale' there was a new replacement to sing the old songs and dance the old dances. Certainly, none of his comrades would be in there tonight. In any case, Trotta didn't feel like looking. For he too was contaminated by the disgrace of Captain Jedlicek, even though he hated serving in the army, and had done for a long time now. The whole battalion was touched by the Captain's disgrace. Lieutenant Trotta's military training was sufficiently strong for him to understand that it was hard to imagine the officers of the battalion continuing to show themselves in uniform on the public street, in the wake of the Jedlicek business. That Jedlicek! Big and strong and cheerful, a good comrade, and a man who needed an awful lot of money. He could take everything that was thrown at him, he was popular with Zoglauer, he was popular with the men. All of them had thought him stronger than the swamps and the frontier. And he had been a spy! From the café came music, a babble of voices, a clinking of cups and glasses, periodically drowned out by the nocturnal choir of the indefatigable frogs. Spring was at hand! But Chojnicki wasn't coming! The only man who, with his money, could have helped him out. It wasn't six thousand crowns any more, it was seven thousand two hundred and fifty! Payable this time next week! If he didn't pay, they would prove some link between himself and Captain Jedlicek. He had been his friend! But then they all of them had been his friends! And even so, that unhappy Lieutenant Trotta was the one to look out for! Fate, his personal fate! This time two weeks ago, he had been a happy and carefree young man in civilian clothes. Two weeks ago, he had run into the painter Moser and drunk a glass of schnapps with him! And today he envied him, envied Professor Moser.

He heard familiar footfalls round the corner, it was his comrades coming home. They were all there, all those who roomed in Brodnitzer's hotel, all in a silent rout. He walked towards them. 'Oh, you haven't left!' said Winter. 'So you've heard! Dreadful! Terrible!' They followed each other up the stairs, each of them at pains to make as little noise as possible. They almost slunk up the stairs. 'Everyone meet in room nine!' ordered Lieutenant Colonel Hruba. Room nine was his room, the largest in the hotel. Heads down, they all filed into room nine.

'We must do something!' Hruba began. 'You've seen Zoglauer! He's in despair! He'll shoot himself! We must do something!'

'That's nonsense, Lieutenant Colonel!' said Lieutenant Lippowitz. He had joined late, after a couple of semesters of law, and could never shake off the 'civilian', with the result that they viewed him with the shy and slightly ironic respect with which they viewed reserve officers. 'We can't do anything at this stage,' said Lippowitz. 'Just keep our mouths shut and do our duty! It's not the first such case in the army. And unfortunately it won't be the last either!'

No one replied. They too conceded that there was absolutely nothing to be done. And yet every one of them had hoped that if they all sat in a room together, they would come up with some possible solution. Now, though, they recognized at a stroke that it was only fear that had driven them together, because each of them was afraid of being left on his own with his own fear in his own four walls; and also that it did no good to be all in a group like this, because even in the midst of his companions, every man among them remained alone with his fear. They raised their heads, looked at one another, and then they let their heads fall again. They had sat like this once before, following Captain Wagner's suicide. Every one of them thought of Captain Jedlicek's predecessor, Captain Wagner, and every one of them fervently wished that Jedlicek had shot himself as well. And to each of them suddenly came the suspicion that their late comrade Wagner had perhaps only shot himself because otherwise he too would have been arrested and taken in.

'I'll get to him, I'll force my way through,' said Lieutenant Habermann, 'and then I'll shoot him myself.'

'Firstly, you won't be able to force your way through!' retorted Lippowitz. 'And secondly, they will take their own steps to make his suicide possible. As soon as they've got everything they can out of him by questioning, they'll give him a pistol and lock him up with it.'

'Yes, that's right, of course!' several of them exclaimed. They sighed with relief. They began to hope that the Captain might even already be dead. And they felt as though it was their own cleverness that had introduced this sensible practice to the work of the court-martial.

'I was this close to killing someone myself today!' said Lieutenant Trotta.

'Who, why, explain?' they variously enquired.

'It was Kapturak, whom all of you know,' Trotta began. He talked haltingly, was lost for words at times, coloured up, and by the time he was done, he was unable to explain why he hadn't given the *coup de grâce*. He felt they wouldn't understand him. They didn't understand him. 'I would have done it!' cried one. 'Me too,' said another. 'Same here,' a third.

'It's not as easy as you think!' interjected Lippowitz.

'That Jewish bloodsucker,' said someone – and then they all

went rigid, because they remembered that Lippowitz's father was a Jew.

'Yes,' Trotta resumed, 'suddenly' – and he was very surprised to find himself thinking of his dead friend Max Demant and his grandfather, the white-bearded king of the innkeepers – 'suddenly I saw a cross behind him!' Someone laughed. Another observed coolly, 'You were drunk!' 'Well, there's an end, gentlemen!' Hruba finally decreed. 'It'll all be reported to Zoglauer in the morning!'

Trotta gazed at one face after another; tired, slack, excited, but even in their slackness and tiredness curiously cheerful faces. If only Demant were alive now, thought Trotta. You could have talked to him, the grandson of the white-bearded king of the innkeepers! He tried to slip out. He went to his room.

The following morning, he reported the incident. He used the language of the army, which, from boyhood he had been used to talking and reporting in, the language of the army, which was his mother tongue. But he could clearly feel that he hadn't said everything and hadn't even said what mattered, and that there was a great and mysterious gulf, a whole curious country, yawning between what had happened to him and the way he described it. He didn't omit to talk about the shadow of the cross that he thought he had seen. The Major smiled exactly as Trotta had expected he would, and asked: 'How much had you had to drink?' 'Half a bottle!' said Trotta. 'Well then!' remarked Zoglauer.

He had only managed a momentary smile, poor, tormented Major Zoglauer. It was another debacle. There were getting to be quite a lot of them now. An embarrassing thing, it would certainly have to be reported to his superiors. That could wait, though. 'Have you got the money?' asked the Major. 'No!' replied the Lieutenant. And they gazed at one another in perplexity, with empty, rigid expressions, with the sorry eyes of people who are not even able to admit their perplexity to themselves. Not everything was in the rulebook, you could go through it front to back and back to front, not everything was contained in it!

Had the Lieutenant been in the right? Had he reached for his sabre prematurely? Or was the fellow in the right who had lent a fortune and wanted it back? And if the Major were to call up all his fellow officers and talk it over with them: who among them would have known what to do? Who was any wiser than the commander of a battalion? And what was the matter with this sorry lieutenant? It had already taken quite a bit of trouble to suppress that business with the striking workers. Calamity, calamity piled up on Major Zoglauer's head, calamity for Trotta, calamity for the battalion. He felt like wringing his hands, Major Zoglauer, only you couldn't wring your hands in uniform. Even if all the officers in the battalion vouched for Lieutenant Trotta, they couldn't raise the sum! And the tangle would only get worse if the sum wasn't paid back. 'What'd you need all that money for?' Zoglauer asked, before remembering a second later that he knew. He motioned with his hand. He didn't want any details. 'First of all, I want you to write a letter to your father!' said Zoglauer. He thought he had come up with an outstanding idea. And that was the end of report.

Lieutenant Trotta went back to his room and sat down and started writing the letter to his father. He couldn't do it without a drink. He went down to the café, ordered a glass of ninety-proof, and pen and ink and paper. He began. What a difficult letter! What an impossible letter! Lieutenant Trotta made a couple of false starts, crumpled them up, started afresh. Nothing is harder for a lieutenant than to describe events relating to himself and his personal safety. Moreover, while Lieutenant Trotta had long hated the service, he realized he still had sufficient military professionalism not to want to be taken out of the army. And as he endeavoured to set out to his father the complicated circumstances, he found himself transformed into the Cadet Trotta who had stood on the balcony of his father's house listening to the sounds of the Radetzky March, and wanting to die for king and country. (So curious, changeable and knotted is the human soul.)

It took more than two hours for Trotta to relate what had occurred in a letter. It was now late afternoon. Already the card- and roulette-players were gathering in the café. And the landlord, Herr Brodnitzer, appeared as well. He displayed unusual, alarming courtesy to the Lieutenant, bowing so deeply that the latter straight away understood that the landlord meant to remind him of the scene with Kapturak, and of his own witness. Trotta got up to look for Onufri. He went into the passage, and called Onufri's name up the stairs once or twice. But no Onufri. Instead, Brodnitzer came out and informed him: 'Your man left early this morning!'

So the Lieutenant set off for the station himself, to dispatch his latter. Only then did it occur to him that Onufri had left without asking for permission. His military training compelled him to be angry with his man. He himself, the Lieutenant, had often travelled to Vienna – and in civilian clothes, and without permission. Maybe the manservant was only following his master. Perhaps Onufri's got a girl waiting for him, the Lieutenant surmised. I'll have him locked up till he's blue in the face! thought Lieutenant Trotta. But as he did so, he realized that wasn't how he talked, and he wasn't serious about it. It was a mechanical response, always available in his soldier's brain, one of many many mechanical phrases that stand in for thought in a soldier's brain and obviate all need for decision-making.

In fact, Onufri the manservant didn't have a girl in his village. He had four and a half acres of land, which he had inherited from his father, and which his brother-in-law was looking after for him, and he had twenty golden ten-crown ducats buried in the ground, next to the third willow on the left of the hut, along the track that led to his neighbour Nikofor's property. Onufri the manservant had got up before sunrise, cleaned the Lieutenant's boots and uniform, stood the boots outside his door, and hung the uniform over his chair. He took his staff of cherrywood and marched off to Burdlaki. He walked along the narrow track where the willows grew, the only track that indicated that the ground was dry enough to bear his weight. For the willows drank up the moisture of the swamp. Either side of the narrow track, the grey, ghostly, swirling morning fogs rose up, surged towards him and forced him to cross himself. Incessantly, with trembling lips, he mumbled the Lord's Prayer to himself. But, for all that, he was of good heart. The large slate-roofed railway depot appeared next, on his left, and that cheered him up because it was more or less where he had expected it to be. He crossed himself once more, this time out of gratitude to the Almighty for leaving the railway depot in its accustomed place. An hour after sunrise he reached the village of Burdlaki. His sister and brother-in-law were already out in the fields. He entered the hut that had belonged to his father, where they lived. The children were still asleep, in cradles on thick ropes hanging from hooks in the ceiling. He took a pick and shovel from the little vegetable patch behind the hut, and set off to look for the third willow on the left. He stood in the doorway, with his back to the door and his eye on the horizon. It took a while for him to establish which his right arm was, and which his left, and then he went left, to the third willow, in the direction of Nikofor's. There he started digging. From time to time, he looked around to make sure no one was watching him. No! Nobody could see what he was doing. He dug and he dug. The sun climbed so rapidly up the sky that he thought it was already noon. But it was only nine in the morning. At last he heard the iron blade of the shovel bite against something hard and ringing. He threw aside the spade, and began stroking the loose soil tenderly with the hoe, then he threw away the hoe, lay down on the ground, and with all ten fingers combed the loose crumbs of moist soil. At first he felt a linen handkerchief, then he looked for a knot, and pulled it out. There was his money: twenty golden ten-crown ducats.

He didn't give himself time to reckon them all up. He buried the treasure in his trouser pocket, and went to see the Jewish inn-keeper of the village, a certain Hirsch Beniower, the only banker in the world whom he knew personally. 'I know you!' said Hirsch Beniower, 'and I knew your father before you! Is it sugar you want, or flour, or Russian tobacco, or money?'

'Money!' said Onufri.

'How much do you need?' asked Beniower.

'A great deal!' said Onufri, and he spread his arms wide, as far as he could, to show how much he needed.

'All right,' said Beniower, 'let's see what you have!' And Beniower opened a large book. In the book it was recorded that Onufri Kolohin owned four and a half acres of land. Beniower was prepared to lend him three hundred crowns on it as security.

'Let's go to the burgomaster!' said Beniower. He called his wife, left her in charge of the business, and went with Onufri Kolohin to the burgomaster.

There he gave Onufri three hundred crowns. Onufri sat down at a worm-eaten brown table, and began to sign his name on a document. He pulled off his cap. The sun was already high in the sky. It was able to thread its already burning rays even through the tiny windows of the peasant hut where the burgomaster of Burdlaki had his office. Onufri was sweating. On his low brow, the beads of sweat grew like transparent crystal boils. Each letter that he formed caused a crystal boil to stand out on his brow. The boils ran down, ran down like tears that Onufri's brain had shed. At last his signature stood on the document. And with the twenty golden ten-crown ducats in his trouser pocket, and the three hundred crowns in paper in the pocket of his tunic, Onufri Kolohin set off on the march back.

It was afternoon when he arrived back at the hotel. He went into the café, asked after the whereabouts of his master, and was standing in the midst of the card-players, looking quite unconcerned, as if he were standing in the middle of the barrack yard, when he saw Trotta. Trotta looked at him a long time, tenderness in his heart, and severity in his expression. 'I'm going to have you locked up till you're blue in the face!' said the Lieutenant's mouth, taking its dictation from his soldier's brain. 'Come up to my room!' said Trotta, and stood up.

The Lieutenant climbed the stairs. Onufri followed exactly three steps behind. They stood in the room. Onufri, still with sunny mien, announced: 'Sir, here is money!' and from the pockets of his trousers and his tunic he pulled out all he had, stepped up, and laid it on the table. On the dark red handkerchief that had hidden the twenty golden ten-crown ducats under the ground for so long, there were still little flecks of silver-grey mud. Next to the handkerchief lay the blue banknotes. Trotta counted them. Then he undid the handkerchief. He counted the gold. Then he laid the banknotes in the handkerchief with the gold, knotted it up again, and returned the bundle to Onufri.

'I'm afraid I'm not allowed to accept money from you, do you understand?' said Trotta. 'It's against the rules. If I take money from you, they'll reduce me to the ranks and throw me out of the army, do you understand?'

Onufri nodded.

The Lieutenant stood there, with the bundle in his upraised hand. Onufri nodded incessantly. He reached out his hand, and took the bundle. It continued to sway in the air a while.

'Dismiss!' said Trotta, and Onufri left with his bundle. The Lieutenant remembered that autumn night in the cavalry garrison where he had heard Onufri's stamping feet behind him. And he thought of the tales from army life he had read in flimsy green-bound volumes in the hospital library. They were full of touching officers' servants, rough peasant lads with hearts of gold. And even though Lieutenant Trotta had no interest in literature, and even though, if he happened to hear the word, he could only bring to mind the drama *Zriny* by Theodor Körner and nothing else, he had always felt a vague resentment against the mournful gentleness of those little story books, and against those golden characters. He did not understand, Lieutenant Trotta, that rough peasant lads with noble hearts really existed, and that many things that really exist in the world were copied and put in bad books; they were bad copies, that's all.

There were a lot of things he didn't understand, Lieutenant Trotta.

## 18

On a fresh and sunny spring morning, the District Commissioner received the Lieutenant's unhappy letter. Herr von Trotta weighed the letter in his hand before opening it. It seemed heavier than any of the other letters he had had from his son. It must be a letter of unusual length, a letter of two pages. The aged heart of Herr von Trotta filled with a mixture of woe, fatherly anger, joy and fearful premonition. The hard cuff rattled against his old hand a little as he opened the envelope. He held his pince-nez in place with his left hand (it had become a little trembly over the last few months), while he brought the letter close to his face with his right, so that the edges of his whiskers brushed the paper with a soft rustle. The evident haste of the handwriting was as alarming to Herr von Trotta as the unprecedented contents of the letter. The District Commissioner even continued to look between the lines for further hidden terrors; he felt this letter was not sufficiently terrifying, as though for a long time, and particularly once his son had stopped writing to him, he had been expecting the most terrible news on a daily basis. And that was probably why he felt calm as he put the letter aside. He was an old man from a past age. Old men from the time before the Great War were probably more foolish than the young men of today. But in situations that seemed terrible to them – and which we, in accordance with the prevailing notions of our times, would probably dismiss with a wise crack – they, these good old men, kept a heroic equanimity about them. Nowadays, the notions of professional honour and family honour and personal honour, by which Herr von Trotta lived, seem nothing more than the final residue of implausible and childish tales. But back then an Austrian district commissioner of the stamp of Herr von Trotta would have been less distressed by the news of his only son's death than by the mere suggestion that he had conducted himself dishonourably. By the lights of that vanished epoch, obscured from our view as by the fresh graves of the fallen, an officer of the K-and-K army who had failed to kill someone who had impugned his honour merely because he owed him money, was a calamity, and worse than a calamity: it was a disgrace for his father, for the army and the Monarchy. And in the first instance what stirred was not Herr von Trotta's feeling as a father, but as it were, his official feeling. And what it said was: Leave the service immediately! Take early retirement. You are no longer fit to serve your emperor! But in the very next instant, his fatherly feelings yelled: The times are to blame! The frontier garrison is to blame! You yourself are to blame! Your son is honest and noble! Only unfortunately, he's weak as well! And now he needs your help!

He needed his help! The father had to save the name of Trotta from being dishonoured and besmirched. And on that point, the two hearts of Herr von Trotta, the father's and the public official's, were in accord. Above all, it was a question of getting the money, seven thousand two hundred and fifty crowns! The five thousand florins which the imperial largesse had granted the son of the hero of Solferino, and the money he had inherited from his father were both long since used up. They had melted away in the District Commissioner's hands, gone on this and that, on household expenses, on the cadet school in Mährisch-Weisskirchen, on the painter Moser, on the horse, on charitable donations, Herr von Trotta had always insisted on appearing richer than he was. He had the instincts of a gentleman. And in those times (and who knows, perhaps even today), there are no costlier instincts. Men laden with such a curse know neither what they earn, nor what they spend. They draw from an invisible well. They don't calculate. They are convinced that their fortune cannot possibly amount to less than their liberality.

For the first time in what was now his long life, Herr von Trotta was in the position of needing to raise a relatively large sum of money very quickly. He had no friends, apart from the fellows he had been to school and later studied with, who were now officials like himself, and with whom he had had no dealings now for years. Most of them were poor. He knew the wealthiest man in the district capital, old Herr von Winternigg. And he started to work his way round to the ghastly notion of approaching Herr von Winternigg, tomorrow or the day after tomorrow, or maybe even today, and asking him for a loan. Herr von Trotta was not overly endowed with imagination. But in spite of that, he succeeded in picturing to himself every single step of that wretched petition. And for the first time in what was now his long life, the District Commissioner was forced to experience the difficulty of being helpless and retaining one's dignity. This experience came down on him like a stroke of lightning, and immediately shattered the pride that Herr von Trotta had carefully tended and looked after for such a long time, the pride he had inherited and was determined to bequeath. Already he felt as humiliated as someone who has been undertaking fruitless petitions for years. His pride had been the strong companion of his early years, then it had become a prop of his old age, and now he had lost it, the poor old District Commissioner! He decided to write a letter straight away to Herr von Winternigg. No sooner, however, had he taken up his pen than it became clear to him that he was not even capable of announcing a call, which ought, strictly speaking, to be called a begging visit instead. And it seemed to the old Trotta that he was perpetrating a sort of deception if he did not from the outset at least hint at the true purpose of his visit. It was not possible, however, to find a form of words that allowed him to do that. And so he remained seated for a long time, pen in hand, pondering and trying out phrases, and rejecting them all. Of course, another possibility was telephoning Herr von Winternigg. But in the time there had been a telephone in the office – not more than two years – Herr von Trotta had only used it on official business. Inconceivable that he might go up to the big, brown, slightly spooky box, crank the handle and ring the bell, and with that ghastly Hello! that almost offended Herr von Trotta (because it seemed to him like a term of infantile high spirits, with which serious people couldn't launch into a discussion of serious topics) begin a conversation with Herr von Winternigg. By this time, it had occurred to him that his son was waiting for a reply from him, a telegram perhaps. And what would the District Commissioner say in his wire! Maybe: Will try all possible, details later? Or: Anxiously awaiting further developments? Or: Try other avenues, no possibility here? – No possibility here. A long, skittering, crumbling sound came after those words. What was impossible? Saving the honour of the Trottas? That had to be possible. That couldn't be impossible! Back and forth, back and forth walked the District Commissioner in his office, just as on those Sunday mornings when he had tested the little Carl Joseph on his term's work. He held one hand pressed against his back, and on the other wrist, his cuff rattled. Then he went down into the yard, driven by the crazy idea that the dead Jacques might still be sitting there, in the shadow of the eaves. The yard was deserted. The window of the little house where Jacques had lived was open, and the canary was still alive. It sat on the window frame, warbling away. The District Commissioner turned back, picked up his hat and stick, and left the house. He had decided he would do something extraordinary, which was to call on Dr Skovronnek at his house. He crossed the little marketplace, turned up the Lenaugasse, looking for a sign on the doors, because he didn't know the number, and finally had to ask a merchant where Skovronnek lived, even though it struck him as rather embarrassing, turning to a stranger for information about a friend. But even that Herr von Trotta endured bravely and optimistically, and he went into the house that had been pointed out to him. He came upon Dr Skovronnek in the little garden at the far end of the passage, sitting under an enormous sunshade with a book. 'Good Heavens!' exclaimed Skovronnek, because he knew that something out of the ordinary must have happened for the District Commissioner to seek him out at home.

Herr von Trotta got through a whole battery of awkward apologies before beginning. He spoke, sitting down on the bench in the little garden, his head down, jabbing the point of his cane into the coloured bits of gravel on the narrow path. Then he put his son's letter into Skovronnek's hands. And then he said nothing, stifled a sigh, and took a deep breath.

'My savings,' said Skovronnek, 'come to two thousand crowns. Please, if they're any use to you, District Commissioner, take them.' He spoke very quickly, as though afraid the District Commissioner might interrupt him, and in his embarrassment, he took away Herr von Trotta's stick, and started jabbing it around in the gravel himself; because it seemed to him it wasn't possible to sit there with idle hands, following such a sentence as the one he'd just said.

Herr von Trotta said: 'Thank you, Doctor, I'll accept them. I'll give you an IOU. If you'll permit, I'll pay you back in instalments.'

'Out of the question!' said Skovronnek.

'Fine!' said the District Commissioner. All at once it seemed impossible to him to use lots of pointless words, as he had with strangers all his life, out of politeness. Time was pressing. The couple of days that were all he had suddenly shrivelled up into nothing.

'The rest,' Skovronnek continued, 'the rest can only be come by through Herr Winternigg. You know him?'

'A little.'

'There's no other possibility, District Commissioner! I believe I know Herr von Winternigg. It seems to me that he's a monster, as people like to say. And it could be, District Commissioner, it could be that he'll turn you down.'

Thereupon Skovronnek was silent. The District Commissioner

reclaimed his stick from the doctor. And, but for the jabbing of the stick in the gravel, there was silence.

'Turn me down!' whispered the District Commissioner. 'I'm not afraid of that,' he said aloud. 'But then what?'

'Then,' said Skovronnek, 'there's one more, rather bizarre recourse, I'm thinking, but probably it's a little too bizarre. Well, perhaps, given your case, it's not as far-fetched as that. If I were you, I would go straight to the old man, the Emperor, I mean to say. Because it's not just a question of money. There is a chance, forgive me for being so blunt with you, that your son may find himself' – he had been going to say 'slung out of the army' – but he said: 'having to resign from the army.'

Once Skovronnek had said it, he straight away regretted it. And he added, belatedly: 'It's probably a silly idea after all. Even while I was saying it, it struck me we're like a couple of schoolboys, brooding over some hare-brained scheme. Yes, old as we are, and worried, still there's something wild and juvenile in my idea. I'm sorry!'

To the simple soul of Herr von Trotta, Dr Skovronnek's idea didn't seem so childish at all. Every time he drew up or signed a document, with every instruction he passed on to his Deputy Commissioner or even to Sergeant Slama, never mind how trivial, he felt he was standing immediately under the outstretched sceptre of the Emperor. And it was perfectly natural that the Emperor had spoken to Carl Joseph. The hero of Solferino had spilled his blood for the Emperor, and so had Carl Joseph in a sense, in that he took up the fight against troublesome and suspicious 'individuals' and 'elements'. According to the simple understanding of Herr von Trotta, it was no misuse of the imperial favour for His Majesty's servant to approach Franz Joseph as simply and trustingly as a needy child his father. Dr Skovronnek took fright, and began to worry about the sanity of the District Commissioner when the old fellow exclaimed, 'Excellent idea, doctor, simplest thing in the world!'

'Not as simple as all that,' said Skovronnek. 'There's not much time. It's not possible to set up a private audience in two days.'

The District Commissioner agreed. And they decided that Herr von Trotta ought to see Winternigg first.

'Even if he does turn me down!' said the District Commissioner.

'Even if he does turn you down!' echoed Dr Skovronnek.

And the District Commissioner set off immediately to see Herr von Winternigg. He took a cab. It was lunchtime. He had had nothing to eat himself. He stopped outside the café, and drank a cognac. He reflected that this was a highly improper undertaking he was embarking on. He will catch old Winternigg in the middle of lunch. But he has no time. He needs a decision by this afternoon. The day after tomorrow, he'll be seeing the Emperor. And he has the cabbie stop another time. He gets out at the post office, and in a resolute hand, he writes a telegram to Carl Joseph: 'Matter is being seen to. Greetings. Father.' He is quite convinced that it will all go well. Because while it may prove impossible to raise the money, it is a greater impossibility that the honour of the Trottas will be impaired. Yes, the District Commissioner imagines that the spirit of his father, the hero of Solferino, is with him, watching over him. And the brandy warms his old heart. It's beating a little harder. He is quite calm, however. He pays the cabbie at the entrance to Winternigg's villa, and with a finger to his hat brim salutes him in the amiable way he always likes to salute the common people. Amiably he smiles at the footman. With hat and stick in hand, he waits.

Herr von Winternigg, tiny and yellow, arrived. He offered the District Commissioner his wizened little hand, fell into a large armchair and was almost drowned in its green upholstery. His colourless eyes stared out of the window. There was no expression in them, or else they contrived to dissemble it; they were dull old mirrors, all the District Commissioner could see was his own little reflection in them. He began, rather more fluently than he expected, with a few well-turned words of apology, and explained why it hadn't been possible to announce his visit in advance. Then he said: 'Herr von Winternigg, I am an old man.' He hadn't meant to say that. The wrinkled yellow eyelids of Winternigg batted up and down once or twice, and the District Commissioner had the feeling he was talking to an old and scrawny bird that did not understand human speech.

'Most unfortunate!' Herr von Winternigg managed, nevertheless, to say. He spoke very softly. His voice had no timbre, just as his eyes had no expression. He wheezed as he spoke, revealing a surprisingly powerful set of teeth, broad and yellow, a stout protective grille that filtered his speech.

'Most unfortunate!' Herr von Winternigg repeated. 'I don't keep any cash!'

The District Commissioner stood up immediately. Winternigg too was rapidly on his feet. He stood, tiny and yellow, in front of the District Commissioner, clean-shaven in front of the other's silver whiskers, and Herr von Trotta felt he was getting taller, and even had the sensation of growing. Was his pride broken? By no means! It was his mission to save the honour of the hero of Solferino, just as it had been the hero of Solferino's mission to save the life of the Emperor. Visits of supplication were as simple as that! It was with contempt, yes, for the first time in his life with contempt, that Herr von Trotta's heart was full, and his contempt was almost as great as his pride. He took his leave. And he said in his old, snooty official's voice: 'My compliments, Herr von Winternigg!' He went on foot, upright, slow, glimmering with the full dignity of his silver, all down the long avenue that led from Winternigg's house to the town. The avenue was deserted, the sparrows skipped across the road, the blackbirds whistled, and the old green chestnut trees bordered the District Commissioner's path. On his return home, for the first time in a long time, he shook the silver table bell. Its jingling little voice ran hurriedly the length and breadth of the house. 'My dear,' Herr von Trotta addressed Fräulein Hirschwitz, 'I would like my suitcase packed and ready in half an hour. Uniform, cocked hat and sword, tails and white tie, if you please! Remember, half an hour!' He pulled out his watch, and clacked the lid open. Then he sat back in his chair and closed his eyes.

His parade uniform hung in the wardrobe on five hooks: frock coat, waistcoat, trousers, cocked hat and sword. Item by item, as though under its own steam, the uniform left the wardrobe, not so much transported by the housekeeper's careful hands as merely escorted by them. The District Commissioner's great trunk with its brown canvas sheath opened its maw, lined with crisply whispering crêpe paper, and swallowed item after item of the uniform. The sword went dutifully into its leather scabbard. The white tie scrolled itself up in a soft paper veil. The white gloves nestled down in the waistcoat lining. Then the trunk closed its lid. And Fräulein Hirschwitz went down to announce that everything was ready.

And so the District Commissioner travelled to Vienna.

He arrived late in the evening. But he knew where to find the men he needed to see. He knew the houses where they lived and the restaurants where they ate. And Government Councillor Smekal and Privy Councillor Pollak and Chief Imperial Audit Councillor Pollitzer and Chief Municipal Councillor Busch and Metropolitan District Councillor Leschnigg and Police Councillor Fuchs: all these and others too saw the extraordinary Herr von Trotta appear on that evening, and even though he was the same age as they were, every one of them was alarmed to see how old the District Commissioner had become. Because he was much older than all of them. Yes, he seemed venerable to them, and they were almost shy of using the *du* form with him. That evening he was seen arriving in many places, and almost at the same time, and they were put in mind of a ghost, a ghost from the olden days of the old Habsburg Monarchy; the shadow of history. And, however extraordinary what he told them sounded to their ears, namely his endeavour to procure a private audience with the Emperor in the next couple of days, still more extraordinary in their eyes was the man himself, the prematurely aged and yet perennially ancient Herr von Trotta, and by and by they came to view his mission as wholly just and natural.

In Montenuovo's office, the office of the Comptroller of the

Household, sat lucky Gustl, whom they envied to a man, even though they knew that his magnificence would come to an abrupt end when the old fellow passed on and Franz Ferdinand came to the throne. They were all of them waiting for it to happen. In the meantime, he had got married, and to the daughter of a Fugger – he, of humble birth, known to them all, from the third row, left side, whom they'd all had to help in exams and whose great 'luck' they had waspishly commented on these past thirty years. Gustl had been ennobled, and had a job in Montenuovo's office. His name was no longer Hasselbrunner, but von Hasselbrunner. His duty was straightforward, child's play, really, whereas the rest of them all had disagreeable and difficult jobs to do. Hasselbrunner! He was the only one who might be able to help.

The following morning, at nine o'clock already, the District Commissioner was standing outside Hasselbrunner's door in the office of the Comptroller of the Household. He was told that Hasselbrunner was away, but there was a chance he might be back in the afternoon. Then, quite by chance, Smetana came by, whom he hadn't managed to see the night before. And Smetana, quick on the uptake and nimble as always, had a few ideas. Hasselbrunner might be away, but there was always Lang next door. Lang was a nice fellow. And so began the indefatigable District Commissioner's peregrination from one office to the next. He was by no means familiar with the secret laws that obtained in all the departments of the K-and-K government in Vienna. Now he was given an insight into their operation. In accordance with these laws, the assistants, deputies or secretaries on whose doors he knocked were grouchy and offhand until he produced his visiting card; then, once they knew his rank, they became ingratiating. The higher officials without exception greeted him with respect and kindness. Every one of them, in the first fifteen minutes, seemed prepared to lay down his career, if not his life, for the District Commissioner. It wasn't until the next fifteen minutes that their expressions dimmed, their faces fell; a great sorrow came over them, and their helpfulness withered, and each one of them said: 'Oh, if it had been anything else but that! I'd have been only too glad! But, my dear Baron Trotta, it's just impossible for the likes of me, well, I'm sure you can imagine it for yourself.' And in these words, or similar, they all talked past the imperturbable Herr von Trotta. He made his way through cloisters and back courtyards, up to the third floor, the fourth, back down to the second, then the ground floor again. And then he decided to wait for Hasselbrunner. He waited till it was afternoon, and then he heard that Hasselbrunner wasn't away at all, he had simply stayed at home. And the intrepid defender of the honour of the house of Trotta took the fight to Hasselbrunner's flat. There at last, there seemed to be a faint glimmer of hope. Together, Hasselbrunner and old Herr von Trotta, they called on this man and that, in the endeavour to reach Montenuovo. Finally, at a little after five o'clock, they tracked down a friend of his in the famous pastry-shop where sybaritic and sweet-toothed servants of the Monarchy occasionally whiled away their afternoons. That his project was unrealizable, the District Commissioner had heard fifteen times already that day. But he remained unwavering in his purpose. And the silvery dignity of his years, and the mildly eccentric, almost a little deranged single-mindedness with which he talked about his son, and the threat to the family's good name, the ceremoni-ousness with which he invariably referred to his late father as the hero of Solferino and nothing else, to the Emperor as His Majesty and nothing else, by and by persuaded his listeners that Herr von Trotta's mission was just and almost rational. If there was no other way, declared this District Commissioner from W., then he, a loyal servant of His Majesty, and the son of the hero of Solferino, would just have to throw himself in front of the carriage in which the Emperor was driven every morning from Schönbrunn to the Hofburg, just like any stallholder on the Naschmarkt. It was left to him, the District Commissioner Franz von Trotta, to resolve the whole matter himself. By now he was so enthusiastic about his mission to save, with the Emperor's help, the honour of the Trottas, that the thought occurred to him that it had taken his son's mischance, as he described the whole thing to himself, to give his long life a proper meaning. Yes, it was purely through that that his life had acquired meaning.

It was the breach of protocol that was the problem. He got to hear that fifteen times over. He replied that his father, the hero of Solferino, had had to break with protocol in his time too. 'He grabbed His Majesty by the shoulder, like this, and pulled him to the ground!' said the District Commissioner. He, who shuddered when he saw sudden or unnecessary actions around him, now stood up, grabbed the shoulder of whichever official he was presently putting in the picture, and tried to reproduce the historic life-saving action there and then. No one smiled. They looked for a way of getting around the protocol.

He went into a stationer's, bought a sheet of regulation office foolscap, a little bottle of ink, and an Adler steel pen, the only type he could write with. Then with flying hand, but in his customary penmanship, which strictly observed the rules of 'hair and shadow', he composed the obligatory request to his K-and-K Apostolic Majesty, not doubting for a moment, or rather, not permitting himself to doubt for a moment, that it would be 'satisfactorily resolved'. He would have been prepared to go and wake Montenuovo in the middle of the night. During the course of the day, in Herr von Trotta's mind, the affair of his son had become that of the hero of Solferino, and thereby an affair of the Emperor's: an affair, more or less, of the fatherland. He had barely eaten anything since leaving W. He looked more gaunt than usual, and he reminded his friend Hasselbrunner of one of those exotic birds in the Schönbrunn zoo, that represent an attempt on the part of nature to replicate the Habsburg physiognomy in a different species. Yes, the District Commissioner reminded everyone who had seen the Emperor of Franz Joseph in person. They were quite unaccustomed to the degree of resolution displayed by the District Commissioner, these gentlemen of the ministries! And the old Herr von Trotta struck them, accustomed as they were to treat altogether graver matters of state with little gossamer witticisms

JOSEPH ROTH

formulated in the coffee houses of the imperial capital, as a character sprung not from a geographically, but from a historically
distant province, the ghost of the history of the fatherland, a pang
of patriotic conscience incarnate. Their invariable propensity to
turn everything into a joke, especially everything relating to
their own doom, was set aside for an hour or so, and the name
'Solferino' awoke in them dread and respect, as the name of the
battle that had first foretold the doom of the Dual Monarchy.
At the spectacle and the speeches of this extraordinary District
Commissioner, they were themselves made to feel a chill. Perhaps
they could then sense the shadow of Death that within a few
months would take them all in its clutches! And across their necks
they felt Death's chill breath.

Herr von Trotta had three more days. And, in the space of a
single night in which he did not sleep or eat or drink, he succeeded
in breaking the iron – or, better, the golden – rule of protocol.
Just as the name of the hero of Solferino could no longer be found
in the history books or the reading primers in Austrian primary
and secondary schools, so too the name of his son is absent from
the protocols of Montenuovo. With the exception of Montenuovo
himself and Franz Joseph's recently deceased manservant, no one
in the world knows that the District Commissioner Franz Baron
von Trotta was received by the Emperor one morning shortly
before his departure to Ischl.

It was a wonderful morning. The District Commissioner had
been up all night, trying on his gala uniform. He had left the
window open. It was a bright summer night. From time to time
he went up to the window. Then he would hear the sounds of
the slumbering city, and perhaps a cock crowing in some distant
farmyard. He smelled the breath of summer; he saw the stars in the
slice of night sky above him, he heard the footfall of the patrolling
nightwatchman. He was waiting for it to be day. He stepped up
to the mirror for the tenth time, straightened his white tie against
the corners of his wing collar, went over the gold buttons on his
frock coat with his white batiste handkerchief again, polished the

golden handle of his sword, brushed his shoes, combed his whiskers, tamed with his comb the few remaining hairs on his bald head
which had a way of sticking up and curling round, and brushed
the skirts of his frock coat once more. He picked up his cocked
hat. He stood in front of the mirror and repeated: 'Your Majesty, I
beg you to have mercy on my son!' In the mirror he saw how the
wings of his whiskers moved, and he thought that was unseemly,
so he tried to say the sentence again, and in such a way that they
didn't move while his words remained audible. He was not in the
least tired. Once more he went up to the window, as though going
up to some sea's or river's edge. He was waiting, yearningly, for
the day, as a man might wait for a ship to take him home. Yes, he
felt homesick for the Emperor. He remained standing in front of
the window until the sky brightened with the grey glimmer of
day, the morning star dimmed, and the confused voices of birds
announced the rising of the sun. Then he turned off the lights in
the room. He rang the bell by the door. He sent for the barber.
He took off his frock coat. He sat down. He had himself shaved.
'Twice,' he told the half-asleep young man, 'and against the grain!'
Then his chin shimmered bluishly between the silver pinions of
his whiskers. The styptic stung, and the powder soothed his neck.
His appointment was for half past eight. Once more he brushed
the greenish-black frock coat. He repeated in front of the mirror:
'Your Majesty, I beg you to have mercy on my son!' Then he
locked the door. He went down the stairs. The whole building was
still asleep. He pulled on the white gloves, smoothed the fingers,
rubbed the leather skin, stopped for a moment in front of the big
mirror on the stairs between the first and second floors, and tried
to catch a glimpse of himself in profile. Then, cautiously, only
touching the steps with the tips of his toes, he descended the red-
carpeted staircase, spreading a silvery dignity, the scent of powder
and eau de cologne and the more pungent smell of shoe polish.
The porter bowed low. A two-horse cab was waiting just outside
the revolving door. The District Commissioner passed his handkerchief across the cab seat and sat down.

'Schönbrunn!' he instructed. And for the whole of the drive, he sat there quite rigidly. The hooves of the horses struck happily against the freshly watered cobbles, and the hurrying white bakers' boys stopped to watch his hackney cab as if it had been a parade. Like the *pièce de résistance* at a parade, Herr von Trotta rolled towards the Emperor.

He left the cab at what seemed to him a suitably respectful distance. And then he walked, with his gleaming gloves either side of his greenish-black frock coat, carefully placing one foot in front of the other to protect his brilliant top boots from the dust on the road, along the straight avenue that led up to the palace of Schönbrunn. In the air above him, the matutinal birds were in jubilant mood. The scents of lilac and jasmine overwhelmed him. From the white chestnut candles, an occasional petal of blossom landed on his shoulder. He flicked it away with his fingers. Slowly he walked up the bright, shallow steps that already looked white in the morning sun. The sentry saluted as District Commissioner von Trotta strode into the palace.

He waited. He was scrutinized, as was the form, by a Gentleman of the Household. His frock coat, his gloves, his trousers, his boots, all were irreproachable. It would have been impossible to detect any shortcoming in Herr von Trotta's appearance. He waited. He waited in the large anteroom to His Majesty's study, through whose six large, arched, still-curtained but already opened windows, the whole wealth of the early summer passed, all the sweet smells and all the wild calls of the birds of Schönbrunn.

He seemed to hear none of it, the District Commissioner. Nor did he seem to notice the chamberlain whose discreet duty it was to examine the Emperor's visitors and give them instructions as to how they were to conduct themselves. Faced with the irreproachable and unapproachable silvery dignity of the District Commissioner, he was silent, and so failed in his duty. Either side of the lofty, white, gold-edged double doors, a couple of very tall sentries stood like statues. The yellow-brown parquet floor, whose centre alone was covered by a reddish carpet, reflected Herr von

Trotta's nether half somewhat unclearly, his black trousers, the gilded point of his scabbard, and the billowy shadows of the skirts of his frock coat. Herr von Trotta rose. With careful, timid, noise- less tread, he walked upon the carpet. His heart was pounding. But his soul was easy. At this moment, barely five minutes before the meeting with his Emperor, Herr von Trotta felt as though he'd been coming here for years, and as though he were in the habit of giving His Majesty Franz Joseph I a personal report every morning on the events of the preceding day in the district of W. in Moravia. The District Commissioner felt perfectly at home in his emperor's palace. At most, he was disturbed by the thought that he might need to run his fingers once more through his whiskers, and that there was no more time in which to pull off his gloves for that purpose. No imperial minister, not even the Comptroller himself could have felt more at home here than Herr von Trotta. From time to time the breeze blew the sun-yellow curtains away from the high arched windows, and a piece of summery greenness crept into the District Commissioner's field of vision. The birds' racket was getting ever louder. Already a few heavy flies were starting to buzz, in the foolish, premature belief that it was midday, and grad- ually the summery heat too was making itself felt. The District Commissioner stopped in the middle of the room, with his cocked hat at his right hip, his left, dazzling-white glove on the golden handle of his sword, his expression directed unwaveringly at the door of the room in which the Emperor was sitting. He stood like that for fully two minutes. The golden chimes of clocks striking in distant church towers wafted in through the open windows. Then all at once, both wings of the double doors were opened. And with head thrust forward, with cautious, silent and never- theless firm tread, the District Commissioner advanced. He made a deep bow, and held it for a few instants, his face to the parquet, not thinking about anything in particular. When he straight- ened up again, the door had been closed behind him. In front of him, behind a desk, stood Emperor Franz Joseph, and it seemed to the District Commissioner that it was his older brother who was standing behind the desk. Yes, Franz Joseph's whiskers were somewhat yellowed, about the mouth especially, but otherwise they were just as white as those of Herr von Trotta. The Emperor was wearing the uniform of a general, and Herr von Trotta that of a District Commissioner. They were like two brothers, of whom one had become an emperor, and the other a district commissioner. Very human, like Herr von Trotta's entire audience with the Emperor, was the movement that Franz Joseph performed at that moment. Fearing he might have a drop on the end of his nose, he took his handkerchief out of his trouser pocket, and wiped it across his moustache. He cast a look down at the file. Aha, Trotta! he thought. Only yesterday he had asked why this audience had suddenly become necessary, but he hadn't listened to the reason. For months now, these Trottas had not stopped bothering him. He remembered having spoken to the youngest scion of the family while visiting the manoeuvres. That had been a lieutenant, an extraordinarily pale lieutenant. This man here must be his father! And already it had slipped the Emperor's mind whether it had been the father or the grandfather of that lieutenant who had saved his life at the battle of Solferino. Had the hero of Solferino suddenly become a district commissioner? Or was this the son of the hero of Solferino he had before him? And he propped his hands on his desk. 'Well, my dear Trotta?' he asked. For it was his duty as an emperor to know – bewilderingly – his visitors by name. 'Your Majesty!' said the District Commissioner with another low bow. 'I beg you to have mercy on my son!' 'What son is that?' asked the Emperor, to play for time, and so as not to betray the fact that he was not conversant with the family history of the Trottas. 'My son is a Lieutenant with the Jägers in B.,' said Herr von Trotta. 'Ah, yes of course, yes of course!' said the Emperor. 'That was the young man I met during the recent manoeuvres! A good fellow!' And because his thoughts had become a little confused, he added: 'He almost saved my life. Or was that you?'

'Your Majesty! That was my father, the hero of Solferino!' said the District Commissioner, with another bow.

'How old is he now?' asked the Emperor. 'The Battle of Solferino. That was the business with the primer, wasn't it?'

'Yes, Your Majesty!' said the District Commissioner.

And suddenly the Emperor clearly remembered his audience with that curious captain. And just as he had done then, when the peculiar captain had been to see him, Franz Joseph I left his position behind the desk, took a few steps towards his visitor, and said: 'Step a little nearer, won't you!'

The District Commissioner stepped nearer. The Emperor put out his thin, trembling hand, an old man's hand with blue veins and little knots on the finger joints. The District Commissioner took the Emperor's hand and bowed. He wanted to kiss it. He didn't know whether he dared to hold it or lay his own hand in it, in such a way that the Emperor could at any time withdraw his own. 'Your Majesty!' the District Commissioner said for the third time, 'I beg you to have mercy on my son!' They were like two brothers. A stranger, seeing them at that moment, would have thought they were two brothers. Their white whiskers, their narrow, sloping shoulders, their matching height and build, gave each of them the impression of confronting his own mirror image. One of them thought he had changed into a district commissioner. And the other thought he had changed into the Emperor. To the Emperor's left and Herr von Trotta's right there were two open windows, also still with the sun-yellow curtains drawn in front of them. 'A lovely day today!' Franz Joseph abruptly said. 'Beautiful!' said the District Commissioner. And while the Emperor gestured towards the window with his left hand, the District Commissioner gestured towards it with his right. And the Emperor thought he was standing in front of his own mirror image.

All at once, the Emperor remembered he still had lots of things to get through before he could leave for Ischl. And he said: 'That's fine then! It'll be taken care of! What has he got up to? Money? Taken care of! Regards to your Papa!'

'My father's dead!' said the District Commissioner.

'Oh, dead is he!' said the Emperor. 'I'm sorry!' And he lost himself in memories of the battle of Solferino. And he returned to his desk, sat down, pressed the button on the bell, and didn't see the District Commissioner leave, head down, sword handle at his left hip, cocked hat at his right.

The morning din of the birds filled the entire room. For all his esteem for birds as some sort of divinely privileged creatures, the Emperor did also at the bottom of his heart, have a certain suspicion of them, a little like his view of artists. And his experiences over the last few years had taught him that these same twittering birds were always to blame for his little episodes of forgetfulness. And therefore he hurriedly jotted down 'Trotta affair' on the file.

Then he waited for the daily visit of the Comptroller of the Household. It was striking nine o'clock already. Ah, that must be him now.

## 19

The awful business with Lieutenant Trotta was buried in a sort of nurturing silence. All that Major Zoglauer would say was: 'Your affair has been taken care of by the very highest authorities. Your Papa's sent the money. We won't waste any more words about it.' Thereupon Trotta wrote to his father. He reported that the threat to his honour had been removed by the very highest authorities. He begged to be forgiven for the unconscionably long time in which he hadn't written, and had failed to answer the District Commissioner's letters. He felt emotional and agitated. He strove to express his feeling. But in his sparse vocabulary, there were no words for remorse, yearning and wistfulness. It was a bitter struggle. He had already signed his letter when he came up with the sentence: 'I am thinking of applying for a furlough soon, so that I may turn to you in person for forgiveness.' This felicitous sentence could not, for formal reasons, be accommodated in a postscript. The Lieutenant therefore set about copying the whole thing out again. It took him another hour. In the process, the external appearance of the letter was much improved. Therewith, it seemed to him that everything had been taken care of, and the whole nasty painful business at an end. He himself was astonished at his 'phenomenal good fortune'. It appeared that the old Emperor was someone the grandson of the hero of Solferino might turn to in any situation. No less encouraging was the now incontestable fact that his father had money. It might be possible, now that the danger of being thrown out of the army was safely over, to resign from it voluntarily, to go and live in Vienna with Frau von Taussig, maybe enter the civil service, wear civilian clothes. It was a long time since he'd been to Vienna. She hadn't been in touch with him. He missed her. He drank a ninety-proof, and missed her a little bit more, but it was that kindly stage of missing that allows a man to cry a little. Of late, the tears had always been there or thereabouts. Lieutenant Trotta looked over the letter once more with satisfaction, a pleasing bit of work, put it in an envelope, and cheerily penned the address. To reward himself, he ordered a double ninety-proof schnapps. Herr Brodnitzer brought it to him in person, and said: 'Kapturak's disappeared!'

A happy day, no doubt about it! The little fellow, who would have been a permanent reminder to the Lieutenant of one of his worst times, had been removed too.

'How so?'

'He was told to leave the country!'

Well now, so far did the arm of Franz Joseph reach, the old man who had spoken to Lieutenant Trotta, with the shining drop on the end of his imperial nose. And so far did the memory of the hero of Solferino reach as well.

A week after the District Commissioner's audience, Kapturak was deported. After the political authorities had received word from above, they stepped in and shut down Brodnitzer's casino as well. There was no more mention of Captain Jedlicek. He disappeared into the silent and inexplicable oblivion from which one could as little return as from the hereafter. He disappeared into the military prisons of the old Monarchy, into the oubliettes of Austria. If his name happened to surface in the minds of one or other of the officers, they were careful to shoo it away at once. Most of them, thanks to their innate gift of forgetfulness, made a great success of this. A new captain arrived, one Captain Lorenz:

a slow-moving, portly, cheerful type, with an invincible tendency to slovenliness, both in person and in the performance of his duty, always prepared to take off his tunic, even though that was against the regulations, and play a game of billiards in his short, patched, sweaty shirtsleeves. He was the father of three children, and the husband of a disappointed wife. He quickly settled in. They got used to him right away. His children, who resembled each other as closely as triplets, came to collect him from the café. By and by the various 'nightingales' – from Olmütz, from Hernals and from Mariahilf – fluttered away. The band now only played twice a week in the café. But even then they were short of verve and spark; in the absence of women wanting to dance, they switched to a classical repertoire, and seemed to spend more time grieving for the old days than playing. The officers were bored again, except when they were drinking, and when they drank, they were sentimental, and overwhelmed with self-pity. It was a humid summer. A second break was instituted during morning drill. The rifles and the private soldiers were covered in sweat. The notes from the trumpeters' cornets struck the dense air and sounded torpid and discouraged. A thin mist, like a veil of silver, or of lead, masked the sky. It lay over the swamps as well, and even stifled the generally exuberant noise of the frogs. The willows did not stir. The whole world was waiting for a wind to arise. But all the winds were asleep. Chojnicki hadn't come home that year. They were all annoyed with him, as though he were some entertainer who had broken his summer contract with the army. To give the lost garrison a fillip, Captain of Horse Zschoch, in the dragoons, had the inspired idea of putting on a big summer party. What made this an even better idea was the fact that the party could serve as a dress rehearsal for the regiment's forthcoming centenary. The regiment wouldn't celebrate its hundredth birthday for another year, but it was as though it was incapable of remaining calm through ninety-nine years without some form of celebration. Everyone said it was an inspired idea. Colonel Festetics said so too, and even imagined that he had coined the expression personally. It was he too who, a few weeks earlier, had begun working on the plans for the great centenary celebration. Every day he went to the regimental office during his hours off, to work on the wheedling letter of invitation that, in six months' time, was to be sent to the regiment's honorary colonel, a petty German aristocrat from an unfortunately somewhat obscure branch of the family. The phrasing of this refined epistle was enough, in and of itself, to keep two men, namely Zschoch and Colonel Festetics, fully occupied. Sometimes they would have furious arguments on points of style. For instance the Colonel approved of the phrase, 'And the regiment, in all due humility and obedience, hereby takes the liberty', while the Captain of Horse was of the opinion that the 'And' was incorrect, and there was something not quite right about the 'humility and obedience' either. They had set themselves to come up with two sentences a day, and by and large they were managing it. Each of them dictated to a copyist, the Captain of Horse to a lance corporal, and the Colonel a staff sergeant. Then they would compare sentences. Each praised the other's effort to the skies. Thereupon the Colonel would lock up the drafts in the large cabinet in the regimental office, to which he alone had the keys. He put the sketches in with other plans he had already made, for the great parade and tournament for officers, and the separate tournament for enlisted men. All these plans lay next to the large, eerie, sealed envelopes containing the secret orders in the event of general mobilization.

So, after Captain of Horse Zschoch had come forward with his inspired idea, they suspended the drafting of the letter to their noble patron, and turned instead to sending out identical invitations in every direction. These concise invitations required less literary effort, and were therefore finished in a matter of days. There were only one or two debates concerning the rank of the guests. For, unlike Colonel Festetics, Count Zschoch was of the view that invitations should be dispatched in order of rank, to the loftiest first, and then to the next lofty, and so on. 'No, all at the same time!' said the Colonel. 'That's an order!' And even though the Festetics were among the best Hungarian families, Count Zschoch drew the inference that the Colonel's blood had given him democratic sympathies. He wrinkled his nose, and sent out the invitations all at once.

The mess superintendent was sent for. He had the addresses of all the reserve officers and those who had retired from the army. All received invitations. Also invited were friends and relatives of the dragoons' officers. These were told that the occasion was a general rehearsal for the next year's centenary celebrations. They were further given to understand that they would have the opportunity to make the personal acquaintance of the regiment's honorary commandant, the German aristocrat from the regrettably somewhat obscure branch of the family. Some of those invited were of more ancient lineage than the commandant. Even so, they were impressed by the chance to meet a mediatized prince. It was decided, as it was to be a 'summer party', to use Count Chojnicki's little wood. This 'little wood' was distinguished from Chojnicki's other woodland holdings by virtue of the fact that it seemed designed by nature and by its owner for parties. It was young. It was made up of small and amusing pines, offered cool and shade, flat paths and a few small clearings that quite evidently existed for no other purpose than to have dance floors laid on them. So the little wood was booked. It was one more occasion for lamenting the absence of Chojnicki. He was invited along all the same, in the hope that he would be unable to resist an invitation to a party given by the dragoons, and that he might even be able to 'bring some more charming persons to the party', as Festetics put it. The Hulins and the Kinskys were invited, the Podstatzkis and the Schönborns, the family of Albert Tassilo Larisch, the Kirchbergs, the Weissenhorns and the Babenhausens, the Sennyis, the Benkyös, the Zuschers and the Dietrichsteins. All of them had some association with the dragoon regiment. When Captain of Horse Zschoch looked over the guest list once more, he said: 'Good gracious, Good Lord!' And he repeated his original oath once or twice more. It was lowering but inevitable that to such a great party some of the plain officers of the Jäger battalion would have to be invited as well. They'll just have to be pushed back against the wall! thought Colonel Festetics. Captain of Horse Zschoch thought the same. While they dictated the invitations to the Jäger officers, one to his lance corporal, the other to his staff sergeant, each glowered at the other. And each blamed the other for the necessity of having to invite officers from the Jäger battalion. Their faces brightened when they got to the name of the Baron Trotta von Sipolje. 'Ennobled after the battle of Solferino,' the Colonel threw in. 'I see!' said Captain of Horse Zschoch. He had the impression that the battle of Solferino had been fought some time in the sixteenth century.

All the regimental clerks were set to twisting garlands of red and green paper. The officers' boys perched on the thin branches of the pine wood and looped wires from one little tree to the next. Three times a week, the dragoons were exempted from drill. They had 'school' in the barracks instead, where they were trained in the arts of making themselves agreeable in distinguished company. Half a squadron was put at the disposal of the cook. The peasants were taught to clean pans, serve trays, hold wine glasses and turn spits. Every morning, Colonel Festetics paid stern calls to kitchen, cellar and mess room. Every enlisted man who was remotely at risk of encountering the guests in any way whatever was provided with white thread gloves. Every morning, those dragoons who had been put up for this demanding distinction at the whim of the sergeants were made to hold out their white-clad hands, fingers spread, for inspection by the Colonel. He tested for cleanliness, fit, stoutness of stitching. He was in a cheerful mood, lit up by a particular, hidden, inner sun. He was astonished and impressed by his own industry, praised it, and solicited more praise from others. He was developing a strange wealth of imagination. Every day he would have perhaps a dozen new ideas, whereas previously he'd got along perfectly well on one a week. And these ideas were not only to do with the party, but the great questions of life, the drill-book for instance, the proper arrangement of dress, and even tactics. In the course of these days, it dawned on Colonel Festetics that he had it in him to make general.

Now that wires had been looped from tree to tree, paper garlands had to be fixed to the wires. They tried a provisional arrangement. The Colonel inspected it. The scene cried out to him for paper lanterns. But seeing as it hadn't rained for a long time, in spite of all the fogs and the humidity, a sudden thunderstorm was a daily possibility. So the Colonel set sentries in the little wood round the clock, and gave them the task of removing garlands and paper lamps at the merest sign of an approaching storm. 'And the wires as well?' he anxiously asked the Captain of Horse. For he knew that great men try to involve their lesser helpers. 'No, they won't come to any harm!' said the Captain of Horse. So they were left on the trees. There were no thunderstorms. It remained humid and close. On the other hand, they realized when some of the guests regretfully replied that they were unable to come, that the Sunday of the dragoons' party was also the day of the party at the renowned Nobles' Club in Vienna. Some of the guests were vacillating between their desire to hear all the latest society news (which could only be guaranteed at the Club ball), and the delightful adventure of visiting the near-mythical border. The exotic was as alluring to them as gossip, as the opportunity to sort out friend from foe, to offer a bit of patronage they had just been asked for, or to secure some that they happened to need just at that moment. A few of the guests promised to communicate their final decision at the eleventh hour, by wire. These replies and the uncertain prospect of wires completely undermined the confidence that Colonel Festetics had acquired over the last few days. 'It's a disaster!' he said. 'It's a disaster!' echoed the Captain of Horse. And they both let their heads droop.

How many rooms should be got ready? A hundred – or would fifty be enough? And where? In the hotel? At Chojnicki's house? He himself unfortunately wasn't there, and had failed to send word either! 'He's a slippery customer, that Chojnicki. I never really trusted him!' said the Captain of Horse. 'You're right there!' affirmed the Colonel. There was a knock on the door, and the orderly announced Count Chojnicki.

'What a capital fellow!' they exclaimed as one.

They greeted him enthusiastically. Privately, the Colonel felt that his genius had lost its way, and needed some support. (Captain of Horse Zschoch felt he had already exhausted his own genius.) Both of them embraced the new arrival, three times apiece, each waiting impatiently for the other's embrace to be over. Then they ordered up some schnapps.

All their deep anxieties were suddenly transformed into easy, pleasant imaginings. For instance, when Chojnicki said: 'Well, let's book a hundred rooms then, and if fifty remain empty, well, too bad!' both of them cried out as one, 'Brilliant!' And they both fell upon the arrival with more, fervent embraces.

In the last week before the party, it didn't rain. All the garlands remained up, and the paper lanterns. Sometimes the non-commissioned officer and four men who camped out like sentries on the edge of the wood, eyeing the west, from where the heavenly enemy was expected, were disturbed by a distant rumble, an echo of faraway thunder. Sometimes pale summer lightnings flickered up in the evening above the blue-grey sky that bunched together in the west, ready to receive the declining red sun. But it was far away, in another world, that these storms emptied themselves. In the quiet little wood, there was a rustling of dry needles and the dry bark of pine trunks. The birds twittered feebly and sleepily. The soft, sandy ground between the trees seemed to glow. There was no storm. The garlands remained up, on their wires.

A few guests arrived on the Friday. They had telegraphed ahead to announce their coming. The officer on duty collected them from the station. The excitement in both barracks grew by the hour. In Brodnitzer's café, the cavalrymen held discussions with the foot soldiers about little or nothing, and with the effect merely of increasing the disquiet. No one was able to remain on his own. Each one's impatience forced him to seek company. They huddled together and whispered, suddenly they were full of fascinating secrets that they had kept silent about for years. They trusted one another absolutely, they loved one another. They sweated companionably in their shared expectancy. The party blotted out the horizon like a mighty festive mountain. They were all of them convinced that it was more than a break from the usual routine, that it was a complete change in all of their lives. At the last moment, they were half afraid of what they had done. The party became autonomous, waving them on, or brandishing its fists in menace. It darkened the heavens, or lit them up. They set to brushing and ironing their gala uniforms. Not even Captain Lorenz in these days would risk a game of billiards. The cosy ease in which he had resolved to pass the rest of his soldier's life was disturbed. He eyed his gala tunic distrustfully, like a slow old horse who has spent years in the shady cool of his stables, and is suddenly forced to participate in a trotting race.

At last, Sunday dawned. Fifty-four guests had arrived. 'Good heavens, great Scot!' Count Zschoch kept exclaiming to himself. He knew perfectly what sort of regiment he was serving in, but surveying the fifty-four illustrious names on the guest list, he thought he had never taken sufficient pride in it before. The party began at one in the afternoon, with an hour-long parade on the exercise ground. A couple of bands had been borrowed from larger garrisons in the vicinity. They played in two open, wooden, circular bandstands set up in the little wood. The ladies sat in canvas-covered baggage carts, wearing summer dresses over stiff corsets and hats as big as cartwheels with stuffed birds nesting in them. Even though they were hot, they smiled, each one an agreeable breeze. They smiled with their lips, their eyes, their breasts secured behind fragrant and tightly fastened clothing; with their filigree lace gloves that went up to their elbows and the tiny handkerchiefs they clutched in their hands, and with which from time to time they liked to dab their noses, softly, softly, so as not to damage them. They sold bonbons, champagne and lots for the wheel of fortune that was spun by the mess superintendent in person, and little coloured bags of confetti that was sprinkled all over them, and that they tried to puff away with flirtatious, pouty mouths. And there was no shortage either of paper chains. They wound themselves round necks and legs, dangled from branches, and transformed all the natural pines into artificial ones. Their green was so much denser and more realistic than the green of nature.

In the skies overhead, the long-awaited clouds had finally assembled. The thunder came ever closer, but the army bands contrived to drown it out. When evening fell over tents, wagons, confetti and dancing, and the Chinese lanterns were lit, no one noticed that sudden gusts of wind set them swaying rather harder than was safe for Chinese lanterns. Although summer lightning lit up the sky with increasing intensity, it still could not compete with the fireworks that the soldiers were setting off behind the little wood, and such flashes of it as were spotted, tended to be taken for misfired rockets. Until all at once someone remarked: 'There's going to be a storm!' And the rumour of the storm began to spread through the little wood.

It was decided to adjourn, therefore, and on foot, on horseback and in wagons, the guests made their way to Chojnicki's house. The windows all stood open. The sheen of candles poured out towards the wide avenue, in a great, flickering fan of luminescence, gilding the ground, and the trees and the leaves looked as though they were made of metal. It was not late, but it was already dark, thanks to the hosts of clouds that were gathering from all sides, and making common cause. The horses, wagons, guests, gaudy ladies and even gaudier officers met again at the entrance to the castle, in the wide avenue and on the gravel-strewn oval forecourt. The riding horses, held by the bridle by soldiers, and the draught horses, controlled with difficulty by the coachmen, grew impatient; the wind passed over their shining hides like an electric comb, causing them to whinny fearfully for their stables, and scrape at the gravel with trembling hooves. The agitation of the elements and of the animals seemed to communicate itself to the humans as well. The lusty cries with which only moments before they had played ball suddenly died. All looked apprehensively to the doors and windows. The large double doors opened, and they made their way inside in groups. Now, whether it was because they were preoccupied with the inherently stimulating, although hardly uncommon, prospect of the storm, or whether they were distracted by the confused sounds of the two bands busily re-tuning their instruments inside the house, no one heard the rapid gallop of the orderly who raced across the forecourt, came to a sudden stop, and in full regulation kit, with glittering helmet, rifle across his shoulders and cartridge pouch on his belt, white lightning flashing around him and purple clouds darkening him, looked not unlike a herald of war in a play. The dragoon dismounted and asked for Colonel Festetics. He was told the Colonel was already inside. A moment later, the Colonel came out, was handed a letter by the orderly, and went back inside. He stopped in the circular hall, which had no ceiling lighting. A footman came up behind him, with a branched candlestick in his hand. The Colonel tore open the envelope. The footman, though trained from earliest youth in the great arts of serving, was nevertheless unable to keep his hand from shaking. The candles he was holding started flickering violently. He made not the slightest effort to peer over the Colonel's shoulder, but the text of the message came within view of his well-trained eyes, a single outsize sentence written very clearly in blue copying pen. As incapable as he would have been of ignoring through closed eyelids one of the flashes of lightning that now were quivering in ever faster succession in every quarter of the sky, so he was of averting his eyes from the terrible, large, blue letters that spelled out: 'There are unconfirmed reports that the heir to the throne has been assassinated in Sarajevo.'

The words struck home, like a single, unbroken word, into the consciousness of the Colonel and the eyes of the footman standing immediately behind him. The envelope slipped from the Colonel's hands. The footman, holding the candlestick in his left hand, stooped down to pick it up with his right. When he stood up straight again, he found himself staring at Colonel Festetics, who had turned round to face him. The footman took a step back. He held the candlestick in one hand, the envelope in the other, and now both were trembling. The flickering candlelight played over the Colonel's face, alternately lighting it and darkening it. The coarse, flushed face of the Colonel, graced with a grey-blond moustache, was now purple, now chalk-pale. The lips trembled slightly, and the moustache quivered. No one else was in the hall, only the Colonel and the footman. From the interior of the house came the sounds of the first muffled waltzes from the two bands, the jingling of glasses, and the murmurs of conversation. Through the door that led out to the forecourt they could see the reflections of distant lightnings, and hear the feeble echo of distant thunder. The Colonel looked at the footman. 'Did you read that?' 'Yes, Colonel!' 'Not a word to a soul!' said Festetics, applying his finger to his lips. He walked off, tottering slightly. Perhaps it was the uncertain illumination that made his walk seem unsteady.

The footman, curious, and as excited at being sworn to silence as by the bloody news he had just learned, waited for one of his colleagues to come and take over his candlestick and position, so that he could go on into one of the rooms and perhaps hear more. Furthermore, though he was a settled and sensible man of middle age, he was also starting to feel a little scared in this hall, which his candles could only barely illuminate, and which seemed to sink into ever deeper and browner darkness following each violent blue-white lightning flash. Heavy waves of charged air loitered in the room, the storm was hesitating. The footman made a metaphysical connection between the sudden storm and the terrible news. It seemed to him that the hour was finally come when the supernatural forces of the world would appear in their full viciousness and unmistakableness. And, holding the candlestick in his left hand, he crossed himself. At that moment, Chojnicki came out and gazed at him in astonishment, and asked whether he was so afraid of the thunderstorm. It wasn't just the thunderstorm, replied the footman. Even though he had promised to remain silent, he was no longer able to bear the burden of his knowledge all by himself. 'What else?' asked Chojnicki. Colonel Festetics had received some terrible news, said the man. And he reported it, word for word.

Immediately, Chojnicki ordered all the windows, which were already shut on account of the storm, to be draped, and then he called for his carriage to be got ready. He was going into town. As the horses were being put to outside, a cab drove up, with its dripping tarpaulin pulled down, evidence that it had come from somewhere where the storm was already lashing down. From the cab stepped the dapper district mayor who had broken up the political protest of the striking brush-factory workers, with an attaché case under his arm. He announced, as though this were the purpose of his visit, that it was raining in town. Thereupon he told Chojnicki that there had been an attempt on the life of the heir to the throne of the Dual Monarchy, in Sarajevo. Travellers who had arrived in the past three hours had been the first to break the news. A little later, a garbled telegram in code had arrived from the government. Evidently the storm had affected wire communications, and so a request for clarification had so far remained unanswered. Besides, it was a Sunday, and not many people were at their desks. However, excitement in town and even in the outlying villages was growing steadily, and people were out in the streets, in spite of the weather.

As the mayor breathily communicated all this, there could be heard from within the sliding feet of the dancers, the bright clinking of glasses, and from time to time a rumble of male laughter. Chojnicki decided he would begin by assembling a few of the higher-ranking guests, those he took to be most cautious and still sober, in a separate room. Using all manner of pretexts, he brought them one after another to the designated room, presented the mayor to them, and told them what had happened. Among those selected were the Colonel of the dragoons, the Major of the Jäger battalion, both with their adjutants, and among the officers of the Jägers, Lieutenant Trotta. The room offered little in the way of seating, so that several of them were forced to lean against the walls, and others, in their ignorance and high spirits, not knowing what they had come to hear, sat down cross-legged on the carpet. But then, even when everything had been said, they remained where they were. Some may have been paralysed by the shock, others were merely paralytic. Others again were by nature indifferent to everything that went on outside them, crippled as it were by their own inborn refinement: they didn't think it was proper to alter their posture simply because of some catastrophe. Some hadn't even brushed the scraps of coloured paper chains and confetti off their shoulders, necks and heads. And their carnivalesque attributes somehow further intensified the horror of the news.

After a few minutes it grew warm in the little room. 'Can we open a window!' said one. Another pulled open one of the tall narrow windows, leaned out, and a moment later jerked back inside. A white hot lightning bolt of extreme violence came down in the park in front of the window. It couldn't be determined precisely where it had struck, but the splintering crack of trees could be heard. There was a heavy black rustling of their toppling crowns. At that, even the casually cross-legged, the apathetic, leaped to their feet and the intoxicated started to reel around, and they all went pale. They felt amazement that they were still alive. They held their breath, looked at one another with stark staring eyes, and waited for the crash of thunder to follow. It was only a second or two, but between the lightning and the thunder, a whole eternity seemed to fit. All of them moved closer. They formed a knot of heads and bodies round the table. For a moment, they all bore a fraternal likeness, different though their individual features were. It was as though they had never experienced a storm before in their lives. In awe and terror, they waited out the brief crack of thunder. Then they breathed again. And, while the swollen clouds that had been sundered by the lightning now started to empty themselves with a jubilant rush outside the window, the men returned to their former places.

'We have to call off the party!' said Major Zoglauer.

Captain of Horse Zschòch, a few sprinkles of confetti on his shoulders and half a paper chain round his neck, leaped to his feet. He was indignant, in his capacity as count, as Captain of Horse, as dragoon in particular and cavalryman in general, and most particularly as an individual of an uncommon sort, in short, as Zschoch. His brief, dense eyebrows bristled up, and two spiny thickets confronted Major Zoglauer. His big, foolish, pale eyes that reflected back things they might have taken in years previously, but only rarely what was before them, seemed now to express the quattrocento loftiness of his Zschoch forebears. The lightning, the thunder, the terrible news, all the events of the past few minutes – these were almost forgotten. His memory retained only the efforts he had put into the regimental celebration, into his inspired idea. He didn't have a good head either; he had been drinking champagne, and his little snub nose was sweating slightly.

'That news is wrong,' he said, 'it's just wrong. I want someone to prove to me that it's true, it's a damned lie, you heard it, it was "rumoured" or "reported" or whatever that vile political tag was!'

'A rumour's cause enough!' said Zoglauer.

Then Herr von Babenhausen, Master of Horse with the reserve, got involved. He was tipsy and fanned himself with his handkerchief which he alternately produced and stuffed back in his sleeve. He peeled himself off the wall, walked up to the table, and narrowed his eyes: 'Gen'l'men!' he said, 'Bosnia's a long way from here. We don't care about any rumours! I shit on rumours! If it's true, we'll learn soon enough anyway!'

'Bravo!' called out Baron Nagy Jenö, one of the Hussars. Even though he was indisputably descended from a Jewish grandfather in Ödenburg, and the barony had only been purchased in his father's time, he was convinced the Magyars were one of the most aristocratic races in the Monarchy, if not the whole world, and he strove, with some success, to forget his own Semitic descent, by aping all the excesses of the Hungarian gentry.

'Bravo!' he repeated. He had trained himself to love or hate things inasmuch as they favoured or hindered the cause of Hungarian nationalism. He had spurred on his heart to hate the heir to the Monarchy, because it was said that he favoured the Slavs and snubbed the Hungarians. Baron Nagy had not come all the way to a party on this desperate frontier, only to have it called off because of some incident or other. To him it was nothing less than a betrayal of the entire Magyar nation if one of its representatives allowed himself to be cheated of the opportunity to dance a csardas – which was a racial imperative – by a rumour. He screwed his monocle in more tightly, as he always did when a patriotic display was called for, just as an old man might grip his stick more tightly when he's about to go for a walk, and in a Hungarian-inflected German that sounded as though he were spelling through his tears: 'Herr von Babenhausen is quite right! Quite right! If one heir to the Monarchy has been assassinated, then there are other heirs to the Monarchy!'

Herr von Sennyi, with more Hungarian blood in his veins than Herr von Nagy, and seized by a sudden panic that an erstwhile Jew might outdo him in Magyar nationalism, got to his feet and said: 'For all we know, the heir to the throne may have been assassinated, but firstly we have no confirmation of the fact, and secondly it's nothing to do with us!'

'It does have something to do with us,' said Count Benkyö, 'but he's not been assassinated at all. It's just a rumour!'

Outside, the rain teemed down with steady violence. The blue-white lightning flashes became rarer, the thunder took itself away into the distance. First Lieutenant Kinsky, born and bred on the banks of the Moldau, claimed that the heir to the succession had represented only a rather slim chance for the

Monarchy – if the pluperfect tense was even appropriate at all. The First Lieutenant agreed with those who had spoken before him: the news that the heir to the throne had been assassinated should be treated as a mere rumour. They were all so far from the so-called scene here, that they could know nothing for sure. The full truth would only – could only – be known long after the party had run its course.

The drunken Count Battyanyi thereupon began to address his compatriots in Hungarian. No one else understood a word. They remained quiet, looked at whoever was speaking, and bided their time, though with a little consternation. But the Hungarians – perhaps it was a national custom of theirs – seemed quite prepared to carry on like that all night. Though the rest of them didn't understand a single syllable, the others could tell from the expressions on their faces that they had gradually forgotten all about everyone else. Sometimes they all burst out laughing together. The others felt offended, not so much because this was no time for mirth, as by their inability to understand what provoked it. Jelacich, a Slovene, lost his temper. He hated the Hungarians as passionately as he despised the Serbs. He loved the Monarchy. He was a patriot. But he stood there in shrugging, gesturing perplexity, an embodiment of love of country, like a banner that wants to be hung out somewhere, but can't find a suitable roof ledge. Some compatriots of his, Slovenes and their Croatian cousins, lived under Hungarian suzerainty. The whole breadth of Hungary lay between Master of Horse Jelacich and Austria, Vienna, and the Emperor Franz Joseph. The successor had been slain in Sarajevo, practically in his homeland, possibly even by the hand of a Slovene like Jelacich himself. If the Master of Horse set about defending the dead man against the attacks of the Hungarians (in this society, he was the only other man who understood Hungarian), he laid himself open to the objection that it was his own fellow countrymen who had done the deed. Indeed, he even felt somewhat guilty. He didn't know why. His family had given loyal and industrious service to the Habsburg dynasty for a hundred and fifty years. But his two half-grown sons spoke of autonomy for the South Slavs and hid leaflets from him that were probably printed in enemy Belgrade. He loved his sons! Every afternoon at one o'clock, when his regiment filed past the gymnasium, they flew towards him, exploding through the large brown school gates with tousled hair and laughter in their wide open mouths, and his fatherly tenderness left him no option but to get off his horse and hug his boys in his arms. He shut his eyes when he saw them reading their dubious newspapers, and he shut his ears to their seditious talk. He was wise, and he understood that he stood powerlessly between his ancestors and his descendants, themselves destined to be ancestors, one day, of an entirely different breed. They had his features, the same colour of hair and eyes, but their hearts beat to a different rhythm, their throats sang new and strange songs that he did not know. At forty, the Master of Horse felt like an old man, and his sons were like bewildering great-grandchildren to him.

It's all one, he thought at that moment, stepped up to the table and smacked his hand down on its surface. 'We should like to ask the gentlemen,' he said, 'to continue their conversation in German.'

Benkyö, who had just been speaking, stopped and replied: 'All right, I can say it in German too: we were just agreeing, my compatriots and I, that it's a good thing if the son of a bitch is dead!'

Everyone leaped to their feet. Chojnicki and the dapper mayor left the room. The guests were on their own. They had been given to understand that there should be no witnesses to any dissension within the army. Lieutenant Trotta stood by the door. He had drunk heavily. His face was pale, his limbs were slack, his mouth was dry, his heart felt hollow. He was clearly intoxicated, but to his surprise there wasn't the usual benign fog in front of his eyes. Rather, he had the impression he could see everything much more clearly, as through a sheet of transparent glass. Faces he had seen today for the first time looked very familiar to him. This hour, this moment, he had seen them before as well, they were the enactment of something he had often dreamed. The fatherland of the Trottas was crumbling and collapsing in pieces.

Home – the Moravian district town of W.: that might still be Austria. Every Sunday, Herr Nechwal's band played the Radetzky March. Once a week, on a Sunday, Austria still existed. The Emperor, the white-bearded, forgetful old man with the crystal drop on the end of his nose, and old Herr von Trotta – they were Austria. Old Jacques was dead. The hero of Solferino was dead. The military surgeon Dr Demant was dead. 'Get out of the army!' he had said. I will get out of this army, thought the Lieutenant. My grandfather left it too. I'll tell them, he thought. As years before in Frau Resi's establishment, he felt the compulsion to act. Was there no picture for him to rescue here? He felt his grandfather's dark gaze boring into the back of his head. He took one step towards the middle of the room. He didn't know yet what he was going to say. Some of them were already watching him. 'I know,' he began, and he still didn't know what would follow. 'I know,' he said again, and took another step forwards, 'I know that His Royal and Imperial Highness, the Archduke and heir to the throne, has been murdered.'

He stopped. He pressed his lips together. They made a tight pale pink line. In his small dark eyes burned a bright, almost white, fire. His black dishevelled hair fell over his low forehead and darkened the furrow over the bridge of his nose, the cavern of fury, the Trottas' inheritance. His head was lowered. His fists hung clenched at the end of slack arms. Everyone looked at his hands. If those present had been familiar with the portrait of the hero of Solferino, they might have thought it was the old Trotta, returned from the dead.

'My grandfather,' the Lieutenant recommenced, and he could feel the old man's stare at the back of his head, 'my Grandfather saved the Emperor's life. And I, his grandson, will not stand idly by while the house of our Supreme Commander is vilified. The behaviour of these gentlemen is scandalous!' He raised his voice. He had never shouted in front of his comrades, or even in front of his men. 'Scandalous!' he said again. The echo of his voice rang in his ears. The drunken Benkyö took a staggering step towards the Lieutenant.

'Scandalous!' shouted the Lieutenant for the third time.

'Scandalous!' echoed Captain of Horse Jelacich.

'The next man to say a word against the departed,' the Lieutenant resumed, 'I will personally shoot down!' He reached for his pocket. As the drunken Benkyö started muttering something, Trotta screamed: 'Be quiet!' in a voice that sounded borrowed to him, a voice of thunder, maybe it was the voice of the hero of Solferino. He felt himself at one with his grandfather. He was himself the hero of Solferino. It was his own picture that was hanging in the gloaming under the ceiling of his father's drawing room.

Colonel Festetics and Major Zoglauer stood up. For the first time in the history of the Austrian army, a lieutenant was ordering captains, majors and colonels to be quiet. Not one of those present still believed that the assassination of the heir to the throne was just a rumour. They saw the heir to the throne lying in a smoking pool of his own blood. They feared they might see blood here, in this room, in another second. 'Order him to be quiet!' whispered Colonel Festetics.

'Lieutenant,' said Zoglauer, 'get out!'

Trotta turned to face the door. Just at that moment, it was pushed open. A mob of guests spilled in, with confetti and paper chains on their heads and shoulders. The door stayed open. Women could be heard laughing in other rooms, and music, and the scuffing steps of the dancers. Someone called out: 'The heir to the throne has been assassinated!'

'The Funeral March!' shouted Benkyö.

'The Funeral March!' other voices called out.

They flowed out of the room. In the two large rooms where there had thus far been dancing, the two army bands struck up Chopin's Funeral March, conducted by grinning, beet-red bandleaders. A few guests ambled round and round in circles, in step to the dirge, with gaudy confetti and paper chains on their shoulders and hair. Men in uniform and others in suits led women on their arms. Their unsteady feet followed the macabre, stumbling rhythm. The bands played without a score, not so much conducted as accompanied by the slow, swishing shapes the bandleaders inscribed in the air with their black batons. Sometimes one of the two would fall behind, and, to try and catch up with the other who had raced on ahead, would skip a couple of bars. The guests marched in a circle round the empty, shining round of the parquet. They went round and round, each one a mourner behind the corpse of the person in front, and in the middle were the invisible corpses of the heir to the throne and the Monarchy. Everyone was drunk. Whoever had not had enough, soon had a spinning head from going round and round. Gradually the bands stepped up the tempo, and the sleepwalking legs fell into a march. The drummers drummed incessantly, and the heavy drumsticks for the big kettledrum were twirling like alert young brushes. The drunken drummer suddenly hit the silver triangle, and at that same moment, Count Benkyö performed a little skip of joy. 'The son of a bitch is dead!' he screamed in Hungarian. But everyone understood him as clearly as if he'd said it in German. Suddenly some started skipping. The bands knocked out the Funeral March at a brisker and brisker pace. And, in between, the triangles tinkled their glamorous, drunken, tinny laughs.

At last, Chojnicki's staff started to clear away the instruments. The musicians grinningly complied. Wide-eyed, the violinists watched their violins disappear, the cellists their cellos, the horn-players their horns. A few still stroked their bows over the unresponsive material of their sleeves and swayed their heads to inaudible melodies still playing in their drunken heads. When they took the drummer's various percussion things away, he continued to beat and swish his various sticks about in the empty air. The bandleaders, who were the most deeply drunk, were finally handed away by two footmen apiece, as if they too had been instruments. The guests laughed. And then there was silence. No one made a sound. All remained where they were sitting or standing, and no one stirred. After the instruments, it was the turn of the bottles. And the occasional guest who was still clutching a half-empty glass in his hands had that taken away as well.

Lieutenant Trotta left the house. Colonel Festetics, Major Zoglauer and Captain of Horse Zschoch were sitting on the steps. The rain had stopped. There was no more than the occasional drop that fell from the depleted clouds or from the projecting roofs. The three men had been given large white cloths to lay on the bare stone. It was as though they were sitting on their own funeral shrouds. Large, irregular patches of damp were evident on their dark blue backs. The wreckage of a sodden paper chain clung loyally to the Captain's neck.

The Lieutenant stood before them. They didn't move. Their heads were down. They might have been a military group in a waxworks.

'Major!' Trotta addressed Zoglauer, 'tomorrow I will ask you for my discharge from the army!'

Zoglauer got to his feet. He put out his hand to speak, and produced not a sound. Gradually it grew lighter, a soft wind tore up the clouds and in the glimmering silver of the brief night, which already carried an intimation of morning, faces could be clearly seen. In the gaunt face of the Major, all was movement. The wrinkles flowed into one another, the skin twitched, the chin wandered this way and that, it seemed to be yawing to and fro, tiny muscles played around the jawbones, the eyelids fluttered and the cheeks trembled. Everything was in commotion, driven by the turmoil of the confused, unspoken and unsayable words in his mouth. A suggestion of insanity haunted this face. Zoglauer pressed Trotta's hand, for seconds, eternities. Festetics and Zschoch continued to squat impassively on the steps. There was a pronounced scent of elderflower. Gentle drops of rain fell, and a mild soughing in the drenched tree tops, and the sounds of animals silenced by the storm were fearfully beginning again. The music inside the house had stopped. Only the sounds of people talking still came through the closed and curtained windows.

'Maybe you're right, you've got your life ahead of you!' Zoglauer said at last. It was a poor and pathetic remnant of all that had gone through his mind in that time. The rest, a large confused tangle of thoughts, he swallowed. It was long past midnight. But in the town, people were still standing talking to each other on the wooden pavements in front of their houses. They fell silent when the Lieutenant passed.

By the time he reached the hotel, day was already breaking. He opened his wardrobe. He packed two uniforms, his civilian suit, his linen and Max Demant's sabre in his suitcase. He was in no hurry, he took his time. He calculated each action by the clock. He made them last a long time. He was afraid of the emptiness that would be left before morning report.

It was morning, Onufri brought in his uniform and his gleaming polished boots.

'Onufri,' said the Lieutenant, 'I'm leaving the army.'

'Yes, sir!' said Onufri. He went out, along the corridor, down the stairs, to the little room where he slept, he packed up his things in a coloured handkerchief, secured it to the end of his stick, and left it all on his bed. He decided he would go home, to Burdlaki, the harvest would be soon. He had no business with the K-and-K army any more. That sort of thing was called 'desertion' and you were shot for it. But the gendarmes only came to Burdlaki once a week, and you could hide. How many had done that! Panteleimon, the son of Ivan, Grigori, the son of Nicholas, Pavel with the pock marks, Nikofor with the red hair. Only one man had ever been caught and punished, and that was a long time ago!

So far as the Lieutenant was concerned, he brought up his request for a discharge from the army at officers' report. He was given a leave of absence, to take effect immediately. He said goodbye to his comrades on the drill-grounds. They didn't know what to say to him. They stood around him in a vague circle, until Zoglauer finally found the formula for the occasion. It wasn't terribly arcane. It was: 'All the best, then!' and everyone else used it after him.

The Lieutenant drove round to Chojnicki's house. 'You can always stay with me!' said Chojnicki. 'I'll take you to the station!' For one fleeting moment, Trotta thought of Frau von Taussig. Chojnicki guessed as much, and said: 'She's with her husband. His latest breakdown will last for a long time. Maybe it will even keep him there. He's quite right. I envy him. I've been to see her, by the way. She's aged, my friend, she's aged!'

The next morning at ten o'clock, Lieutenant Trotta arrived in the District Commissioner's residence. His father was in his office. He saw him as soon as he opened the door. He was sitting next to the window. The sun came through the green blinds, and drew narrow stripes on the burgundy carpet. A fly buzzed, a clock ticked. It was cool and shady and quiet, as it had once been in the summer holidays. Somehow, there was the feeling of an odd new gloss lying over everything in the room. He didn't know what it was. The District Commissioner got up. The strange new shimmer seemed to come from him in some way. The pure silver of his beard tinted the muffled green daylight and the reddish hue of the carpet. It gave out the mild luminescence of an unknown, possibly otherworldly light that had begun to dawn right in the middle of Herr von Trotta's terrestrial life in the way that the mornings of this world break even while the stars are still visible in the night sky. Many years ago, when Carl Joseph had come from Mährisch-Weisskirchen to spend his holidays here, his father's whiskers had still been parts of a small black forked cloud.

The District Commissioner remained standing beside his desk. He allowed his son to approach, put his pince-nez down on some files, and opened his arms. They embraced quickly. 'Sit down!' said the old man, pointing to the armchair where Carl Joseph had sat as a cadet, on those Sundays between the hours of nine and noon, his cap on his knees and his gleaming snow-white gloves on his cap.

'Father!' began Carl Joseph. 'I'm leaving the army!'

He stopped. He felt right away that he would be able to explain nothing while he was sitting down. So he stood up, and faced his father across his desk, and looked at his silver whiskers.

'In the wake of the tragedy,' his father said, 'that befell us all the day before yesterday, such a departure is more in the nature of – of – of a desertion.'

'The whole army has deserted,' replied Carl Joseph. He left his place. He began to walk to and fro across the room, with his left hand at his back, using his right to gesture as he spoke. Many years ago, the old man had used to walk like that across the room. A fly buzzed, a clock ticked. The beams of sunlight on the carpet grew more and more pronounced, the sun was rising fast, it must already be high in the sky. Carl Joseph broke off his explanation to look at the District Commissioner. The old man sat there, his hands dangled down from the armrests of the chair, half covered by the stiff, round, shiny cuffs. His head slumped on to his chest, and the wings of his whiskers rested against his lapels. He is young and foolish, thought the son. He's a sweet young white-haired fool. Maybe I'm his father, the hero of Solferino. I've grown old, he's merely sunk in time. He walked back and forth, and he proclaimed: 'The Monarchy is dead, it's dead!' He shouted, and then he stopped.

'I expect you're right!' murmured the District Commissioner.

He rang, and instructed the beadle: 'Tell Fräulein Hirschwitz that we're lunching twenty minutes later than usual.'

'Come along!' he said, and he stood up, took down his hat and stick. They went to the park.

'A bit of fresh air never hurt anyone!' said the District Commissioner. They avoided the kiosk where the young blonde served soda water with raspberry syrup. 'I'm tired!' said the District Commissioner. 'Let's sit down!' For the first time in Herr von Trotta's tenure of office, he sat on one of the ordinary park benches. He traced some meaningless scribbles in the dust with his stick, and said quietly: 'I went to see the Emperor. I didn't mean to tell you, but I did. It was the Emperor who settled your affair in person. Now, not another word!'

Carl Joseph pushed his hand under his father's arm. He felt the old man's skinny arm as he had felt it years before, on their evening walk in Vienna. He left his hand there. They stood up together. They went home, arm in arm.

Fräulein Hirschwitz appeared in the grey silk she kept for Sundays. A strand of hair in her lofty coiffure now matched its grey. In spite of the short notice, she had managed to produce a Sunday lunch: noodle soup, boiled beef and cherry dumplings.

But the District Commissioner didn't say a single word about it. It was as though he were eating a common or garden chop.

## 20

A week later, Carl Joseph said goodbye to his father. They
embraced in the hall, before getting in the cab. The older
Herr von Trotta did not approve of such intimacies being performed on railway platforms, in full view of any stray person
who happened along. It was a quick embrace, as they generally
were, in the damp atmosphere of the passage and the chill that
came off the flagstones. Fräulein Hirschwitz was already in
position on the balcony. Herr von Trotta's efforts to explain to
her that this was no occasion for waving had been unavailing.
That too might be something to do with her Prussian sense of
duty. Even though it wasn't raining, Herr von Trotta opened
an umbrella. A mildly overcast sky was sufficient cause for him.
Moreover, Fräulein Hirschwitz would be unable to see him
from the balcony. He didn't say a word. Not until his son was
on the train did the old man raise a hand with outstretched
finger: 'It would be a good thing,' he said, 'if you were to leave
on medical grounds. It's always better to have a reason to leave
the army.'

'Very well, Papa!' said the Lieutenant.

Moments before the train pulled out, the District Commissioner
left the platform. Carl Joseph watched him go, with his upright

walk and the furled umbrella pointing up like a drawn sword. Herr von Trotta didn't turn back to look.

Carl Joseph was given his medical discharge. 'What will you do now?' his comrades asked. 'I've got a job!' said Trotta, and they didn't ask any more questions.

He enquired after Onufri. He was told in the regimental office that his batman Kolohin had deserted.

Lieutenant Trotta went to the hotel. Slowly he changed his clothes. First he unbuckled his sabre, the emblem and weapon of his honour. He had been afraid of that moment. To his surprise, it passed without a pang. There was a bottle of ninety-proof on the table, but he didn't even need a drink. Chojnicki was coming to pick him up, there was the signal of his whip outside; then he was in the room. He sat down and watched. It was afternoon, three o'clock struck from the church tower. All the rich voices of summer flowed in through the open window. Summer itself was calling to Lieutenant Trotta. Chojnicki, in his pale grey suit and yellow boots, his yellow bamboo whip handle in his hand, was an envoy of summer. The Lieutenant passed his sleeve over the dull sheath of his sabre, pulled out the sword, breathed over it, wiped it with his handkerchief, and laid the weapon in its case. It was as the washing of a corpse before the burial. Prior to strapping the case to his suitcase, he balanced it one last time on the palm of his hand. Then he put Max Demant's sword in with it. He read the inscription carved under the hilt. 'Get out of the army!' Demant had told him. Well, now he was getting out of the army . . .

The frogs croaked, the crickets thrummed, outside the window Chojnicki's chestnut horses were whinnying, pulling a little at the light wagonet, so that its axles complained. The Lieutenant stood there in his unbuttoned coat, the black rubber neck-band peeping through the open green facings of his tunic. He turned and said: 'The end of a career!'

'The career no longer exists!' said Chojnicki. 'The career itself is finished.'

Then Trotta took off his coat, the coat of the Emperor. He

stretched the tunic over the table, as he had been taught to do at cadet school. First he folded the stiff collar, then the sleeves and laid them in the lining. Then he folded up the lower half of the tunic; already it looked like a little parcel, with grey shimmering silk lining. Over it came the trousers, twice folded. Now Trotta put on his grey civilian suit; he kept his belt, last memento of his career (he had never got along with braces). 'My grandfather,' he said, 'would have packed up his army life just like this in his day too!'

'I dare say!' affirmed Chojnicki.

The suitcase was still open, Trotta's army self lay inside it, a corpse folded up in regulation style. It was time to shut the suitcase. Now the pain suddenly came over the Lieutenant, the tears welled up in his throat, he turned towards Chojnicki to say something. He had gone to army school at the age of seven, at ten he was a cadet. He had been a soldier all his life. The military Trotta had to be buried and mourned. You didn't put a body into the ground without tears. It was good to have Chojnicki sitting by.

'Let's have a drink!' said Chojnicki. 'You're feeling sad!'

They drank together. Then Chojnicki got up and closed the Lieutenant's suitcase.

Brodnitzer personally carried the suitcase to the carriage. 'You were a model guest, Baron!' said Brodnitzer. He stood, hat in hand, next to the carriage. Chojnicki already had the reins in his hands. Trotta felt a sudden surge of affection towards Brodnitzer. Farewell! he wanted to say. But Chojnicki clicked his tongue, and the horses pulled, raising their heads and their tails at once, and the light, elegant wheels of the carriage crunched along the sandy street as though it were a soft bed.

They drove through the swamps, set echoing now by the noise of the frogs.

'This is where you'll live!' said Chojnicki.

It was a little house on the edge of the woods, with green shutters like those on the windows at home. Jan Stepaniuk was living there, an under-forester, an old man with long drooping moustaches of tarnished silver. He had served twelve years in the army. He addressed Trotta as 'Lieutenant', returning to his military mother tongue. He wore a coarse linen shirt with a narrow collar with red and blue stitching. The wind puffed out its wide sleeves, making his arms like wings.

And there Lieutenant Trotta stayed.

He was resolved not to see any of his comrades again.

By the light of a flickering candle, in his wooden chamber, he wrote to his father on fibrous, yellowish office paper, the salutation four fingers' breadth from the upper edge, the body of the letter two fingers from the lateral edge. The letters resembled one another like official missives.

He didn't have much work to do. In large green ledgers with black bindings he kept a record of the names of the wage-labourers, their wages, the requirements of the guests who were staying at Chojnicki's. He added up the figures, well intentionedly but incorrectly, reported on the condition of the poultry, the pigs, the fruit that was sold or kept for household consumption, the little field of yellow hops, and the hop-kiln that was hired out to a buying agent.

He knew the local language now. He could more or less understand what the peasants said. He traded with red-haired Jews, who were already beginning to buy in wood for the winter. He learned the different prices for birch, fir, pine, oak, linden and sycamore. He was mean. Just like his grandfather, the hero of Solferino, the knight of truth, he counted out hard silver coins with his hard, bony fingers when he travelled into town of a Thursday, to the pig market, to buy saddles, hames, yokes and scythes, whetstones, reaping hooks, hoes and seed. When he chanced to see an officer passing by, he ducked his head. It was an unnecessary precaution. His moustaches grew and grew, the stubble stood tough and black and thick on his cheeks, he was unrecognizable. Preparations for the harvest were already in full swing, the peasants stood outside their huts, whetting their scythes on round, brick-red stones. All over the country sounded

342

the chafe and scrape of steel on stone, drowning out the song of the crickets. At night, the Lieutenant would occasionally hear music and noise from Chojnicki's 'new castle'. He took those sounds into his sleep with him, they were no different from the occasional crowing of the cocks at night, or the dogs barking at the full moon. At last, he was contented, lonely and at peace. It was as though he had never led any other sort of life. When he couldn't sleep, he got up, picked up his stick, walked through the fields, through the polyphony of night, and awaited the morning when he'd greet the red sun and breathe in the dew and the gentle song of the wind that portends the day. He felt as fresh then as he did after a good night's sleep.

Every afternoon, he walked through the surrounding villages. 'Praise be to Christ Jesus!' said the peasants. 'For ever and ever, amen!' replied Trotta. He had the same bent-kneed walk as they did. That was the way the peasants of Sipolje walked.

One day found him walking in the village of Burdlaki. The tiny church tower, the finger of the village, pointed up into the blue sky. It was a quiet afternoon. The cocks crowed sleepily. The mosquitoes danced and buzzed up and down the length of the main street. Suddenly a peasant with a heavy black beard came out of his hut, stood in the middle of the road, and greeted him: 'Praise be to Christ Jesus!'

'For ever and ever, amen!' responded Trotta, making to walk on. 'Lieutenant, remember Onufri!' said the bearded peasant. The beard covered his face, a dense, black, thickly feathered fan. 'Why did you desert?' asked Trotta. 'Only go home!' said Onufri. There was no point in asking such stupid questions. He understood Onufri. He had served the Lieutenant, as the Lieutenant had served the Emperor. The Fatherland no longer existed. It was crumbling, it was breaking apart. 'Aren't you afraid?' asked Trotta. Onufri was not afraid. He was staying at his sister's. The gendarmes passed through the village once a week, without looking round. They were Ukrainians as well, peasants like Onufri. So long as no one sent in a written accusation to the sergeant, there was nothing to worry about. And in Burdlaki people didn't denounce one another.

'Farewell, Onufri!' said Trotta. He carried on up the curving road, which emerged unexpectedly into a landscape of wide fields. Onufri followed him to the bend in the road. He heard the tramp of hobnailed soldiers' boots on the pebbled road. Onufri had taken his army boots with him when he went. Trotta was going to the Jew Abramchik, who ran the village tavern. From him you could get soap, schnapps, cigarettes, loose tobacco and postage stamps. The Jew had a flame-red beard. He sat outside the arched gateway of his tavern, and spread a glow that you could see down the road a mile away. When he grows old, thought the Lieutenant, he'll be a white-haired Jew like Max Demant's grandfather.

Trotta drank a schnapps, bought tobacco and postage stamps, and went on. From Burdlaki, the road led past Oleksk, to the village of Sosnov, then on to Bytok, Leschnitz and Dombrova. He walked this road every day. It crossed the railway lines twice, on two bleached, black and yellow level-crossings, and a glassy, incessant ringing came from the crossing-keepers' huts. Those were the joyous sounds of the world beyond, which no longer interested Baron Trotta. The world beyond was wiped out, as with a sponge. Wiped out were the years with the army, as though he had always walked over fields and country roads, always with his stick in his hand, and never a sabre at his hip. He lived as Grandfather had done, the hero of Solferino, and like Great-grandfather, the invalid in the castle grounds at Laxenburg, and maybe like all his nameless, unknown forebears, the peasants of Sipolje. Always the same route, past Oleksk, to Sosnov, to Bytok, to Leschnitz and Dombrova. These villages made a ring around Chojnicki's castle, they were his villages. It was still early. If he walked a little faster, he would reach him before six o'clock, and be sure of not meeting any of his former comrades. Trotta lengthened his stride. He stood under the window and whistled. Chojnicki appeared in the window, nodded and came out.

'It's happened at last!' said Chojnicki. 'It's war. We have been expecting it for a long time. But it will surprise us, even so. It appears that no Trotta is allowed to dwell in peace for long. My uniform is ready. In a week or two, I think we'll all be sent to the front.'

Trotta had the sense that Nature had never been so peaceful as it was at this hour. You could already look at the sun with a naked eye, it was going down in the west so quickly you could see it falling. A strong wind came out to greet it, curled the little white clouds in the sky, tousled the corn and wheat fields on the ground, and caressed the red faces of the poppies. A blue shadow hovered over the green pastures. To the east, the little wood sank in black-ish violet. Stepaniuk's little white house where Trotta was living, glowed at the edge of the wood, the melting light of the sun burn-ing in its windows. The crickets thrummed more noisily. Then the wind carried their sounds off into the distance; there was silence for a moment, you could hear the earth breathing. Suddenly, up above, there was a hoarse, distant screaking. Chojnicki raised his hand. 'Do you know what that is? It's the wild geese! They're leaving us early. It's still the middle of summer. They can already hear the shooting. They know what they're about!'

It was a Thursday, the day for the 'little gatherings'. Chojnicki turned to leave. Trotta slowly walked back to the glittering win-dows of his cottage.

That night, he couldn't sleep. About midnight, he heard the hoarse cries of the wild geese. He got dressed and stepped outside. Stepaniuk in his nightshirt was lying on his back by the thresh-old, his pipe glowing. He lay flat on the ground and said, without moving: 'It's not possible to sleep tonight!'

'The geese!' said Trotta.

'That's right, the geese!' affirmed Stepaniuk. 'In all my life, I've not heard them this early in the year. Listen, listen!'

Trotta looked up at the sky. The stars blinked as usual. There was nothing else to be seen. And yet there were incessant hoarse cries coming from up there. 'They're practising,' said Stepaniuk. 'I've been lying here for a long time. Sometimes I can see them.

They're just grey shadows. Look!' Stepaniuk pointed up at the sky with his glowing pipe. At that moment, you saw the tiny white shadows of the wild geese against the cobalt sky. They were rippling among the stars, a small skein of brightness. 'And that's not all!' said Stepaniuk. 'This morning I saw many hundreds of ravens. I've never seen so many before. Strange ravens, coming from distant parts. I think they've come from Russia. We have a saying in my language that the ravens are the prophets among the birds.'

To the north-east, there was a wide band of silver on the horizon. It grew perceptibly brighter. A wind got up. It wafted a few confused sounds of merriment from Chojnicki's house to them. Trotta lay down on the ground next to Stepaniuk. Sleepily he gazed at the stars, listened to the cries of the geese, and finally fell asleep.

He woke at sunrise. He felt he had been asleep only half an hour or so, but it must have been more like four hours. Instead of the usual twittering of birds greeting the day, there was the black croaking of hundreds upon hundreds of ravens. At Trotta's side, Stepaniuk got up. He took the pipe out of his mouth (it had gone cold while he'd been asleep) and pointed with the stem at the trees all around. The big black birds sat stiffly on the branches, like eerie fruits that had come down from the sky. They sat there impassively, the black birds, and cawed. Stepaniuk threw a few stones at them. But the ravens just flapped their wings once or twice. They squatted on the branches as if they were fruit that had grown there. 'I will shoot them,' said Stepaniuk. He went inside, got his shotgun, and started shooting. A few of the birds fell, the rest remained squatting on the branches, and seemed not even to have heard. Stepaniuk picked up the black corpses, he had killed over a dozen of them, he carried his booty back to the house in both hands, the blood dripped on to the grass. 'Strange ravens,' he said, 'they don't budge. They are the prophets among the birds.'

It was Friday. In the afternoon, as ever, Carl Joseph took his walk through the villages. The crickets were not thrumming, the frogs did not croak, only the ravens screamed. They were sitting everywhere, on the lindens, on the oaks, on the birches, on the willows. Maybe they come before the harvest every year, thought Trotta. They hear the peasants sharpening their scythes, and then they gather. He walked through the village of Burdlaki, secretly hoping Onufri would be there. Onufri was not there. The peasants stood in front of their huts, sharpening the steel against the reddish stones. Sometimes they looked up, the cawing of the ravens bothered them, and they aimed black oaths against the black birds.

Trotta came past Abramchik's tavern, the red-haired Jew was seated outside his gate, his beard glowing. Abramchik got up. He doffed his black velvet cap, pointed up in the air, and said: 'Ravens have come! They have been screaming all day! Wise birds! A man should be careful!'

'Yes, maybe, maybe you're right!' said Trotta, and carried on walking the usual path between the willows that led to Chojnicki's house. He stood under the windows. He whistled. No one came.

Chojnicki was probably in town. Trotta took the road to town, the road through the swamps, so that he didn't run into anyone. Only the peasants used this road. A few of them came towards him. The path was so narrow that there wasn't room for two to pass abreast. He had to stop and let them by. All those coming towards him today seemed in a greater hurry than usual. They greeted Trotta more fleetingly. They took longer strides. They walked with their heads down, like people with something important on their minds. And suddenly, Trotta could see the excise gates at the edge of the town, the numbers kept growing, and a group of twenty or more were filing on to the path. Trotta stopped. He saw that they were workers, workers from the brush factory who were returning to their villages. Among them, perhaps, were men he had shot at. He stopped to let them pass. They hurried by in silence, one after the other, each with a knotted bundle over his shoulder on the end of his stick. Evening seemed to be falling faster than usual, it was as though the haste of these people were contributing to the darkness. The sky was slightly overcast, the sun went down small and red and a silvery grey fog climbed up over the swamps, like the clouds' terrestrial brother hurrying to be reunited with them. Suddenly all the bells in town started to toll. The workers stopped for a moment, listened and then went on. Trotta stopped one of the last of the column and asked why the bells were tolling. 'It's on account of the war,' the man replied, without raising his head.

'On account of the war,' repeated Trotta. Of course. There had to be war. It was as though he had known it since this morning, since last night, since the day before yesterday, since his discharge and the dragoons' ill-omened party. It was the war he had been preparing himself for since he was seven years old. It was his war, the war of the grandsons. The days and the heroes of Solferino had come round again. The bells tolled without cease. There were the excise gates. The guard with his wooden leg stood in front of his little hut, surrounded by people, and a gleaming black and yellow poster was pinned on the door. The first words of it, black on yellow, were legible from far off. They stood like heavy roof beams over the heads of the assembled crowd. They said: 'To my peoples!'

Peasants in short, strong-smelling sheepskins, Jews in flapping, greenish-black kaftans, Swabian farmers from German enclaves in green loden suits, middle-class Polish merchants, craftsmen and civil servants thronged the hut of the excise guard. Each of the four walls had one of the large posters on it, each in a different local language, each beginning with the Emperor's address: 'To my peoples!' Those who were literate read the text aloud. Their voices mingled with the booming chant of the bells. Some went from one wall to the next, reading all the different versions. When the sound of one bell had died away, another one rang out. People streamed out of the little town, on to the wide road that led to the railway station. Trotta passed them as he walked into town. It was evening by now, and, its being a Friday, candles were burning in the little houses of the Jews, throwing their light on the pavements. Each little house was like a tomb. Death itself had lit the candles. Louder than on other Jewish feast days the singing rose from the houses where they were praying. They were saluting an extraordinary Sabbath, a Sabbath of blood. They stormed out of the houses in hurried black swarms, assembled at the crossroads, and soon their lamentations rose for those of their number who were soldiers and would have to join their units tomorrow. They shook hands, they kissed each other on the cheeks, and wherever there were two embracing, their beards united as for an especially fervent leavetaking, and the men had to part their beards with their own hands. The bells rang out over their heads. Between their chimes and the cries of the Jews the metallic voices of the trumpets in the barracks spoke up. They were sounding taps, the final lights-out. Already night was at hand. There were no stars to be seen. A low, lightless, murky sky hung over the little town!

Trotta turned for home. He looked for a carriage or cab, there was none to be had. He walked with long, rapid strides to Chojnicki's house. The gate was open, the rooms all lit up, as for one of the 'parties'. Chojnicki met him in the entrance hall, in uniform, with helmet and bullet-pouch. He had his horses already harnessed up. His garrison was three miles away, he wanted to be there that night. 'Wait a moment!' he said. For the first time, he said *du* to Trotta, perhaps negligently, perhaps because he was already in uniform. 'I'll drive you back, and then take you into town.'

They drive to Stepaniuk's cottage. Chojnicki sits down. He looks on as Trotta takes off his civilian clothes, and gets into his uniform. Item by item. Just as only a few weeks ago – but it feels like an eternity! – he had watched in Brodnitzer's hotel as Trotta took off his uniform. Trotta returns to his army clothes, it is like a homecoming. He pulls his sabre out of its case. He buckles on the sash, the huge black and yellow pompoms stroke the glittering metal of the sabre. This time, Trotta shuts his suitcase.

They don't have much time in which to say goodbye. They stop outside the Jägers' barracks. 'Adieu!' says Trotta. They shake hands for a very long time, time passes almost audibly behind the broad, motionless back of the coachman. It's as though it's not enough merely to shake hands. They feel they should do more. 'We always kiss,' says Chojnicki. So they quickly embrace, and kiss one another. Trotta climbs out. The sentry outside the barracks salutes. The horses start to pull. The barrack gate falls shut behind Trotta. He stands still a moment, and listens to Chojnicki's carriage driving away.

## 21

That very night, the Jäger battalion marched to the north-eastern frontier at Woloczyska. It began raining, gently at first, then harder and harder, until the white dusty roads were turned to silvery grey mud. The mud smacked together over the boots of the soldiers, and spattered the spotless uniforms of the officers marching to their regulation deaths. Their long sabres got in their way; the magnificent, long-haired pompoms dangling from their black and yellow sashes were now tangled, wet and mired by thousands of little spots of mud. At daybreak, the battalion reached its destination, joined up with a couple of other infantry regiments, and fell into extended order. They waited like that for two days, and there was nothing to be seen of the war. Sometimes they heard isolated, distant shots from somewhere to the right of them. There were little frontier skirmishes between cavalry units. From time to time they caught glimpses of wounded revenue officers, and occasionally a dead border guard. Medical orderlies removed the casualties, dead or wounded, under the eyes of the waiting troops. The war refused to start. It hung fire, as occasionally thunderstorms will hang fire for days before breaking out.

On the third day came the command to withdraw, and the

battalion got into marching order. Officers and men alike were disappointed. A rumour spread that two miles east of them, an entire regiment of dragoons had been pulverized, and that enemy Cossacks had already broken through into the interior. The troops marched westward in grim silence. They soon realized that this was an unplanned retreat, because at the crossroads and in the villages and small towns on their route, they encountered a confused mixture of all sorts of forces. The high command issued contradictory orders. Most of these were to do with the evacuation of towns and villages, and the treatment of pro-Russian Ukrainians, Orthodox priests and spies. Hastily formed courts martial handed down hasty judgments. Secret informants supplied unverifiable reports on peasants, priests, teachers, photographers, civil servants. There was no time. They were in a hurry to retreat, but also in a hurry to punish the traitors. And while ambulances, baggage columns, field guns, dragoons, uhlans and infantrymen met up in various configurations under the incessant rain on the softened roads, while couriers galloped this way and that, while the inhabitants of the little towns fled west in endless hordes, surrounded by the white terror, laden with chequered white and red feather beds, grey sacks, brown chairs and tables, and blue oil lamps – while all this went on, in the little church squares of the villages and hamlets, the shots of hastily assembled firing squads executed the hasty death sentences, and ominous drum rolls accompanied the monotonous judgments of the courts martial, and the wives of the slain lay screaming for mercy in front of the muddied boots of the officers, and flickering red and silver flames shot out of huts and barns, sheds and outbuildings. The Austrian army's war began with punishments, with courts martial. For many days the real or supposed traitors were left dangling on trees in the church squares, as an example to the living. But far and wide, the living had fled. Fires burned round the hanging corpses, and the leaves caught, and the fire was stronger than the continuous, drizzling rain that ushered in a bloody autumn. The old bark of the ancient trees slowly turned to charcoal, and tiny, silver, smouldering sparks darted out between the little ridges of it, like fiery worms, and licked at the leaves; the green foliage shrivelled up and turned red, then black, then grey; the ropes loosened, and the corpses fell to the ground, with blackened faces and bodies untouched.

One day, they stopped in the village of Krutyny. They had got there in the afternoon and were due to leave the next morning, before daybreak, on their westward route. That day, the rain had let up, and a late September sun spun a kindly, silvery light over the wide, still unharvested fields, the living bread that would never be eaten. An Indian summer drifted slowly through the air. Even the crows and ravens were quiet, deceived by the brief peace of the day, and hence without hope of any carrion. The troops had been in the same clothes for eight days now. Their boots were sodden, their feet swollen, their knees stiff, their calves sore, their backs too locked to bend. They found billets in some huts, tried to pull dry clothes out of their kit-bags and wash in the few wells. It was a clear, calm night, but for the noise of abandoned dogs howling with fear and hunger in the isolated farmyards; the Lieutenant was unable to sleep. He left the hut where he was billeted. He walked down the long village street, towards the church tower which pointed its Orthodox double cross at the stars. The church, with its shingle roof, stood in the middle of a small graveyard, ringed by crooked wooden crosses that seemed to dance in the night. Outside the wide, grey, open gates of the graveyard three bodies were hanging, a bearded priest flanked by two young peasants in sand-coloured jackets with coarsely woven straw shoes on their motionless feet. The priest's black cowl reached down to his shoes. Occasionally, the night wind caused his feet to brush against his priestly robe like the clapper of a bell, but without making any noise.

Lieutenant Trotta went up to the hanged men. He looked at their swollen faces. He thought he could recognize in the three of them various of his men. They were the faces of people with whom he dealt on a daily basis. The broad black beard of the priest reminded him of Onufri's beard. That was what Onufri had looked like, the last time he'd seen him. And who knows, maybe this hanged priest was Onufri's brother. Lieutenant Trotta looked around. He listened. There were no human sounds to be heard. In the bell tower of the church, there was the rustle of bats. The abandoned dogs barked in the abandoned farms. The Lieutenant drew his sabre, and one after the other, cut down the three hanged men. Then he shouldered one body after the other and carried them to the graveyard. With his shining sabre, he began to loosen the soil on the paths between the graves until he thought he'd made enough space for three bodies. He laid them in the hole, all together, scraped the earth over them, with sabre and scabbard, trampled it down with his feet and trod it firm. Then he made the sign of the cross. Not since the final mass in the cadet school of Mährisch-Weisskirchen had he made the sign of the cross. He wanted to say a Lord's Prayer as well, but he only moved his lips soundlessly. Some unknown night bird screamed. The bats rustled. The dogs howled.

The following morning, they were on the march again before sun-up. The world was swathed in the silvery fogs of an autumn morning. Before long, though, the sun came through, glowing like high summer. They became thirsty. They were marching across a sandy, abandoned plain. From time to time they had the illusion of hearing the sound of running water. A few soldiers ran in the direction of the sound, only to turn back soon enough. No streams, no ponds, no wells. They passed through a couple of villages, but their wells were choked with the corpses of shootings and summary justice. The corpses, some of them bent double, dangled over the wooden rims of the wells. The soldiers didn't bother to look into the depths. They rejoined the company. They marched on.

Their thirst grew. Noon approached. They heard shots, and flung themselves to the ground. The enemy had presumably overtaken them. They crawled forward on their hands and knees. Ahead of them, they could see already, the road widened. There was the gleam of an abandoned railway station. The tracks began there. At a trot, the battalion reached the security of the station; for a few miles from there, they would be covered by the railway embankments. The enemy, perhaps a swift sotnia of Cossacks, might be just alongside them, on the other side of the embankment. Depressed and silent, they marched along between the embankments. Suddenly a man cried: 'Water!' And a moment later, they had all seen the well on the embankment slope, next to a watchman's hut. 'Halt!' ordered Major Zoglauer. 'Halt!' the other officers ordered. But the thirsty men could not be stopped. One by one to begin with, then in groups, the men charged up the slope; shots rang out, and the men fell. The enemy cavalry the other side of the embankment shot at the thirsty men, and more and more thirsty men ran towards the fatal well. By the time the second platoon of the second company approached the well, there were already more than a dozen bodies on the green slope.

'Platoon halt!' ordered Lieutenant Trotta. He stood aside and said: 'I'll get you water! No one move! Wait here! Get me a bucket!' He was brought a couple of waterproof canvas buckets from the machine gun section. He took one in each hand. And he walked up the slope, towards the well. Bullets whistled around him, clattered at his feet, flew past his ears and his legs and over his head. He leaned over the well. On the other side of the slope he saw two rows of Cossacks firing at him. He wasn't afraid. It never occurred to him that he, like the others, might be shot. He could hear the bullets before they were shot, and, at the same time, the first drumming bars of the Radetzky March. He stood on the balcony of his father's house. The army band was playing below. Now Nechwal raised the black ebony baton with the silver head. Now Trotta dipped the second of his buckets into the well. Now the cymbals clashed. Now he pulled the bucket up. With a brimming bucket in either hand, with bullets fizzing around him, he put out his left foot to begin the descent. He took two steps. Now it was only his head that wasn't covered by the slope.

And now a bullet struck his skull. He took another step and fell. The buckets toppled and swayed and emptied themselves over him. Warm blood poured from his head on to the cool earth of the embankment. From down below the Ukrainian peasants in his platoon chorused: 'Praise be to Christ Jesus!'

For ever and ever, amen! he wanted to say. They were the only words of Ruthenian that he knew. But his lips could no longer move. His mouth gaped open. His white teeth grimaced against the blue autumn sky. His tongue slowly went blue, he could feel his body cool. And then he died.

That was the end of Lieutenant Carl Joseph, Baron von Trotta. So simple and so inappropriate for literary treatment in the primers of the K-and-K elementary schools of Austria was the death of the grandson of the hero of Solferino. Lieutenant Trotta died, not with sword in hand, but with a couple of buckets of water. Old Trotta read the letter a couple of times, and let his hands sink. The letter fell from his hands, and fluttered down on to the burgundy carpet. Herr von Trotta did not remove his pince-nez. His head trembled, and the wobbly pince-nez, with its oval glasses, fluttered like a glass butterfly on the old man's nose. Two heavy, crystal tears fell simultaneously from Herr von Trotta's eyes, smeared the glasses of his spectacles, and ran on down into his whiskers. His body remained still, only his head trembled back and forth and from side to side, and all the time the glass wings of his pince-nez were aflutter. The District Commissioner sat at his desk like that for an hour or more. Then he stood up, and walked through into his house, quite normally. He took his black suit out of his wardrobe, his black tie and his black crêpe mourning ribbons that he had worn on his hat and sleeve following his father's death. He changed, not looking in the mirror as he did. His head was still trembling. He did his best to tame his unruly head. But, the harder the District Commissioner tried, the more his head trembled. His pince-nez still sat fluttering on his nose. At last, the District Commissioner gave up all his endeavours, and simply allowed his skull to tremble. In his black suit, with his black mourning ribbon on his sleeve, he went into Fräulein Hirschwitz, remained standing in the doorway, and said: 'My dear, my son is dead!' He quickly shut the door, went into his office, from one room to the next, stuck his trembling head in all the doors and announced everywhere: 'My son is dead, Herr Suchandsuch! My son is dead, Herr Suchandsuch!' Then he took his hat and cane, and went out on the street. All the passers-by greeted him, and were bemused by his trembling head. The District Commissioner would stop the occasional one of them and say: 'My son is dead!' And he didn't wait for the other to show consternation and sympathy, but walked straight on, to Dr Skovronnek. Dr Skovronnek, now in the uniform of a colonel in the army Medical Corps, was spending his mornings in the garrison hospital and his afternoons, as before, in the café. He rose when the District Commissioner walked in, saw the old man's trembling, and looked at his unsteady head and fluttering pince-nez. 'My son is dead!' repeated Herr von Trotta. Skovronnek kept his friend's hand for a long time, for minutes. Both remained standing there, hand in hand. The District Commissioner sat down, Skovronnek moved the chess board on to an adjacent table. When the waiter came up, the District Commissioner said: 'My son is dead!' And the waiter bowed very low, and brought him a cognac.

'Another, please!' ordered the District Commissioner. At last, he removed his pince-nez. He remembered that the notification of his death was still lying on the carpet in the office, and he got up and returned to his residence. Dr Skovronnek followed him. Herr von Trotta appeared unaware of it. But nor was he at all surprised when, without knocking, Skovronnek opened the office door, walked in, and stopped. 'This is the letter!' said the District Commissioner.

The old Herr von Trotta did not sleep that night or on many of the following nights. His head continued to tremble and shake, even when it was resting on pillows. Sometimes the District Commissioner would have dreams of his son. Lieutenant Trotta would stand in front of his father, with his officer's cap filled with water, and say: 'Drink, Father, you're thirsty!' The dream recurred more and more frequently. And eventually the District Commissioner learned to summon his son every night, and some nights Carl Joseph came to him more than once. In consequence, Herr von Trotta began to long for night and bedtime, the day made him impatient. And when spring came, and the days grew longer, the District Commissioner would darken his room in the mornings and evenings, and so seek to prolong the nights artificially.

His head would not stop shaking. And he himself and everyone else gradually became used to the continual shaking.

The war seemed not to concern Herr von Trotta very much. He would only pick up a newspaper in order to conceal his trembling head behind it. There was never any discussion of victories and defeats between himself and Dr Skovronnek. Usually they just played chess, and in complete silence. But sometimes one would say to the other: 'Do you remember the game we played two years ago? You were just as careless then as you are now.' It was as though they were talking about events that had transpired decades before.

A long time had passed since the news of the death, the seasons had relieved one another in accordance with the old and immutable laws of nature, though mankind barely felt them under the red veil of war, and, of all men the District Commissioner felt them perhaps the least. His head was still trembling like a large, though light fruit on the end of a thin stem. Lieutenant Trotta had long since rotted away, or been eaten by the ravens who circled that day over the deadly railway embankment, but old Herr von Trotta continued to feel as though he'd learned of his death only yesterday. And he kept the letter from Major Zoglauer, now also deceased, in his inside pocket; every day he read it and it retained its terrible freshness and novelty, just like a funeral mound that is kept and tended by grieving hands. What did Herr von Trotta care about the hundred thousand dead who had since followed his son? What did he care about the hasty and confused decisions taken by the people above him, that were issued on a weekly basis? And what did he care about the end of the world, which he could now see approaching with even greater clarity than once the prophetic Chojnicki could? His son was dead. His job was over. His world had ended.

# EPILOGUE

All that remains is for us to relate the final days of District Commissioner Trotta. They passed almost like a single day. Time flowed past him, a broad, even river, with a monotonous sound. The news from the Front and the various extraordinary decrees and promulgations from the government hardly concerned the District Commissioner. He would have gone into retirement long ago. He only continued in his post because of the war. And so he sometimes felt he was living a kind of pallid, second life, and his real, first life was long over. His days – it seemed to him – were not chasing towards the grave, like everyone else's. The District Commissioner stood, turned to stone, on the bank of his days, like his own monument. Never had Herr von Trotta so resembled the Emperor Franz Joseph. Sometimes he even had the temerity to compare himself to the Emperor. He remembered his audition at the palace of Schönbrunn, and in the manner of simple old men talking about some shared calamity, he spoke silently to Franz Joseph: If someone had said that was our lot? Eh, what about that! Two old boys like us!

Herr von Trotta slept very little. He ate what was set in front of him, without noticing it. He put his signature to documents without reading them properly. It happened sometimes that he arrived in the café, and Dr Skovronnek wasn't there yet. Then Herr von Trotta would pick up a three-day-old newspaper, and read it all over again. But if Dr Skovronnek happened to speak of some very new developments, the District Commissioner would merely nod, as if he already knew.

One day, a letter came for him. A certain Frau von Taussig, not a name that meant anything to him, working at present as a volunteer nurse in the Viennese lunatic asylum at Steinhof, wrote to tell Herr von Trotta that Count Chojnicki, driven mad by his experiences on the battlefield a couple of months before, talked about the District Commissioner a great deal. In his confused ramblings he would keep insisting he had something important to communicate to Herr von Trotta. If it so happened that the District Commissioner was planning to visit Vienna at any time, his visit might effect a sudden transformation in the condition of the patient, such things had been known to happen. The District Commissioner consulted Dr Skovronnek. 'If you can stand it, I mean, if it's really no trouble to you ...' Herr von Trotta said: 'Nothing's any trouble.' He decided to set off right away. Maybe the sick man would have some important information about the Lieutenant. Maybe he had some memento or message from his son. Herr von Trotta travelled to Vienna.

He was shown to the asylum's military wing. It was late autumn, a gloomy day; the asylum wallowed in the grey precipitation that had been descending on the world for the past several days now. Herr von Trotta sat in the gleaming white corridor, gazed through the barred window at the denser, finer mesh of the rain, and thought about the slope of the railway embankment where his son had met his end. He'll be getting all wet now, thought the District Commissioner, as though the Lieutenant had died today or yesterday, and his corpse was still new. Time passed slowly. People passed, with crazed expressions or with cruelly contorted limbs, but for the District Commissioner madness held no terrors, even though it was his first visit to an asylum. The only terrible thing was Death. Shame! thought Herr von Trotta.

If Carl Joseph had been driven mad instead of dying, then I could have nursed him back to sanity. And if that had been beyond me, nothing could have kept me from going to see him every day! He might have had a hideously withered arm like this lieutenant here, but you can stroke a withered arm just as well as a sound one. You can look into twisted eyes as well! So long as they're the eyes of my son. Happy those fathers whose sons are insane!'

Finally, Frau von Taussig came, a nurse like so many others. He only noticed her uniform, why would he look at her face! She, though, looked at him long and said: 'I knew your son!'

Only now did the District Commissioner raise his eyes to her face. It was the face of a now middle-aged woman who was still beautiful. Yes, her nurse's bonnet had a rejuvenating effect on her, as such things always do, because it's in a woman's nature to be rejuvenated by goodness and compassion, and hence also by their external trappings. She must have been in society before this, thought Herr von Trotta. 'How long ago is it,' he asked, 'that you knew my son?' 'It was before the war!' said Frau von Taussig. Then she took the District Commissioner by the elbow, led him down the corridor in the manner in which she was used to leading invalids, and told him softly: 'We were lovers, Carl Joseph and I!' The District Commissioner replied: 'Forgive me, was it on your account, that awful trouble?'

'Partly on my account!' said Frau von Taussig. 'I see,' said Herr von Trotta, 'partly on your account.' Then he pressed the nurse's arm gently, and continued: 'I wish, on your account, that Carl Joseph were still able to get into trouble!' 'We're almost with the patient!' said Frau von Taussig. She felt tears coming to her, and she believed she wasn't allowed to cry.

Chojnicki sat in a bare room that had had everything taken out of it, because he would sometimes fall into rages. He sat on a chair that had all four legs bolted to the ground. When the District Commissioner entered, he stood up, advanced towards the visitor, and said to Frau von Taussig: 'Valli, leave us! We have an important matter to discuss!' Then they were all alone. There was a peephole in the door. Chojnicki went over to the door, blocked the peephole with his back, and said: 'Welcome to my mansion!' His bald head seemed even balder for some reason to Herr von Trotta. An icy wind seemed to gust forth from the large, blue, protuberant eyes of the patient, a coldness that wafted over the yellow, shrivelled and at the same time swollen face, and over the expanse of the skull. From time to time, the right corner of Chojnicki's mouth twitched. It was as if he wanted to smile just with the right corner of his mouth. His ability to smile had settled in the right corner of his mouth, and quit the rest of him for ever. 'Have a seat!' said Chojnicki. 'I sent for you, because I have something important to tell you. You mustn't tell anyone! You and I are the only ones to know. The old man's dying!'

'How do you know?' asked Herr von Trotta.

Chojnicki, still backed against the door, pointed up at the sky, then pressed his finger to his lips, and said: 'From upstairs!'

Then he turned, opened the door, called: 'Sister Valli!' and said to Frau von Taussig, who had immediately appeared: 'The audience is over!'

He bowed. Herr von Trotta walked out.

Accompanied by Frau von Taussig, he walked down the long passages, down the broad steps. 'Maybe it did some good!' she said.

Herr von Trotta took his leave, and went to see Railway Councillor Stransky. He didn't really know why himself. He went to see Stransky, who had married a Koppelmann. The Stranskys were at home. They didn't recognize the District Commissioner immediately. Then they welcomed him, with a mixture of embarrassment and melancholy and chilliness, as he thought. They brought him coffee and cognac. 'Carl Joseph!' exclaimed Frau Stransky, née Koppelmann. 'When he was made a lieutenant, he came to see us right away. He was a sweet boy!' The District Commissioner combed his side whiskers and didn't speak. Then in came Stransky junior. He had a limp, it was hideous to behold. Carl Joseph didn't used to limp! thought the District

Commissioner. 'They say the old man's dying!' observed Senior Railway Councillor Stransky suddenly.

At that the District Commissioner stood up and left. He knew the old man was dying. Chojnicki had said as much, and Chojnicki had always known everything. The District Commissioner went to see his boyhood friend Smetana, in the Comptroller's Office. 'The old man's dying!' said Smetana.

'I want to go to Schönbrunn!' said Herr von Trotta. And he drove to Schönbrunn.

The indefatigable, thin drizzle shrouded the palace of Schönbrunn, just as it shrouded the asylum of Steinhof. Herr von Trotta walked down the long avenue, the same avenue he had walked down a long, long time ago to the secret audience on his son's behalf. His son was dead. And now the Emperor was dying. And, for the first time since Herr von Trotta had been notified of his son's death, he believed that his son had not died in vain. The Emperor cannot survive the Trottas! thought the District Commissioner. He cannot survive them! They saved his life, and he will not survive the Trottas.

He remained outside. He remained outside, among people of the lower orders. A gardener from the Schönbrunn park came along, in his green apron, shovel in hand, and asked those standing around: 'How is he now?' And those standing around, foresters, coachmen, lower officials, porters and invalids, like the father of the hero of Solferino, replied to the gardener: 'No change! He's dying!'

The gardener trudged off; he went off with his spade to dig flowerbeds, to dig the everlasting earth.

It was raining, softly still, but more and more heavily. Herr von Trotta took his hat off. The junior officials standing around him took him for one of themselves or perhaps a postman from the Schönbrunn post office. And one or two of them said to the District Commissioner: 'Did you know him, then, the old bloke?'

'Yes, I did,' replied Herr von Trotta. 'He spoke to me once.'

'He's dying now!' said a forester.

Just then the priest entered the Emperor's bedroom with the Last Sacrament.

Franz Joseph had a temperature of 39.3; it had just been taken. 'I see, I see!' he said to the hooded figure of the Capuchin. 'So this is death!' He sat up on his pillows. He heard the indefatigable sound of the rain out of the window, interspersed with the occasional crunch of feet on gravel. The sounds seemed to the Emperor alternately very far off and very close. Sometimes he understood that it was the rain that was causing the gentle pattering outside the window. A little later, he had forgotten that it was the rain again. And he asked his personal physician a couple of times: 'What's that humming?' Because he couldn't say the word 'patter' any more, even though it was on the tip of his tongue. After he had asked after the cause of the humming, he believed it was a 'humming' that he heard. The rain was humming. The footfalls of passers-by outside were humming. The Emperor took more and more of a liking to the word and the sounds he thought it designated. In any case, it made no difference what he asked, because no one could hear him. He merely moved his lips, but he had the impression he was speaking out loud, audibly for everyone, if a little quietly, but no differently, really, from on the past few days. At times he was puzzled that he didn't get a reply. Moments later, he would have forgotten both his question and his bemusement at the silence of the people he asked. And once more he gave himself up to the gentle 'humming' of the world that all around him was living while he was dying – and he was like a child, giving up all his resistance to sleep, soothed and overcome by the lullaby. He shut his eyes. After a while, though, he opened them again, and saw the plain silver cross and the dazzling candles on the table, awaiting the priest. And then he knew that the Father would be there soon. And he moved his lips and began, as he had been taught as a child: 'In rue and humility, I confess my sins.' But that too no one heard. Just then, he saw the Capuchin was already there. 'I've had to wait a long time!' he said. Then he thought about his sins. 'Pride!' it occurred to him. 'I've been proud!' he said. He went through the sins one after the other, as they were listed in the catechism. I've been Emperor for too long! he thought. But he believed he had said it out loud. 'Everyone has to die. Even the Emperor must die.' And he had the impression that somewhere, far away, the imperial part of him was dying. 'War is a sin too!' he said aloud. But the priest didn't hear it. Franz Joseph was baffled again. Lists of casualties were published every day, the war had been going on since 1914. 'Make an end!' said Franz Joseph. No one heard. 'I should have died at Solferino!' he said. No one heard. Or maybe, he thought, I'm already dead, and I'm a dead man speaking, and that's why they can't hear. And he fell asleep.

Outside, among the people, waited Herr von Trotta, the son of the hero of Solferino, hat in hand, in the incessant drizzling rain. The trees in the park at Schönbrunn were rustling and soughing, the rain lashed them, mildly, patiently, diligently. Evening fell. More onlookers came. The park filled up. The rain didn't abate. The crowd seemed to take it in turns, some went, others came. Herr von Trotta stayed. Night came, the steps emptied, people went to bed. Herr von Trotta pressed himself against the gate. He heard carriages drive up, now and again someone opened a window somewhere above him. Voices called. The gate was opened, and shut again. The rain trickled down, indefatigably, gently, the trees rustled and soughed.

Finally, the bells began to clang. The District Commissioner went away. He walked down the shallow steps, along the avenue to the iron gate. That night it had been left open. He walked all the way back into the city, bareheaded, hat in hand, without meeting anyone. He walked very slowly, as if following a hearse. As day was breaking, he reached his hotel.

He went home. It was raining in the district town of W. as well. Herr von Trotta called for Fräulein Hirschwitz and said: 'I'm going to bed, my dear! I'm tired!' And for the first time in his life, he went to bed in the daytime. He couldn't sleep. He sent for Dr Skovronnek. 'Dear Dr Skovronnek,' he said, 'would you get me the canary?' The canary was brought from old Jacques's house. 'Give him a lump of sugar!' said the District Commissioner. And the canary was given a lump of sugar.

'Dear creature!' said the District Commissioner.

Skovronnek echoed: 'Dear creature!'

'It'll outlive us all!' said Trotta. 'Thank God!'

Then the District Commissioner said: 'Send for the priest! But mind you come back as well!'

Dr Skovronnek waited for the priest. Then he went in again. The old Herr von Trotta lay quietly back on his pillows. His eyes were half shut. He said: 'Give me your hand, my dear friend! Will you fetch me the picture?'

Dr Skovronnek went to the drawing room, clambered up on a chair, and lifted the portrait of the hero of Solferino off its hook. When he returned, holding the painting in both hands, Herr von Trotta was not able to see it. The rain drummed softly on the window panes.

Dr Skovronnek waited, with the portrait of the hero of Solferino on his knees. After a few minutes, he got up, took Herr von Trotta's hand, bowed over the District Commissioner's chest, took a deep breath, and closed the dead man's eyes.

It was the day they lowered the Emperor into the Capuchin Vault. Three days after that, Herr von Trotta was lowered into his grave. The burgomaster of the town of W. spoke over the grave. His funeral oration, like most speeches at the time, began with the war. The burgomaster went on to say that the District Commissioner had given his only son to the Emperor, and nevertheless had continued to live and to serve. All the while, the indefatigable rain came down on the bare heads of those gathered about the grave, and there was a rustling and soughing of the wet bushes and wreaths and flowers all around. Dr Skovronnek, in the unfamiliar uniform of a territorial medical officer, tried very hard to remain standing to attention, even though he found it to be a less than adequate expression of piety and grief. – He was just a civilian. After all, Death isn't a staff surgeon! thought Dr

Skovronnek. Then he was among the first to step up to the grave. He refused the spade that was held out to him by a gravedigger, but bent down, and broke off a sod of wet earth, crumbled it in his left hand, and with his right scattered a few crumbs of it on the coffin. Then he stepped back. It occurred to him that it was afternoon, the hour for their chess game was approaching. Now he didn't have a partner any more; nevertheless, he decided to go to the café. As they left the cemetery, the burgomaster invited him to ride in his carriage. Dr Skovronnek climbed in. 'I would have liked to say in my address,' said the burgomaster, 'that Herr von Trotta couldn't have outlived the Emperor. Don't you agree, doctor?' 'I don't know,' replied Dr Skovronnek, 'I don't think either of them could outlive Austria.'

Dr Skovronnek asked to be dropped outside the café. He went to his regular table, as he did every day. The chess board was there, quite as if the District Commissioner hadn't died. The waiter came to clear it away, but Skovronnek said: 'No, leave it there!' And he played a game with himself, smiling and shaking his head from time to time, looking at the empty chair opposite, in his ears the gentle rushing sound of the autumn rain, which still pattered indefatigably against the window panes.

# THE LEGEND OF THE HOLY DRINKER

## *Joseph Roth*

Translated by Michael Hofmann

'Encapsulates Roth's wit, keen ironic sense and his limitless humanity' *London Review of Books*

'It is both funny and magical ... a poignant work' *Paris Voice*

Andreas is an alcoholic vagrant living under a bridge. As a man submerged at the very bottom of society, any change would be an improvement – but a run of exceptional good luck lifts him marvellously, briefly, onto a different plane of existence. This haunting novella, published after Roth's death in 1939, is an unforgettable testament to his wit and compassion.

'Good things come in small packages – that's certainly true of this gem of a book ... magically told' *Daily Express*

# THE EMPEROR'S TOMB

## *Joseph Roth*

Translated and with an introduction by Michael Hofmann

'A new translation by the peerless Michael Hofmann, this is the troubled, troubling account of a young man struggling to fit into Vienna in the wake of the first world war, a time when the Nazis' behaviour is slowly becoming evident' *Sunday Herald*

'This is a kind of sequel to Roth's pre-First World War masterwork, *The Radetzky March* – so this recommendation is really a ruse to make you read both books. Roth is Austria's Chekhov. The same secular modern spirit, the same deadpan humour, the same wry understanding of the human condition and its random injustices – but set in the twilight years of the Austro-Hungarian Empire. Unforgettable, really great literature – and so rare to have it so expertly rendered into English. Treat yourself' William Boyd, *Scotsman*

'An urgent and deceptively moving lamentation of stark emotion ... an inspired variation on the traditional coming-of-age narrative ... a profound farewell gesture of love and sorrow' Eileen Battersby, *Irish Times*

'One can see *The Emperor's Tomb* as a sort of sequel to Roth's masterpiece *The Radetzky March*. But as Michael Hofmann notes in his excellent introduction, the differences between the two books are more interesting than the similarities ... What is breathtaking however is the power of Roth's prose. In despair, battling with poverty and illness, he nevertheless manages to create one astonishing scene after another ... you are unlikely to find a better novel this year' *Jewish Chronicle*

# JOB

## The Story of a Simple Man

## *Joseph Roth*

Translated by Dorothy Thompson

'*Many years ago there lived in Zuchnow, in Russia, a man named Mendel Singer. He was pious, God-fearing and ordinary, an entirely commonplace Jew . . .*'

So begins Roth's novel about the loss of faith and the experience of suffering. His modern Job goes through his trials in the ghettos of Tsarist Russia and on the unforgiving streets of New York. Mendel Singer loses his family, falls terribly ill and is badly abused. He needs a miracle . . .

This modern fable, told in Roth's tender and musical prose, is both a striking evocation of the tumultuous era Roth lived through and a timeless exploration of hope and despair at the extremity of experience.

'There are some books that seem sacrosanct
and one of them is *Job*'
*Independent*

'It is not possible to do justice to *Job*'s poetic subtlety, but I
can vouch for its extraordinary merits'
Thomas Mann

# WHAT I SAW

## Reports from Berlin 1920–33

## *Joseph Roth*

Translated and with an introduction by Michael Hofmann

'These brilliant and quixotic pieces immortalize the everyday
life of 1920s Berlin ... An instant classic'
Roy Foster, *Financial Times*

'A supreme observer, a cynical romantic with a flair for prophecy
and an understanding of the slow fester of moral outrage ...
Outstanding' Eileen Battersby, *Irish Times*

'His slivers of Berlin life during the Weimar Republic catch a
city juddering with a sense of its own modernity, even as he
listens for sighs escaping through the cracks. Tender, caustic
[and] thrilling' David Jays, *Observer*

'Marvellous ... proof that [Roth] is as brilliant and original a
journalist as he is a storyteller, casting his eye and cocking his
ear where lesser writers never venture' *Sunday Times*

'Nonstop brilliance, irresistible charm and continuing
relevance ... A book that gives so much delight without
resorting to fraudulent means or shoddy thinking. The hardest
thing about writing this review is that I want to quote every
sentence' Jeffrey Eugenides, *New York Times*

# THE HOTEL YEARS

## Wanderings in Europe between the Wars

### *Joseph Roth*

Translated by Michael Hofmann

In the 1920s and 1930s, Joseph Roth travelled extensively in Europe, living in hotels and writing about the towns through which he passed and the individual and idiosyncratic characters he encountered. Collected here for the first time, these tender vignettes form a series of literary postcards from a bygone world, heading towards world war.

'A hugely significant and wonderfully haunting collection'
William Boyd

'Thanks to the expert translations of Michael Hofmann, Roth is on track to canonical status ... The writing is so consistently incisive that we devour the lot, compulsively, from cover to cover' *Independent*

'This wonderful selection of journalism from the Weimar years, a period Roth spent in Paris, Germany and on the road, displays his genius from every angle, as a rebel, a loyalist and a man of compassion' Jan Morris, *Daily Telegraph*

'[Roth's] journalism creates a vivid sense of a continent on the brink of change' *Independent on Sunday*

'Joseph Roth has emerged as one of the greatest, certainly the most prescient, of the German writers of the entre-deux-guerres' *TLS*